Deep Zero

a Dana Hargrove legal mystery

V.S. KEMANIS

ISBN-13: 978-0-9997850-9-6
ISBN-10: 0-9997850-9-5

℞ **Opus Nine Books**
• **New York** •

the county and state levels and brings her personal knowledge of the investigation process into the story. Her overall attention to detail makes the work a true page-turner." — *Kirkus Reviews*

In *Seven Shadows*, "tension mounts and leads to a climactic confrontation that is surprisingly different from what one might expect. Kemanis has created an engaging plot on which to build her narrative—one chock full of technical legal expertise. Yet it is the emotional tributaries that flow from that plot that give this story a greater sense of literary weight." — *The U.S. Review of Books*

"In *Homicide Chart*, V.S. Kemanis weaves three separate plot lines into a compelling tale. Her characters are well defined, very authentic, painted with a deft hand. This is Ms. Kemanis' real talent. She makes us care for the characters." — *Online Book Club*

Forsaken Oath is "clever, immersive… Kemanis, a talented weaver of scene and exposition, keeps the reader engaged with each new twist and bit of evidence." — *Kirkus Reviews*

Power Blind "is a family saga, mystery, and legal tale all rolled into one… The author did a fantastic job drawing me into the story through compelling observations, descriptions, and dialogue… Frankly, there is a lot to like in this one." — *San Francisco Book Review*

"Kemanis writes in a style that adeptly dramatizes legal arguments while also finding moments of stark lyricism… [*Deep Zero*] is a well-drawn legal thriller." — *Kirkus Reviews*

In *Deep Zero*, Kemanis "vividly portrays the difficulties of balancing the intricacies of the practice of law with the intimacies of the practice of parenthood. Her principal players seem particularly real… This is a confident author as at home with courtrooms, legal briefs, and summary judgments as she is with bedrooms, term papers, and adolescent anxiety." — *The U.S. Review of Books*

"*Forsaken Oath* is a terrific legal thriller, written by a prosecutor who knows her way around the legal trenches. Kemanis's expertise brings wonderful authenticity to a twisting plot." — Allison Leotta, author of *The Last Good Girl*

Also by V.S. Kemanis

Dana Hargrove Legal Mysteries

Thursday's List
Homicide Chart
Forsaken Oath
Seven Shadows
Power Blind

Story Collections

Dust of the Universe, tales of family
Everyone But Us, tales of women
Malocclusion, tales of misdemeanor
Love and Crime: Stories
Your Pick: Selected Stories

Anthology Contributor

The Crooked Road, Volume 3
The Best Laid Plans
Me Too Short Stories
Autumn Noir

Visit
www.vskemanis.com

CONTENTS

PLAN

Monday, February 9, 2009, 3:05 a.m.

COLD, DEEP TO the bone. Numbing, painless. With all physical sensation gone, the rest of it is now almost a memory, not even that. The remaining bits float away into the vast, sucking expanse of black sky over the river. Naomi lets them go.

There was pain as recently as an hour ago. In the warmth of her bedroom, she convulsed on the cloudy surface of her down comforter, the fabric wet with tears. The lights were off, but her room wasn't entirely dark. The glow of the laptop pulsed and electrified the air. *Permanent.* Declaring a life of its own.

"Whatever you post, it will never go away. Think about *that.* It will be there forever."

Her mother's voice was part of that forever. Naomi had listened to her advice, but maybe the others didn't have mothers to guide them. Or maybe they didn't listen, just didn't care.

Even worse, maybe their mothers were laughing right along with them.

The glow pulsed powerfully, receded, and surged again. Naomi's vigilant hand kept the screen alive with ceaseless, repetitive work. Searching, clicking, finding the trash, trying to erase it, powerless against the tide, rushing over an infinite plane beyond her control. Who had seen it, commented, or shared?

Finally, she simply couldn't do it anymore. She was done. In a blink, the pain vanished. The release was sudden, like pulling the plug in a tub of dirty water. The vortex swirled and hypnotized and emptied into a deep, dark netherworld, a final gurgle echoing up.

Inertia created a void ready to be filled. Cold logic and reflexive action crept in. A plan revealed itself. A few things had to be done, a few people contacted, a few people told off.

Detached from the world, perched above her bedroom on a still blade of her ceiling fan, a spectral Naomi surveyed her regret. Down below, heaped on the messy bed clothes, she saw the sad lump of a girl, shrouded in black from shoulder to toe. The girl was sorry and would tell them so. Mom, Dad, and Olivia. Maybe less sorry about Olivia? Naomi hadn't seen her older sister since Christmas, when she'd been home during the month-long break between college semesters. Even then, they hadn't really talked because Olivia was out with her old high school friends most of the time. It didn't matter anyway. How could anything be explained to the older, perfect one, the first-born daughter who'd inherited the "skinny jeans"?

From her distant perch, Naomi's plan came into focus, even as the stern voice of logic scolded her for remaining mute. If it weren't for this new, icy numbness, she might be in tears, thinking of everything awful and wonderful she'd ever felt for Olivia: admiration, love, connection, resentment, longing. Now, there was only regret. A simple fact. And regret never led to sweet endings.

Mom and Dad were the biggest regret. Naomi was an utter disappointment to them, even if they wouldn't find out about it until tomorrow. She inspected her shame, analyzed it, and found it lacking in power. Not enough to change the plan. Should be enough, but it wasn't. Eventually they'd see that it was better this way. Better for everyone. She would apologize. Regret was all she had left to offer.

Naomi floated down from the ceiling and faced the glowing light once more. She opened her e-mail and started to compose a message to her family: "Dear Mom, Dad, and Olivia…"

She stopped because the next words were going to be, "I love you." An odd thing for a numb person to write. Yet, she saw the truth in it. "I love you" was the correct opening line, so she typed the words fast, making it permanent. Then she added the rest. "I'm sorry, but there's no other way. I think you'll understand when you see what happened. Please forgive me. Love, the Gnome."

Funny name, that. Olivia, at age three, was trying to say Naomi and it became Nome. Then, sometime in elementary school, it turned into Gnome when Olivia discovered the word. After that, even though they didn't mean it that way, the nickname sounded like a joke they were playing on her. The little elf? Dwarf? Garden gnome? So little. So funny.

The Gnome took a moment to read the message again, black letters in relief against an illuminated background. In the lower right corner of her screen, the time jumped instantly from "2:11 AM" to "2:12 AM." She entered the commands needed to delay sending the message until seven in the morning. By then she would be gone.

The next part was not as difficult. She closed her e-mail screen, uncovering the profile page underneath. A photo of herself stared back. Of course. For a month now, she'd never logged out.

It was a good picture, just her face, taken more than a year ago when she was prettier. The camera captured her in a straightforward, honest look. Behind the photo was a larger one, the "wallpaper." She changed it frequently, alternating between photos of landscapes or buildings or water, never photos of herself. Two days ago, after seeing the worst message—the truly horrid one—she'd changed the background to a sweeping aerial view of the Bear Mountain Bridge.

Other girls wouldn't think of posting a photograph of the outdoors unless they were prominently displayed in the foreground. Always about themselves, those photos. Head tilted slightly to the left and down, lips provocatively pouty, mascaraed eyes peeking out from under a waterfall of shiny hair. Or a body shot, full length, the lower back pertly arched or a hip jutting. Naomi knew two girls who were prime examples, but she was done with looking at their Facebook pages. Forever.

Her fingers moved.

The message came easily.

Tap, tap, tap.

"Surprise. Yes, I can. See if I won't."

After typing these words, they seemed to belong inside that little box at the top of her page where they would remain forever. She realized then that the words had been on her mind for at least two days, coinciding with her choice of new wallpaper, the picture of the bridge.

She sat back and read the post again, fully satisfied with it. Nothing more, nothing less. She made the setting "public." They would know. Not just the two girls but everyone, really, would know it was her response, and they would understand where to place the blame.

Naomi's finger hovered. She wasn't sure how to delay a post, or if it *could* be delayed like she'd delayed the e-mail to her family, but what did it matter? The intended recipients and their "friends" were probably asleep right now, but even if they saw it tonight, what could they do? Something, maybe, but there was absolutely nothing they *would* do.

She hesitated, her heart thudding rapidly. There was moisture under her arms, on her upper lip, in the V between her legs. These reminders of her living body puzzled her and contradicted the numbness. She fought the distractions. Relief was near, and the message would be the first step.

With a tap on the pad, she made it permanent and found her peace of mind. It was a small satisfaction, knowing she had set things straight.

Finally, it was time to press the power button. She shut the machine down, killing this useless virtual life.

Almost completely dark now. All around, the house was still. Down the hall, her parents were fast asleep. Many times, Naomi had been awake in the middle of the night, hearing nothing but the faint sound of her father's snore.

When her eyes adjusted, she rose from the bed. Moving automatically, without hesitation, she maneuvered around the furniture. She'd spent her entire seventeen years in this room. Her sixth sense avoided the sharp edges and tripping hazards and took the exact number of steps needed to reach the chair in the corner. More from habit than anything else, with no thought or fear of the cold, she pulled her jacket off the chair and put it on. She patted the outside of the right pocket to feel the hard contour of her cell phone. Another habit. There was no one she wished to call.

In the hallway, and again downstairs, she stopped to listen. No one stirred. She found the keys where they were always kept, in a dish on a small table near the door to the garage. She wouldn't be asking permission this time. It's her mother's car she usually borrows, an aging Honda Civic.

The noise from the garage door opener might awaken them, so she disengages the chain and pulls the door up by hand.

Her mind controls the body without thought. She gets into the car and starts it up.

Twenty minutes pass, a blank space that's lost to her. She was there, now she's here.

The Civic is tucked into a dark, ill-used corner of the large parking lot at Bear Mountain Park, backed into a tall mound of snow plowed up from the last storm.

A ten-minute walk in the biting cold, but she doesn't notice. She's already numb.

Naomi blinks and stands on the bridge, midspan.

The night is overcast, no moon or stars, her body masked in black to match it. A single car passes without stopping. Then no one.

Numbing, painless. All physical sensation gone.

The guardrail is high, coming up past her abdomen.

She should just…

She couldn't even…

LOL!

Oh, yes, I can. Naomi pulls herself up with a strength she rarely uses. Taking a moment to balance on the night, she lets the icy wind rock her. It pushes, she sways, the river beckons.

The next step is easy. She takes it.

1 » *DRIVE*

"GOOD MORNING, WESTCHESTER!" The chipper voice of radio personality Lacey Greer jazzed up the dreary Monday commute.

On the dot of seven, traffic was still medium light on the parkway, building steadily. Most of the southbound commuters were headed for Manhattan. For Dana and many others, the destination was White Plains, the business hub of this suburban county. She liked to get a jump on the world and beat the worst traffic. By seven thirty, she'd roll into the underground lot at the County Courthouse, happy to leave the clogged parkway behind.

A familiar tune played under Greer's voice. "Coming up this hour, the Great Recession and rising substance abuse: Is there a link? We'll let you know what the experts are saying. Next, we'll pay a visit to the Dolan household in Yonkers where those adorable quints are celebrating their first birthday! And stick around, you chocolate lovers! We have a special Valentine's Day recipe for a treat you can share with your sweetheart: peppermint nut-fudge love knots! All of that right here…"

Dana held back from changing the station, not because of the quints or the love knots, but to hear the report on substance abuse. Local news programs reflected the pulse of the community, and it behooved her to listen. Of course, there could be interruptions. The Bluetooth was enabled to receive calls from home or the office. There were always plenty of both, spanning a broad spectrum of emergencies.

The phone rang now. "Natalie" appeared on the lighted display, cutting off the radio. Dana punched the knob on the console. "Hi, sweetie. What's up?"

"You know your white, fluffy hat?"

"Mm-hmm, sure…"

"I couldn't find *my* hat, so I…"

"That's fine. You need something on your head. It's seventeen degrees outside." Dana looked at the clock. By now, Travis should be at the corner of their cul-de-sac, Dovecote Lane, waiting for the bus to Stone Ridge High School. Natalie had another twelve minutes before she would have to catch the middle school bus.

"I know, but there's just one thing about it."

"What's that?"

"Well, there's kind of a spot on it…"

"Oh-*kay*…"

"It was on the table when I was drinking my juice, and maybe a little bit splashed onto it. I'm really sorry." Cranberry, of course. Natalie's favorite. "The spot isn't too big, and you won't even see it if you fold the edges!" Her amplified voice remained bright and sunny, even as she confessed her negligence.

"All right, sweetie, thanks for telling me. Just try to be more careful next time."

"I will!"

"And get down to the bus stop." There was no backup plan today if Natalie missed the bus. Evan usually saw the kids off (and sometimes spoiled Natalie by driving her to the corner), but he'd already left the house. He had a long drive this morning and a particularly challenging day ahead.

"I'm going now. Bye-bye, Mommy, I love you!"

"Love you too."

Emergency call? Hardly this one, but Dana encouraged the kids to contact her about anything they considered "important." Naturally there were degrees of importance, and Natalie's judgment tended to place more of her daily activities toward the higher end of that scale. Travis, at the other extreme, rarely called. At sixteen and a half, he was independent and self-assured. That's not to say he wasn't a loving son, but he didn't have a need to be reminded of his connection to the family. Natalie, three years younger than her brother, was communicative and transparent. She liked to share what was happening, spontaneously, in the moment. It was not unusual for Dana to receive a phone call or two from her during work hours every day.

When the call ended, Lacey Greer's voice resumed in mid-sentence: "…prescriptions for pain killers and sleep agents are soaring, and overdoses are on the rise…"

Dana understood the attraction to pills. She was an occasional insomniac herself and had toyed with the idea of taking medication to help her unwind. The pressure was constant, so much to do: fine-tuning the organization of the office, updating policies and priorities, devising strategies for prosecuting high-profile crimes. Could she take a pill to temporarily obliterate the thoughts that teemed in the middle of the night? At the urging of her younger sister Cheryl (who swore by Ambien), Dana had tried the sleeping pill once, only to find that she was headachy and dizzy the next day. Not a good idea for the chief law enforcement official of the county.

"…and what does our new district attorney say? *'It's a big problem, doctors over-prescribing, making it easy for illegal peddlers of pain killers. And child-proof bottles won't stop teenagers who find these drugs in the medicine cabinet at home…'*"

The last thing she expected! Greer had pulled the sound bite from a press conference in January, shortly after Dana was sworn in as the new DA. *"Substance abuse and addiction are hitting this county hard, splitting up families, contributing to domestic violence, larceny, intoxicated driving and vehicular manslaughter..."*

Not a bad excerpt, but something about it nettled Dana. She'd been told that her voice was distinctive, that it had a pleasing, reassuring quality, but now, hearing the sound bite again, she wasn't impressed. Her voice struck her as oddly disembodied, not as warm and passionate as she would like it to sound. Did people understand how much she really cared? Did they know the strength of her commitment? This was the community in which she and Evan were raising their children.

The radio program continued with an interview of the coordinator of a volunteer outreach program. Now *here* was a voice that resonated genuine compassion! The contrast led Dana to suspect the source of her discomfort about her own sound bite. Was she starting to sound like a politician?

She didn't think of herself in that way. The job of district attorney had virtually fallen into her lap. She'd been an assistant DA her entire career, more than twenty years, first in New York City, then in Westchester, ever since moving here with her family in 2003. She'd served as chief of the homicide bureau, then as the top executive ADA to District Attorney William Davenport. When Bill announced that he wouldn't be running for reelection in 2008, he endorsed Dana, making her a shoo-in as his successor. There wasn't much need for political maneuvering or campaigning. A couple of fundraisers, a few hands to shake. Little competition, and she won the election handily. Dana was sworn in on New Year's Day 2009 and got right to work, despite the holiday. The young DA, forty-seven years old, had the energy to tackle big problems.

A promise was a promise, whether made by a politician or not. Dana believed in action, the proof of integrity. In this sprawling county of nearly a million, home to people of every socioeconomic class, ethnicity, race, and political persuasion, the problems were varied and complex. Commentator Lacey Greer was right to be questioning a link between the financial crisis and rising substance abuse. Last year's crash of the housing and stock markets was taking its toll. The evidence was everywhere. Houses in foreclosure, mothers and fathers out of work, and the symptoms of familial breakdown: more drunk drivers, overdoses, domestic violence, and directionless teenagers committing petty crimes, despondent about a world without a future. Besides these problems, there was gang activity down county, cybercrime, public corruption, organized crime in the carting and construction industries. And, this county was not immune to the ultimate crime, although the murder rate here was modest compared to what Dana had "grown up on" as an ADA in New York City. "Only" forty-one homicides in Westchester last year, but she'd never seen the likes of some of them. Today she expected to get an update in the investigation of a particularly gruesome case…

The phone cut off the news program a second time. "Evan" was on the display. She punched the knob and said, "Hi. How's the drive?"

"Another thirty or forty minutes to go. I'm not fond of this road."

"Be careful."

"Did Natalie call you?"

"Yes. She called you too?"

"Yup. Asked if I thought you would want to hear about a mishap involving your favorite winter hat."

"So, now she's testing the waters before calling me. Am I that scary?"

"Not in the least. She's just beginning to understand how important you are."

"That's very sweet of you to say, darling. I hope you like your new job, screening my phone calls!"

"Anything to get my daughter to call me first. So why aren't you wearing your favorite hat?"

One less step, she could tell him. No need to deal with "hat hair," the rearranging of her chin-length hairstyle, still proudly dark chocolate in color, free of gray. Instead she replied, "The outdoors doesn't exist for me. I'm in the car with the heater on, and then I park in the garage and take the elevator up—Hey!" she yelled and honked. A black BMW cut into her lane, nearly side-swiping her Ford Escape.

"What's going on?"

"A sports car just cut me off. I should've gotten the plate number and called County."

"You're just jealous. Let me buy you a sexy car to go with your new position."

"Ha ha. I'm keeping the Escape, thank you." Dana liked her SUV, especially in the winter. It pushed through fluffy snow like it was nothing. But…what was that? Up ahead, the BMW fish-tailed. Speed or black ice? Dana slowed as she approached the spot. She felt the slip! An instantaneous loss of control, enough to push her heart up into her throat. She sucked in her breath, loud enough for Evan to hear.

"Dana…?"

"I'm okay. Just a little black ice."

"Be careful. I'm hitting plenty of slick spots. More of them, the farther north I go."

"It's too cold for the salt to melt the ice."

"I'd say it's time for you to reconsider your stubborn asceticism."

"Hmm, don't think so." She understood his meaning. As a top county official, Dana was entitled to have her own driver, an officer who would take her to work, meetings, trips, wherever she needed to go. She'd refused. Why waste taxpayers' money when she was more than willing to drive herself? She'd been doing so for more than six years. She made an exception whenever she visited crime scenes. Usually, she called on her right-hand person to drive, Indigo Raines, confidential investigator to the district attorney.

Some said Dana was crazy for rejecting this perk of the job, but she doubted that she would ever get used to having a chauffeur. Part of it was a control thing, she would admit. She liked to rely on herself. Winter weather added to the stress, however, and at times like this, her past life in Manhattan seemed like the good old days. Descend into the subway, rattle through a tunnel, and come out in a different place. Wouldn't *that* be easier, now that Travis was learning to drive? Learning in the wintertime! She was fine with leaving the driving lessons to Evan.

"You think about it, Madam District Attorney," said Evan.

"All right, I will."

"I've heard that before."

"I'm good at mulling things over. Right now, I'm curious about your deposition. Good luck with it."

"Thank you. I need it. A first for me."

"Tell me about it tonight. I want to know everything."

"You bet."

They clicked off. The radio program came up again, but she'd missed the rest of the report on substance abuse. Greer was interviewing the harried mother of the Dolan quintuplets. Time to change the station. Classical music, Mozart. The piece was snappy and soothing all at once.

Not much longer to go, nearing the exit to White Plains, she slowed to thirty miles per hour. Her wheels came close to the shoulder and caught another slick spot. A quick shimmy — did she imagine it? Deep breath. Calm, calm. The Escape was her faithful chariot.

Five minutes later, she pulled into the driveway reserved for county officials and stopped at the entrance to the underground lot, an impenetrable portal with a full-size metal gate. Her favorite guard was standing outside, beating his gloved fists together, exhaling clouds of vapor. He wore a hat with earflaps, a navy, padded jacket, and a mustache above his ready smile. Quick to act when he saw Dana's car, he pushed a remote inside his pocket to start the slow, upward roll of the metal gate.

She opened her window and smiled up at the armed guard. Besides the frozen look, the red cheeks and frost on his mustache, his eyes expressed something—relief? She suspected he'd been looking out for her arrival. Almost every day at seven thirty, regardless of the weather, he waited for her outside, shunning the relative comfort of the small control booth with its powerful, blasting heater.

"Good morning, Pete!"

"Good morning, Your Honor. How was the drive?"

"Not bad. A few icy patches."

"Got word of a four-car pileup on I-287."

"Glad I don't have to take the expressway."

"Yes, ma'am, a good thing, I'd say." Dana smiled to herself. In the first week of her term as DA, Pete had addressed her, on one occasion, as "Miss Hargrove." His face colored immediately with doubt as to possible mistake or a perceived lack of respect. Ever since then, it had been "Your Honor" or "ma'am."

"Thanks, Pete. Get inside and warm up!"

She rolled into the garage and stopped at the intersection before turning right. In her rearview mirror, Pete's shins and feet were visible, glued to the same spot on the other side of the gate as it completed the slow roll downward, finally closing with a decisive, echoing boom.

Dana was halfway through her second cup of coffee when Confidential Investigator Indigo Raines opened the door and walked into her office without invitation, the only warning a single, hard-knuckled rap. She didn't bother to close the door behind her.

"Damn this freeze is killing me," Indigo declared, rubbing her hands, then inspecting them. "All ashy. I'm going back to Alabama."

"Not until we finish digging up the dirt on muscle man."

"I need some sun."

"Haven't you heard? It's so cold they even had snow in Birmingham."

Indigo sat down, overwhelming the chair. "Nothing close to a New York winter." Her rich voice spoke so assuredly that no one could debate the point. Not many women dwarfed five-foot-eight Dana (five-ten in business heels), but Indigo was six feet tall and always dominated the room, not just physically, but also with her unique brand of verbal acuity.

"What's new on the mental health of our loving husband?" Dana asked.

Just then, First Deputy DA Ted Brevoort knocked on the jamb of the open door. "Come in," Dana said. "We're just getting started on Perry Rigger." As an executive assistant, Ted no longer carried a regular caseload, but Dana had assigned him to prosecute *People versus Rigger* because she needed her best on this one. The trial started tomorrow with a hearing on the defense motion to suppress the defendant's statements to the police. After a three-day manhunt ended in his arrest, Rigger had talked to the cops in a big way, full of excuses and explanations.

Ted lowered his athletic, wiry frame into the seat next to Indigo, ready to add his usual incisive understatement to the meeting. "The more we find out, the nuttier he gets."

"Battier you mean," Indigo said with a big smile.

Ted shot a scolding glare at her through his black-rimmed glasses. "Very original," he said wryly—his way of showing that he enjoyed Indigo's humor. The bat jokes were nothing new in this murder case against a man who'd told investigators that he just "snapped" when his wife said she wanted to invite her parents over for dinner. Didn't she understand the stress he was under? His failing business, a vitamin and health supplement store, was going into bankruptcy, and he just couldn't face having the in-laws over to the house. Mercifully, according to the medical examiner, the first blow of the baseball bat rendered the victim unconscious, unable to feel the thirty blows that followed. Dana had never seen such a grisly murder, even when she was working the homicide chart years ago, during the crack epidemic in Manhattan.

"Not nutty or batty enough, apparently," she said. Rigger's attorney, Frederick Carlyle, had rejected a plea of not responsible by reason of insanity, and the court had found Rigger competent to stand trial. "The only question is whether he's going to raise the defense of extreme emotional disturbance—EED."

"He'll go for it," Ted predicted. "He doesn't have any other options that I can see. Even if he gets his statements suppressed, the physical evidence proves he killed his wife. EED won't beat the case for him, but…"

"Very original!" Indigo mimicked.

Ted's mouth twitched as he pretended to ignore her. "As I was saying, the EED defense won't *acquit* him," Ted's eyes darted toward his foil, "but the jury could convict him of manslaughter instead of murder. He has to show a personality disorder that made him 'snap' involuntarily."

"We all snap, baby," said Indigo, "but no one snaps with a baseball bat unless he wants to kill someone. Where I grew up, murder was murder, and crazy was crazy. Only people in Scarsdale get these fancy 'diseases.' Narcissistic, paranoid personality disorder, megalomaniacal tendencies." She clucked and shook her head in disdain. "Can't hardly fit those words in your mouth."

"It's a difficult defense to win," said Dana. "You also have to prove a good reason for snapping. A plausible trigger that sets off your mental disorder. The only defense cases *I* know of with any kind of success are paramour situations…"

"Yeah, it's okay to go bat crazy when you find the wife in bed with another man," offered Indigo.

"Mm-hmm. Cases like that," Dana agreed. "Inviting the in-laws over for dinner doesn't cut it."

"Or beat it," added Ted.

"I don't know, Mizz DA," said Indigo. "You never met *my* in-laws. Why'd you think I had to get out of that marriage?"

Dana laughed. "Should we be looking for bodies?"

"I'm clean. Didn't have a bat handy when I needed one."

"Good to know." Dana's big smile changed into a firm set of her mouth. "Time to get serious here. What did you learn about Rigger this weekend?"

"I can't say, not if we're getting all serious here. I had *way* too much fun working overtime this weekend."

"Try me."

"Went to the gym where Rigger pumps iron. What a stink in that place, but the *bah-dies*, my God girl, pecs and abs glistening everywhere. The owner said he suspected Rigger was using steroids—"

"I can believe it."

"I spoke with a couple of the hunks over there, handling the barbells. They went on and on about how Batman just loved himself, standing in front of that big mirror in the exercise room, examining his bod while he lifted weights. Hair dyed jet black. Such an asshole, they said. He was always accusing everyone of messing with his gym bag. A weird guy, but he knew what he was about. A control freak, they said, always wanted his muscle shirt to fall just so on his chest," she demonstrated, "wiped the barbells with Purell before he touched them, chewed these tablets, some kind of health crap, exactly half an hour into his workout. Really strange, but in total control. This is a dude who knows what he's doing."

"More than capable of forming the intent to kill," Ted mused. "Did you apply your usual charm on these witnesses?"

"You bet. Two of 'em gave me their numbers just like that!" She snapped her fingers. "Might use those numbers myself sometime…"

"Restrain yourself," Ted intoned. "I may need those witnesses for rebuttal if the defendant takes the stand."

"Sounds like a plan. Anything else, Indigo?" Dana asked.

"That's it."

"Okay, good work. I think we're done with Mr. Rigger for now."

"Back out into the cold," Indigo said in her drama queen voice. She pushed up from the chair, and Ted started to do the same.

"Hold on a minute, Ted." He stayed seated while Indigo left the room. Dana wanted to talk to him about Evan's civil case against a prisoner Ted had prosecuted. "Evan's on his way to Green Haven this morning to depose Yusuf Nashid."

"Yes, he told me."

"Any thoughts on his case?"

"He's not going to have any problem that I can see. I gave him everything we had, the public stuff, anyway, not the privileged material." Discovery rules protected an attorney's "work product," including any notes of theories and impressions of the case. "He should be able to win it on summary judgment. The victim's widow is entitled to that money."

"Proof of the crime isn't necessary…"

"Right, it isn't. The crime is proven. The defendant's guilty plea took care of that." Ted's manner and tone were offhand, but then he paused, placed his hands on the back of the chair, and looked directly into Dana's eyes. An intellectual mind meld.

"You're thinking that it's another case involving extreme emotional disturbance."

"It's in the back of my mind. Wasn't that a possible defense? The reason for the negotiated plea?"

"We anticipated a defense of EED or crime of passion. Intentional murder was tough to prove, so Bill agreed to a plea to the lower charge." Ted was referring to Dana's predecessor, DA William Davenport. "But for Evan's purposes, the plea doesn't matter. The defendant is doing time for manslaughter, and the conviction itself provides the basis for Evan's lawsuit."

"Okay, thanks Ted. He really appreciated your help on it."

"Any time."

As Ted walked out of her office, Dana's preoccupation with Evan's case lingered. Why she should have a sense of unease, she didn't know. Perhaps it had to do with memories of the old days, the cases she'd litigated against Evan's adversary. Defense attorney Vesma Krumins always used to come up with an interesting theory, whether it was something completely off-the-wall or eminently reasonable.

Unpredictable, that's what she was.

2 »   *SLICE*

THE DRIVE TO Green Haven Correctional Facility was a harrowing start to an unpredictable day, enough to raise the blood pressure—but not by much. Not for a person like Evan Goodhue. Steadfastly cheerful and optimistic, Evan recovered from each slip and near miss with a whistle and a quick laugh of relief. Not much rattled him.

The Taconic State Parkway, designed for a quieter era, was once a two-lane, north-south road to be taken at medium speed. A beautiful drive with climbing and descending grades, hairpin twists and turns. The parkway had expanded to accommodate increased traffic, swallowing the shoulder on either side to make four "lanes." Any big snowfall was a challenge, impossible to push completely off the road. The lanes were so narrow that mere inches separated cars traveling side-by-side and in opposite directions. There were also plenty of fools who ignored the 50-mph speed limit, even in this weather.

Evan had grown up in Westchester and knew the roads, but he rarely drove north on the TSP through Putnam and Dutchess Counties. Today's adventure seemed almost surreal, a stark contrast to his usual routine as a civil litigator in the courtrooms and conference rooms of the concrete metropolis. His early career in criminal prosecution was now a distant memory. Yet here he was, on a treacherous drive to a maximum security prison, to keep an appointment with a murderer! He laughed and burst into song: *"If I can make it here…!"* The windows in the empty cabin of his Subaru shook. Sinatra he wasn't.

On a usual Monday, Evan would have seen the kids off to their school buses before leaving for work. He missed that today. Travis and Natalie didn't exactly "need" his supervision (they'd made it clear enough), but he loved their brand of teenage chaos and grabbed every possible opportunity to be with them. On this icy morning, there'd been some thought that the schools might delay opening. Before the kids were up, he checked the school website. Everything on schedule. The school district had decided it was safe, and who could possibly come to harm on a hulking yellow school bus?

Dana, on the other hand, was more skittish when it came to driving in the winter. On the phone just now, he picked up on her stress. Not that she would admit it. Dana was a person of perpetual reasonableness, even in the jaws of calamity, but Evan could hear the slightest constriction of her throat under the smooth mellifluous tone. He believed that his own voice and positive disposition had a calming effect on her. He liked to think of it as his own unique contribution to their relationship. Maybe this was pure fallacy, a search for an equalizer. Maybe the calming effect flowed the other way.

Evan's usual weekday routine took him on the same route as Dana, south to White Plains. The satellite office of his law firm, Belknap, Rose, & Goodhue, P.C., was on the seventeenth floor of an office building a few blocks from the County Courthouse. There'd been years of commuting by train to the headquarters of BRG in Manhattan before Evan spearheaded the idea of opening an office in the suburbs, where he served as senior partner to a small staff. After the move, the Goodhue-Hargrove family lifestyle relaxed a little. Evan spent less time commuting, and the proximity of his office to Dana's allowed them occasional lunches together or springtime walks in the park. This year, Dana's new position as DA had stressed things up a bit. But Evan had come to learn that the ship of their nineteen-year marriage could cut a steady line through the roiling sea of changing variables. Never a dull moment with Dana Hargrove.

"Maybe *that's* why I married you," he mused out loud. The frosty windshield made no reply.

Thirty minutes remained to his destination. Maneuvering the curves and slick spots, he used the time to think about his case, *Hafeez versus Nashid*. This lawsuit had as many unexpected twists and turns as the parkway. Evan's client, the plaintiff Malikah Hafeez, was the widow of Almed Nashid, the victim of an "honor" killing, brother against brother. The murdering brother, Yusuf Nashid, was in his ninth year of a sixteen-year sentence at Green Haven. Yusuf had been damn lucky to get such a light sentence. He owed it all to the plea-bargaining skills of his attorney, Hernando Ramirez, a respected name in criminal defense. The charge of second-degree murder had been reduced to first degree manslaughter with a sentence in the middle of the range. The ADA on the case, Ted Brevoort, had agreed to this compromise as the best outcome under the circumstances. Yusuf was not seen as a threat to the public at large, and the People's case was weak on the *mens rea* element. Was it cold-blooded intent or extreme emotional disturbance? The crime had been personal.

"They were close," Malikah told Evan months ago, during the initial intake interview. She was a woman of contrasts: a brightly flowered head scarf and dignified bearing, intelligent eyes, a bitter and vengeful edge to her voice under the veneer of her receding nature. Malikah, Yusuf, and Almed had grown up in Mount Vernon, the first-generation children of two families of Yemeni immigrants. "Despite everything about Almed—and I knew everything—Yusuf loved him. You could see it. They got together every week, and they observed all holidays with their parents."

"Then it must have been…"

"Yes. A shock. Yusuf freely admitted the killing and was proud of it. Maybe it was the closeness that made him so proud."

Because they were so close. A strange quirk of culture or personality beyond Evan's grasp, but he accepted it nonetheless. Malikah's telling of the story was so clearly uncontrived.

As part of his mental preparation for today's deposition, Evan conjured Yusuf's mugshot from his arrest in 2000, trying to visualize his face and probable demeanor. It was impossible to know how he would respond when questioned under oath. For present purposes, Evan didn't need to ask him about the facts of his crime. This lawsuit was simply a fight over money. Yusuf's sister-in-law Malikah was suing him under the Son of Sam law, which required convicted felons to compensate the victims of their crimes. The law reached more than just the ill-gotten gains from the crime itself. All property and income of the defendant was fair game, even if the defendant acquired the property years after his crime. When the victim suffered, the culprit had to pay.

If he had the money. That was the catch.

Most convicted felons were penniless, and Yusuf was no exception. He'd been utterly judgment proof—until now. Just recently, he'd come into a very large sum of money, and its source was one of those interesting twists in the case. A twist of the knife.

Although Evan didn't intend to delve into the murder at the deposition, if asked, Yusuf might have this story to tell. From the day that his brother Almed married Malikah, Yusuf knew that the marriage was a sham, a cover for Almed's homosexuality. This knowledge was implicit, gleaned from observation and intuition. Almed had never admitted his sexual orientation and did his best to hide it. Yusuf could blot the shame of Almed's sin from his mind as long as it remained a secret. All of that changed when Almed's true colors came to light, unintentionally but publicly.

He was seen at a gay bar. Not just seen, but photographed, unbeknownst to him, by a patron who was taking a picture of a group of friends. Almed happened to be in the background, his likeness clear enough to see. When the photographer posted the picture on social media, Almed was identified, bringing shame to the family.

Evan knew these facts of the case from his conversations with Malikah and the prosecutor, ADA Brevoort. He'd reviewed all the paperwork: the police reports, medical records and autopsy report, the DA's file, and court transcripts. It was enough to patch together an incomplete silent film, one that morphed, with the aid of Evan's imagination, into full color and surround sound.

In his mind, he replayed that movie now.

On February 22, 2000, Yusuf arranged to meet Almed at a teahouse in Mount Vernon. The owner was Yusuf's close friend, a man named Tadeo, whose complicity later would be suspected but not confirmed. The shop was convenient for Yusuf's purposes, an unassuming storefront. Behind the store was a service alley for deliveries, dumpsters, and garbage pickup.

"We have to talk about this shame," is what Yusuf said to Almed on the phone. "I don't want to be seen with you. Come in the back door. There will be a booth for us in the rear."

"You don't understand—"

"We will talk."

"How can I know you'll keep an open mind? Listen to me—"

"No! You listen. I'll tell you how to make this right."

The meeting was set, but their teatime was short. Their "booth" was not in the teahouse proper but in Tadeo's back room, away from prying eyes.

"What of our mother and father?" Yusuf asked.

"You're the one who told them! They knew nothing until then. They don't have a computer and still haven't seen the picture."

"They had to be told."

"This is *my* life. I'm doing nothing to hurt you."

"And not Malikah? Are you not shaming her with this filth?"

"I care for Malikah. That's none of your—"

"It *is* my business!"

"I can see there's nothing to talk about." Almed rose to leave and turned to the door leading into the main room of the tea-house. Yusuf stood and blocked him. Tadeo suddenly appeared in the doorway, an impenetrable obstacle. There was only one exit, out into the alley.

"*I'll* tell you how we'll make this right! Go!" Yusuf followed him out.

Yes, the brothers were very close. And because he loved his brother, Yusuf was carrying a nine-inch hunting knife. Because he loved his family, Yusuf unsheathed that knife as he followed Almed into the alley.

It was 8:04 a.m. when Evan pulled into the visitor parking lot at Green Haven. Nearly an hour remained before the deposition was scheduled to begin, but he was unsure if he'd allowed enough time. There would be screening and security procedures for him and the others: the stenographer, video technician, and his opposing counsel, Vesma Krumins.

The correction officers in the screening area were efficient and stern, not mean spirited. They had a job to do. Evan was "wanded" and came up clean, despite his beating heart. An officer searched his briefcase, removed his cell phone, placed it in a plastic box, and whisked it away into a security room, giving him a claim tag in return. Evan put the little square in his jacket pocket, a poor substitute for his phone. Stripped of instant contact with the outside world, he felt a twinge of panic and had the urge to protest, but primal needs quickly prevailed. At a maximum security prison, it's wise to toe the line. In a few hours, his freedom and possessions would be restored to him. He'd be miles away from this place—the prisoners would not.

Fingering the edges of the claim tag, Evan wondered what he'd do if they needed a phone to contact the judge for a ruling during the deposition. Obliquely, he looked for signs of accommodation in the profile of the correction officer who escorted him through a dank, linoleum-floored, cement-walled corridor. Heels clicked and reverberated, nostrils pricked from the faint odor of sewage barely masked by a strong disinfectant. They came to a door with a small, square window at face level. The deposition room. The officer waved his electronic key. Evan stepped inside, where a man and a woman were already setting up, the stenographer and video technician. And there it was: a clunky, square-buttoned telephone sitting on the end of the table closest to Evan.

The officer nodded toward the apparatus. "Dial 9 before you make a call. Everything's recorded."

"Understood. Thank you."

"This door stays locked. If you need one of us, hit star 88." The officer stepped out and locked him in. *Hit star 88…* Somehow, Evan wasn't reassured. A murdering felon would soon be joining them in this locked, ten-by-twelve room.

On the wall, an antiquated, round-faced clock let him know that forty minutes had passed since he'd left his car in the lot. The little hand and big hand were both approaching the nine. In two seconds of silence before speaking, he heard just as many clicks of the second hand. "Good morning," Evan said, a bright voice at odds with the environment. Introductions were made, business cards exchanged. Carter, the video technician, Teresa, the stenographer. He'd arranged for these professionals from the court reporting service but had never met them. He followed up with the obvious question, just to say something. "So, Ms. Krumins is yet to arrive?"

"Haven't seen her," said the young video guy.

Teresa glanced around the room with dancing eyes and said, "Guess not. But she's a hard one to miss." A wry, knowing smile. No doubt Teresa had worked with Vesma Krumins before.

Evan suppressed a chuckle, set his briefcase at one end of the long table, and took out his notes. The room was a dull white without decoration, furnished only with the rectangular table and six chairs. A half dozen plastic bottles of water had been placed in the middle of the table.

A minute later there was a "beep" of the electronic key at the door, and Vesma was shown into the room. Evan noticed a difference. Her usual style had taken a hit for today's outing to the pen: a conservative pantsuit and mandarin-collared blouse. Her ash-blonde hair was twisted and pulled up in a knot at the back of her head instead of loose and messy to mid-back, the way she liked to wear it. The tough, plain features were made even more so without the trademark red lipstick.

"Good morning," she said to the group. Three voices returned the greeting. Evan walked up and extended a hand, noticing his new superior height. Another difference. She was wearing squatty-heeled shoes today.

Still at the open doorway, the officer asked, "When do you want him?"

Evan caught Vesma's eye. "About ten minutes?"

"That should do it," she said. There were stipulations to discuss.

"Okay. Call star 88 when you're ready. We'll bring him in over there." The officer motioned to a door on the opposite side of the room. Perhaps he saw the question in Evan's eye because he added, "An officer will stay in the room with him."

"No restraints," Vesma said. It was a directive rather than a question. Weeks ago, she'd made this request to the warden in writing, copy to Evan. He trusted her judgment on this because she knew her client well enough, not only from this lawsuit but from another, the one that had filled her attorney escrow account with over a million dollars. Frozen dollars. By order of the court, no one could touch those funds until this Son of Sam lawsuit was resolved.

"He doesn't give us any trouble," was the officer's response. Evan took that as a "yes" to Vesma's demand. A trouble-free murderer. Really? Today, this felon might not be so pleased, a formerly docile prisoner now simmering with rage over Malikah's grab at his money…

They got down to business. Evan nodded at Teresa. "We're on the record." He announced the name of the case and the purpose of their gathering and identified the people in the room. He turned to Vesma. "Did you review the proposed stipulations? I'll read them into the record—"

"Not so fast," Vesma said. "I don't agree with all of this." The paper was in front of her on the table. "I'll stipulate to the first part of number one. 'On September 14, 2000, Yusuf Nashid was convicted on his plea of guilty to manslaughter in the first degree and was sentenced to a term of sixteen years.' I won't stipulate to the rest of it."

Evan was miffed but not entirely surprised. Vesma never liked to give an inch. "What's there to dispute? Your client stabbed and killed his brother Almed on the night of February 22, 2000. It's in the public record."

"Then use the public record. The indictment. The transcript of the guilty plea. I'm not going to characterize what he did or didn't do. It was a plea deal. He pled guilty. That's it."

"Okay. And what about the medical malpractice case?"

She read from the paper again. "I'll stipulate to this much: 'In the case of *Nashid versus Agarwal*, on June 28, 2007, the jury awarded the plaintiff $100,000 in future medical expenses, and $1,000,000 in pain and suffering. Judgment was entered in the principal amount of $1,100,000, plus post-verdict interest, and the

Appellate Division affirmed the judgment on December 17, 2008.' That's it."

Very fine. Vesma was making his job difficult. The rest of the stip, couched in proper language, conveyed the messy facts of the med mal case: On February 22, 2000, Yusuf presented with a knife wound to the lower abdomen, Dr. Parth Agarwal botched the emergency surgery and a follow-up attempt at repair, and Yusuf was left holding the bag.

"I'm not stipulating to anything further about that case," said Vesma. "As you say, it's part of the public record."

Evan placed an open hand on his bald pate and stroked back to the cleanly-shaved lower cranium. An unconscious habit, often triggered by the hardball tactics of opposing counsel.

In the end, it didn't matter much. Evan didn't need to retry the med mal case. Still, he wasn't quite sure what Vesma had up her sleeve. His suspicions about an underlying agenda dated back more than a month, when he sent her the notice of deposition. He'd expected her to respond with a demand to cancel the deposition. This case easily could be resolved on a set of stipulated facts and opposing summary judgment motions. The outcome hinged on pure questions of law: Who was entitled to the money sitting in Vesma's escrow account? A quick resolution seemed to be in her interest. She'd taken Yusuf's med mal case on a contingency basis and hadn't been reimbursed for her expenses or legal fees, close to a quarter of a million. When Evan filed this action, the court froze the entire amount in escrow, ignoring Vesma's claim.

Was she worried about recovering her fee? Under the Son of Sam law, crime victims could recover the defendant's civil judgments, minus attorney fees. But an argument could be made that other provisions of the law were in conflict. Attorney contingency agreements were based on obtaining results for the client. If Malikah won the Son of Sam lawsuit, then Vesma literally hadn't recovered anything for Yusuf. All the money belonged to Malikah, and Vesma's claim was a matter of private contract between her and her client. It was a weak argument, and Evan hadn't played that card. Yet. He figured that Vesma deserved to be paid for her work. Still, he hadn't dismissed the tactic entirely. He'd see how things were going.

As far as the facts were concerned, only the basics were in the public record. It made no sense for Vesma to be so obstinate about refusing to sign the stipulation. Many facts were undisputed. This was an "honor" killing that hadn't gone as smoothly as Yusuf intended. Almed defended himself, struggled, twisted his brother's arm back, and managed to slice him in the gut. Yusuf overcame Almed's resistance and plunged the knife deep into his brother's chest and neck, again and again, four times. Tadeo summoned an ambulance, telling the authorities (truthfully or falsely?) that he discovered the bloody combatants when the fight was over. It was too late for Almed, but an optimistic prognosis for Yusuf. He underwent emergency surgery in the wee hours of the morning. Was Dr. Agarwal incompetent or simply not at his best, shaky from lack of sleep? Maybe he felt an insidious subliminal influence—the knowledge of Yusuf's crime. In a slippery slice of the scalpel, the doctor completely severed Yusuf's colon where merely a nick had been wanting repair. A subsequent surgery, also by Dr. Agarwal, failed in the attempted resection.

Clear malpractice, something that might have won an even larger verdict if the plaintiff hadn't been a convicted felon, a fact that snuck out during the trial. This was the kind of case that might have garnered two or three million for a more sympathetic plaintiff.

"So, we're done." Evan crossed out wide swatches of the page and handed it to Vesma for her signature before giving it to Teresa. "Please mark this as joint exhibit one, stipulations of counsel."

They were ready to call star 88.

No one spoke in the five minutes it took for the delivery of the deponent. A beep of the electronic key at the other end of the room announced the prisoner's arrival. Arms loose at his sides, Yusuf Nashid ambled in, followed by a correction officer. "Sit here," the guard told the prisoner, motioning to the chair closest to the door. Yusuf complied. "I'm Sergeant Demmings," the uniformed man told the group. "I'll be staying." He closed the door—an automatic lock, no doubt—and took up an authoritative stance next to it.

Yusuf was cool and aloof under a half-lidded gaze. His eyes darted toward Vesma in a moment of recognition. Maybe neediness. The prisoner looked plenty healthy to Evan, who momentarily flashed on a probable image of Yusuf's abdomen inside that orange jumpsuit. Curiosity merely. Who would be satisfied with one-point-one million (minus attorney fees) to live with that?

Carter directed the camera, Teresa administered the oath, and the deponent swore to tell the truth. Everyone remained seated during the questioning. Yusuf's answers were efficient, single words and short phrases, and he showed no hesitation in responding. Evan laid the groundwork, establishing that Malikah was Yusuf's sister-in-law, that he'd been convicted of manslaughter for killing his brother Almed, that he'd used a knife to kill him, and that he'd acted alone. Yusuf also testified that Almed cut him during the altercation, that he'd undergone surgery, and that he'd sued the surgeon for malpractice, went to trial, and obtained a judgment in his favor. Vesma voiced no objections to any of this.

"Mr. Nashid, were you awarded a large sum of money in your lawsuit against Dr. Agarwal?"

"Yes."

"Is that sum composed of one hundred thousand dollars for future medical expenses and one million dollars for pain and suffering?"

"Yes. I have suffered."

"But your victim has suffered also. Are you aware that, under the law, you're obligated to compensate the victim of your crime to the extent of your ability?"

"I have no ability. Almed is dead." His eyes shot in the direction of his attorney.

"By ability I mean the large asset, the jury verdict. Are you saying that the jury didn't award that money to you?"

"It is mine."

"And when you killed Almed, you hurt his widow. Malikah is a victim of your crime, is she not?"

"I'm going to object," Vesma cut in. "Don't answer that Yusuf."

"Grounds?"

"These are legal questions for the court."

She was right, of course, and Evan wasn't going to call the judge on this one. He'd gone this far only to see what he could get out of the prisoner, to learn something about his personality and state of mind. "I won't fight you on that, counselor. Your witness."

Vesma's eyes remained fixed on Evan's for a fraction of a second too long, conveying a hint of disbelief. He'd done very little with this witness, but what was there, really, that he had to prove?

"Hello, Yusuf," she began.

"Hello."

"How're you holding up?"

Evan raised his eyebrows but said nothing.

"I'm okay."

"I'd like to ask you about your guilty plea. Were you originally charged with murder?"

"Yes."

"Did your attorney, Hernando Ramirez, work out a deal for

you, a guilty plea to manslaughter?"

"Yes."

"Did you take that plea deal because you were guilty?"

"No."

Here it comes, Evan thought. Something was coming. He could feel it. He still couldn't place his finger on it.

"Were you aware when you pled guilty that you were forfeiting all possible defenses? Giving up your defenses?"

"Yes."

"Then why did you take the deal?"

"Because my attorney got me sixteen years. I could have done twenty-five or more. The evidence didn't look good."

"Did you believe you were innocent of murder?"

"Yes."

"If you had gone to trial, what would your defense have been?"

"Justification."

Okay. They'd arrived. This was it.

"Please explain the basis for this defense."

"Almed had dishonored our family. I confronted him, we fought, and he cut me badly."

"You mean, he took your knife during the fight?"

"No, no, no. He came at me first. He had his own knife."

3 »   *VICTIM*

VESMA HEARD HER own voice in the earpiece: "Hello, you've called the Kavanaghs. We can't come to the phone right now…" She replaced the receiver, crossed her arms, and remained standing at the edge of her desk.

It was 3:50, and Ginger wasn't home. Vesma wasn't quite sure where she was. Not an uncommon situation, but no real cause for concern. The girl ran with a "good" crowd at Stone Ridge High and was active in extracurricular clubs. Today, for some reason, Vesma felt an impulse to call. Maybe it was the strangeness of the day, the early morning visit to the maximum security prison.

"Gingie." Under her breath, Vesma absently muttered the favorite nickname. She picked up the receiver again and tried her daughter's mobile phone, imagining it deep inside the backpack under three textbooks and a ruin of crumpled homework. After four rings, the call went to voicemail. Although the recording was only six months old, it played back the voice of an infantile stranger: "Hi, this is, um, Gingie? [to her friends in the background, "what do you want?" — giggles] um, leave a message?" More giggles and a beep. Vesma opened her mouth to speak but ended the call instead. It was useless to leave a message.

Now, going on four years after her divorce from Tynan Kavanagh, Vesma was just beginning to realize how much she'd relied on her son Sean. He'd been a real comfort, the man of the house, counted on to keep an eye on his little sister. An unfair burden to place on a teenager, but unavoidable. Ty was perpetually noncompliant with child support, and after years of staying home with the kids, Vesma was back at work, reinventing her law practice. A year and a half ago, they moved out of the city to this northern suburb, a better environment for teens. Maybe they were the poor kids on the block, but their bungalow was cozy and affordable, and the high school was academically strong in a diverse school district. There'd been one year's peace of mind when Ginger was a sophomore, Sean a senior. This year, her son was away at college and Ginger was on her own.

Vesma envied those mothers and daughters who seemed to have a natural, unthinking closeness. Relationships weren't crafted by force. In her early career as a criminal defense attorney, Vesma had learned to choose her questions wisely when interviewing a client. Over-examination often backfired, eroded the trust, and elicited information that, maybe, she didn't need or want to know. The third degree was best saved for the opponent.

Still, even this mother was not without rules. At the start of the school year, Vesma had imposed a single guiding principle: "Let me know your plans." More often than not, the facts weren't volunteered. Questions led to vague answers, floating out in cheery, spacey obliviousness to the benefits of certainty. "I'll be home after school," the girl might say, having omitted, "after a SADD meeting." Students Against Destructive Decisions, her favorite club. Late buses were taken and rides magically arranged without the need of parental knowledge. It wasn't deliberate deception, but simply a life lived in the moment, the moments ever changing, presenting new opportunities or suddenly remembered commitments. Vesma understood how the teen mind worked and remembered the pleasures of living life in the present. But a phone call to Mom would also be nice. In the moment.

Vesma didn't doubt that, tonight, when she got home at six, Ginger would be there, doing her homework or instant messaging with friends on the computer. One such evening, not long ago, she'd asked Ginger about her afternoon, and this is how the conversation went:

"Did you have a SADD meeting today?"

"Yup."

"How'd you get home?"

"Devraj drove us. Me and Sarah."

"Devraj has a license?"

"Of course, Mom!"

"Then it must be a restricted license. He shouldn't have more than one passenger in the car."

"Devraj is, like, one of the older juniors. He's almost seventeen!" A slip of the tongue, proof of guilty knowledge. Ginger was too sharp not to know the rules. She'd had her driving permit since mid-September and was eligible for a restricted license next month when she was sixteen and a half. She was also smart enough to argue every plausible exception to the rules in her case, to avoid taking the school bus. She'd been spoiled by her big brother, her own personal chauffeur. When he went off to college, Sean took the "preowned" Kia with him—another point of contention. Since Mom had given Sean a car, shouldn't she do the same for her daughter?

"Ginger. Too many kids in the car is a distraction. There's a reason for these restrictions. Aren't you and Devraj talking about stuff like that during your SADD meetings?"

"How can you compare this to drunk driving! I would *never* get in a car with a drunk driver!"

Vesma felt the sting of guilt. Was it any wonder that her daughter was such a dedicated member of a student group against drunk driving? Vesma didn't like to remember the many times that Ginger had unknowingly (or knowingly?) gotten into a car with a certain, beloved drunk driver. Thankfully, those worries were over. Ty claimed to be rehabilitated, and although Vesma entertained doubts about that claim, it didn't matter. Ginger had refused to see him for nearly two years now, despite the court-ordered visitation schedule.

"We're the good kids, Mom, remember? We're working on SADD together and the bus is gone and how else are we supposed to get home? You're all at work." She waved her hand in the air. *All you absent parents.*

"You can always call me. I'll leave work and come get you."

"It would ruin your day, and I'd be waiting for, like, an hour. You wouldn't believe how safe Devraj is. I mean, people honk at him all the time because he's going the speed limit!"

Years ago, in a blur of crazy youth, Vesma had ignored some of the rules too—far bigger rules than the little ones that Ginger sometimes forgot. Much of what Vesma had done during that era was now kept to herself.

Four o'clock. Glancing around her small office, eyeing the clutter at the edges of the desk, she was reminded that there was still time to be productive. Best to remain on track and get home at a decent hour.

The intercom buzzed. "Yes?"

"Package just delivered for you."

"Okay, thanks."

Vesma walked out to the central reception area of the suite of offices she shared with three other solo attorneys. Anna Ciriglio was at the front desk, talking into her headpiece. A vital member of the professional group, Anna wore many hats, as receptionist, secretary, and paralegal. She looked up and pointed to a six-inch thick mailer on the corner of her desk. Vesma glanced at the sender's address and didn't need x-ray vision to know what the package held: a thick trial transcript, an indictment, pretrial motion papers, and a probation report with the mug shot of her new client. Would the photo display an angry face of poverty and ignorance or a smug face of misdirected privilege? She didn't know anything about the case yet, and this was just the first. Others would be coming her way.

As she lifted the package, her heart gave a nervous flutter of excitement or dread or some of both. She hadn't represented a criminal defendant for…had it been that long? Nearly seventeen years. Her last trial was in June of 1992, when she was seven months pregnant with Ginger and Sean was a toddler. The case pitted Vesma against Dana Hargrove in the "battle of the bellies," as their colleagues dubbed it. Ever conscious of her appearance, Vesma invented her own mental game, "the battle of the maternity fashions," winning that one hands down. As for the important part of the battle, the attorneys split the difference: one conviction and one acquittal on the two murder counts against late-term abortionist Dr. Grant Spellman.

Their respective bosses at the Legal Aid Society and the Manhattan District Attorney's Office claimed that the match was a product of the random rotational assignment systems of their offices. Vesma and Dana were skeptical. These two trial stars, both noticeably pregnant, ended up on opposite sides of the courtroom in the high-profile murder case, conveying a mix of subliminal messages. Hargrove personified community outrage at the alleged horrific acts Spellman had committed against the near-term unborn. Krumins conveyed a comfort with her own choice and the choices of other women in similar circumstances.

For Vesma, the emotionally charged trial brought to a head the near impossibility of juggling new motherhood with professional demands. Sitting next to the smarmy Dr. Spellman within his cloud of anxious body odor and cheap aftershave, she came to a decision. The day after the verdict, she walked into her boss's office and gave notice. It was time to stay home with the babies.

Ty would support them. Hopefully.

Fast forward to 2009 and those seven-month fetuses of the trial stars were now attending the same high school. This time, it was pure coincidence. Vesma hadn't given a thought to Dana in years, and so it came as a surprise, months after moving to the suburbs, to learn that Dana's kids were in the same school district. Until recently, there was no reason to think that the kids knew each other, but then Ginger mentioned Travis's name when she was talking about a SADD meeting. The girl was aware of a connection between the mothers, but Vesma hadn't said much about any of her cases against Dana, including *People versus Spellman*. It was not a trial she liked to talk about.

Now, Vesma's return to criminal law was not entirely a matter of choice. It was her area of expertise and the logical path to take. The first step in this direction came when her officemate, Hernando Ramirez, referred Yusuf Nashid's medical malpractice claim to her. It wasn't criminal defense, but it was the closest she'd come to a convicted felon in years. She was grateful for the break but suspected that it had been a "pity" referral. Hernando was aware of Vesma's financial desperation since the crash of 2008, when her meager plate of small-potatoes civil cases started to dwindle. The slam-dunk med mal case was a godsend, a huge jury verdict that gave her a boost in spirit (and money!) but not for long. Slapped with the Son of Sam lawsuit, filed by Dana Hargrove's husband no less, Vesma wasn't allowed to touch any part of the million-plus dollars until Malikah's claim was settled.

Because of her financial bind, Vesma decided to take court appointments for criminal appeals. As she stood at Anna's desk eyeing the package, she couldn't name her feelings, a mix that instantly pulled back the sights, sounds, and emotions of her early days with the Legal Aid Society, the clients, colleagues, and Tynan, a top defense investigator for the Society. Maybe she could recapture some of the good part of those days, the energy and idealism. She knew it could never be the same. Coming back to it now, she didn't have the energy for another trial, so she'd chosen appellate practice. The experience would be more antiseptic, a greater distance from the client and a loftier immersion in the law.

Turning from Anna's desk, she walked straight into the path of Hernando, also out looking for the afternoon mail. "Hi, Nando."

He glanced at her and pulled his chin back in mild surprise. Instantly, she understood what he'd noticed. Her face was exposed, the hair pulled back in a librarian bun, and her shape was straightened and shortened in the conservative pantsuit with low heels. A new look for this morning's visit to Green Haven, where her usual style would have been too provocative. He said nothing about it and shifted his eyes to the package in her hands. "Special delivery?"

"A case in the Appellate Division."

"I didn't know you were doing appeals now." Anna, still talking into her headset, caught his eye and thrust a short stack of envelopes in his direction.

"A new thing. A court appointment." Vesma looked down, taking a sudden interest in her package. "I signed up for the 18-B panel."

"Ah-ha!" Nando grinned with genuine pleasure. "A criminal appeal? Since when did you come back to the dark side?"

"I guess you buttered me up with Yusuf." It was awkward. She'd often ribbed him about some of his big, bad clients while expressing a desire never to do criminal defense again. Interesting that Hernando, a former prosecutor, seemed to relish his current specialization in criminal defense, while Vesma, despite her experience in the field, had been averse to the thought of making a living that way again.

His eyes sparkled with laughter, but not in a mocking way.

"Actually," she went on, "I just need to pick up a little more income…"

He frowned. "Too bad about the freeze." They both knew what he meant.

"I'll get my cut eventually."

"You will. The court can't make you work for free. How did the deposition go?" Obliquely, he eyed her outfit.

"Not bad. Do I still smell like prison?"

He laughed and was about to respond but seemed to think better of it.

"If you really want to know," she said, "your man Yusuf was very cooperative. Do you have some time to talk about it?"

"Sure! Come by my office in a few minutes. I have to make a quick call first."

"Okay."

He winked and turned away. Did he do that on purpose? It was so natural, his keen attention, the instant inclusion.

Vesma walked out of reception and entered the next open door, her office. With money still on her mind, the room seemed shabbier than usual. Hers was the lowest rent office in the suite. An almost square eleven by twelve, the dimensions were slightly askew, as if the structure had decomposed into a misaligned skeleton. The building had been constructed long before the days of corporate extravagance, and the neighboring building blocked most of the light passing through the small, perpetually dirty window.

Feeling the weight of her "special delivery," she walked up to her desk, dropped the bundle in the middle, and stared at it for several seconds. The new case could wait. She'd rather discuss *Hafeez versus Nashid* with Hernando. On the edge of her desk, an accordion folder held the case file, including Nando's papers from the criminal prosecution in 2000. She picked it up and walked out.

He might still be on the phone, so she ignored the direct route through the conference room and took the long way around, passing the nicer offices, the ones she'd rather have. The first corner office belonged to Keiko Tanaka, who specialized in estate planning and probate. The door was shut, but muffled voices could be heard. Keiko was inside, working with a client. The other corner office belonged to Jerome Feinberg, the oldest attorney in their suite. He specialized in civil litigation, had decades of experience, and had given Vesma invaluable guidance during her med mal trial against Dr. Agarwal. The door to his office was closed, all quiet. Jerry was probably in court.

Next came Hernando's office, directly across from hers on the other side of the conference room. "Everyone calls me Nando," he'd said that first day. His door was wide open, and he sat with feet propped up on his desk, phone to ear, gazing out his own dingy window. Left hand held the phone, right hand cupped the back of his head over the dense, black, collar-length hair. He spoke rapidly in animated Spanish, not noticing her presence in his doorway. Here was a man very easy with his job, doing it well, without second thoughts.

She didn't stand in the doorway for long. He ended the call, lifted his feet off the desk, planted them on the floor, and swiveled around. "Enter!"

She came in and sat down across from him on the other side of his desk, holding the case file in her lap. The wooden chair lacked upholstery and felt hard under her thighs. Nando didn't like his clients to be too comfortable, and she had her own reasons for feeling uneasy. A week ago, she'd visited Yusuf at Green Haven to prepare him for the deposition. Maybe she'd laid a few hints, helping him along with an idea for his defense of the case. She hadn't told Nando about that conversation. Should she?

"So," he started, "what did our man say about the night that put him in prison for sixteen years?"

"He testified that Almed pulled a knife on him first and he defended himself. If he'd gone to trial, he would have presented a justification defense."

Hernando lifted his eyebrows. "Surprise, surprise. I guess he's had a lot of time on his hands. Gets the imagination going."

"It certainly surprised my adversary." She glanced down at the file in her lap and gave Nando a guarded look from under a lowered brow. "Although, it *does* seem to fit your notes. There was something in there about a knife."

"Hmm. Let me see those papers again." He motioned toward the file. She opened it and pulled out a single page with his handwritten notes.

He scanned it, stopping midway to read out loud. "'Almed: pocketknife.' That's what I wrote, all right."

Vesma could see the puzzlement on his face. She didn't want to give the impression that she doubted him or his defense strategy of nine years ago, when he represented Yusuf. "Maybe Yusuf said something to you during an interview?"

"Apparently. But I *do* know that I never saw a pocketknife or any record of the police recovering a knife other than the murder weapon."

"Well, maybe, if Almed was carrying a knife, it could've been returned to Malikah. Take a look at this…" She pulled another paper out of the file. "The hospital record says that the police took the decedent's clothing as evidence, but his 'personal effects' were released to his wife."

Hernando leaned back in his chair, elbows on armrests, fingertips touching. "I see where you're going…"

"There's a chance the DA knew about this and didn't say anything. That's improper."

"But still, we're talking about what Yusuf told me. If I thought there was a viable justification defense, I wouldn't have been so quick to recommend that he take the plea. As I recall, Yusuf was eager to accept his punishment. He was conflicted about killing his brother. He was proud of it and ready to stand up and say, 'I did it,' because he was righteous about protecting the family name. But he also felt remorse and regret. Either way, it all added up to a guilty plea, so I got him the best deal possible. He never told me it was self-defense." Nando shook his head. "I would have remembered something like that."

"Then how did the pocketknife come up?"

He gazed off into the distance. "I think he mentioned it when I asked how he got cut. At first, I assumed it was a knife fight. Maybe my question gave him an idea. He said something about his brother always carrying a pocketknife, but he was quick to add that Almed would never use it against him or anyone else. He used it to peel fruit! Something like that." Nando shifted his gaze again, and their eyes locked. "Nope. If there was any self-defense that night, it was Almed trying to defend himself from Yusuf's attack. Almed managed to turn Yusuf's knife on him."

"Well, it was a different story today."

"He's had plenty of time to work on a new strategy." Hernando leaned back in his chair, eyes to the ceiling, hands interlaced behind his head. "Money is a good motivator."

They sat in silence for a moment until Hernando leveled his gaze, meeting her eyes. He seemed to see right into her mind. She felt his tacit approval, enough to cancel out the discomfort of her vulnerability. Or guilt. If he suspected that she'd encouraged Yusuf in his new ideas, he wasn't bothered by it. There was enough room for doubt here, and criminal law was all about doubts. A reasonable doubt always won the case for the defense.

"Tell me how you're going to use this new theory," he said with a little smile. He was already guessing.

"Here's the argument." She straightened up and put the accordion folder on his desk to use her hands while talking. "The purpose of the Son of Sam law is to compensate victims. A person like Yusuf who's injured in the act of self-defense is a victim. He's twice a victim because of the med mal, and that money should compensate *him*. The fact that he pled guilty doesn't change that. It was merely a negotiated deal. He gave up his right to a trial in exchange for a lower sentence. He said what he had to say in court to make that deal. Now, in the Son of Sam case, we can litigate the self-defense theory because it was never decided in the criminal case."

"Okay, very nice, but…"

"You're skeptical."

"Your opponent, Mr. Husband of the DA…"

"Evan Goodhue."

"How could I forget? He'll argue that Yusuf is precluded from using that defense. When he pled guilty, he admitted on the record that he committed the deed."

"I've read the transcript. He admitted to stabbing Almed, but that's it. He simply omitted the details, that he stabbed Almed in self-defense."

Nando laughed and shook his head. "That's a tough argument to make. Good luck!"

"Not so tough. We could file a motion to vacate his guilty plea based on newly discovered evidence."

"What's new here? That he remembered his defense after stewing in prison for nine years?"

Vesma faltered. "I…I'll need to get Malikah or the DA to confirm what we suspect. Almed had a pocketknife, and it was returned to his wife. Or, if we can't get that much, I'll demand an admission from Malikah that her husband used to carry a pocketknife, like Yusuf said. *That's* the new evidence. Something never disclosed to us."

"A neatly closed pocketknife in his pocket…"

"We don't know where it was or what it looked like when the doctors and nurses were trying to save Almed's life."

He smiled. "Okay. It's something. You only need to throw a wrench into the works to put Goodhue on the defensive. But even if you establish it, Yusuf might not want his plea back. Did you think of that? It's *his* choice to make. If the court vacates his plea, he's back to square one, still under indictment. There's a risk of conviction after trial and a heavier sentence." Hernando leaned forward and slapped the desk. "*But*...he'll have a million bucks!"

She laughed. "That's the idea. I don't know. He still might not think it's worth it."

"Right. But how about the ex post facto argument, the one you told me about?"

"Oh, I haven't given up on that one. It's my backup argument. Yusuf stabbed Almed in 2000, but the Son of Sam law wasn't enacted until 2001. If the court applies the law retro-actively, it's punishing him twice for the same crime. That's unconstitutional."

"It's plausible, but I can see Goodhue reminding the court that restitution to the victim isn't considered a criminal punish-ment under the law. Paying money isn't the same as doing hard time."

"Right about that." Her voice trailed, and she hung her head. Not much to be done. This was a losing case. Money, money, money. She should get back to her office right now and start work-ing on the new case, something to pay the bills. All she really wanted out of *Hafeez versus Nashid* was...

"Your fee," Nando said. "That's what I'm wondering about. Who cares whether Yusuf or Malikah gets the money? You just have to get your fee out of escrow first. Upfront."

"But Yusuf's my client."

"Right, okay, you're his lawyer, go ahead and zealously advocate for him. Do your best. But that doesn't mean that you forget about your fee. Where does that stand right now? Goodhue really hit you hard with that freeze order. Seems he should've been nicer and let you extract your fee. What kind of attorney is this guy?"

"Almost too nice. That's what gets me. When he applied for the attachment order, he didn't say anything about my fee. I think the judge froze the whole amount just because it was easier."

"That's worse. No thought went into it. But Goodhue didn't run back into court and say, 'Judge, you made a mistake.'"

"No, he didn't. And he's not going to, and we know why not."

"Leverage, pure and simple. But what's his argument?"

Vesma had thought about this aspect of the case long and hard. She was quick to answer. "I get no fee because the jury awarded the money to Yusuf, not to me. My fee is a private arrangement between attorney and client. I'm a creditor, like everyone else, and Malikah's claim takes priority."

Hernando wrinkled his brow. "Pretty weak. It conflicts with the Son of Sam statute."

"Right. I'm drafting a motion to release my fee, citing the statute and staying a thousand miles away from the word 'creditor.'"

"You think Goodhue's going to oppose? How do you think he'll respond?"

Vesma didn't answer. She was unsure.

"I thought you said he was a nice guy."

"I've been burned by nice guys before. They're the ones you have to look out for."

Nando's silence, and the warmth in his regard, told her everything. The room, with its hissing radiator, was suddenly hot.

Finally, he said, "I've never seen your hair like that before."

4 »   TEENS

Excitement was in the air at Stone Ridge High School, shattering the winter doldrums. Finally, there was something to look forward to: The Valentine's Day Dance! How perfect the date fell, Saturday, February 14, the start of a three-day weekend going into Presidents' Day. With five days left until the dance, the decorations committee was busy creating a vision. On the big night, the gymnasium would be transformed into a tunnel of love with cardboard hearts, crepe paper streamers, and cabaret lighting.

Between classes, the corridors reeled with the buzz of pent up energy, the dazzle of manic smiles, bursts of physical jousting, laughter, loud whispering and stolen glances under veils of long hair. Small explosions of action and sound reverberated against the gray-green walls and buffed linoleum floors. Teenage insecurities were on display. The established couples had their dates lined up, but what about everyone else? Infatuations were tested with timid invitations, accepted with soaring hearts, or rejected to dashed hopes. Members of solid cliques pretended not to care. They would go as a group and dance together. The only kids left out would be the loners, the few teens who had no one.

Parents and teachers prayed for clear weather.

Teens prayed for killer outfits.

"Everyone" was going.

Not Ginger, however, and she was fine with it. As the duly-elected vice president of Students Against Destructive Decisions, she was dedicated to the mission of her organization. Saturday was going to be a big night, the culmination of months of planning and fundraising, car washes and bake sales. The inaugural night of Call Central! Ginger had volunteered to take calls on SADD's brand-new Samsung Gravity mobile phone, a cool aqua color with slide-out keyboard! They hadn't raised enough money for one of those new iPhones, but hey, who needed the Internet? Calling and texting was all they needed.

Some of the other SADD members *would* be going to the dance, mixing fun with business. It was an opportunity to deliver their message. Monday, during lunch break, Ginger and friends paraded into the office of high school principal Arthur Beggs to discuss their plan. Dylan Radner, SADD's president and senior classman, was followed by three juniors, vice president Ginger, secretary Alicia Jones, and treasurer Travis Goodhue.

Dylan was an articulate boy, top of his class, and someone to listen to. He made their case. "Mr. Beggs. Please. We need the stage *two* times, once at the beginning of the dance and once at the end, before anyone gets into a car and drives home." Dylan's open expression and enthusiasm stirred Gingie to breathlessness. She bobbed her head in support of his statement and, with effort, pulled her gaze from his shining profile, so irresistible it was almost scary.

"We're proud of your efforts, Dylan. Your message is important. I just don't want you to dominate the event—"

"But this is the perfect time to spread the word about Call Central. Practically the whole school will be there, and some of those kids are going to be drunk or high."

"Well, I don't know about that..." Mr. Beggs gave a nervous little laugh.

Ginger's amber eyes came to rest on the principal's florid complexion, where the impact of Dylan's zeal was showing in those thousands of tiny red capillaries under the aging skin. Sometimes she wondered why she had to see so much, so many of these microscopic details that surrounded her, the molecules of matter plugging the emptiness and filling her with sadness one minute, happiness the next. Why?

"Please, Mr. Beggs," popped out of Ginger's mouth. "You always said the school is behind us a hundred percent!" Fine particles of spray shot from her mouth into the white winter light streaming through the window, making miniature rainbow dances in midair. Why?

"Exactly," the principal began anew, scrunching his brow in earnest. "But I think that one time on the stage should be adequate. You'll have a full five minutes in the middle of the evening, when the band takes a break. That's more than enough time to talk about Students Against Destructive Decisions and your student ride program."

"No one will be listening then," Dylan insisted. "It has to be when they're looking at the stage, waiting for the band to play. The first time, before the music starts, we'll remind them to make good choices, to avoid being tempted, before it's too late. There'll be people at the dance who sneak pills and hipflasks into the gym to share with their friends."

"You hold a very grim view of your fellow classmates, Dylan."

"I'm just saying it like it is."

"Even so, I don't think anyone would risk doing something like that. Our friends, the state troopers, will be providing extra security."

"That won't stop some people. I wish we could stop them. It seems impossible, but at least we can try to keep them from driving. That's why we also have to make an announcement about Call Central at the end of the night, when they're looking at the stage, waiting for the last song to start. We'll give them the phone number to call for a ride and they can add it to their contacts. No one should get behind the wheel if they're drunk or stoned."

"Hmm. I don't know if your plan will have any more success than mine. You might just aggravate the kids when they're trying to have fun!"

Ginger locked eyes with Travis and smiled, remembering last week's SADD meeting, when he did that funny imitation of the cheerful Mr. Beggs. A dorky smile and, "Kids just want to have fun!" Travis didn't joke around very much, but when he *did*...wow, he was so funny! Something about being so serious most of the time made him even funnier.

She didn't think their joke was any sign of disrespect because, in fact, Ginger really loved the principal, who looked like a huge teddy bear. But he *did* seem clueless at times. She could see that Travis was thinking the exact same thing! He had that little crooked corner of his mouth and a raised eyebrow. So cute! Travis was the absolute best, her new, very good friend (even if their moms had a strange, mysterious past that had to do with criminals). Right now, he looked like he was anxious to say something...

"Mr. Beggs," Travis spoke up. "I don't think one time during the break will work. When I'm at a dance, the minute the band stops for a break, everyone starts talking to each other. They aren't listening to announcements."

"Right," added Alicia. "I know I wouldn't be listening then."

"Okay, I'll tell you what," said the principal. "I'll give it some good thought, how's that? Now, why don't you go and work on your speech, and I'll let you know the plan by Friday." With a cut-out smile, Mr. Beggs stood and dismissed them.

Before leaving, Ginger gave him an amiable, bright-eyed smile because, well, what else was there to do? She turned, and suddenly the principal was history, no longer in her consciousness. She was walking behind Dylan and noticed that her eyes were exactly level to the most noticeable vertebra at the base of his neck, above the edge of his shirt. Alicia was behind her, and then Travis, as they filed out of the room. These were the people she was with, and these were the people that mattered to her right now, at this moment.

Dylan's healthy good looks, the dark hair, olive skin, and hazel eyes, drew many people to him, but he also put a lot of people off, the kids who thought he was too squeaky clean. Imagine: a gorgeous boy, smart and quick and friendly, who'd reached senior year without having tried even a sip of beer or a puff on any kind of cigarette. He wasn't even religious! How could a boy like that be so irresistible and so clean at the same time? He was too good to be true.

Ginger used to wallow in her crush on Dylan, but that was already ancient history, ever since he started going out with a senior classmate, Myra. Now that he was taken, he seemed different to Ginger, as if her eyes were fitted with a new pair of 3-D glasses, magically fallen from the sky onto the bridge of her nose. His sharp features were layered, his intensity a little too electric, his height teetered on gawky, his intelligence bordered on nerdiness. Far from perfect, he was still their esteemed leader, and Ginger admired him without lapsing into the old dreaminess.

Sweet! Dylan Radner, a normal kid after all! At SADD meetings, Myra was always tight against his side, pressed up like a suction cup. They would whisper intently, with their heads gently touching. Ginger was not a bit jealous, just happy for them. Myra was perfect for Dylan. She had a genius IQ, spoke in big words naturally without looking as though she'd planned them, and was cute, or maybe the right word was sexy. A rich, heavenly dessert, Myra had cinnamon hair, chocolate irises in marshmallow whites, and vanilla-caramel skin with strawberry cheeks.

Walking down the corridor after their meeting with the principal, Ginger grabbed Alicia's hand and swung it playfully, her pale, red-freckled skin against Alicia's dark mahogany. "Hey, what do you think? Did they even have pot when Mr. Beggs was a teenager? I bet he thinks no one at his high school ever got drunk or stoned."

Alicia giggled. "Yeah, and he's never even heard the people here who call Stone Ridge 'Stoner High'!" They laughed, and Ginger gave Alicia's hand a final, big swing before dropping it and running up to their president. "Dylan! That was epic! I know Mr. Beggs is going to agree with us."

Dylan glanced sideways, catching her eye just long enough to say, "Thanks Veep! I hope you're right." She loved it when he called her "Veep"! His profile was strong and happy, showing that she'd pleased him with her praise.

Wow, I love these guys! Ginger fairly skipped with glee in her store-faded jeans, glossy auburn hair against the nearly matching rust-colored sweater. How could anyone be any happier? What could be better than doing the right thing with the right people?

Later that day, after the final bell rang, fifteen hundred Stone Ridge students streamed into the corridors. Privileged upper-classmen walked out to their cars, others took school buses or shamefully ducked into their mothers' minivans, and some, like Ginger, stayed after school for clubs or sports. Others did their usual loitering at favorite spots just beyond the school property: behind the pizza shop across the street, or in the woods next to the custodians' maintenance garage. That Neverland of skulking youth, full of smoke and shadow.

Above the colonial façade of the main building, the big clock struck three. Outside, the icy wind whistled. Inside the over-heated building, the SADD officers and members met in the art room, propped on high stools along the length of a paint-splattered table.

"Let's get started," said Dylan brusquely. "I have to get to work by four." Another reason to admire him: Dylan had a black belt in martial arts and coached at a taekwondo studio after school.

Dylan and Myra, to his left, were suction-cupped together at the head of the long table. Myra's friend, Chrissy, sat on her other side. Ginger perched on a stool near Dylan, around the corner of the table. It was the spot she deserved as vice president, chosen for her dedication and bright ideas.

A quick evaluation of Dylan's face left her puzzled. What had happened in the last few hours? He'd been so happy at lunchtime, and now, what was that look? Worry, or even anger. Maybe he was just discouraged about the slow pace of progress. He'd started out the school year with such bright ideas for SADD, programs for education and outreach to keep kids away from drugs and alcohol. Some of this had helped, but not really. They were left with Call Central, a realistic project aimed at preventing drunk and stoned teens from killing themselves and their friends on the roads.

Seeing his downcast look, Ginger tried to make it light. "Everything's under control for Saturday, Prez!" He responded with a wan smile. Myra squeezed his arm.

Ginger mentally did a head count. Not as many people as last week, and only half of the people on her list of everyone who'd ever shown up to a meeting. To Ginger's right sat one of her good buds, Devraj, and across from them were Alicia and Travis, all of them juniors. Further down the long art table were sophomores Sarah and Cameron, and on the other side, a few newer members, freshmen Larissa and Dawn.

Dylan, Myra, and Chrissy were the only seniors among them. Was *that* the reason for Dylan's sour mood? For weeks, he'd been trying to recruit more of his classmates, frustrated by their apathy. "Senioritis" he called it. SADD needed more drivers who were at least seventeen years old. Anyone under that age had, at most, a limited license and wasn't allowed to drive after nine o'clock at night. Myra and Dylan, the perfect couple, the gorgeous couple, would be making the announcements at the dance. They were also, along with Chrissy, the only volunteer drivers scheduled for Saturday night, but the three of them had only two cars available. Myra was "working on" her parents for permission to use the family sedan.

"Let's have the reports," Dylan said.

Alicia and Travis rummaged through their backpacks and pulled out their notes.

"What are the figures, Travis?" Dylan asked.

"We paid for the phone and the first three months of the call plan. The money left over is twenty-two dollars and fifty-four cents."

"Not very good. Some of the gas money is going to come out of our pockets unless we have another fundraiser."

"Since you're driving, maybe the rest of us can chip in with a little money," offered Ginger cheerfully.

"Thanks, Veep. We'll see how much we spend." He did *not* sound happy. Not at all.

"My Dad set up the phone account," Travis reported. "We got the number we wanted: 736-7433. 736-RIDE. And I added the contacts to the phone, all the SADD members' cell numbers."

"You double-checked that list of numbers?" Dylan asked Larissa, the girl responsible for giving Travis an updated list.

Larissa nodded. "Yeah, 'course," she said. "I even changed Connor's number this week. His old phone fell in the toilet." They all laughed, probably louder than if Connor had been there. Maybe his interest in SADD had fallen into the toilet too.

"Did you set the ringtone?" Ginger asked Travis. She was excited about that. Last week's well-attended meeting was devoted to a debate on the musical ringtone. The final vote was ten to three in favor of "I Drove All Night."

"Yup. It sounds good too!"

Dylan thanked Travis and said, "Alicia, can you read the minutes?" Still so glum!

"Okay, word," Alicia said, using her favorite expression. She pulled out her notes. "February 2, 2009, president Dylan Radner called the meeting to order at 3:10…" Alicia spoke in a silky voice. Ginger watched her mouth moving around the words, a flat pink tongue, full lips pushed outward by big teeth, a pretty overbite of contrasting white against her dark skin. Dylan was looking at Alicia, his eyes unfocused. What was there to read in his face? Ginger caught Travis's eye and they exchanged smiles. He was her new best friend, a considerate, serious boy, and very smart.

Alicia was still reading. "…Dylan, Myra, and Chrissy volunteered to drive, Ginger and Travis volunteered to take calls and dispatch the rides from 9:00 PM to 2:00 AM. After two, Dylan will get the phone from Travis and Ginger and take any calls. That's about it."

They were sure that calls would come in after two, but Ginger and Travis didn't feel they could volunteer for the whole night. Wouldn't their parents throw a fit? But two o'clock was no biggie. They were usually up that late on Saturdays anyway. And the best part was that they'd be together for it. Maybe Dylan had emerged in 3-D, but Travis had become newly visible to her in the fourth dimension. She felt like she'd known him forever and couldn't figure out why. This imaginary element of time added a depth greater than anything she could immediately, outwardly see.

"The only foible in the plan could be the destinational issue," Myra said.

Dylan cast loving eyes on his very articulate girlfriend. "They've studied the map," he suggested. He turned to Ginger. "Right? And you'll be online?"

"Don't worry. I'll be logged onto Google Maps." Of what other use was the phone person? Receive the call. Contact the driver. If the driver needs directions, provide them. At first, it was suggested that the phone person be the driver. But the non-drivers also needed something to do, and besides, it was better to spread the responsibilities around, to build a network. If the driver didn't know how to get to an address, it wasn't wise to rely on the drunken fool in the back seat. The available cars didn't have navigational systems, and SADD didn't have the money for a TomTom. "If they're really lost, I can even stay on the phone with them while they drive—"

"Can't do that," Dylan cut her off.

"Moving violation. Liability issues," said Myra.

"Okay, well…"

"Tell them to pull over if you want to talk on the phone."

Should she just say it? Should she let them know they're already a couple of uptight old folks? Chill, guys! But she loved them! Loved everyone in this room, especially the boy across from her. Travis saw the joke, and they exchanged sparks in the fourth dimension.

"Okay. Anyone else here have a lead on drivers?" Dylan scanned their faces. "We have only three."

"There's seven on the list," said Devraj, the person in charge of maintaining that list. "Aren't a few of these over seventeen?" He handed the paper to Dylan.

"Two of them, but they said they can't drive. They're going to the dance and an after-party." He shook his head in mild disgust.

Ginger was about to suggest that anyone with upperclassmen for brothers or sisters just *had* to get their siblings involved, but Dylan kept talking. "I need some help with this. Myra and I asked tons of people today, but only a few agreed to be backups. That's it. We aren't a hot topic. Every senior is *obsessed* with this Facebook slander that's been going on."

"I heard about that," said Alicia.

Chrissy was nodding, and so was Travis and half the others. They knew. Everyone seemed to know! "What are you talking about?" The question flew out of Ginger's mouth before she could think. The room went silent. She scanned the faces around the table, her cheeks growing hot. A minute ago, all these people belonged to her, and suddenly they were strangers again. It was always this way, back and forth like this. Why? Why didn't that ever stop?

"Two girls are posting mean comments about Naomi Steuben," Dylan explained. Ginger didn't know the name, probably a senior. "It's infantile," he added.

"The Facebook thing is the newest part," Chrissy said. "It started in history class with the 'fat ass' comments behind her back. Naomi is just a quiet girl, and she never talks back to them."

"She doesn't know how to stand up to those two. She didn't come to school today. Maybe that's why."

"She needs a good rhetorical comeback," Myra suggested.

Devraj cut in. "Who're the two girls?" Ginger was thankful that he asked the question, because she wasn't eager to highlight her own ignorance again. She planned to log onto the family computer the minute she got home, to look up the Facebook pages of those girls.

"Chloe Dyckman and Taylor Sloane."

"The beauty queens," Alicia added. "You should've seen Taylor's boyfriend in the hallway today. He had his arm around her, defending her like, 'It's a free country! Taylor can say whatever she wants about that gross cow!' It was totally sick!"

Ginger froze in a memory. She was ten. Daddy's arm was slung, dead weight, around her mother's shoulder, and the palm of his other hand was brushing across Ginger's bangs. She felt his dry, hot skin, ghostlike. *It's a free country!* He swayed and spewed the words at the top of his lungs, that smell oozing from his pores.

Travis rolled his eyes and shook his head. "Julian Yarnell.

That notorious bad mouth."

"He isn't worth mentioning," Dylan said, signaling the end to the conversation. "I'm disgusted with the class of 2009!"

Cruel, thoughtless people always hurt others, but what about people who didn't *mean* to hurt someone else but did it anyway? Ginger looked around the room at her perfectly perfect group of friends and felt included again. The question she'd blurted out was forgotten, or never even noticed in the first place. These were people who cared about others, who never meant to hurt anybody. She wondered what had called them to action and brought them here together, on a mission to fight destructive decisions. What were their secret stories, the hurts they'd felt, and the people who'd hurt them? What were the embarrassing things they couldn't say out loud?

Their stories couldn't possibly be as bad as hers, the day-to-day uncertainty she'd felt, always on alert, watching her father, listening, guessing what he might do if she did this or said that. It was a relief when it was over, she kept telling herself. Then why did she miss him so much? For a while, Sean helped her to forget. They relied on each other for a few nice years, but now her brother was gone too, and she was left with two empty spots. This group, these friends, were everything to her. Home held nothing until six or seven or whenever Mom got back.

Everything was so much better than a few years ago. Wonderful, really. These were the good kids, the ones who loved her and she loved them. Absently, she moved the palm of her hand delicately back and forth over the top of the round metal corkscrew in her spiral notebook. Back and forth, pleasingly metallic and bumpy, then, *ow!* A prick. The sharp tip on the end was exposed and dangerous. She lifted her palm to see the spot of blood. If everything was so wonderful, then why did her eyes feel hot, close to tears? It was this ecstatic happiness, she decided, but she fought the tears, not wanting the others to see…

"Oh, Dylan, guys, everyone, I have such a good idea!" The sound of her own voice startled her, and the others turned to look. Had she interrupted something? She wasn't entirely sure who'd been talking.

Dylan turned completely away from Myra to look at her. "That's great, Veep. Watcha got?" He smiled, and maybe she hadn't interrupted anyone. His smile told her that everything was better now, that he wasn't feeling as down as he'd felt a minute ago. But what was it that she wanted to say? A suggestion for the group, something about their brothers and sisters...

Dylan was waiting, and now she felt someone else's attention. She turned away from Dylan and saw Travis, looking at her expectantly.

There was a brief disagreement, not quite an argument, as they got into the car in front of the school. Travis was trying to convince his grandmother to let him drive.

"I have my permit with me," he said, "and I'm taking the driving test next week for my license."

"That's wonderful, dear heart!" his grandma said in her singing kind of way. In the driver's seat, with her hands on the steering wheel, she was barely tall enough to see over the top of it. She didn't look like she was going to get out or move over for him.

"Dad took me out for two hours yesterday. He said I was doing great."

"And I'm sure you are!" She turned her head over her shoulder and said "Hello, there!" to Ginger, who was getting into the back seat as Travis got into the front passenger seat.

"Hello..." Ginger wasn't sure whether she should say "Mrs. Goodhue" or "Mrs. Hargrove." Travis's parents had different last names. The grandmother solved the problem by saying, "I'm

Brenda. What's your name?"

"Ginger."

"Oh, I *love* that name! It looks *just* like you too."

Travis was still trying to convince her as he closed the door. "And it's even easier driving today than yesterday. Look at the driveway." He pointed out the front windshield. "It warmed up and it's just wet on the road."

She started to drive. "I'll just leave all of that to your dad. How's that?" She laughed a little, like they were all having fun.

Travis had told Ginger that his grandmother occasionally liked to "treat" him or his sister Natalie to a ride home, especially on days when his parents would be getting home late from work. Then, his grandmother would hang around the house or even fix them dinner. Ginger didn't know whether Travis thought of "late" as six or seven, which was the time her mom usually got home, or if his parents had even later hours. For her, there were many afternoons when the five o'clock hour seemed to last forever.

A few months ago, thinking of Travis and his grandmother, she got on a public bus after school and visited her grandfather. He lived only a fifteen-minute drive away (which took a half hour on public transportation). The visits soon became her own occasional habit. She didn't tell her mother and doubted that Mom would ever find out. It would be different if Mom ever wanted to visit or call Grandpa, but she always made up excuses. There was something strange between Mom and Grandpa that Ginger didn't quite understand. Why couldn't she have a normal grandparent like Travis?

Travis had offered her a ride home after SADD meetings many times, but she'd always said "no." He told her it wasn't out of their way, and it really wasn't. Not very. Her house was closer to the school, kind of on the way to his house, with just a short detour of a few blocks. But she felt bad that she couldn't ever make the same offer in return. Her mother was never around, and her grandfather didn't have a car. But that wasn't the biggest reason. It had to do with where they lived. When Travis first told her his address on Dovecote Lane, she knew immediately where it was; she babysat for a family that lived two houses away from him. It was a beautiful cul-de-sac with clean two-story houses. His house wasn't scary-huge, but it was sure a lot nicer than her single-story cottage with a scruffy yard in front. He would be seeing it for the first time today.

"How're the plans for the big dance?"

"All good, Grandma…"

"How wonderful! You and Ginger will be *dancing* the night away!"

They should have set her straight, but then Brenda started singing in her very high, trilly voice about "funny" valentines or something. There was such a happy feeling in this car that Ginger wanted the ride to last forever.

"That was a red light, Grandma."

"No, dear heart, it was only yellow."

"Geesh! It turned red before we got through!"

Maybe they'd all be safer if Travis drove. Brenda went back to singing, and Ginger's fleeting unease was quickly forgotten.

5 »   *TENDRILS*

A LOW CEILING of thick gray clouds pressed down overhead, narrowing the space between heaven and earth. Gretchen Fleischer and Deke Blandenberg were traveling south on Route 9W, along the Hudson River.

At the wheel, Gretchen nodded left over her shoulder and mused, "Beautiful, isn't it?"

Deke gazed out the windshield for a long moment, taking in the white and gray expanse. "I'd say you don't have to take that trip to Alaska now. Save the money."

She smiled. "Still going."

"Take a photo of this instead. Post it in June, and say you just got back from the Yukon."

"Cute. But I'm already paid up. No refund."

The river was a hodgepodge of stacked and moving ice floes, white-capped with fallen snow. On the far shore, bleak cliffs jutted up from river's edge, densely quilled with barren trees.

Gretchen and Deke, in a department-owned SUV, were headed for Iona Island to continue their water monitoring project for the Department of Environmental Conservation. As usual for a Tuesday early afternoon, they encountered little traffic along this route. A few cars were parked in the turnouts along the edge of the river. These belonged to the nature diehards. Winter bird-watchers peered through binoculars past Doodletown Bight to the island beyond, looking for bald eagles nesting there, overwintering. Hikers had parked near the access points to snow-covered trails through the woods, up from the river toward Bear Mountain. A couple of river gazers stood motionless, awestruck by the powerful beauty of those chunky, haphazard ice floes, ever shifting and swirling across the wide expanse.

Those nature lovers were barred from Iona Island at this time of year. Set off from the mainland by brackish tidal marshes, shallows, and mudflats, the island and surrounding waters provided a fragile habitat for waterfowl and aquatic life, a site for the Hudson River National Estuarine Research Reserve. Even this far north from the sea, the river was a tidal estuary, where salty sea water met freshwater runoff from the land. "The river that flows both ways," Native Americans first called it.

As environmental scientists for the DEC, Gretchen and Deke were permitted entry. Gretchen turned onto the poorly plowed access road over Salisbury Meadow, bumping and skidding along. A minute later, she pulled into the cleared edge of the small parking lot. They'd hike the rest of the way to water's edge.

Stepping out of the car on either side, they walked around to the back to collect their gear. "Damn, that wind stings! Where's my hat?" Gretchen pushed items around in the hatch area, looking for her hat, regretting that she'd left it in the back. Deke's head was already well covered. He eyed her obliquely and said, "I thought you were already wearing it."

"Ha ha." She found the fleece-lined cap, pulled it over her own dense bush of curly hair, and unfolded the earflaps. "And I thought you had the quatro cable."

"Always snooping around in my pack!"

"You're lucky I checked."

Their style of exchange, full of friendly barbs and insults, had developed from their close working relationship. They'd taken innumerable trips together, mucking knee-deep in silt, pushing through tall reeds in the summer, comparing results on data loggers, recording their findings in the lab. More than just colleagues, Gretchen and Deke were best friends who'd almost forgotten their brief, embarrassing attempt at something more, three years ago.

Gretchen opened her backpack, checked the contents, and nodded with approval. Her multi-probe data logger, handheld unit, and all sensors, cables, and sample tubes were accounted for. Inventory complete, she pulled on her gloves. Deke had grabbed his own pack and was standing a couple of yards away, gazing up into the heavens. "What're you doing?" he asked her, apparently talking to the sky. "Getting ready for the prom?"

Gretchen slung her backpack over a shoulder and closed the hatch door. Her eyes followed Deke's gaze upward. "Hawks don't go to the prom. Didn't see any at my prom, anyway."

"What a thought. You in a prom dress!" But Deke was still watching the hawk.

They both paused, not moving despite the cold. What wouldn't they give for that experience, to feel it in more than just the imagination? The hawk circled majestically, wings spread in a buffeted glide through fickle air currents, overseeing a vast panorama of water and land below.

The walk was only about half a mile, up to the northern edge of the island, off Doodletown Bight. Their boots crunched through the thin ice layer that had formed over hard-packed snow. In a blink, Gretchen lost her footing. "Whoa!" Deke caught her arm, and she felt a little ridiculous, not even sure how she'd slipped. The treads on her boots were better than a black bear's claws, made to grip anything.

At water's edge, they stopped and searched for a spot. "Where can we go in? The ice is stacked up over here."

"Further up," Deke pointed. "There's water between the floaters."

They walked further along, to a spot where the river's current dashed the ice floes against the shore. Further out, in the middle of the river, the wind whipped up the clear water into whitecaps between the floating mini bergs. They unloaded their backpacks and assembled the equipment. Although their thermal gloves were thin and malleable, it was nearly impossible to grasp the cables, attach the sensors and the handheld unit. They'd be measuring dissolved oxygen, pH, temperature and ORP, shorthand for oxidation reduction potential.

"I can guess the DO level without even measuring." Gretchen shook her head. "This is winterkill, big time." Fish needed oxygen to live. Oxygen entered the water from the surrounding air and photosynthesis. Prolonged ice cover was killing the fish.

"Not a problem. I'll pull out a few frozen bass for dinner. You're invited."

"Not my idea of a good meal."

"Don't worry. Indian Point corpses don't float this far up."

"Oooo. You're sick. How'd I get *you* for a partner?"

From where they stood, they couldn't see the bald heads of the cement reactor domes. Indian Point was just south of them, around a bend in the river. The aging nuclear plant sucked water from the Hudson to cool the reactors and pumped it out again twenty-five degrees hotter, killing a billion fish and aquatic organisms every year in the process. Built in 1962 in a quieter era, the troubled nuclear plant was now surrounded by a densely populated suburb, only thirty miles north of the eight million people in New York City. In 2005, leaks from a pool of spent fuel were discovered. Plumes of radioactive contamination spread into the groundwater, making a tasty cocktail of Strontium-90, tritium, Cesium-137, Cobalt-60, and Nickel-63. Gretchen and Deke were tasked with monitoring samples of river water. So far, their studies hadn't shown any dangerous levels of radioactive contaminants in the river. The Big River.

With the handheld data logger in his left hand, Deke, like an ice fisherman, gently tossed the cable with the sensor away from him, into a free patch of water a few feet out. Gretchen took her handheld and assembly and walked further on, looking for another area to read. She found a spot of shoreline where the wind had swept most of the snow away. Tendrils of marsh grass were pushed up against the edge by the ice floes. It gave her a bit of frozen, grassy ground to walk on, to get closer to her intended goal, the square of gray-green water moving between the lodged ice chunks. Her feet crunched on matted brown grass, long and razor thick. She spotted, a bit further out from the shore, a softer-looking vegetation of a different brown color, the curled tendrils frozen in the ice.

She was about to toss the cable when a round, white shape caught her eye. "Hey Deke!" she called out. "I just found your frozen fish dinner!"

"Pry it out of the ice for me."

"No way!" She looked at the shape again, the visible part of something larger suggested by a dark shadow under the ice. Perhaps the white underbelly of an Atlantic sturgeon? The Hudson spawned some mammoth bottom-feeders…

Gretchen gasped and stumbled backward, coming down hard on her tailbone.

Concentrating on his data logger, Deke glanced at her askance. "Do I have to come over there and pick you up *again*?"

She couldn't answer, couldn't speak, for what she'd seen was unmistakable. Above the waxy white skin of a bloated cheek, a human eye, startled open in death, stared back at her.

Dana got the call from Indigo at about two o'clock. A body had been found and identified. Everything added up quickly in her mind. She was personally stricken, more than the usual case. A child was dead, a teenager close in age to Travis, a girl from his high school. A girl who'd been reported missing yesterday. An apparent suicide.

Dana's office tracked every missing person in the jurisdiction, investigating suspicious circumstances that could mean abduction or murder. Yesterday, a police report crossed her desk about a girl named Naomi Steuben. The girl's parents had called the police at 7:10 that morning, frantic about their daughter's disappearance in the middle of the night. She'd taken the mother's car, and the county police were searching for it. When Dana got the report, she'd reviewed it quickly and put it aside. There were other, more pressing matters on her plate, the Perry Rigger trial for one, Evan's Son of Sam case for another.

But today, a few startling details were coming clear. Over the phone, Indigo reported what she'd learned after speaking with the witnesses who'd found the body, the police officers who responded to the scene, and Naomi's parents. By all appearances, pre-autopsy, the girl had jumped from the Bear Mountain Bridge. The mother's car was found parked in a corner of the lot at the nearby state park. "The parents say she wasn't the kind of girl to kill herself. Said she wouldn't do a thing like that."

"Understandable," Dana said, not without compassion, but because she'd heard this before, many times. The loved ones of suicide victims often expressed such disbelief.

"This is a little different. They're saying two of her classmates are to blame. Two girls."

"They pushed her off the bridge? That's pretty hard to do without someone seeing them."

"Pushed her, yeah, but not literally. There was no way they could do that. You saw Naomi's description."

"Right," Dana said vaguely, not completely sure of Indigo's meaning. Where *was* that report now? She grabbed it out of her inbox as Indigo kept talking into her ear. "...you'd need four people to lift her over the rail and push her off." Dana scanned the description on the page: "Seventeen years old, shoulder-length brown hair, brown eyes, 5 feet 5 inches, 240 pounds."

She blinked and focused on the curved numbers, their heartbreaking significance. "What are they saying the classmates did?" she asked, even as the likely answer came untethered at the back of her mind.

"They bullied the girl to death. Said some downright nasty things about her at school and on Facebook. Even dared her to kill herself. The parents knew about some of the taunting at school, but they didn't know about all the online activity until they looked at Naomi's laptop after she was gone. Now they want blood! They want to press charges."

A connection clicked in place. Last night at dinner, Travis had mentioned a "juvenile Facebook war" going on, but he quickly backpedaled the moment it came out of his mouth. "Don't worry, Mom! They aren't *my* friends. Two girls named Taylor and Chloe are saying stuff about another girl. They're all seniors." Travis was new to Facebook, having recently opened an account with the reluctant go-ahead from Dana and Evan. Social media was a stressor for any parent of a teenager, but it was doubly stressful now that Dana was in the public eye. It would take just one poorly worded message, anything that reflected badly on the character of the district attorney's children, and the press would be all over it. Travis was sensitive to this. For a sixteen-year-old kid, he was way ahead of his peers when it came to foresight and restraint. And, as it turned out, he hardly posted anything at all, preferring to read the messages posted by kids he liked.

"If they aren't your friends on Facebook, how did you find out about it?"

Natalie burst in, "They made everything public! Even *you* could see it, Mommy!" She had a cake-eating grin on her face, delighted to show off her know-how. Natalie had been lobbying for her own Facebook account ever since she reached the minimum age of thirteen, but Evan and Dana were doing their best to hold her off. Travis hadn't even expressed an interest until he turned sixteen. He was a studious and introspective boy, content with a handful of very close friends, the real kind, not the virtual. But Natalie was their social butterfly, anxious to connect with all the people of the world whenever and however she could. She was an avid fan of instant messaging, but times had changed. Facebook was now the thing.

"So, I guess you saw all of this too?" Evan asked his daughter with the laid-back tone that always eased the kids into opening up. Dana regarded her husband with admiration. *Masterful.*

"Sure, I saw it. Travis showed me!"

Travis rolled his eyes. "I did it just to show you a *bad* example," he said to his sister. To his father: "It was some really mean stuff those girls posted."

"That's a valuable lesson," Evan said, making his son's eyes light up with pride. "Words can be hurtful, and the damage is a hundred times worse when it's broadcast to the world in a public forum."

Travis shook his head in mild disgust. "I don't know why people have to treat each other like that."

They all nodded in agreement.

Conversation over, lesson learned. The subject was dropped, and they said not another word about it for the remainder of the dinner hour.

Now, after hearing Indigo's report of the suicide, Dana wished she'd gotten more details from Travis last night. He hadn't revealed the name of the victim, but he must have been talking about Naomi Steuben. Mere curiosity was no longer an issue. This was a potential criminal prosecution. *The parents want to press charges.* But what kind of charges would fit here?

"I'd better meet with the parents," Dana said.

"Oh, you won't be able to avoid it! They're demanding a meeting. The father kept slamming his fist into his hand and cursing under his breath, turning fire red in the face. He's a big, beefy guy. I thought he'd bust a gut. And the mother was almost hysterical. They were ready to drive over here and beat down your door. I held them back."

"Okay. I'll arrange an appointment. Probably tomorrow. First, I want to process everything we've got. What else do you know?"

"Like I said, the online stuff was new to them. The Steuben parents looked at Naomi's Facebook page and saw a strange message she posted right before her death. Their older daughter Olivia, who's away at college, seemed to think it was a reply of some kind. She looked at the Facebook pages of the two likely bullies and found horrific things. You wouldn't believe what they called this girl. 'Blimp,' and 'Jellyroll,' and 'Lard Butt,' and they made up little sick fantasies about what she'd do with all that fat in bed. With herself and with other people. I brought the laptop back with me. It's down with the techies."

Dana clamped the phone receiver between chin and shoulder as she swiveled her chair around to the computer monitor on her desk. "I have to see this." She started to type. "I'm bringing up Facebook now. Let me see Naomi's page first." She spelled the name aloud as she typed it in.

"If you get more than one person with that name, her page is easy enough to pick out."

"Well, yes, looks like at least three Naomi Steubens are coming up. I'm going to guess it's this one..." She placed the cursor and clicked. "Oh no! God in heaven, really?"

"Looks like you found it."

"Her background photo is the Bear Mountain Bridge!"

"Yup. The tech crew will be able to tell us when she posted that photo. It might say how long she'd been thinking of doing this."

"And I see her last message here at the top." Dana read it to herself. *Surprise. Yes, I can. See if I won't.* "See if I won't jump off the bridge?"

"Yup. Taylor Sloane practically dared her to do it. She and Chloe Dyckman are the bad girls."

"Okay. I'll try Taylor's page." Dana spelled the last name out loud, and Indigo corrected her. "It's with an 'e' at the end."

"A couple of people…much older…not from New York. I don't find her. Let me try Chloe's." Indigo confirmed Dana's spelling of that name. "Same thing. A couple of people that couldn't be her. Nothing."

"That's crazy. I saw their pages this morning. Plenty of dirt."

"I don't see anything, but maybe I'm a complete computer ditz…"

"Or maybe…"

Five seconds of silence elapsed.

Dana knew exactly what Indigo was thinking. "They've deleted their accounts."

"Giving us evidence of their guilt, right there."

"So, they're feeling guilty, but we can't prosecute a guilty mind. We need a guilty act. That's the question. What's the crime?"

"Dig into the Penal Law. There's gotta be a statute that fits. Meanwhile, the tech crew can work on recovering the data. We can also subpoena Facebook."

"Fat chance!" Instantly, Dana regretted the word. She hurried on. "They'll move to quash, to protect their users."

"Maybe, but meanwhile, I can tell you exactly what the last few messages said. I remember them."

Dana turned away from her computer screen and pressed the phone receiver hard to her ear, not letting a decibel of sound escape.

Indigo recited the evidence from memory. "First, Chloe posts a message like this: 'Certain people just don't get the message.' Taylor writes back, 'Someone should tell her to end that miserable fatness right now. So gross. She should jump off the Bear Mountain Bridge.' Then Chloe says, 'How would that work?' and Taylor replies, 'Yeah. She couldn't get her fat butt over the railing.' Chloe finishes it off with an 'LOL.'"

And this was Naomi's response. *Surprise.*

Funny how she acted when she got home, not like herself at all. Dana had an honest, realistic approach to parenting and didn't shy away from the evils of the world. She avoided explicit details but didn't sugarcoat when discussing things like death and murder with the kids. They'd had open conversations about drugs and crime and why people hurt each other and hurt themselves, the futility of finding any sense in senseless acts.

But something about Naomi Steuben's case threw Dana into another dimension. A kind of shock. After seeing the girl's photo on the computer, it stayed on her mind all day. That round face, so pretty underneath the weight, too much to be saddled with at such a young age. No longer young, or maybe forever young, Naomi's existence was now frozen in memory as unrealized potential. Life, ephemeral. A suicide, a high school student bullied into jumping off a bridge.

When Dana got home, she took Evan aside and told him about the case. They agreed that she should talk to Travis. But she said nothing all evening. Why was that? In the back of her mind she envisioned the inevitable talk that would fill the halls of Stone Ridge High the next day, and she wanted to be the first to give him the news. Yet she stalled. Was suicide a more difficult subject than murder? Maybe it was the cruelty of those girls that so unsettled her.

A strange stillness gripped the household, an awareness that there was something different about this day. Quiet. Tiptoeing. The barest minimum of superficial conversation at dinner, even surprisingly little from chatterbox Natalie. Travis had a down-turned mouth. After dinner, they each went about their own activities in different corners of the house. All the long evening, Dana's mind was fixed on Naomi's face.

At ten o'clock, Travis stepped into the living room, where Dana was pretending to read. "Good night, Mom."

He paused. She looked up. "Good night, sweetheart."

He didn't move for another second, then he turned to go.

Maybe now she was ready. "Travis?"

"Yeah?"

"Can we talk in your room for a moment?"

They walked into his enclave, a relatively neat room for a boy his age, but appropriately stuffed with paraphernalia: Little League and varsity baseball trophies, a science fair project, plastic models of starships (from a younger age), baseball bat and glove, books (mostly science fiction), disconnected pairs of socks and sneakers. Dana started out in a halting manner, trying to find the right words. It had been eight hours since she'd gotten the news about the body. "There's something I think you should know, Travis. Remember what you told us last night about the Facebook war? Well, this afternoon..."

"They found her floating in the river. I heard about it, Mom."

Of course he had. "How did you hear?"

"It was after school, on the bus."

Three o'clock, only an hour after Dana had heard. News traveled so much faster than in her day. "Who was talking?"

"Somebody on the bus. A sophomore. I don't know her name. She said, 'Did you hear about that girl who jumped off the bridge?' And there was another kid with an iPhone who looked it up and started reading things out loud. No one on the bus really knew her. None of the seniors ride the bus, you know."

It was true. The seniors did everything in their power to avoid the embarrassment of riding the big yellow school bus. They had to have cars or be riding in friends' cars.

"When I got home," Travis went on, "I looked up the news story on the computer. And there were also some people posting things on Facebook." As he spoke, his doleful eyes searched the room, melting her with that blue confusion of youth.

"My heart goes out to her family," Dana said. Ineffectual words. She brushed his smooth cheek with the back of her fingertips. He was two inches taller than her and had started to shave, just his mustache and chin. "How do you feel about it?"

"It's sad," he said, but there was something other than sadness in his voice. A tough defensiveness. "Are you going to tell Nats about it? I didn't know if I should say anything."

"Don't worry about that. I'll talk to her."

"I mean, she doesn't know any of these people anyway."

"But the news might filter down. I'll talk to her."

"I guess the police told you right away, after they found her."

"They did. I got the report at about two o'clock."

"So, you already started working on the case..."

"Yes, that is, we're reviewing the situation."

She saw the tension rising from his hands, into his chest and face. "You've got to do something about it, Mom. It's been bothering me all night!"

"I'm not sure what we can do. I don't know if this is even the kind of case my office should get involved in. Usually there's no one to prosecute for a suicide."

"But they made her do it! I just know it! She couldn't face those people at school anymore. She wouldn't have jumped if they hadn't said all those things!" A deep, guttural sound exploded in his throat. It was the man inside of him, fighting against an admission of powerlessness.

6 »   *SIBLINGS*

"Ted Brevoort please. This is Evan Goodhue."

"I'm sorry. Mr. Brevoort is unavailable. May I take a message?"

"Please have him call me when he's able. It's about the case of Yusuf Nashid." Evan gave his number and ended the call.

It was only five minutes to nine, too early for court, and Evan had hoped to catch Ted in his office. Most likely, he wasn't taking any calls that weren't related to his trial. Ted was prosecuting a headline-making case against Perry Rigger, a man accused of killing his wife in a distinctly gruesome manner. Thanks to Dana, Evan knew the details of the court proceedings. Yesterday, Ted had prevailed at the suppression hearing, and Rigger's statements to the police were ruled admissible at the trial. They'd picked a jury, and Ted was starting the People's case today.

Under the circumstances, it would be pure luck if Ted returned the phone call today. Evan would just have to wait before quizzing him about his alleged omission. Ted hadn't mentioned a second knife. Why?

"Because there *wasn't* any other knife," Evan announced to his empty office. "The only knife was the murder weapon."

This was Evan's new habit, talking to himself. The suburban satellite of Belknap, Rose & Goodhue, P.C., was quieter than the headquarters in Manhattan, with only a few attorneys. A little too tame and sedate for Evan, who enjoyed bouncing ideas off his colleagues. When no one was around, he took sides against himself, sometimes in full voice.

He gave a second look through the papers on his desk. Vesma hadn't wasted any time. Yesterday afternoon, less than twenty-four hours after their meeting at Green Haven, she'd served him with notices to admit, interrogatories, and a notice of deposition for his client, Malikah Hafeez. All of it was aimed at getting Malikah to admit that her husband Almed had been in the habit of carrying a pocketknife, and that he was armed with that knife on the night of the confrontation with his murderous sibling.

"So what if Almed was armed?"

The invisible adversary answered, "It supports a self-defense claim," and Evan retorted, "It still doesn't matter." Legally, Yusuf's inventive new defense made no difference to the outcome of the Son of Sam case. The manslaughter conviction itself supported Malikah's claim to Yusuf's assets. It was too late for the convict to back out of his guilty plea. Evan had convinced himself of this, but… "Could this new strategy really work for her?"

Evan was about to file a summary judgment motion, hoping for a quick win on papers, but Vesma had thrown a wrench into the game plan. She was making things difficult, sniffing along a cold trail for phantom evidence to support a bogus defense. Evan should be angry about her tactic, but it made him smile instead. He had to admire Vesma's gumption and ingenuity. Maybe she would back down if they worked out a deal to release her attorney's fees from escrow, the money she'd earned for representing Yusuf in the medical malpractice action. But Evan wasn't quite ready to give up that leverage.

As these thoughts swirled, the distinct, scratchy ping of ice pellets on glass met his ears. He turned to face the plate glass window, opening onto a panorama of the city from a height of seventeen floors. It had started to sleet.

Evan recalled his meeting with Ted several weeks ago. There'd been no mention of a pocketknife. The portion of the DA's file he'd handed over contained no notes or reports about it. Yusuf's deposition testimony about self-defense had come as a surprise. On the night of the murder, in the alley behind the teahouse, Almed supposedly threatened Yusuf with the open pocketknife and lunged at him, aiming straight for the jugular. Yusuf claimed that he'd pushed the knife away from his throat and defended himself with his own knife, not well enough to prevent being stabbed in the gut while he was swinging at Almed.

"A ridiculous story. No way it happened like that!" The wounds Yusuf had inflicted on Almed were not defensive but deep and deliberate, four of them, right lung, left side of the neck, left pectoral, heart.

Unaware of any possibility of a second weapon, Evan had never raised the subject with Malikah. In Vesma's discovery demands, he found a clue. In the notice to admit, Vesma was demanding that Malikah admit to having received the pocketknife from the hospital, as one of Almed's personal effects. Evan confirmed the source of Vesma's belief in the hospital records that Ted had provided.

With nothing else to go on, he called his client.

"Ms. Hafeez? It's Evan Goodhue."

"Hello, Mr. Goodhue. How are you today?" Malikah was always cordial, dignified, and proper.

"Just fine, thank you. And you?"

"Very well. I'm surprised to hear from you again so soon." He'd made a brief call to her Monday afternoon to let her know that the deposition had been held, but he hadn't mentioned Yusuf's claim of self-defense. It seemed irrelevant at the time.

"Yes, sorry for the intrusion, but I've just received several discovery demands from the defendant's attorney. Mainly, she's asking for information about a pocketknife." He paused intentionally, to get her reaction. The first thing he heard was a small intake of breath, followed by halting speech, unusual for Malikah. "You—" she started. "You say, a pocketknife?"

"Exactly. I take it that Almed liked to carry one around."

"Yes, that's right. I keep a room in my house devoted to the memory of my husband. The pocketknife is in there, along with his other things."

How interesting! Wouldn't Vesma like to get her hands on the actual knife. But she hadn't gone so far as to ask for it. "So, you still have the knife? Am I assuming correctly that it's the same one that the hospital returned to you on the night Almed died?"

"Yes," she said without hesitation. That sealed it.

He paused in thought, perhaps longer than he realized. Long enough for her to ask, "Is there a problem?"

"No, not at all."

"When I picked up Almed's things at the hospital, there was no blood on the knife, if that's what you're thinking."

Well, no, he hadn't been thinking about blood, but apparently, she had.

Bernard Steuben was a large man, not as physically massive as Indigo had suggested, but he carried a monstrous weight of grief and anger. Dierdre Steuben was of average size, disheveled and dazed. If she'd been hysterical when Indigo met her, the hysteria was now under control. Cloudy, unfocused eyes suggested that the calm was chemically induced, perhaps with the help of a sedative prescribed by her doctor.

The Steubens were waiting for Dana in the small conference room. They stood when she entered and were properly respectful, participating in the rituals of hand shaking, exchanging words of introduction, and receiving condolences from the district attorney. As soon as the three settled into their seats, Bernard launched into the purpose of their visit.

"It's been two days since those girls murdered our child, and we want to know why there hasn't been an arrest." His double chin shook, and his cheeks were aflame. "It's no secret what happened. Everyone knows who did this. It sickens us to have them going about their lives as if nothing happened, and we sit here, doing nothing! You don't know how many times I've thought of going to the parents of those girls and just..." He let it fade. Talk of revenge was not wise in the presence of the district attorney.

Mrs. Steuben spoke into the pause. "Our girl was such a happy child," she murmured through trembling lips, gazing into the distance. Her spacy affect transported the edgy vibe in the room toward an ethereal plane.

Dana had difficulty reconciling Dierdre Steuben's comment with the information she'd received that morning from the high school. Naomi's calculus teacher said that the girl was a brilliant student but troubled, sluggish and morose. An English teacher provided Dana with some of Naomi's creative writing assignments from the current school year, a litany of melancholic prose.

"Both of our girls," corrected the father, patting his wife's hand in her lap.

"Another daughter?" Dana asked as if she didn't know, hoping to add a hopeful note to the conversation.

"Naomi has an older sister, Olivia," he said. "She's absolutely devastated by her sister's death."

"She'll be coming home soon...," the mother added wistfully.

"She's upstate, in her second year of college," said Mr. Steuben. He turned to his wife, patted her hand, and said, "She'll be here." Turning again to Dana, he said, "Olivia could give you an earful about that Dyckman clan. A rotten bunch! Chloe has an older brother who was in Olivia's class. Tim Dyckman. I'm sure you have a record of him. He's been arrested for…for assault. The parents couldn't give a damn what their kids do. And that other girl Taylor is a piece of work too. She's an only child, spoiled silly from what I hear. Princess of the day, a snotty beauty contestant. You should throw Taylor and Chloe into the clink and see how they like it!"

"I understand your concern, Mr. Steuben…"

"Concern? We're talking about murder!" He fairly jumped out of his seat, making Dana regret her decision to meet with them alone. Indigo had offered to accompany her, but Dana hadn't wanted the parents to feel overwhelmed by a show of authority. Clearly, Bernard Steuben was far from intimidated. "Those girls drove our daughter to this! They wanted her dead and made sure of it!"

"As good as pushed her," Naomi's mother whispered, ghost-like.

"I know some of the law myself," her husband went on. "My brother's a lawyer in Texas. Not really in criminal law, but he's a smart guy. He says this is murder, pure and simple. It's an intentional killing he says."

A civil attorney in Texas with an opinion on New York criminal law. Dana wouldn't tell the grieving father what she thought of that opinion. "I understand your point. I want you to know that we're actively investigating every aspect of this case, and we're taking a very broad view of it. But 'murder' is a strong word. Murder involves not only an intent to kill, but also an act to go along with that intent."

"Like the taunting at school and the Facebook posts. Multiple acts, if you ask me. And they knew —" He stopped short, seeming to reconsider his words. "They knew that Naomi was a sensitive girl. Anyone could see it."

"It's horrible conduct. Reprehensible. You have my total agreement on that." Dana would have liked to tell him then and there that arrests were forthcoming, but she held back from making a promise she couldn't keep. It would only add to their misery. "We're looking for a statute that fits that conduct. *If* there's a law on the books, they will be charged. So far, however, it's clear that there've been no cases like this in New York that were prosecuted as murder."

"It's a first, then. There always has to be a first. No one ever heard of this Facebook until a few years ago."

"That's true. Sometimes the law takes a while to catch up to changes in technology and trends in society. But we can't charge people with crimes if the charges aren't going to stick, if the evidence doesn't match the legal standard we have to prove in court. That would make things worse, don't you think? To charge them and then have the case dismissed?"

Mr. Steuben hung his head and shook it and said nothing as Mrs. Steuben searched the room impassively, her half-lidded eyes finally coming to rest on a right angle where two walls met. Solid. Secure. Permanent.

Dana sat on the couch, Natalie cross-legged on the carpet in front of her. It was nine thirty, and they'd forgotten all the troubles of the last few days, fully immersed in a time-honored grooming ritual. Dana was brushing Natalie's dense thicket of hair, admiring the variety of natural colors in it, from sandy to chestnut to honey. She loved the feel of it, the soft weight and coils in it. Difficult to manage, but it was Natalie's best feature, nothing like Dana's dark mink-smooth hair.

This blonde child was Evan's in so many ways. Photos of him as a young teenager in the early seventies usually caught him with a goofy grin on a round face half covered with bountiful locks the same color as Natalie's. Dana wondered how Brenda felt about her son's long-haired hippie phase. She'd never asked her mother-in-law. She smiled to herself now, imagining Brenda's likely response—a laugh of delight and a full-voiced, trembling rendition of "Aquarius," mostly on key.

"Make a French braid, Mommy. From the top, straight down the middle. Then my hair will be ready for school in the morning. I can just get up and go!"

"I'm not so sure it will look very neat after you sleep on it…"

"Sure it will! I'll just dab some water on it to smooth down that wispy stuff."

Dana didn't need much coaxing. She traded the brush for the comb she'd placed on the couch and used the pointed edge to divide her daughter's hair into the starting sections of the braid, one on the right, another on the left. Interlacing the strands through deft fingers, she began to weave, working tightly. Smooth and intricate.

"You know why I like a French braid in my hair?"

"Because it's pretty and different from everyone else?"

"No. Well, yes. But also because it makes my face look thinner."

Dana was taken aback. She blurted, "I don't think so." Didn't think what? That the hairstyle made Natalie's face look thinner, or that her daughter should be having such worries?

"It definitely *does* make a difference. I've done 'before and after' in the mirror."

"Why would you ever want your face to look thinner?"

"Because of these cheeks." Raising both hands to her face, she clawed the round parts of her cheeks and shook them.

"Hey, calm down! You made me mess up." One of the strands slipped, causing a bulbous protrusion.

"That's okay, just do it over again!"

They sat in silence for several seconds as Dana sectioned and crossed and pulled.

Finally, Natalie said, "It's impossible, anyway."

"What's impossible?"

"To get thinner. I like to eat too much."

Oh no. This really *was* on Natalie's mind. Did their recent conversations about the bullied girl have anything to do with it? No comparison. Natalie might be described as pleasingly plump, but only when judged by the perverse standard of a skeletal fashion model. "You don't need to get thinner. You're a healthy weight, and you eat a well-balanced diet."

"Cookies. Come on, Mommy. You know I can't stop with cookies sometimes. I'm just like Daddy."

It was true that Natalie's metabolism more closely resembled her father's, while Travis took after Dana, able to eat and not gain a pound. Coincident with this thought, the tall beanpole walked through the living room on his way to the kitchen. Undoubtedly, he was on a mission to find a bedtime snack. Dinner was never enough for that boy. He was a bottomless pit, growing like a weed, thin as a rail but starting to fill out in the shoulders and torso.

"I bet he's going to get cookies. Me and Daddy each had only one after dinner. He said he'd help me cut down."

"He did, did he?" Evan was perpetually struggling with his weight, more or less keeping it under control as long as he kept up his jogging, at least three mornings a week.

"Yup. He's been giving me his dieting secrets." She patted the top of her head, feeling the pattern of the braid. "How's it look? It's so nice and tight."

"I'm doing a perfect job, if I do say so myself. Your hair is such a beautiful mix of shades, light brown to blonde. You can see the streaks when it's woven like this."

"Just like Daddy's was, right? So, does that mean I'm going to go bald too?"

"Hey, I heard that!" Evan's voice came from the hallway. "Talking about your bald old man! Don't you know I have feelings?" He walked to a corner of the living room and plopped down in the recliner. "I wasn't bald when I met your mother. You can blame her for that."

"*Daddy!*"

"I disclaim responsibility," Dana said. "You were well on your way when I met you, darling." They'd met in 1988, when Dana was twenty-six and Evan was thirty-one. At that time, the sand-dollar sized porcelain spot at the top of his head foretold the hairless globe to come, a reality for him now, at age fifty-two.

"Say," Evan said, "That hairstyle is *really* cool. I think you found your calling, Dana. We'll open a hair salon. You do the styling, and I'll shave all the kerfuffle off the bald guys' heads."

"Where've you been?" Dana asked.

"Down in the basement, checking on that drip from the hot water heater."

Natalie jumped up and looked at her reflection in the plate glass window facing the pitch-dark backyard. "Do you think this braid will last until Saturday? Sammy invited me to sleep over. Can I go?"

"Samantha Bohr," Travis said tonelessly as he stepped into the living room. In one hand he held a huge tumbler of milk, in the other, a plateful of oatmeal cookies.

"What do you mean, 'Samantha Bohr'? Why don't you like her? She's my best friend." Natalie got down on the floor again, this time at her father's heels.

Best friend? This was news to Dana, who recalled only two after-school get-togethers: one at Samantha's house and one at the Goodhues'.

"I'm not saying I don't like her." Travis set the tumbler and plate on the coffee table and sat in the chair next to the couch. "She just has a moron for an older brother. Michael Jr. They call him Emjay."

"Moron is a strong word," Evan remarked.

"Okay, I take it back, but you wouldn't like him, Dad."

"What's the big problem with Emjay?" Evan asked.

"Just the way he acts around school."

"What grade is he in?"

"He's a senior, but he's not too bright and he takes classes that sophomores and juniors usually take. His family is rich and he's a sports star, both football and wrestling. I'm glad he doesn't like baseball." Travis's sport. "Emjay and his football buddies walk around school like they own everybody. They're kind of loud and belligerent."

"Belligerent?" Evan caught Dana's eye. They could be proud of Travis's vocabulary.

"I saw him get in an argument once."

"Well, he wasn't even there when I went to their house," Natalie said. "And he won't be there Saturday night either because you guys have a dance. It'll just be me and Sammy." She twisted around to look at her father. "Can I go, Daddy?"

Sleepovers (or, rather, "non-sleepovers") were kept to a minimum because of the sheer disruption to schedule. After being awake twenty-four hours, Natalie was usually close to comatose the next day. She knew it was best to ask permission from her father, the soft touch.

"Sure, I don't see why not, do you, Dana?"

How could she say 'no' after that? "I guess you haven't had a sleepover in a while."

"It's been forever!"

"Okay, I'll call Mrs. Bohr to confirm."

Natalie rolled her eyes at the suggestion of parental involvement but said nothing, knowing she'd won the battle. Travis stuffed a cookie in his mouth, having said all he wanted to say about the Bohrs, fulfilling his responsibilities as older brother.

"How about you, Travis?" Dana asked. "Are you still sched-uled for the ride phone on Saturday, or did you decide to go to the dance instead?" As late as last week, there'd been some indecision on this point.

He swallowed and said, "I'm on Call Central with Ginger."

"Ginger Kavanagh?" Dana asked, although there couldn't be another Ginger. She'd been under the impression that Travis, on his own, would be taking calls on the new cell phone that Evan had purchased with SADD's funds. "You need two people taking calls the same night?"

"Right. We're backing each other up. We'll be on call until at least two, maybe three."

Evan coughed and clutched his neck. "In the morning?"

"Oh, Daddy!" Natalie laughed.

"I thought the dance was over at eleven."

"People will be going to after-parties and we want to be on call. We can't make any mistakes on the first night."

"Where are you going to *be* when you do this?" Dana asked.

"We haven't decided which house, hers or ours."

Dana and Evan exchanged looks.

"Let's have Ginger over here," Dana said. "It would be nice to meet her."

"Yeah!" Natalie said. "I want to meet her too! Oh...forget that. I'll be at Sammy's house."

"It's okay by me to have her here," Travis agreed, scooping up another cookie. Judging by his expression, he viewed Saturday night as pure business, his shift on Call Central with a coworker. What would the two of them be doing together all night, waiting for calls?

"You think her mom will come pick her up at two or three in the morning?" Evan asked with another cough.

"Sure, or you can take her home."

"A gracious offer on your part, son, but I think I'll have a talk with Vesma about this. How convenient that we have a date in court tomorrow."

"Better watch out, Mommy," Natalie said with a gleam in her eye. "Daddy is having dates with strippers!"

"What are you talking about, young lady?" Dana was sure she'd never told the kids that story about Vesma's wedding to Tynan in night court, when she surprised everyone by taking off a bulky suit to reveal her wedding dress underneath.

"She did some kind of striptease in the courtroom. Travis told me that Ginger told him…"

"Nats!"

"…and *you're* complaining about *my* friends!"

7 »   *SAM*

Evan HEARD THE report of Vesma's three-inch heels, signaling her approach. He pocketed his BlackBerry and looked up. One hundred eighty degrees from Monday, she looked nothing like the dowdy woman who'd deposed the prisoner at Green Haven. She wore a thigh-gripping skirt of not-exactly-purple, and her ash-blonde hair was loose, swaying freely with each definitive step. A stony gaze and tough, compelling features. She was back to attention grabbing, her trademark persona.

Evan had arrived a few minutes early, hoping to catch her in the corridor to discuss a few things in private before they entered the courtroom of the Honorable Friedrich Tenzler.

"Good afternoon, Vesma," Evan greeted.

"Hello," she said dryly. Perhaps warily.

"You've had a chance to look at our responses?" He'd had the papers delivered to her office that morning.

"Yes. Very interesting. Thanks for making my case for me."

Absolutely wrong, and stridently cocky to boot. All a game. Evan smiled amiably and said, "We'll see what Judge Tenzler says on summary judgment."

"I still get to depose your client first."

"We're done with discovery. She's given you the admission you were angling for. There's no more fish in the pond." He looked at his watch. "Listen. We have, maybe, two minutes left, enough time to go off topic."

"What's the off topic today?"

"Our kids."

"Hmm." She studied him with her made-up eyes, lashes, liner, and shadow. The careful craftmanship betrayed a desire to impress—or to conceal. "I suppose you're talking about Students Against Destructive Decisions."

"Yup. I'm sure you know that Travis and Ginger are planning to work together on Saturday night."

Her blasé expression didn't indicate whether she knew about it or not. "The night of the big dance."

"Right. And it's also launch night for Call Central."

"Do you and…Dana have a problem with it?" There was a miniscule pause before the deliberate injection of Dana's name, clearly enunciated.

"Not at all."

"I guess you wouldn't. I understand that you purchased the phone for the kids."

"With their hard-earned money. It's a worthwhile project, and we're behind it a hundred percent. I just wanted to square away the arrangements for Saturday."

"Do the kids need arranging?"

"It's more like the adults who need to make arrangements. Travis is happy to have Ginger over to our house—"

"You'll be home Saturday night? You and Dana?"

"Yes, both of us. You'll just need to drop Ginger off and pick her up again at about two in the morning."

The black liner bounced upward in a brief widening of the eyes. Perhaps she hadn't anticipated this detail. "I'm sure we can arrange it. But let me talk to Ginger first. I'll call you tomorrow, and we'll nail down a plan."

"Sounds good. Shall we?" He motioned toward the door and pushed it open, allowing her to precede him. The audience section of the courtroom was empty, amplifying the sound of Vesma's clacking heels along the length of the center aisle. The only other person in the courtroom was the clerk, shuffling papers at his table. He looked up and said, "Are we all here?"

"You bet," Evan answered. "Ready to go."

"I'll call the judge." The clerk picked up the phone receiver.

As they waited at their respective counsel tables, Evan took stock of the case. *Hafeez versus Nashid* was proceeding at a pace he liked, something all too rare in the world of civil litigation. This week had been especially brisk with Monday's deposition, Tuesday's discovery demands, Wednesday's revelations (from Evan's own client), and today's scheduling conference. If this were an ordinary case, they'd leave today's meeting with a scheduling order, setting deadlines a few months hence to complete discovery and make summary judgment motions. But Evan was ready to move faster, and he planned to make that pitch to the judge. Would Vesma be on board? He was betting she needed to collect her fees out of that escrow account sooner rather than later.

There was whispering in the distance, a one-sided conversation, then a stronger voice broke the silence. "Judge Tenzler wants you in chambers," said the clerk. "This way." The attorneys rose and followed him out the private door behind the bench, into a narrow passageway to an office in back. The clerk rapped twice on the door.

"Come in," a voice bellowed from within.

As the clerk let them in, the judge swiveled around in his high-backed leather chair to face them.

"Good afternoon, Your Honor," the two attorneys said in stereo.

"Come in and sit." He motioned across the desk, open-handed, to indicate the two empty chairs awaiting them. "Just got off the bench. I wasn't about to get robed up again for our little conversation. You're lucky today's trial settled before closing arguments. Otherwise, you'd be sitting in the courtroom, waiting for someone to inhale between a noun and a verb. It's a wonder those yappers reached an agreement. The jury was good and sick of 'em, I can tell you that!"

Speaking of yappers, the judge was a man who liked to talk. His large head, topped with a sparse comb-over, featured a shining forehead and a perpetually open mouth, whether it was emitting sound or not. He was in the habit of using his square-fingered hands to illustrate. A thumb and stiff fingers mimicked the snapping jaws of an alligator to show the talking heads he'd endured in his courtroom this morning.

Evan enjoyed the show and considered himself lucky that Judge Tenzler was assigned to this case. His style and track record boded well for the plaintiff. Vesma smiled politely at the judge's garrulous manner as her eyes flitted around the room, taking in the computer monitor, law books, green banker's lamp, and the old-fashioned heavy-slatted venetian blinds on the window.

"Wipe that worried look off your face, Ms. Krumins! We don't need a steno in here today. I'll put everything down, right here, in my order." He pulled a preprinted form out of a drawer, slapped it on the desk, and unscrewed the cap of a fountain pen. "I'll even insert the caption and the date." He wrote quickly and (from what Evan could see) illegibly. "So, where are we? What've you got for me Mr. Plaintiff's Lawyer?"

"We're moving right along, Your Honor. We deposed the defendant on Monday, and the plaintiff has answered all of Ms. Krumins's interrogatories and requests for admission. I'm just about ready to file the plaintiff's motion for summary judgment…"

"How's next Tuesday?" Judge Tenzler scribbled a note. "Monday's a holiday."

"That works for me. I'll be ready with my papers."

Vesma opened her mouth to speak, but the judge beat her to

it. "Fast work counselors! Just what I like to hear. Why waste everyone's time with endless discovery and trial posturing? This is a simple case. The law is the law. The statute is straightforward. The facts are clear. The defendant killed his own brother and pled guilty to manslaughter. His money should go toward compensating the victim's wife. We've been through all this before when Mr. Goodhue made his attachment application. I froze the funds. Why? Because the plaintiff's case is pretty darn strong. Now it's time to decide who gets that money. We don't need to drag this on."

Well. It looked like the judge had already made up his mind. Evan liked the sound of it, but still, an air of unease settled on his shoulders. This was a bit too much. A judge should remain fair and impartial to the end, and today, there would be no official transcript of the proceedings to bear witness.

As the judge spoke, Vesma squirmed infinitesimally in her tight skirt, a sign of her rising anger, an internal fight for control. As ostentatious as she liked to appear, she never crossed the line between professionalism and demagoguery, at least as far as Evan had seen. She was smart and principled enough to know how far she could go to get what she wanted.

"Your Honor," she blurted into the pause. "Respectfully, the defendant has *not* completed discovery. At a minimum, I need to depose Mr. Goodhue's client, Malikah Hafeez. Just today, I received her admission that her husband came to the altercation with his own knife. The hospital returned it to her after her husband died. And my client testified at his deposition that he was defending himself from a knife attack—"

"Hold on a minute, Ms. Krumins! This court isn't about to relitigate the criminal case. Your guy admitted the crime and he's already done nine years in the pen. Now that a million bucks is on the table he's claiming self-defense? That's a good one!"

"The prosecutor withheld the evidence, Judge. My client's

attorney on the criminal case, Hernando Ramirez, never got it. The prosecutor even withheld it from Mr. Goodhue."

"No such thing," Evan rallied. "I received most of the file from the assistant DA who handled the prosecution, Ted Brevoort. We've spoken a few times, including yesterday."

After a long day in court, Ted had returned Evan's call and cleared up a few misconceptions. Evan realized now that, months ago, when they'd first spoken about the case, Ted hadn't withheld any information. He'd simply related what the physical evidence proved, that the defendant's nine-inch blade had caused all the wounds, the defendant's and the victim's. "Oh, yes," Ted acknowledged during yesterday's call, "I knew about a pocketknife. Malikah told me. It wouldn't have helped the defense, so I wasn't legally required to tell Ramirez about it." *Borderline*, Evan was thinking, trying to tamp down new worries about prosecutorial incompetence or misconduct. But then, Ted set him straight: "Even though I had no obligation to disclose it, I told him anyway. I'm sure that I did, but you'll have to take my word for it. You aren't going to find any written record of the disclosure."

With this conversation in mind, Evan told Judge Tenzler, "Ted confirmed there was no evidence that a second knife caused any of the injuries. The only person in a defensive mode was the victim. He fought off the defendant's attack and managed to turn the defendant's own knife on him before the defendant stabbed him to death. The physical evidence bears that out. And Mr. Brevoort released the hospital records to Mr. Ramirez. Nothing was withheld. The records say only that the decedent's 'personal effects' were returned to his wife. Just because we've determined that those effects included a closed pocketknife..."

"Supposedly closed. Supposedly clean. I have the right to depose your client and cross-examine her about the knife because she's a hostile witness. I'm also going to locate the hospital employees who handled that knife—"

"Whoa! Counselor!" The judge was shaking his head and waving his hands. "Nine years have gone by, and you're going to dig up the emergency room staff? Even if you find them, no one's going to remember this. And the plaintiff doesn't know anything about the crime. She wasn't there when your client stabbed her husband. I'm not allowing this! No further depositions or discovery."

"Exception, Your Honor. I object. This discovery is relevant to my case." Vesma eyed the blank spot next to the judge's desk where a stenographer should have been sitting, recording her objections. "If this case ever goes up on appeal…" She looked at Evan.

"Your exception is duly noted."

"No appellate court would ever sanction such a wild goose chase, Ms. Krumins." The judge's face, open and affable, showed no signs of concern. "What else do you have?"

"I plan to file a motion to vacate my client's conviction based on newly discovered evidence and prosecutorial misconduct. Brevoort should have investigated the second knife and disclosed the details to the defense."

"A pocketknife." The judge smiled broadly and demonstrated a space of six inches between thumb and index finger. "I don't need to see your papers on that one. Don't waste your time. Motion denied."

"Respectfully, Judge, that's a decision for the criminal court to make. The civil court has no jurisdiction. This case will have to be stayed pending the outcome of the defendant's motion in criminal court to vacate his conviction."

"I'm not granting a stay. Where's the law that says I have to give you a stay?"

"In fact, the law is to the contrary, Your Honor," Evan stated confidently, having researched every potential argument ahead of time.

"Exactly!" The judge threw up his hands. "I'm not holding up this case for a baseless motion in criminal court. There's nothing new here. No prosecutorial misconduct! If your guy had a defense, he knew about it and should have raised it nine years ago."

"He was facing twenty-five to life on a murder charge and negotiated a deal for a reduced sentence. Anyone with a viable defense, even an innocent man in that situation, would have taken the deal. He's just as much a victim as the plaintiff's husband…"

"That's your argument? He's a *victim*?"

"Yes, he's three times a victim." For each of the three ways, she flourished a shiny, crimson-tipped finger: index, middle, and ring. "He was a victim during the knife fight. He was a victim again in the hands of an incompetent surgeon who severed his colon beyond repair. And now, we're victimizing him a third time. There was no Son of Sam law in 2000 when he was prosecuted and sentenced. Years later, his assets are being seized. This violates his constitutional right not to be subjected to enhanced punishment, after the fact."

"So, now we're talking the constitution?"

"It's an unconstitutional ex post facto law. At the very least, since my client is also a victim under the Son of Sam law, a chunk of this money should be earmarked for his future medical expenses."

"Okay, okay, okay. I've heard enough." The judge started to scribble on the pre-printed scheduling order.

"And I have another application, Judge. Some of that money in escrow doesn't belong to my client. It's my fee from the medical malpractice case. Two hundred thousand dollars should be released to pay my bill!"

Less than Evan's estimate. Perhaps she thought that a more reasonable demand would yield quicker results.

The judge didn't look at her. He focused on the order he'd

started to craft and recited its provisions as he wrote them. "The parties have completed all relevant discovery. Defendant's additional requests, including a deposition of the plaintiff, seek irrelevant, immaterial matter, and are denied. Escrow to continue pending judgment. In the interim, defendant's request for release of alleged attorney's fees is denied, without prejudice to renew the application upon submission of proof of the claim…"

"I have that proof here, now, the retainer agreement…"

The judge continued to ignore her. "…including proof of a legal basis for the claim, beyond mere creditor status. Plaintiff's motion for summary judgment is due Tuesday, February 17, defendant's response or cross-motion is due…"

"Objection."

"You have your exception…due February 19…"

"Two days!"

"That shouldn't be a problem for you, Ms. Krumins. It sounds like you already know your evidence and arguments by heart. You can take the two days to write them down."

"That violates the Civil Procedure Law!"

"We'll see about that. I have the discretion to expedite the schedule."

"But I can't even get my client's deposition transcript by then!"

The judge looked at Evan as he reached for the phone receiver and pressed a single number on the pad. "You'll stipulate to whatever this man testified to?" It wasn't a question.

"Be glad to, Your Honor."

"These folks are ready to leave," the judge said into the receiver. To them: "My clerk will give you a conformed copy of this." With a smile on his big mouth, he slapped the order and waved it in the air.

* * *

Leaning against the doorjamb, arms crossed, Hernando looked at Vesma with concern written on his face, oblivious to his own perfection. That's how it seemed to her. He was achingly etched in living marble, a citadel resting on pillars of intelligence and compassion. "I can see it didn't go well today," he said.

She almost couldn't look at him. It wasn't him. It was the anger and frustration and also, she hated to admit, her fear of incompetence. She kept it cool by directing her gaze over his left shoulder. "Not the best. As you know, my case sucks." Laying blame elsewhere might help.

"Did you get your arguments before the judge, at least?"

"Sure. I had a good time racing ahead at ninety miles an hour, straight into a brick wall."

"Bet that was a good feeling."

"Judge Tenzler is the worst."

"I've never appeared before him, but I hear he makes it abundantly obvious when he doesn't like your case."

"Understatement of the year. I'm seriously considering filing a recusal motion, or better yet, a grievance with the judicial conduct committee."

"Now, that's serious."

She inhaled deeply and didn't respond immediately. He took it as a cue to pass the threshold. "Tell me about it," he said, walking to her desk and sitting across from her.

"Good chance there's a little sexism mixed in. Evan Goodhue was Prince Charming, and I was the viper stripped of all human rights. Apparently, the Civil Procedure Law doesn't exist for me or my client. I was denied any further discovery related to the pocketknife, and he granted me a generous two days to file a cross-motion for summary judgment."

Nando shook his head and whistled, filling her small office with sound. Skillful at whistling, like everything else. She would have liked to see Judge Tenzler's reaction if Nando had made her arguments today.

"That's undeniably wrong," he said. "But I would hold off on a recusal motion or a judicial grievance."

"I know. It could backfire."

"Sad but true, especially with that kind of judge."

"I wasn't completely serious."

"Just frustrated, I know. Still, there's no way he can deny your counsel fees for the med mal."

"Oh, yes he can!" Laughter bubbled up to surprise her, and once it got started, it wouldn't stop. The nerves and tension and ridiculousness of that man's face with his big mouth and arrogance just flew out of her in fits and waves, a seismic release. Nando picked up the cadence and laughed along with her until their eyes filled with tears. She settled down, grabbed a tissue and dabbed at the corners of her eyes, careful not to smudge her mascara.

A little better. The tension had gone out of her. "None of this is really very funny."

"We have to laugh at something." He leaned forward and knocked once on the edge of her desk with a tight fist of hard knuckles. He stood and said, "Gotta go," but didn't take a step. Their eyes locked, and he lingered. "Listen," he said. "We've been officemates for how long?"

"Over a year. A year and a half."

"What do you say we… Are you free Saturday night? I'll take you to dinner."

A flutter in her chest was a sign that she'd been hoping for this despite her efforts to accept its impossibility. Had he really been thinking about her in this way? Could a younger man, at least five years younger, really be interested in a divorcée pushing fifty? Embarrassed to think of it now, she'd looked for clues as to his romantic or marital status and had found no evidence of attachment, no photos in his office, no ring on his finger.

He waited for her answer with a new side of his personality on display. There was a dab of boyishness and vulnerability she'd never seen before. Her answer was easy. "Yes," she said. "That would be nice."

8 » *MISDEMEANOR?*

TED WAS EXCELLENT at this, he really was. Sitting in the packed courtroom, watching her top assistant examine a witness, Dana felt a twinge of jealousy. She missed the days of being on trial, the impossible stress of assembling a thousand details and the constant looming threat of disaster: witnesses who never showed up, jurors with secret biases, testimony that collapsed under cross-examination by the defense. There'd been hundreds of mornings when she practiced in front of a mirror, evaluating what the jury would see that day, details of clothing and physical appearance, mannerisms, tone and inflection of voice, a professional image meant to inspire confidence.

A performance. What was real under the surface?

The man at the defense table had committed a brutal murder but claimed he was afflicted with a fruit salad of neurotic disorders. Narcissism, paranoia, megalomania. He'd like the jury to think he was uniquely sensitive to even the smallest slight, primed to "snap" into a murderous rage. *We all snap, baby.* Extreme emotional disturbance, a mitigating defense. Nothing intentional. Not my fault.

Yeah, sure, right.

Eerily calm, with glassy eyes, Perry Rigger placidly stared at the witness on the stand, the police officer who'd arrested him. Beneath the veneer of the defendant's studied demeanor, his mind was active. He was the focal point of attention at this trial, every person in this room thinking about him. Did this spectacle feed his illusions that his "disease" would get him off the hook for murder? What part of him was real? His appearance had changed in the many months since his arrest, when he was incarcerated and remanded without bail. No more tanning salons or hair dye or barbells or steroids. The formerly fake black hair had reverted to its natural gray, and his back and shoulders seemed to have shrunk slightly, as far as could be discerned under his baggy clothing, suit and tie.

"Officer Wesson, please tell the jury what happened when you approached the defendant."

The officer had just told of an all-night manhunt, followed by a low-speed car chase weaving through the early morning commuter rush. The defendant had parked his car on the Tappan Zee Bridge, got out, and climbed onto the railing. Another spectacle. Traffic was tied up for miles, news helicopters circling with the thrum of chopper blades.

"When I got about ten feet away, he yelled, 'Stay back or I'll jump!' I stayed where I was. He was crying, and before I could say anything, he said, 'Oh God, I killed her! I killed her!'"

Oh God, is right. Dana had come to the courtroom this morning to observe and to offer Ted advice, if need be. She'd also wanted, maybe, to forget Naomi Steuben for an hour or more, but how could she forget? Here was another bridge with a potential jumper, this one saved. Between Naomi and Perry, it should have been the other way around.

Ted was doing fine and didn't need a backseat driver. Dana got up from her spot in the front pew of the audience and tiptoed down the aisle to the door. Half an hour remained before her next meeting on the Steuben investigation.

Back at her office, Dana's desk was just as she'd left it, three newspapers lined up in a row. She leaned over them, supporting herself with hands cupping the edge of the desk, elbows locked. The headlines stared back. Two local papers and the *New York Times*. It was unusual for a Westchester County case to attract the attention of a reporter from the *Times*, but Naomi's story offered so many sensational angles: heartbreak, scandal, and a person to blame.

At the moment, Dana was that person.

MOM AND DAD DEMAND JUSTICE FOR TEEN'S DEATH

TRAGIC END TO TEEN BULLYING GOES UNPUNISHED

DA HARGROVE TIGHT LIPPED ABOUT CHARGES IN STEUBEN CASE

True, true, true, her mind screamed back.

She stepped away from the desk and paced the room. Naomi died early Monday morning, her body was found Tuesday afternoon, the parents made their demands on Wednesday, and this was Thursday, a day of decision. Or not. Nothing seemed to fit.

Her desk phone rang once. She walked over and pressed the speaker button. Her trusted administrative assistant, Leticia Townes, came over: "You have a call."

Dana knew her assistant well, right down to that tone of voice. Leticia, or Lecia as everyone called her, had been with Dana from the time she was a bureau chief in the Manhattan DA's office. When Dana offered Lecia this job in the suburbs, she accepted immediately, barely masking the depth of her loyalty with offhand remarks about the benefits of "reverse commuting." Lecia lived in the Bronx and drove north to White Plains every morning, against the tide of commuters traveling south, down to Manhattan.

"Who is it, Lecia? Another nosy reporter?"

"Worse," she said. "It's Mrs. Sloane, Taylor Sloane's mother.

You want me to tell her you're unavailable?"

This was tricky, and Lecia knew what Dana was facing. A thousand thoughts raced. Should she speak to the mother of a potential defendant? Were there any conflicts? How would it look?

At the moment, there was no conflict of interest. No one had been charged. There was little risk in talking to Mrs. Sloane, and Dana wanted to know why the woman was calling. This was the mother of the "princess," that "snotty beauty contestant," as Bernard Steuben had described the girl.

"I'll take the call, Lecia. Wait a sec." She pressed the speaker button to turn it off and took a deep, restorative breath before picking up the receiver. "Okay," she said. "You can put her on now."

A faint click sounded, then a tentative, "Hello?"

"Hello, Mrs. Sloane. This is District Attorney Dana Hargrove."

"Okay. Hello. Maybe I'm surprised. I thought your secretary would send me to some underling. David?" She'd turned her head away from the receiver to call out in a louder, less amplified voice. "Pick up the other line." Back to Dana, "I want my husband to hear what's going on. Do you mind?"

"Not at all." Dana rolled her eyes heavenward. "How can I help you?" She heard another click, and then, the sound of congested breathing close to the mouthpiece. A maleness in the nasal rasping.

Mrs. Sloane launched into a tirade full of hurt. "Every newspaper is printing this horrible stuff about our daughter! We can't go anywhere, to the supermarket or the office, without someone glaring at us or saying something nasty. We've been holed up inside our house since Tuesday afternoon!"

"I'm sorry to hear that."

"Taylor is the sweetest girl you'd ever want to meet. You

don't know her like we do. Everyone loves her. She's pretty and popular! From the minute she was born, a blessed light of beauty has been shining on her. You've got to put a stop to this! Every time we turn on the TV, the parents of that girl are screaming that they want our girl arrested, and you haven't said a word about it! Everyone imagines you're busy cooking up some kind of criminal case against Taylor. I don't see how you could even *think* of such a possibility! My daughter has a right like everyone else to express her opinions. Just like those Steubens are spouting off on TV. That's free speech!"

Mrs. Sloane ran out of breath, and Dana jumped into the pause. "I appreciate your thoughts on this, but you might have missed the news stories with my statement to the press. This investigation is ongoing. Nothing has been decided in this situation, so I can't say anything else until the investigation is concluded."

"What is there to investigate? She jumped off the bridge. End of story."

"It's my obligation to—"

"Very sad of course. I don't want to sound like I'm uncaring, but the girl took her own life. Why do we have to suffer for it?"

"—my obligation to gather information from anyone who might know something about this. Would you both like to come down and give statements? Perhaps Taylor could come with you. I'll speak with you personally."

"Absolutely not!" the husband bellowed. "If you want a statement, ask that other kid. If you want to charge someone, charge her. If it's anyone's fault, it's that girl Chloe Dyckman. Those Dyckmans are bad apples to the core. We've told Taylor to stay away from her more than once."

"Yes, we have," agreed Mrs. Sloane, "but the same rules about free speech apply to Chloe too, dear. I'm sure the district attorney would agree." To Dana, "We voted for you, you know.

You're our representative too!"

The soapboxing about "free speech" was very interesting, given that Taylor and Chloe had shut down their Facebook accounts, erasing all their public posts. Had the parents been behind it? "You're right, Mrs. Sloane. I serve all the people in the county, and I'll certainly take everything you're saying into consideration. As I said, you're welcome to come to my office to give statements. Beyond that, I can only say that you'll be informed as soon as the investigation is complete." *In fact, Taylor and Chloe could be the first to know — that is, if arrests are made.*

Dana carefully extricated herself from this conversation. As soon as she was off the phone, Lecia called to say that people had arrived for her next meeting. The attorney handling the Steuben investigation was ADA Linda Marquette, head of the Bias Crimes Unit, a career prosecutor, ten years Dana's senior. She walked into the office with Mohammed Bitar, affectionately known as "Bytes," the tech wizard from IT who'd done the forensics on Naomi's computer.

Dana invited them to sit at the round table tucked into a right angle of her large office, where the windows on either side faced south and east. This was the corner Dana often went to when she was alone, a good place to think or to make a phone call to Evan, as she gazed at his window on the seventeenth floor of his building a few blocks away.

"Did the M.E. issue a report yet?" Dana asked Linda.

"Just got it this morning." She pulled some papers out of the accordion folder she'd carried in. "Nothing unexpected. Cause of death was massive internal injuries. The height of the bridge is 155 feet above the water at the point where she jumped. She was alive when she hit. From that high up, it's like slamming into concrete."

"Ouch," Bytes said. He was a small, wiry youth of twenty-six, going on nineteen. The sparkling brown eyes and bobbing curls of thick hair made him look like a kid about to burst with exciting news. He'd placed a manila folder on the table in front of him and was fidgeting with the corners and edges.

"No injuries inconsistent with the fall," Linda said. "No medical evidence of foul play beforehand. Toxicology was clean."

Dana turned to the computer geek. "Okay, Bytes. Watcha got?" It was hard not to smile. She really loved this guy.

"Retrieved everything! I have the report right here." He pushed the folder toward Dana. "Go ahead! You can have this one. Linda has another copy."

Dana opened the folder and started to peruse the printouts from Facebook. "You have posts here from Taylor and Chloe. How did you manage that? They closed their accounts and everything was taken down."

His eyes flashed excitedly. "Oh, we have a lot of tricks! Archive tools, and actually, a lot of this was in the cache of Naomi's computer." He searched Dana's face expectantly. Finding a blank, he explained, "The temporary files stored in her browser. Every time she opened a webpage, whether from Facebook or anywhere else, an image was stored. The archival tools also store web content, exactly the way it looked on a particular day. It's virtually impossible to erase this stuff."

"I wonder if Taylor and Chloe knew about that when they closed their accounts."

"Whether they knew it or not, they were trying to cover their tracks," Linda said. "It's obvious."

"These pages are like snapshots," Bytes went on. "I got tons of these and didn't include all of them here, but I can get the rest for you. I made a summary at the end of the report."

Dana's eyes finished scanning the first page and turned to the next. And the next. "This is vile stuff..."

Sat behind Fat Ass in history. Blubber squishing out between her pants and shirt. Butt crack showing!

Blub, blub.

"...really horrible."

She smells like old bacon grease. Oily hair. Disgusting.

"These girls just didn't stop."

She needs one of those thingies to pull her out of bed in the morning. A crane. If I were that fat, I'd kill myself.

"Relentless."

Could tie the arms down but wouldn't do any good. She'd just eat out of a bowl like a dog!

"Pictures of hot dogs and pigs.

Don't ever go in the bathroom when she's in there. The noise. The smell.

Word.

One time she walked out of the stall looking like she just came. Must be a relief unloading all that sh...

Dana couldn't read any more.

"How many people could see this? Naomi had only fifteen Facebook friends."

"But Taylor and Chloe each had hundreds. And it was set to 'public,' so you didn't even have to be a friend to read it."

"Naomi was clearly worried about who was seeing these posts," Linda added. "She clicked on their pages dozens of times a day."

"What's the time frame? How long was this going on?"

"The first post was January 23."

"Just a couple of weeks before her death."

"She was constantly trying to find a way to erase this," Bytes said. "Her search engine shows she was asking questions like, 'How do I erase other peoples' Facebook posts about me?' There's no way to do this. After Naomi died, before her body was found, a few friends of Taylor and Chloe even 'liked' some of their posts before they shut down their accounts."

"What do you mean 'liked'?"

"It's a new feature Facebook activated on February 9."

"The day Naomi jumped!"

"A sad coincidence. It's a thumbs-up button you can click to show that you read someone's post and liked it."

"What will they think of next? Were you able to retrieve every relevant post?"

"There could be more. The archival system isn't foolproof."

"If there's anything else, we'll have to get it from Facebook." Dana turned to Linda. "Any luck with the subpoena?"

"I've already gotten an answer."

"That was fast."

"I'm not saying it was a *good* answer. Facebook's counsel called me and said he would move to quash. 'We value the privacy of our account holders,' he said. 'When they close their accounts, they're asserting their privacy interest.'"

"Don't think so," Dana muttered. "They sure as hell weren't concerned about privacy when they were bullying this poor girl." She skipped several pages in the report to a section that had printouts of older posts. "This is stuff Naomi posted last fall. Is it relevant to our case?"

Bytes was squirming again. He leaned closer to Dana and jabbed a finger into the document. "She'd just opened her account that month and was posting almost every day."

"I think she was excited to have a brand-new means of communication," Linda said. "It must have been an outlet for her at first."

Dana shook her head. "That's what I don't get. Privacy? Kids are using this site like a personal journal, but it's open for public view. AIM was the thing a few years ago, but now it's Facebook. I just saw some statistics. The number of users doubled from one hundred million in 2008 to two hundred million this year. When I was a kid, all I had was a diary with a little clasp and a tiny key. You know the kind, Linda?"

"I had one just like it."

"That miniscule lock could be jimmied by anyone, but we still had the fantasy that it was private."

Bytes laughed nervously but kept his mouth shut in deference to his esteemed superiors. Quaint, he could have been thinking. Dana gave him a knowing wink. "Of course, no one's going to be digging up my secrets in an archival system. That diary is long gone, at the bottom of a landfill." She turned her eyes again to his report. "The words 'trash' and 'delete' have been diluted from their original meanings."

"Follow along here," Bytes said, pointing. "She didn't come right out and say it, but…you'll see!"

October 20, 2008. *Is a hammer and chisel the right way to operate on wisdom teeth? I think that's what the doctor used. My mouth is a construction zone! My whole head hurts and he gave me chipmunk cheeks!* Photo of a chipmunk to go with.

Dana thought of Natalie, the French braid, the before and after.

October 21. *Don't ever get your wisdom teeth out if you can help it. This pain won't stop! Time for another pill.* Underneath was a single comment posted by Naomi's sister, Olivia: *Get better soon!*

October 24. *Unbearable pain in my mouth. Everything sucks at school. It's raining, no one's around, nothing's happening this weekend. Good thing we refilled the script. How many percs does it take…? They say it's a good way to go, LOL.*

"Is this what I think it is?" Dana asked.

"Yup," Bytes confirmed. "That same day, she was also searching for information on drug overdoses, specifically Percocet."

"She was thinking of suicide."

"Not only thinking of it," Linda said. "Attempting it."

"Really? How could her parents not know about that? 'Naomi was such a happy child,' they said."

"I called the Steubens yesterday and asked about this. Got them both on the line. They admitted there was an episode in October when they rushed her to the emergency room. Claimed it was an accidental overdose of pain killers. She was in a lot of pain from the surgery and developed a post-surgical infection."

"I guess they never looked at her Facebook page."

"They were oblivious to that. Never looked at it until Monday."

"We'll have to get those medical records."

"The Steubens gave me an authorization. I should have the records later today. Indigo is at the hospital now. You know how persuasive she can be."

"Indeed, I do.

"The parents also said they were aware of the harassment but didn't know the extent of it until this week. Naomi had mentioned a few instances of taunting at school and some text messages."

"Did we recover anything from Naomi's phone?" Dana asked Bytes.

"It's waterlogged and ruined. But Linda got the call log from AT&T."

"It shows incoming texts from Taylor's number," Linda said. "Nothing came in from Chloe's phone. And if you look at the Facebook comments closely, you'll see that most of the bad ones are written by Taylor."

Dana glanced at one of the pages again. Little encouraging replies by Chloe in between the longer posts by Taylor.

"We don't have the actual text messages from Taylor's phone yet," Linda continued. "That will take a while, and we might run into litigation with AT&T."

Taylor's phone only, Taylor's active imagination on Facebook. There went Mr. Sloane's claim that Chloe was the rotten apple. True, though, that Chloe was a willing participant. Dana considered the possibility of getting a search warrant for Taylor's cell phone, and maybe even Chloe's. It would be useful to see any communication between the two suspects. But the tactic would tip their hand. Did they really need those messages to build their case?

In the brief silence, the only sound was a dull drumming. Bytes was playing piano on the tabletop with his nail-bitten fingertips.

"I'm just not sure what we have here," Dana said, finally. "We don't yet have a law specifically aimed at cyberbullying. It's a big problem, but the legislature moves at the pace of a garden snail."

"There could be federal laws that apply," Linda said.

"Oh, I wouldn't refer this case to the feds. They didn't have much luck in that recent case against the Missouri mom. She helped her kid to set up a fake MySpace account, and they used it to taunt and humiliate a girl into committing suicide. The mom was acquitted of the felony charges and convicted of some computer hacking-type misdemeanors that were thrown out on appeal. What do we have under New York law?"

"Certainly a misdemeanor. At the very least it's harassment…"

"That's such a low-level offense, it doesn't reflect the severity of this conduct. Not to my mind."

"Stalking is another possibility," said Linda, "but I'm not sure the elements fit. We'd have to prove that their conduct caused Naomi to fear physical injury from them. These girls were inflicting mental anguish and harm to Naomi's reputation."

"I agree. How about felonies? What are the possibilities?" Dana had already lined up the more serious crimes in her mind, each one a borderline case. Because of this, her criticism of the federal prosecution of that Missouri mom wasn't entirely fair. Her own chances of a felony conviction under New York law were next to nothing. But she kept quiet about her doubts, not wanting to influence Linda. She needed an unbiased opinion.

"Starting at the higher end, there's the class C felony of manslaughter in the second degree under a theory that they intentionally caused or aided Naomi in committing suicide. I don't think we have the evidence for this one."

"How do you see it?"

"To begin with, the statute is rarely used, and you need strong proof of intentional aid. Like putting a loaded gun in the victim's hand and urging her to pull the trigger when she says she wants to kill herself. Those are the facts of the only prosecution I've seen in the case reports. There's also a civil case that interpreted the statute to prohibit physician-assisted suicide. Not relevant here."

"Okay. Any other possibilities?"

Linda glanced at Dana before continuing. If she thought that her boss had already made up her mind, she didn't let on. Just as Dana wanted an unbiased opinion, Linda wanted to hear Dana's reaction to the theories she'd developed. Bytes had stopped drumming the table and was rapt, following the discussion with keen interest, tinged with nervous energy. He seemed eager to contribute but held his tongue, for now.

"Two other possible theories. Manslaughter in the second degree for recklessly causing Naomi's death, and the lower-level class E felony, criminally negligent homicide."

"Causation is difficult to prove, don't you think?" Dana asked. "Their conduct has to be a direct cause of her death, and—"

"That isn't the most difficult hurdle—"

"—they'll argue that Naomi was depressed and would have chosen suicide anyway."

"But she killed herself in the specific way they directed!"

Dana grimaced and nodded in agreement. "True. They dared her to jump off the Bear Mountain Bridge and she did."

"So, I'd say the mental state is the harder element to prove."

"For recklessness, we have to show that they were aware of the risk that Naomi would kill herself and they consciously disregarded that risk. For criminal negligence, we have to prove that they didn't perceive the risk and they should have." Dana paused, turned, and looked Linda directly in the eye. "Go jump off a cliff."

Linda regarded Dana with a glimmer of levity in her intelligent eyes. "Excuse me?"

"No, really. I mean it! And Bytes is my witness." Dana turned to him. "I'm Linda's boss, and I just ordered her to jump off a cliff. Aren't you going to turn me in? Have me arrested and prosecuted?" Dana picked up the manila folder with his report inside and slapped the tabletop for emphasis. "Oh, I get it. There's no way in heaven you think that I believe she's going to follow my order! Or that I'm negligently blind to a risk that she'll do it. I don't have the mental state for the crime."

"Maybe if you knew that Linda was vulnerable and suicidal," Bytes exclaimed, looking pleased with himself. Suddenly, his expression turned to embarrassment and horror. "Sorry, Linda! I didn't mean to suggest that!"

"I'm not offended in the least." She smiled.

"I get your point, but what does it have to do with our case? We just don't have that kind of evidence." Dana slapped the table with the report again, less forcefully, more resignedly.

Linda and Bytes looked at each other, a bit of knowledge passing along the airwave between them.

"What?" Dana asked.

"Show her," said Linda.

"May I?" he asked, holding his hand out for the report. Dana slid it along the table and Bytes gently pulled it away. It didn't take him long. He flipped the pages, knowing exactly where he was headed. "You stopped reading the report just about here, before you got to this part." He folded the pages back and pushed it her way again.

"I couldn't go any further. It was rather hard to stomach…" Casting her eyes downward, Dana read the page, turned it, read the next page and turned it, finding herself caught up in another never-ending stream of sickness, the meaning very clear. Taylor and Chloe knew about the overdose, every fact, down to the number and kind of pills Naomi had taken, how long she'd been in the hospital, what she looked like when she returned to school. How did they know all these details? Not from Naomi's Facebook posts alone. There must have been other sources, other ways. It didn't matter. Dana's investigators would find out. What was important, right now, was the fact that Taylor and Chloe knew just how emotionally fragile Naomi was.

It was enough. Not a strong case, but legally enough. This was a question she could put to the voice of the community.

"Linda." Dana lifted her eyes from the page. "I'd say you're going into the grand jury with this. Tomorrow. We'll help you get ready. Your star witness is sitting right here." She reached over and patted the IT wizard's shoulder.

Bytes fairly beamed.

9 »   *GINGER*

WHEN THE LAST bell rang, Travis was the first out the door of his AP English class. He needed to make a run to his locker, get his calculus and Spanish homework, and jump into the school bus before it pulled away from the curb. Ten minutes. There was no one to drive him home today, and he couldn't stay over for the late bus.

In the next ten minutes, he also hoped to see Ginger.

They shared only one class together in the morning, and sometimes they had lunch at the same table in the cafeteria with the other SADD members, but not today. Off and on, her face would come to mind, or he'd hear things she'd said, spoken in her voice. When that happened, he could forget other things that were getting him down. He was achy and tired, probably from the extra hard workout in gym class, but it was more than that. Ever since Tuesday, there'd been a heavy weight pressing down on his head and shoulders. It wasn't just him. The whole school had fallen into a dark mood. All the excitement about the Valentine's Day dance had vanished into the thickening air.

Travis had never met the girl, but he couldn't stop thinking about what it must have been like for her, standing on the railing of that bridge in the dead of night and stepping off into the blackness. Erasing herself. It was the very last thing he would ever consider doing, and the thought of her up there on the bridge made him angry. Nothing could be done about it now. It was too late for anybody to do anything.

Those two girls were a constant reminder. Today, he saw them in the hallway, talking and laughing like they were actors on stage. He didn't know them, but he remembered seeing them before this ever happened, at a time when they owned the hallways, hanging on the arms of their boyfriends, wearing tight jeans and tossing their shiny hair. Now, they pretended to do the same, with their eyes full of fear, darting into the shadows.

Seeing Ginger always made him feel better. He didn't know why. It wasn't a crush or a physical attraction. At least, he didn't think it was. She had a quality he wanted to be around, something he wished he had. A kind of strength that comes from being better than other people without even knowing you are.

They'd been getting to know each other. There were plenty of opportunities to talk, before and after the weekly SADD meetings, at driver's ed classes, and sometimes at lunch. The other day, he'd been surprised and happy when she agreed to let Grandma drive her home. She lived in a small, single-story house that was completely dark inside when they drove up at five o'clock, in the fading winter light. Grandma waited at the curb until she went inside and turned on a light.

Ginger had told him a little about her life, not much, only hints about her father and the divorce. She didn't go on and on like some girls. She held most of it back, he could tell. It was almost like he knew how much she'd gone through just by how much she *didn't* say. But the most amazing thing about her was that she didn't let anything get her down. She had a smile that could knock the entire world out of your mind because all you could see were those white teeth and dimples and freckles and shining green eyes.

Was that happiness? More like caring about other people. She was the most dedicated member of SADD, even more passionate about their mission than their leader Dylan. She didn't explain where that came from, but Travis knew, and it was another reason to admire her. Other people might get stuck in the anger, but she got energy from it for positive action. What kind of father would fail and disappoint an amazing daughter like Ginger? Maybe Travis was feeling the anger *for* her. What a rotten dad.

With his loaded backpack on his shoulder, Travis left through the school's main entrance and looked down from the top landing of the broad cement stairs. Six or eight yellow buses were lined up at the curb, their engines humming, hundreds of students milling about on the sidewalk. He surveyed the sea of heads and spotted her. You couldn't miss her. That's what he realized. She was easy to find with that hair, a color that no one else had. And when you walked toward her and she saw you, the smile was something else you couldn't miss.

As if reading the radar, she looked up, straight into his eyes. He made his way through the shifting bodies and found her.

"Hi!" she said. "I haven't figured out what to do. You want to stay after? I know there isn't a meeting or anything…"

"I can't. I mean, I want to, but I have too much homework."

"Maybe Dylan should have called another meeting. Do you think we're ready for Saturday? I mean, not really us, but the others?"

"We've got the three drivers. I think it will work out. And…I asked my dad if you could come over on Saturday. To my house."

Ginger looked away and gave a little laugh. "Okay!"

"My dad was supposed to talk to your mom about it today."

"Okay. Really?"

"Yeah. If she can't drive you, we'll pick you up." He wasn't quite sure of this, but he would make it happen. It had to happen.

Her face seemed to light up. "Cool. Word. I'll see what my mom says tonight."

He hesitated and glanced around. Only a minute had passed, but the sidewalk was nearly empty.

She looked at him with a little furrow in her brow, as if she was noticing something about him. This just didn't feel like a normal day.

"Are you taking your bus?" he asked.

She waved a hand in the air. "Maybe I'll wait 'til the late bus."

"Okay. See you tomorrow." He turned and sprinted to the third bus in line, number 73, just as the lead bus was starting to pull away. The doors closed behind him.

After saying goodbye to Travis, Ginger walked down the front lawn to the road and kept walking to the county bus stop. She didn't want to go home. Weekday afternoons were deadly. Ever since the divorce, and after Sean moved away to college, the house had become one huge echo.

Ginger believed her visits to Grandpa were still secret. Mom and Grandpa never seemed to talk, and if they did, Grandpa was likely to forget. The last time they'd all been together was at their house, at Christmas, when Sean was home. Since then, Ginger had been coming to Grandpa's house on her own after school, one or two days a week.

After the first few afternoons, she began to notice how much he forgot and how much he remembered at the same time. It was mind-boggling. One minute he'd be calling her Vesma instead of Ginger, and the next, he'd jump back to his boyhood a million years ago, remembering things like they happened yesterday. He would describe the farm he grew up on and his favorite horse and the Russian tanks rolling across the countryside and bombings and people disappearing in the middle of the night. Half of it was so fantastic she thought he patched it together from that crazy corner in his mind where old people jumble up everything they've ever seen and done.

Grandpa had lived in the same house ever since Ginger could remember. It was a dirty color of white, even smaller than her house, in the middle of a row of similar houses without much room between them. Hugging the yard was a steel fence made of wire twisted into diamond shapes and a gate with a metal lever she lifted to open the latch. It was the type of fence that should have a dog behind it. She heard a few of them barking at houses down the block. When she stepped onto the cement walkway inside, the gate closed itself behind her with a metallic click.

At the front door she knocked, using the metal knocker. There was also a doorbell, but she preferred the knocker. Her own house didn't have one, and she especially loved this feature of Grandpa's house. Sometimes she would lift it as high as it would go and just let it fall, other times she would take it in hand and apply all her might to produce the loudest possible sound. Either way, she was prepared to wait. He needed time to get to the door.

Finally, she heard the big click as the bolt lock slid away, echoing back into the front hall. The door crept open six inches, and most of Grandpa's face peered out from the darkness like a raccoon in the night. The next moment he said, as he always did, "Well, well!" and opened the door wider. "Come in, come in!" Things were usually said in twos at the beginning.

"*Sveiks!*" greeted Ginger in the only Latvian she knew.

"My goodness! *Sveika!*" He chuckled a little. The way he said the word sounded so much better than her version, and he always added a different ending.

The smell of the place always hit her right away, a closed-in odor, the opposite of an open meadow. She'd gotten used to it and liked it because Grandpa was part of it. She followed him in, took a step and came to a halt, stepped again and stopped, adapting to his shuffle. This kind of stuff used to drive her crazy when she was a kid, but now it was almost a relief just to calm down and become really…really…slow.

They entered the kitchen, and she sat on one of the yellow vinyl chairs that bounced slightly on its aluminum "S" frame.

"Some milk?" he offered.

"Sure." She didn't like milk very much unless it was chocolate, but she always managed to drink it. She let him serve her. He seemed to enjoy it. He took his time getting a glass out of the cabinet, opening the refrigerator, bending back the carton spout, and pouring from the quart container. She looked at his profile as he did the pouring. The corner of his mouth was turned upward, and his nose was bulbous and covered with bumps. When he shuffled over and set the glass on the table his face moved into the light from the window, close enough for her to see. Was that… dust inside the cracks and folds of his skin?

He looked at her with a secret in his eyes and waited, but she only smiled back. After a moment he spoke. "I have some cookies too! I know you like cookies."

Excited now, he shuffled a little faster back to the counter, picked up the tin, and brought it to the table, pushing it toward her. The lid was on tight and he couldn't open it himself. She'd seen him try. He always had the same kind of cookies, an assortment, some with slivers of almonds on top, some with jelly in the middle, some very thin and brown and hard. Nothing like chocolate chip, but she always ate one or two and replaced the top loosely with a corner pushed up. Maybe, when she was gone, he would be able to open it himself and have a few.

He sat down in the yellow chair opposite her at the tiny table. He hunched over a bit like he always did, his hands in his lap with the fingers interlaced. She couldn't see his hands under the table, but she knew that's how they were. "How was school today?" he asked.

The recent tragedy crossed her mind, but she decided not to

tell Grandpa about it. Why should she? It might only upset him as much as it had upset her. "Good. We've been having a lot of meetings about Call Central. But not today."

"Call Central?"

"You know. I told you we're working on a ride network. I'm going to be the dispatch person for the first night!"

"My goodness." His eyes, with the slack, diagonal lids over the outside edges, were watery and almost whitish looking on the rims of the gray pupils. She just couldn't tell what he remembered right now.

"I'll be with my friend Travis. This Saturday. Day after tomorrow."

"Tomorrow, yes. Day after." Little backward phrases like that, and the sharp "t's," reminded her he was from somewhere else.

"The school is having a dance, and some of the kids will need rides home that night." She decided not to mention SADD's mission to prevent teens from driving drunk or stoned.

"A dance!" He lifted his arms above the table and twisted right and left, with a little smile on his lips.

She laughed. "I won't get to dance this time. Call Central is more important."

"Oh, yes." He nodded his head. There was no longer a smile, but he didn't look unhappy.

They sat for a while in silence. Ginger drank her milk, trying not to make loud gulping noises. In between swallows she heard the kitchen clock ticking. She took out a cookie covered with hard, white frosting and bit down, holding her other hand underneath to catch the crumbs. Then she heard the sound of her own teeth chewing inside her head.

"Yes, Gingina."

She hadn't said anything, but she'd been thinking a lot of things. She swallowed her mouthful of cookie and spoke. "I like it when you call me that."

"What, Gingiņa? That means my little Ginger."

"In Latvian?"

"Yes, my little Ginger. Like your mama calls you Gingie."

"You were telling me last time about when you had to move, you know, when you had to leave your home in Latvia."

"Oh, yes. A terrible time. So terrible."

He looked down at his hands in his lap, then up and away from her. She was afraid she shouldn't have asked him this. He seemed to be looking out and seeing everything from that time. He was in the middle of it. She wished she hadn't asked.

"I'm sorry," she said.

"Sorry?" He sat up straighter and his eyes were pulled up and open by the raising of his scraggy eyebrows. "Why are you sorry? You aren't German or Russian."

This sounded so funny she almost laughed. He must have seen it in her eyes and a twinkle came into his.

"Yes, it was terrible, but it was so long ago. The Germans and Russians were fighting in our backyard. We ran. Everybody did. We grabbed what we could…," he made swiping motions over the tabletop, gathering imaginary things, "…and we piled it all in the wagon, but when we got to the boat, we couldn't take any-thing with us to Germany. Nothing at all."

"Why couldn't you stay on your farm?"

"Stay with the Russians in our house? We didn't like either of them, but if we had our choice, it was the Germans, not the Russians."

This sounded wrong to Ginger, who had a memory from history class poking around in her mind, but what did her teacher know? Grandpa had been there.

"And you really couldn't bring anything with you? Nothing? What were you going to wear?"

"What we had on, of course! We piled the clothes on our

bodies. It was cold anyway. And we each took one small satchel. I had one book I read over and over again for a whole year."

"And nothing else?"

"We put the pictures in our satchels. My mother, my father, my sister, we all had some." His head drooped, and he was quiet for a while. She saw the brown spots on his scalp under the brittle strands of white hair.

Without warning, his head bounced up again. "Go get the pictures."

"The pictures?"

"The pictures, yes!"

This was the one thing she was allowed to do for him. The first time, he'd taken her to his bedroom to show where he kept the box, but the second time, he suggested she go by herself while he stayed in the kitchen. It became their little ritual.

She went down the short hallway, past the bathroom, into his bedroom at the end of the hall. The smell of Grandpa's whole house was concentrated in there more powerfully, right around the bed. It was very dark with the rolling shades pulled down, and she flipped the light switch on the wall, sending electricity into a dim, yellow bulb under a dirty frosted-glass ceiling fixture.

The shoebox was on a shelf in his closet, as if it contained shoes. Maybe this was his way of hiding it. She knew the pictures were precious to him, and he kept them in the bedroom so he could look at them at night, in bed. She hadn't asked him this. She just knew, partly because he kept his glasses on the bedside table next to a little lamp. Her mission was to retrieve both the glasses and the shoebox and return to the kitchen.

When she got back, he put on the glasses, a kind that nobody ever used anymore. They had heavy black rims and very thick lenses, and his eyes bugged out behind them. He didn't like to wear them all the time, especially when he was walking, because they made him dizzy.

The photos, mostly old, brown or gray, were curled at the edges and of all sizes and shapes. Some were taken in Latvia before and during the war, some in the German DP camp, and some in the United States. "You pick first," he said, the corners of his mouth twitching.

"Okay." She took the top off the shoebox and put her hand inside while looking up at the ceiling. Sometimes she could tell by feel which ones were the oldest, the ones she liked the most because they were so mysterious. She settled on a medium-sized one and pulled it out, happy to find an old snapshot she had never seen before. The edges were curled, and the image had faded. It was probably from Latvia, not Germany, and depicted a girl sitting on a sturdy, broad-chested horse with very thick, furry hooves. The horse was more prominent than the girl, whose body seemed tiny in comparison, but her country-girl square face beamed out to the world with a well-fed, healthy and happy look, framed by neck-length wavy hair held back on one side with a barrette. If the picture had been in color, her cheeks and lips would have been rosy.

"Who's that?"

"Let me see, let me see."

He took the snapshot from her and examined it at varying distances from his nose. Finally, he said, "Vesma, on her horse."

"That's Mom?"

"My sister. And that is her horse."

"Your sister's name is Vesma too?"

"Did I say Vesma? Tekla. That is my sister Tekla. Yes, it is."

Ginger had heard the name before. She took the picture back from him and examined it, trying to find a resemblance between this girl and Grandpa. She might have been twelve or thirteen. How happy she looked! How wonderful to live on a farm with horses, cows and pigs! "She came with you too, when you left Latvia?"

"Of course, yes she did."

"What happened to the horse?"

Grandpa looked away and shrugged his shoulders, enough to say that the horse had not fared well.

"Was your sister in the camp in Germany too?"

"Yes. But then she got married and moved to Canada."

"Oh. Then I never met her."

Grandpa thought for a moment. "You did meet her. Yes. You were very young, a baby. Your mother took you to Canada. But then, there was no opportunity for you to know her. Tekla died very soon after that."

They sat and let this information sink in.

"Your turn!" she said, breaking the silence.

He took the box and rummaged around inside, making a big show of it like he'd entered the drawing for the grand prize, then pulled one out and held it in both hands, resting them on the table. Ginger leaned toward him and looked over the top. She knew this one. It was a very old, studio portrait of a young couple, their images artistically blurred around the edges. The woman's hair was pulled back in a low bun with the sides in a wave tight against her head and covering her ears. Ginger wondered how she could have gotten that wave into it. Her face was sturdy and square, like Tekla's. The man was behind her, taller, with a long face and stern expression. The first time she saw the picture, she guessed it was Grandpa when he was young, but she'd been wrong.

"I know that one!" she said.

"Why? But certainly, yes, you do." He handed it to her.

"Your mother and father."

"Yes."

"What were they like?"

"Well, my mother was a schoolteacher, and my father was a customs agent in the civil service. This was a problem, you see, when the Russians came. People with those kinds of jobs...well, we had some friends. They just disappeared. My father said to us, we have to leave."

"Where do you think your friends went?"

"Siberia. Or killed. The Germans killed certain people and the Russians killed others. We had to leave."

Ginger felt outrage. "How could they just come into your country and kill people? I wish they hadn't done that. I wish you never had to leave."

Grandpa took off his glasses and smiled at her with his real eyes. "But if I hadn't left, we wouldn't be sitting here right now, would we?"

The question opened a flash flood of generations in her mind, from Grandpa's parents, to Grandpa and Grandma, their children Andris and Vesma, Grandma dying, Uncle Andris and Aunt Stephanie childless, Mom and Daddy with Ginger and Sean. Daddy leaving them. And whose fault was that? Mom always said it was "nobody's fault."

"It's your turn," Grandpa said, waking her up.

Ginger quickly pulled out a photograph near the top of the box. The moment she saw it, her heart jumped. If she'd taken the time to sort through, the texture of the photo paper might have given her a clue about this picture before pulling it out. They had dozens like it at home, now tucked away in a drawer and avoided by her mother. Ginger would never look at them unless she was in a happy mood, feeling especially strong.

"What's that?" asked Grandpa.

"Christmas, when I was little."

"A picture of you? What luck!"

Do you like it?

I love it, love it, love it, Daddy.

What are you going to call it?

I think…

Come here, patting his lap.

"What's in the picture? Let me have a look."

She handed it to Grandpa. He held it in one hand, using the other to put on his glasses again after a couple of fumbling attempts. Now she understood why he kept those big, out-of-date glasses. The ones with thin frames would have been impossible for him to put on. He examined the photograph with bug eyes and a scrunched nose. "I remember. Vesma took this one."

"We have the same one at home."

"Vesma, she would mail the copies to me. You are maybe five years old?"

"Six." She remembered every minute of that Christmas. Daddy asked if she had a name for her new stuffed animal while he tugged on a pigtail under her ear and stroked the top of her head, putting little kisses into the part on her scalp. There was a smoky smell on his lips and fingers and that other smell on his breath. A glass with his favorite brown liquid sat on the table next to him. A confused feeling. She wanted and didn't want to be on his lap. He might drape himself over her and talk funny and exhale onto her face.

"And that is your father. You were always on his lap. What are you holding?"

"That's Floppy." The stuffed bunny she still slept with every night. It was soft and white and had long droopy ears with pink insides. Now there was a little rip in the seam between the body and one of the legs.

Her eyes started to sting.

Look at those ears. So floppy.

That's Floppy. That's her name, Daddy. Floppy.

What a good name!

Grandpa's head seemed stuck, looking down at the long-ago Christmas, the tree lights in the background, Ginger holding Floppy, sitting on her father's lap in the picture her mother had sent to him. They lived only fifteen minutes away, but Mom had mailed it to him.

And suddenly it was clear as daylight, the half-conversation she'd overheard only last week, the half that was spoken by her mother. Ginger had been standing outside the bedroom door. It was ajar, and she was about to knock, but she stopped herself, wanting to hear. Mom was lying on her bed talking on her cell phone with Uncle Andris, using the kind of hushed voice reserved for dark secrets. Ginger's ear strained at the crack in the door:

I should visit more often, I know…

…I guess it just became a habit…

…He never liked him and was so angry when we married…

…Maybe I should have listened to him…

Ginger's stomach hurt as she watched Grandpa examining Daddy under his veil of drooping eyelids. She wanted to grab that photo, yank it from his hand! *We wouldn't be sitting here right now, would we?* This is what he'd said only a few minutes ago, knowing all the while…*he never liked him*… Never wanted her father in the family, and that meant he never wanted her. Their stolen afternoons together would have never happened and never been missed.

Now, this one was surely spoiled.

The tears welled in Ginger's eyes, threatening to fall. Grandpa didn't seem to notice. He picked up the picture of Tekla again. His eyes went from the photo of her daddy in one hand to the photo of his sister in the other and back again, while his grayish skin and elephant eyes just made her feel sadder. What was he thinking, remembering?

She turned away and bent down, pretending to pick something off the floor. She sniffed and wiped the tears away. When she sat up, he was staring at the Christmas picture. "Your daddy." He chuckled low. "How he loved his little girl!"

A rush of warm feeling replaced the sickness in her stomach and the burning in her eyes. Maybe Mom saw things one way and

Grandpa saw them another way. Suddenly, she wanted to jump up and kiss him and say she was sorry! But she held back, thinking it would only confuse him.

It was only four thirty when Ginger got home to the huge echo. She'd left Grandpa's early because Uncle Andris showed up unexpectedly. It rattled her, to be discovered.

She had homework to do, but no motivation to start it. She sat in the kitchen and thought of the things she could eat but didn't feel hungry.

Last year at this time there were plenty of afternoons like this, but it was different. Sean was in the house. If she wanted, she could talk to him, or they could keep to themselves and it didn't matter because the house felt different, just because he was there.

She wondered what he was doing right now, so far away. It was his freshman year at Stanford in California, on the other side of the country. So smart, he'd gotten a full scholarship. Did he ever think about her? She remembered how he always used to know when it was important to listen to her. Other times, he might say something completely random that would turn out to be true or right. Like any sister, she'd get mad at him sometimes, but never because she thought he was wrong.

There was a lot Ginger could tell him. So many things were happening at school, both horrible and awesomely amazing. She dug down in her backpack for her cell phone. Did Sean miss her? They hadn't talked since Christmas. Why hadn't *he* called? She punched in the shortcut to Sean's phone, but nothing happened. Silence. No light, no life, and she knew she'd plugged it in last night. The oldest flip phone in the world, it should be in a museum. She'd been warning Mom about it acting up, asking for a new one, but the answer was always "no money."

She went into the living room to the little desk in the corner that held the family telephone and the computer she shared with her mother. She dialed the shortcut for Sean's number, waited through a million rings, and heard the outgoing message. *Hello, you've reached Sean Kavanagh. I can't take your call. Please leave a message.* Was this adult really her brother? She hung up without leaving a message. What would she say?

She sat at the desk, thinking. Maybe she could get up the nerve to call Daddy. At times like this, her resistance wore thin. It had taken her years to build up the protective behaviors, the ways to prevent or minimize disappointment from his missed visits and thin excuses, and finally, she stopped seeing him at all. Sean had been the biggest influence on her in making that decision.

But Daddy had tried to keep up the communication, leaving voicemails, sending letters, cards, and e-mails. She'd responded by e-mail a few times; she couldn't remember when. A phone call? It was easier to write an e-mail.

She turned on the computer. What she found surprised her. A notification. An e-mail from Daddy! This had to mean something. There'd been that photograph at Grandpa's, and her idea to call or write, and here was a message from him, just waiting for her! They were thinking of each other, practically at the same time.

His note was longer than usual, and it ended this way: *Gingie. You can call me anytime. I know you're busy at school and have all kinds of activities, so I won't bother you with calls, but please call me. Anytime. Your Daddy.*

Funny that she could never remember Sean's cell phone number, but she could recite Daddy's number in her sleep, even though she hadn't called it for a very long time.

After a second reading of the message, while trying to compose a reply, she heard the car pulling into the garage. The car door slammed, the garage door closed on its electronic track, and the back door to the kitchen opened. It was only a little after five o'clock. Mom was earlier than usual.

"Gingie? You here?"

"In the living room."

Mom walked in and dropped a fat accordion folder onto the little table next to her easy chair.

"What's that?" Ginger asked.

"My new case. A criminal appeal. I have to read this transcript and write a brief. I figured it's something I can do at home, so I left the office early. What's new with you?" She kicked off her high heels and settled into the chair.

Ginger hesitated a moment before she confessed. "Daddy sent me an e-mail. I was just reading it."

Mom lifted her eyebrows. "What does he have to say?" Her forearms were relaxed along the sides of the easy chair and her voice was flat, closer to an uncaring tone than it used to be.

"He says he wants to give me a car for my seventeenth birthday this summer."

Mom's expression changed so slightly that only Ginger could see the skepticism and distrust. She could read her mother's thoughts—*I will not come between father and daughter*. Mom had never stood in the way of the visits and had actually tried to encourage them, always making sure the arrangements were safe, never letting Ginger get into a car with Daddy. She would drive Ginger to the planned meeting spot, a restaurant, or the movie theater, or Daddy's apartment, but he was the one who sabotaged the plans most of the time, canceling or forgetting the dates. Both Ginger and Sean finally refused to see him, despite his efforts to prove his complete rehabilitation.

"It's a very generous idea, honey, just like all his ideas, but I wouldn't get my heart set on it."

"He thinks it's unfair that Sean got the extra car when he went to college..."

"It's impossible for Sean to get around where he lives

without a car."

"I know. I just meant that Daddy really sounded serious about getting me a car."

"Even if he's serious, he couldn't afford it. I don't know if he told you—he ran out of his paid medical leave and he's been on an unpaid leave of absence for several months."

Ginger considered this. "That means he'll go back, right? I mean, you aren't on 'leave' unless they want you back."

"I would guess so. I really don't know. He was a top investigator for the Society." The Legal Aid Society is what she meant. He investigated cases for the criminal defendants they represented. Daddy had told her stories about his work. She wasn't sure if he was exaggerating, or even showing off, but some of it didn't sound very nice, almost scary. Going into run down, dangerous neighborhoods and talking to witnesses who had criminal records themselves.

Ginger had also overheard enough about the family finances to know that Daddy was obligated to pay child support but had failed to make the payments many times since the divorce. "He said it would be a used car."

"Okay, honey. Okay. I wish *I* could buy you a car."

"Maybe you can buy me a new phone at least? It's totally broken."

"I'll see. Maybe I can."

"You need to keep in touch with me."

"But do you ever call me back?" Her voice was sweet, not judgmental, and she smiled softly, with a kind of dreaminess in her face, her eyes full of light and shine. Cheeks rosy. She seemed different, mysteriously so.

Ginger looked at the computer screen again and clicked on the "x." Daddy's e-mail disappeared. It was better to empty her mind of him, for the millionth time. "I'm done with the computer if you want it."

"Thank you, but I don't need it right now. Do you want dinner?"

"Sure."

"All right. I'll make something." But she didn't get up from the easy chair. Her gaze drifted away, and she spoke to a corner of the room. "I saw Travis's father today in court. He said you're going over to their house on Saturday night."

Ginger's heart gave a strange flutter. "I have to go, to be with Travis. I mean, we're on Call Central together. It's the first night."

"Right," Mom said and stopped, still looking off into the distance. Everything she did seemed to be in slow motion. After a moment she said, "I can drive you, but we'll have to coordinate the times. I'm going to be…busy that night."

"Are you going somewhere?"

She turned to Ginger and smiled contentedly, like she'd just eaten a big bowl of ice cream. "I'm going on a date."

The word "date" punched Ginger in the gut and shocked her into a dizzy spin. "You mean a *date* date?"

"Mm-hmm. I'm going out to dinner. Hernando Ramirez asked me out."

10 »   *WAITING*

DANA SAT IN her favorite corner of the office, gazing at Evan's window in the distance. Mentally, she reached out to him. It was eleven o'clock. Her cell phone and a copy of the Penal Law were at hand, on the table next to her. None of this warranted a phone call, the emptiness and angst that came with waiting.

If she called him, it would be out of weakness. She had nothing new to say. Everything going on this morning was just ordinary stuff. High-profile cases. Worries about the children. Evan was fully up to date on the facts and details. Outcomes were in the hands of other people. What could a phone call accomplish? Why should she distract Evan from *his* work? She gazed out across the gray sky and imagined his silhouette in that tiny square of glass.

"Strong." "Courageous." "Judicious." These were the adjectives flung around during her campaign for DA, spoken by people who knew her well. Her first boss, former Manhattan District Attorney Patrick McBride. His successor, District Attorney Jared "Denzel" Browne. Even her former nemesis, Legal Aid attorney Seth Kaplan, had endorsed her. "Impartial and independent," he'd said, huge concessions for Seth, champion of the underdog. More meaningful to her were the expressions of gratitude and the testimonials from victims of crime. "A true public servant." "Compassionate." "Fair and just." She'd inspired faith in many people. She couldn't let them down when the going got rough. Couldn't let herself down.

The Steuben and Rigger cases dominated the news this morning, with Steuben taking a slight lead. When would the DA do something about cyberbullying? On Wednesday, a snarky commentator came up with a catchy label: "The Mean Girls." But today's op-ed in the county newspaper shot down that moniker as inadequate. This wasn't just mean. This was murder. Was Madam DA holding back because Taylor and Chloe were in the same school district as *her* children? If the reputation of Stone Ridge High plummeted, so did the property values. Bad high school, bad college prospects for Travis and Natalie Goodhue.

Yes, the newspaper even printed their names. It was a shock. Normally the editor showed restraint. Dana was a public figure, fair game. Her children were not. The minute she arrived at the office, her first call was to the editor. Indignant and seething, she stopped just short of threatening a lawsuit. "You will *not* mention my children again! Ever!"

"It's an opinion piece."

"Ever!"

The editor conceded her mistake and offered a retraction.

"No! That will just call more attention to them."

"All right."

"Just—never again!"

Dana hung up, grudgingly satisfied that she'd done what she could. Time to move on.

Eleven fifteen. ADA Marquette's presentation in the grand jury shouldn't take very long. Bytes and Indigo were the main witnesses, and the medical examiner would make a brief appearance. The key evidence came from Naomi's computer. Linda and Dana thought it was enough to get an indictment, but more would be needed for trial to prove guilt beyond a reasonable doubt. A parade of possible witnesses came to mind: doctors who'd treated

Naomi for the overdose, family members who were aware of the suicide attempt, Bernard and Dierdre Steuben, maybe even Olivia Steuben, and Naomi's classmates, anyone who'd witnessed acts of bullying at school. An ugly scene of protracted investigation and legal process. Avoided. For now. *Let's see if the girls are charged first.*

Dana caught herself. She would have to stop thinking of them as "girls." They were both seventeen, which made them "adults" under New York's Penal Law. Tried as adults, sentenced as adults, sent to state prison. Bedford Hills. Never mind that New York lagged woefully behind the rest of the country in its juvenile justice laws! Every psychologist on the planet now recognized that teenagers were prone to heightened risk taking, their brains not yet fully developed to make rational decisions with long-term consequences in mind. Other states were raising the age to eighteen or nineteen, but in New York, anyone over the age of sixteen was charged as an adult. In some cases, even kids as young as thirteen who committed serious felonies could be tried as "adults."

But there were other options open to Dana. If Taylor and Chloe were convicted of felonies, she could recommend "youthful offender" status. Their criminal records would be erased as if they never existed, and state prison wasn't mandatory—probation was an option. Would that be the "fair" and "impartial" choice here? "Compassionate" for all concerned? But any recommendation she made would be just that, a recommendation. The judge would make the final call. The only way to ensure a slap on the wrist would be to charge them with misdemeanors.

What was too lenient? Too harsh? Why couldn't she make up her mind what she thought about these girls and their cruel acts? These "women" and their "crimes"?

Manslaughter felt even more ridiculous when she compared this case to Rigger's. Could both cases end up with manslaughter convictions? There was no comparison. If Perry Rigger convinced the jury to buy his defense of extreme emotional disturbance, the verdict for his heinous bat bludgeoning could be reduced from murder to manslaughter. Man one, not man two like Taylor and Chloe, but still manslaughter. Ted was finishing the People's case this morning, and the defense case could start this afternoon. Rigger planned to testify. Maybe she'd go watch the trial this afternoon if Linda still didn't have a result in the grand jury.

Dana glanced at her desk where three sets of papers were neatly lined up. Two of them were the beginnings of press releases. One announced that the grand jury had not returned an indictment. The other announced an indictment against Taylor Sloane and Chloe Dyckman for reckless manslaughter (slash) negligent homicide (slash) harassment, depending on the outcome. The third set of papers included search warrants for the girls' cell phones and laptops, to be executed at the time of their arrests—*if* there was an indictment. The phone company had reported that the text messages from Taylor to Naomi were no longer available. Chloe's phone was also of interest because, although there was no record of Chloe texting Naomi, any texts between Taylor and Chloe about Naomi would be relevant.

Dana checked her mobile phone. Eleven twenty-two. Her focus on these murder and manslaughter cases had pushed other thoughts from her mind. Avoidance was merely a temporary salve, ultimately ineffective.

Travis hadn't been his usual self this morning. Slept past his alarm, not by much, only ten minutes, but enough to mean something. He was normally alert and punctual to a fault, unlike Natalie, who had to be coaxed out of bed. Any change in his habits meant that something was going on.

Dana had to knock on his closed door to wake him. She'd just read the newspaper and was still in her out-of-body state, the aftermath of the jolt at seeing the names of her children in print. It was six thirty. Evan was in the basement on the treadmill, his indoor exercise substitute when the pavement was too icy for his morning jog. Dana liked to be on the road before seven, but today she would wait. She had to talk to Evan about this. Should they warn the kids? Say anything to them? If they decided to discuss the news, the family should be together.

When Travis opened the door, she asked, "Are you feeling all right?"

"Okay. A little tired."

He seemed to be holding back, leaving something out. The boy internalized everything, and she feared that he was still upset about the suicide. Perhaps he was depressed, but she found it easier to pretend it was something else. "Are you coming down with a cold?" She felt his forehead. "You feel a little warm." But he'd just gotten out of a warm bed. "Maybe you should stay home today."

"No, Mom. I'm fine."

"Your voice sounds a little scratchy."

"I just got up. Let me get ready for school."

"Okay. I'll make you some toast." She backed off and closed the door to let him get ready. She would do the same thing. Not feeling well? Go to work. Staying home got nothing done. Solved nothing. He took after her in this way. There was a lot of pressure on the kids in their junior year, with AP tests and regents exams to study for. Travis couldn't miss a day.

Evan came upstairs, sweating, pressing a towel to his forehead. She told him about the news articles and op-ed column. They decided to speak to the kids. Evan took a shower, Dana coaxed Natalie out of bed, and the family sat down to breakfast together. Travis looked glum and chewed listlessly, leaving half his toast unfinished. *Very* unusual for him. Natalie ate a single piece of toast with a thin layer of butter, clearly wanting more, fighting the urge.

"There's something in the newspaper today I want you to be

aware of in case anyone says something to you about it," Dana said.

"Is it about that suicide case?" Natalie blurted. If she was distraught, there was no indication of it. She was open about nearly everything, would rather talk than keep it in.

"Yes. Some news reports and articles have been suggesting that my office should bring criminal charges…"

"Well, they should…," muttered Travis.

"What was that, young man?" Evan asked.

Dana glanced at Evan askance, sending a silent message to tread lightly. What was it about this morning? Now Evan was acting strange. He usually didn't take that kind of tone with the kids. Maybe the news coverage was getting to him too.

"We're working hard on it, sweetheart. It's my job to try to do the right thing under the law. What I wanted to warn you about is an editorial in today's newspaper. It implies that my decision could somehow be influenced by the fact that you two," she looked at Travis and Natalie in turn, "are students in the same school district as the girls who were involved. The newspaper mentions you by name…"

"Really?" Natalie brightened. "I'm in the newspaper!"

"Your names are mentioned, but the only thing about you is that you attend school in this district. I plan to call the editor about it because it's completely inappropriate to print anything at all about you, even that little bit."

"And you should know that your mother makes her decisions in any criminal investigation based on the law and the facts of the particular case. That's it. Nothing else." Evan crossed his hands in the air and sliced them outward, erasing everything but the law and the facts. "The people writing these editorials don't know diddly-squat." He crossed his eyes and stuck out his tongue.

Natalie laughed, but Travis barely cracked a smile. "May I be excused?" he asked. "I don't want to miss the bus."

"Of course," Dana said.

"Mommy, did you talk to Samantha's mom about tomorrow?" Natalie was already past their discussion and moving on to her own priorities.

"Not yet. I left a message for Mrs. Bohr, but she hasn't called back. I'll take care of it today."

"I can still go, can't I?"

"Yes, we already said…"

"Thank you thank you thank you!" She jumped up and wrapped her arms around Dana's neck, then ran out of the room, calling, "I've gotta get ready too!"

Evan and Dana looked at each other and shrugged.

At two, Dana was at her desk when Linda called on the office line. The grand jury had just started deliberating. She predicted that, unlike most run-of-the-mill cases, the vote would not come back quickly. There were twenty-three grand jurors, and they needed a simple majority of twelve to indict. No judge in the room—Linda was their legal advisor.

Many of the jurors had asked Linda questions about the charges submitted to them for a vote: reckless manslaughter, criminally negligent homicide, and harassment. Did Taylor and Chloe have to believe that Naomi would kill herself in that specific way? Did the bullying have to be the *only* reason that Naomi jumped, or just one of the reasons? One juror even asked this: "What's coming next? If I just *think* hard enough that I want someone dead you'll charge me with manslaughter?"

"Wow!" Dana exclaimed. "That's a doozy. Kinda sounds like they won't indict."

"Oh, I'm not so sure about that. The juror who asked that question is the one, you know…"

"Not *that* one?"

"Yes. The one who demanded to see the judge last week. Said the others were picking on her because of her questions and the way she voted on the cases. I'm guessing she hasn't voted once to indict anyone this term, but the judge kept her on. Said he was satisfied with her answers, that she was fair and impartial."

"I wonder what she said to convince him of that!"

"She knows what to say when it's important."

"So, that's one vote not to indict. The twenty-two others could come back with anything."

"I'll keep you posted."

"Call me on my cell. I'm not sure where I'll be."

When Dana hung up, she got a text from Ted that the defense case was due to start at two fifteen. She decided to go up to the courtroom, but first, just one more look at those press releases…

The desk phone rang again. Lecia had a caller on the line.

"Please, no reporters," Dana said.

"I wouldn't do that to you. She gave the name Sandra Bohr. I asked what it's about, but she said it's personal. Do you know this woman?"

"Yes, she's okay. Didn't she say she was returning my call?"

"No, nothing like that. Just, 'It's personal.'"

"Okay, thanks, I'll take the call. She's the mom of one of Natalie's friends."

During this brief exchange, Dana was reminded, with some surprise, that she'd given her office number to Sandy Bohr. Usually she gave out her cell number for personal calls related to the kids. The two numbers left subtly different impressions, mom versus elected official. For some reason, in this instance, Dana was injecting her professional self into the projected image. Part of her understood this, without quite knowing why.

This was, maybe, only the second time they'd ever spoken, but she decided to go for first names. "Sandy? Hi, it's Dana.

Thanks for calling back."

"No problem." A bit surly.

"Natalie tells me that Samantha has invited her for an overnight tomorrow night. I just wanted to confirm with you."

"Sure, fine. She can have whoever she wants."

"I just wanted to make sure it doesn't interfere with any plans you might have." Were Sandy and her husband the type of couple to make special plans for Valentine's Day? Dana didn't want to suggest anything too personal. "I suppose Samantha's brother will be at the high school dance, and you…"

"Emjay will be out. You're not interrupting anything for us."

"Great. If those girls are up all night talking, feel free to tell Natalie to pipe down!"

"I'm sure they'll be fine."

An awkward silence. Dana envisioned that sprawling estate on three acres, the Bohrs' "McMansion." She supposed that two chattering teenage girls in Samantha's bedroom wouldn't be heard in the living room or the parents' bedroom. Sandy's husband, Michael Sr., was a successful plastic surgeon, who'd provided well for the family. "Is eight o'clock all right? Evan will drop Natalie off." *Perhaps the men can have a chat about liposuction or tummy tucks.*

"Fine, no problem."

"Thanks. Okay, then. Nice talking to you, Sandy."

"Sure. Bye now."

And that was that. Why didn't it feel quite right?

Dana walked out of her office, stopping briefly at Lecia's desk to let her know where she'd be. "When you get back, give me all the gory details!" Lecia's eyes flashed.

"Maybe we should switch places for a day."

"Oh, I'm still good with vicarious thrills. You can handle all that in-your-face stuff, and I'll handle the public and the reporters."

Dana pressed her hands into prayer position and tilted her face heavenward. "Thank you! You're my lifesaver."

Down the hall to the secure elevator she went, her mind abuzz. Now her thoughts centered on Natalie and Samantha Bohr and Sandra Bohr. Natalie had invited Sammy over to their house once, and Dana had found her to be polite and intelligent. Perhaps their friendship would change in the fall, when middle school was behind them. Natalie would be going to Stone Ridge High School, and Samantha was already accepted to an exclusive, private high school. The Bohrs had the money to send Michael Jr. to private school as well but, the word was, they'd given in to his wishes to stay in the public system. Emjay wasn't academically strong and was more interested in sports. The Stone Ridge football team, the Titans, was first in the state, and the wrestling team was ranked third. Emjay was a star on both of those varsity teams.

Dana didn't really know Michael Sr. and Sandra Bohr other than the scattered times she'd seen them at school functions. Funny how parents of school kids in a suburban community can simultaneously know and not know one another. Names and faces, homes, the vague outlines of lives, the children's activities, all became familiar in a back-of-the-mind sort of way, impressions formed from intermittent sightings, a word or two exchanged, photos and captions in local newspapers and school newsletters.

Dana played back the phone call in her mind. What was it in that woman's voice? Indifference, arrogance, or...judgment? Maybe she was conveying a subliminal message about the criminal investigations in the news. If Sandra Bohr were on the grand jury, would she indict Taylor and Chloe for manslaughter or set them free? Dana didn't know how to read her. The voice and attitude didn't fit the image she'd crafted of Sandy, based on what Natalie had told her (repeating Samantha's words). Curiosity had gotten the better of Dana, and she'd done a Google search under Sandy's maiden name—or was that a stage name? Sandra Steele was formerly a Broadway performer, dancer, singer, and actress. Just like Cheryl.

Dana stepped into the elevator and pressed the button for the eleventh floor of the courthouse. The doors closed her in. Ever since learning of Sandy's former career, she'd been meaning to ask her sister about it. Cheryl was at least ten years younger than Sandy, and certainly their careers on Broadway had never intersected, but Cheryl might know an interesting tidbit or two. If nothing else, Dana owed Cheryl a phone call. They needed to catch up, and Cheryl had mentioned that she might be free to get together tomorrow afternoon.

Wouldn't that be nice? A Saturday afternoon get-together, just the girls, Dana, Natalie, and Cheryl. Valentine's Day at that. Dana had been wanting to do something special for Natalie, and anything involving her favorite aunt would be the thing. Lunch and shopping, and maybe a new outfit for Natalie to brighten up this dreary, freezing weather.

A boost to her self-esteem.

Moving on autopilot, her mind immersed in thought, Dana arrived at the courtroom. Before opening the door, she made sure that her cell phone was on vibrate in her jacket pocket. She entered and tiptoed down the aisle, finding a seat in the first row. Judge Madeleine Sinclair acknowledged her with a glance and a nod. Everyone was on the tip of readiness. The jury sat in the box, the stenographer's fingers were poised. Rigger's attorney, Frederick Carlyle, stood and said, "The defense calls Perry Rigger."

Carlyle looked down at his client and, with his eyes, encouraged him to get up, out of his chair. As Rigger stood, his moment of hesitation was replaced with an overconfident air. The contrast between the men was striking. They both stood brick-wall straight, but Carlyle towered a full head over Rigger, and his rich brown skin was a pleasing sight next to his client's pasty pallor.

Rigger's eyes skittered across the jury panel as he swaggered to the witness stand. Although he'd been remanded without bail during the trial, he was allowed to wear civilian clothes instead of institutional garb. His suit was now a size too big for him, a sign of his distaste for prison cuisine. As Indigo had reported to Dana and the team, in former, pre-murder days, Rigger was known at his health club to guzzle raw vegetable juices of orange and green and beet red. Among his fellow body builders, he espoused the benefits of a pure organic diet with plenty of free-range, grass-fed beef. Any health benefits from these habits were undoubtedly canceled out by the toxic amounts of vitamin supplements, illegal steroids, and psychotropic drugs he took for depression, anxiety, and sleeplessness. Indigo had dug up a lot of this information, and the rest was revealed in medical records, which Carlyle had openly disclosed to the prosecution.

Rigger's modest stature of five foot seven no longer displayed the compensating enhancement he'd worked so hard to attain: the body-builder muscles. He was now physically shrunken but still full of himself, showing plenty of ego, arrogantly puffing his chest out as the court clerk administered the oath. "I do," Rigger said, as if that proved his case. The jury couldn't possibly disbelieve him now. His self-importance had a wary edge, receding as soon as he asserted it. He wilted slightly as he sat, slumping a quarter of an inch on the hard, wooden chair.

Carlyle led his client through a half hour of background information. His marriage to Violet. Two children, now young adults. His vitamin and health supplement store. And then, the beginnings of his financial ruin, a business partner who ripped him off, impending bankruptcy, despair, sleeplessness, trips to the emergency room. Carlyle was letting him talk at length, interjecting a question here or there. Ted sat calmly, conveying mild skepticism, but not objecting. Dana agreed with this tactic. Let Rigger keep talking until he was cross-eyed. There would be plenty to shoot down on cross.

There were more defense witnesses in store, judging by Carlyle's list filed with the court. He planned to call Rigger's doctors, family members and friends who could attest to his supposed deteriorating mental state. But Rigger was the first witness for the defense.

Dana pondered the defense strategy. In most cases, attorneys advised their clients not to testify. But in Rigger's case, there was no doubt he killed his wife. His only defense was a hoped-for reduction of the murder charge to manslaughter. Extreme emotional disturbance. He could attempt to prove the defense with other witnesses and medical evidence, but the jury would be left wanting to hear from the man himself. This was his chance to gain their sympathy.

Not working so far. Not for me.

The defendant spoke in a chillingly quiet voice, measured, almost creepy, his eyes moving back and forth before he answered each question. Studied. Rehearsed. Planned. Narcissistic. The whole world revolved around him. His mind was plotting the impression he wanted to leave on the jurors, even as he spoke.

That's how it looked to Dana. But she wasn't sitting on that jury. Would Rigger impress them as a man whose mental impairments excused his uncontrolled barrage of violence? Would the trigger point be credible? Carlyle would have to rely heavily on the testimony of the medical experts to create this impression.

Dana felt a buzz in her jacket pocket and pulled her phone out far enough to see the face of it. A text from Linda. An hour had passed since the deliberations started. Unusually long. "GJ still out. War and Peace!" Dana smiled and suppressed a laugh. Linda's code was based on a story Dana liked to tell about a grand jury proceeding in Manhattan, 1992. The jury was considering murder charges against the late-term abortionist, Dr. Grant Spellman. During deliberations, shouting could be heard through the walls of the grand jury room, followed by a muffled scream and a loud "thud." A court officer rushed in to find a hardbound copy of *War and Peace* on the floor. Upon seeing the officer, the juror standing next to the volume immediately clutched her upper arm, as if the book had hit her. On the other side of the room, the opposing camp sided with the man who'd flung his coffee-break reading material and claimed that the "injured" person was lying.

Dana replied to Linda with the single letter "y," her own code to indicate she'd received and read the message.

"Perry, could you please tell the jury about the events of June 26, 2008."

The defendant's eyes shot over to the jury and back to his attorney before he answered. "Do you mean that night or after midnight?"

"Start at the beginning. Did you and Violet have a conversation?"

"Yes."

"About what time did that start?"

"Ten o'clock."

So precise. Practiced, even though his attorney tried to lead him into a generality.

"What did Violet say to you?"

"She said she hadn't seen her parents in a long time and she wanted to… No, she didn't want to invite them, she already *did* invite them for dinner that coming Saturday. In two days. They were coming over. Without asking me first if it was okay, they were coming over. End of story. I said, 'What do you mean? I can't believe you did that without asking me!'"

Oh, brother.

"How did this make you feel?"

"I hadn't slept in weeks. She *knew* what I was going through! I couldn't have any company to the house at all. No one. Especially not her parents. I knew what they would do. Make little snippy comments about my business, why didn't I move on to something else, go out and make some money, hinting around that I was bringing everyone to wrack and ruin… You don't know these people. Their eyes, just the way they look at you, and Violet knew I couldn't do that, I just couldn't do that. I was at the end of my rope. 'Call it off,' I told her. She refused. I couldn't stand it, so I went and took—"

"Take a breath, Mr. Rigger," Judge Sinclair directed from the bench. "Speak clearly." The stenographer had been shaking her head in distress as Rigger's speech accelerated and slurred.

A performance.

"Okay. Sorry, Your Honor." His forehead glistened with sweat.

"Do you need a moment, Perry?" Carlyle asked.

A sideshow.

"I'm okay."

"Please go on. You said that you took something?"

"I took a couple of extra pills, I can't remember which ones, they were some of the antidepressants. You know that the police found the pill bottles in the bathroom, right? I took a bunch, and you can compare the prescriptions to the bottles to see what I took. I just can't remember exactly. The whole thing about her parents depressed me, but now that I look back on it, I should have taken something to calm me down, like Valium or, or maybe just an herbal tea. I was completely on edge, just needed to sleep, you know, being so wound up, no sleep for days. The pills seemed to make it worse. My hands were shaking."

Here he was skating the line. His defense wasn't based on intoxication or overmedication. He wasn't claiming that the medicine prevented him from forming the intent to kill. He was claiming a mental disorder and circumstances that made it "reasonable" for him to "snap." What would the jury think about this business with the pills?

"So then, after I took the medication, I said to myself I had to talk her out of it. By then it was almost midnight, and she was in the living room, ignoring me, sitting there reading a magazine like everything was normal. She didn't even look up when I came in the room and told her to call off the dinner, I just couldn't handle it right then, at that point in my life..."

Dana felt a buzz in her jacket pocket as Rigger continued talking, nonstop. She looked down at the screen. "True bill." The jury had returned an indictment. It was a relatively quick end to *War and Peace* after all.

She stood and acknowledged the judge with eye contact and a subtle nod. Turning, tiptoeing down the aisle, she had no regrets about missing the rest of Rigger's story. His testimony was coming out in predictable fashion, consistent with his statements to the police. Violet didn't want to talk to him, tried to ignore him, refused to engage. She retreated. He followed. It was galling to be ignored. He had to make her understand the stress he was under, how impossible it was for him to have any company over to the house, especially her parents. He was at a breaking point, and she just didn't care. She kept turning her head away, refusing to listen, walking away from him, into one room then another. When she entered the mudroom, on the way to the garage, he thought she was going to get the car and drive away. It was there that he demanded, for the last time, that she call off the dinner plans. Unfortunately for Violet, a baseball bat was propped up against the wall, conveniently at hand the moment he "snapped." And what was the trigger? Her final words, in a mocking tone: *"Are you crazy? Are you out of your mind?"*

Would the jury think that the district attorney was turning her back on his defense? Would Carlyle accuse Dana of making a little show of her own by leaving the courtroom? Maybe, but she couldn't worry about that right now. She had to finish writing her press release and set the arrests and search warrants into motion. She had to be prepared for the public reaction to her announcement of criminal charges against two teenage girls.

Linda hadn't said what those charges were.

Outside the courtroom, in the hall, Dana texted Linda: "My office in five."

On her way to the elevator, mobile phone in hand, she felt the buzz again and looked at the screen. Cheryl was calling. What timing! But the urge to answer was irresistible. She'd much rather talk to her sister than rush back to the news awaiting her at the office.

"I'm not interrupting anything, am I?" Cheryl asked.

If only she knew. But Cheryl would find out soon enough, just like Dana and the rest of the world. "Not at all. Actually, I've been thinking about you and was about to call. Are you still free tomorrow?" Dana paused outside the elevator to finish the conversation.

"Until six. Then I'm going on a hot date."

"Uh-oh."

"Hey, it's Valentine's Day. Aren't you and Evan going to do something romantic tomorrow night?"

"It will have to be something like watching TV while we chaperone Travis and a girl he's having over to the house."

"Uh-oh back at you."

"It isn't supposed to be a date for him. He's working on a club project. I'll tell you all about it tomorrow. Can you meet me and Natalie for lunch and some shopping?"

"I'd love that! An afternoon with my favorite sister and favorite niece."

"Your *only* sister and *only* niece."

"She's my sweet, sweet girl. Thank you so much for having that girl, Dana! She's the best thing you ever accomplished."

"I'm glad I'm good for something."

11 »   CANCELED

AT ONE O'CLOCK the pain was so bad, Travis couldn't bear it. There were two more class periods in the day, but he couldn't face them. On the other side of the principal's office was a door marked "Nurse." This would be the first time he'd ever open that door and walk inside.

"You're burning up," the nurse said after one touch of the forehead. She peered into his eyes, ears, and throat, and handed him a glass of water. "Rest here. I'll call your mom." She seemed to consider what she'd just said and quickly added, "Or how about your dad?" In this big high school, everyone seemed to know him and who his mom was and what she might be doing today. He'd already gotten a few comments about the article in this morning's newspaper.

"No!" He almost couldn't speak from the burn in his throat. "Call my grandma please," he croaked. "She'll come." Luckily, Grandma Brenda was on the approved call list. Within twenty minutes she was there.

"You don't look too chipper, young man," she said when they'd gotten into her car.

"I'll be okay. I just need to go home."

"Oh, no you don't! I'm taking you to the doctor first."

"Argh!" He didn't need a doctor. If he could just sleep, he'd be better by tomorrow. He had to be better by tomorrow.

"Your mom would *kill* me if I didn't take you to the doctor!" Grandma's shaky vibrato had a very dramatic flourish. If he didn't feel so bad, the funny sound of it would make him instantly happy. "I should just pull over right now and call her," Grandma added, glancing at his face.

Stubbornly, he set his gaze directly ahead, out the windshield. "You can't. She's..."

"Busy. I know, I know. But what is she going to say when she finds out I kidnapped you from school?"

He pursed his lips and shook his head.

"Alrighty. I'll just have to take my punishment later. How about your dad then? I'll call him instead."

"No, please don't."

She kept her eyes on the road and laughed briskly. "Okay, I'll give you the benefit of the doubt just because your heart's in the right place. You don't want to worry them. Is that it?"

"They'll see me when they get home. I'm not dying."

"No, you're not, but you look mighty sick. Off to the doctor we go."

He didn't have the strength to protest and was beginning to agree with her judgment of his condition. He prayed it was nothing. He couldn't be sick right now. Tomorrow night couldn't be canceled.

Hours later, after a very long wait in the doctor's office, the exam, the diagnosis, and a trip to the pharmacy, he was finally home again, sitting on the living room couch with Grandma. She handed him a pill and a glass of water. Down went the first dose of a powerful antibiotic.

He didn't feel up to doing anything. Reading or homework were out of the question, and there was plenty of time for that later. It was only Friday, and the weekend was ahead. "I'm going to stay in here and watch TV." He toed off his sneakers, grabbed the clicker from the coffee table, and pressed the power button.

"Okay. Lie down while you watch."

Travis lifted his feet and slid them behind Grandma, leaving her a narrow space to sit. She reached for the afghan on the arm of the couch and draped it over him as he pulled a pillow under his head. The room was spinning. He didn't bother to change the channel on the TV. A nature documentary was showing, and that was just fine.

Natalie came in the front door, fresh off the school bus. "Hi Grandma! Are you staying for pizza tonight?" Friday was the traditional pizza night at the Goodhues.

"I don't think your brother will want any pizza."

Natalie came closer and eyed Travis. "What's with you?"

"Stay away!" Grandma warned. "Strep throat over here!"

"Eeuw!" Natalie needed no encouragement to leave the room. On her way out, she twisted around, stopped, and said, "You'd better stay away from him too, Grandma! Don't you have your play pretty soon? You can't get sick." Grandma's part in a local theater production had been big news around the house. Everyone would be going.

"Oh, don't you worry. That's not until March, and anyway, I *never* get sick."

Natalie scrunched her brow in confused disbelief and vanished into the hallway.

Brenda stroked Travis's forehead and started singing about "my melancholy baby" while the soothing baritone voice of a male narrator enlightened them about the habits of predators. Travis closed his eyes and drifted on the strange harmony of voices intertwined in a mysterious duet. *Every cloud must have a silver lining,* sang the soprano over an ominous bass line: *The gray wolf relies on the teamwork of the pack for a successful hunt…*

Taylor gazed at herself in the full-length mirror on her bedroom wall, not completely satisfied with what she saw. There was still a day left to change her mind, to find something else in her closet.

It would be convenient to blame her mood on Friday the thirteenth. Maybe that would make everything else that was bad in her life disappear. Put a spell on it. When she and Chloe were in middle school, they'd gone through a witch phase. The idea had been Chloe's, like everything else they did together. Chloe had been reading about the witches of Salem, supernatural phenomena, and black magic. She devised potions and brews, performed hexes and voodoo, and directed Taylor in her part of it. Doubt and indecision weren't allowed because Chloe was absolutely sure of the necessity and correctness of their mission. There was that boy they didn't like who became seriously ill. *See. That proves it.*

Two raps sounded on her bedroom door, and then it opened. Dad would've waited until Taylor invited him in, but Mom never did.

Taylor's entire body tensed as her mother stepped into the room. Mom eyed the dress from top to bottom, pausing at the parts of her daughter that seemed to matter to her. "That looks nice on you," she said, but her voice carried that little downturn of criticism at the end, like it almost always did.

"I don't like it anymore."

"Come on, honey. We paid an arm and a leg for it. Julian will like it. I guarantee you."

Skintight, that's why. She recalled the trip to the mall, the dress shop, modeling one style after another for her mother. When Taylor was a little girl, Mom would make her model the new dresses for her father in the living room. "Twirl around!" Big bow tied in the back of the waist. Mom would prompt, "Isn't she so pretty?" Dad would agree, with an appreciative gleam in his eye. Now, Mom was dressing her for the boyfriend. *Julian will like it.*

"The color looks hideous." Hot pink with red hearts, a ruffle at the waist, clingy miniskirt, long-sleeved with cutouts at the shoulders, a low back. Taylor swiveled in a half circle, changing her view from front to profile to back, twisting her head around to see the compact roundness of her rump in the mirror.

"It's perfect for Valentine's Day…"

"Yeah, but I bet everyone thought of the same thing."

"You'll be the prettiest. Believe me. You always are."

Prettiest or sexiest? She had the body to show off in this second skin. But the color wasn't right for a blonde. A brunette, maybe, like Chloe, but not someone with her coloring, fair, with pale, winter-white skin. From babyhood on she'd been a towhead, and Mom had made sure it stayed that way, supplying the bottle of color when her hair started to darken a few years ago. "Maybe it'll look better with the shoes," Taylor said.

"Go put them on. I want to see the whole look." Her mother leaned up against the wall with her arms crossed, looking like she had nowhere else to go. A fake casual air. Just another regular day. But the effort was apparent in the jiggle of her leg, a sign of the nerves. Taylor could see the flesh under her mother's tight jeans. It was jiggling too. Fat, but not so much.

Ever since that big girl jumped off the bridge, Mom and Dad wouldn't go away. Hovering one minute, glued to her the next. Their eyes were constantly darting her way. A precaution. If they stopped watching her, she might disappear. They pretended it had never happened. They said nothing, didn't scold or punish her, didn't ask how she was feeling, didn't say anything about what they knew. Kept the TV off when she was around. Hid the newspapers. But the news couldn't be hidden. It was everywhere, on every screen.

The way they deliberately didn't mention Naomi kept her right there in the room with them. Taylor couldn't really remember anymore what that girl looked like. In her mind, a set of frames endlessly repeated in flickering succession, like an old-time movie. A hulking shadow, perched and teetering, a step off the edge, a slow-motion fall. Pitch black, icy plunge, deep zero.

For the last three days, Taylor had been coming home immediately after school. Mom and Dad didn't have to say it. She could read their minds: Come home so we can see you and make sure you haven't disappeared and that everything is the same as always. Nothing has changed, nothing is canceled, you're still going to the dance tomorrow, still the prettiest.

The red digital numbers on her clock radio said 5:16. Didn't Mom need to finish making dinner or something? Taylor walked to the closet, squatted against the strain of the tight material on her thighs, and scooped up the shoes. She really didn't want to put them on. The whole look was wrong. She stood and said, "What's that smell? Is something burning in the kitchen?" Maybe Mom would take the hint.

"I don't think so. Let's see the shoes."

Tall, skinny heels. Red. They dangled from Taylor's fingers by the backstraps. "Here. You wanted to see them. I don't want to put them on."

"Well, *I* don't want them!" Mom laughed, sounding phony, with darting eyes. "Okay. You'd better take that dress off anyway. You can't wear it to the table. We eat in fifteen minutes." With another lingering look, she turned away.

Finally gone. Mom had left the door open, and Taylor closed it. As much as she hated these intrusions, she felt just as bad, or worse, when they were over. She was left with nothing but herself. The room, the mirror, the dress, the shoes. She flung them at the closet, but they hit the wall instead and landed on their sides, pigeon-toed.

The mirror. Nothing had changed from a week ago. Her hair was still long and shiny. She'd applied eyeliner carefully this morning, using the high-quality kind that didn't smudge. She hadn't cried today, so the mascara was still affixed to her eye-lashes.

There was nothing exactly wrong with her face, but she looked like shit.

At school, she was getting stared at, but this was nothing new. The stares had always been a big part of her image. Standing with Chloe or Julian, a picture of what everyone else wanted to be, she absorbed the glare and lunched on the admiration of smaller people who couldn't hide their hearts full of envy. Funny that the attention was now very much like it had always been. Eyes skittering her way with the flash of little smiles. Trouble looking away again. But now, there was something different that made her feel dirty. A shine. A little twist of the mouth. Fascination, all the same. Was this a new kind of envy? *Arrest them. They killed the girl.* She'd heard this, but there was nothing to it, just gossip, rumor, and the thrill of scandal. Impossible. How could she be arrested for talking the truth?

She'd had some doubts about this. The truth part of it. She wouldn't admit her doubts and tried to hide them, but Chloe could tell. Chloe saw everything because she understood better than anyone how the world was put together. She'd always given Taylor the best explanation for who they were: the chosen, the physically perfect, the cleverest, the top one percent. Take a step down, just a notch below them, and the vast ocean of ordinary people stretched out in all directions, the edges splashing up at their toes, a tide that kept trying to rise but never could. Further down, in the mud of the ocean floor, the bottom-feeders lurked, the people who simply shouldn't exist, never should've been born. They added nothing of value to the world, and whenever they rose high enough to be seen, simply got in everyone's way.

Eighteen minutes had passed since she'd put on the dress. Doubts were circling again. Chloe would have the answers, like she had from the very beginning. There was nothing to doubt back then. Chloe had been right to identify Naomi as one of the bottom-feeders. Was right to come up with a plan and to guide Taylor through it. This is the way it was, as Taylor remembered it. This is what they were supposed to do. No need to think about it…until now. In the last few days, Chloe had been saying things that didn't seem exactly right, that made Taylor question her memory…

You were the one sitting behind that girl in class.

Well, that part was true.

She wasn't in any of my classes. You were the one who told me about her.

Maybe that was true. Taylor remembered asking Chloe, "Is she one of the ones you meant?"

You remember the first time. You spoke to her in the hallway, in front of those people.

Maybe so, but Chloe had planned it, had told her what to say, hadn't she? Chloe didn't have a reason to go up to Naomi and say anything because they didn't have a class together. Naomi sat in front of Taylor in history, blocking her view of the world map. They'd laughed about that, Chloe the hardest. She was the one who came up with that joke about the map and urged Taylor to say it to Naomi's face, in front of a group of people.

After the first time, you had a lot of ideas about what to say to her.

But what about Chloe's ideas?

Taylor wandered around her bedroom, gazing longingly here and there, finally settling on the discarded red shoes. Maybe they would make her feel better. She put a hand on the wall to steady herself, bent down, and pulled them on. Three inches taller now. The mirror. Her legs really *were* nice.

She eyed her cell phone on the bedside table and walked over, taking small steps in her high, high heels and tight, tight skirt. She'd tried to ignore her phone, but twenty minutes was the limit of her resistance. By now, there should be another text from

Chloe, and sure enough, there was. A response to the message she'd sent twenty minutes ago that she was going to try on her dress for the dance and see how it looked.

I'll bet you look killer in that dress! Mine sucks.

Ha ha, Taylor replied.

Everything normal. Or was it? What did Chloe mean by that?

Hot and close, shoulder to shoulder in feral stride, loping, hunting, panting, they charged ahead to the kill. The rank odor of wet fur and sour breath pricked his nostrils, the metallic taste of blood invaded his mouth. The pack surrounded him, squeezed his chest and neck, constricting, strangling, suffocating. Submerged, he was drowning, twisting underwater, wrestling his way up to the surface out of this tragic and grand death. Naomi Steuben. Not a grand death, a grand jury. Negligent homicide.

Travis lurched upward and swayed off-kilter in a stranglehold of twisted afghan. He was soaked with sweat. The room had grown dark, lit by the gray-green glow of the television screen. He stared at his mother, but she didn't stare back. Her eyes floated above the heads in the room, fixed on no one.

"Is that Dana?" Grandma came running in.

The district attorney stood behind the official podium bearing the seal of her county office, framed on either side by the flag of the State of New York and the flag of Westchester County. In a flash she disappeared, replaced by the façade of the County Courthouse, a female reporter standing in front, stylishly bundled up but red-nosed from the cold, speaking into a handheld microphone.

"Heavens to Betsy! Just missed it! I could hear her clear as day from the other room." Grandma's voice sang out, full of awe and pride.

"Mommy said the grand jury came in with an indictment,"

Natalie reported. Unlike other kids, Natalie and her brother had been schooled from an early age in the meaning of terms like "grand jury" and "indictment."

Not until his sister spoke did the feverish boy notice her, sitting cross-legged on the floor, head tilted up to the TV. How long had she been there?

"Indicted who?" Travis was still fuzzy, in a dream. Soon enough, the newscast set him straight. The scene changed to a familiar suburban neighborhood, an upper middle-class home. A tall, slender girl walked down the front steps with a defiant air, shiny brunette ponytail bouncing. She wore tight jeans with fashionable frayed rips along the thighs and a short, puffy down jacket. A uniformed female police officer gripped her upper arm, near the elbow.

"Hey, that's right near Samantha's house!" Natalie exclaimed.

"Just minutes ago," the reporter said, "Chloe Dyckman was taken into custody at her home on Thistle Court," the scene changed, "and on Baxter Lane, officers arrested her classmate, Taylor Sloane." In front of a more modest home, the blonde teen stepped from the walkway toward a waiting police car. Without warning, she lost her footing and nearly tumbled to the ground, saved from catastrophe by the police officers on either side.

"What is that young lady wearing?" Grandma exclaimed.

Her Stone Ridge High sweatshirt was, apparently, hastily donned, leaving it askew and unzipped, showing enough of the skin-tight, red and pink minidress underneath, a ruffle pushing the sweatshirt out at the waist. Taylor's spike heels were blatantly crimson against the snow-lined walkway.

"I simply don't see *how* she can manage to walk in that getup!"

Travis shook his head, confused. "Why didn't the police let her change the shoes?"

"Why would she *want* to change them? I *love* those shoes!" Natalie jumped up and strutted around the living room taking tiny steps on tiptoe, hips swaying. Suddenly, with a high-pitched "Oops!" her foot slipped and flew up into the air, precipitating her theatrical fall to the carpeted floor.

Grandma laughed. "Oh, really, Natalie Rebecca Goodhue!"

"It isn't funny," Travis intoned.

12 »   VALENTINE

CHERYL LIVED IN Manhattan, but that wasn't the only reason Dana chose NYC for their lunch-and-shopping excursion on Saturday. It was a good day to get out of Westchester. The rampant media attention to the Dyckman and Sloane arrests was filling her imagination with visions of unpleasant scenes: reporters rushing at her in the shopping mall, accosting her with handheld recorders shoved into her face, Cheryl and Natalie caught on camera.

Manhattan, with its teeming streets and shops, would provide a shield of anonymity.

At ten thirty on the morning of Valentine's Day, mother and daughter boarded a Metro-North train and took an hour-long ride along the Hudson River down to the city. Chunky ice floes jammed the shoreline, covered with a topping of snow from the latest storm, and further out, in the middle of the wide river, small bergs floated haphazardly. Here and there, a winter bird came to rest, to enjoy the float. It was a bleak and beautiful scene. It was… a reminder. A photo had been taken before Naomi was removed from the river. A bloated face, open eye, tendrils of hair frozen into the ice.

The sideways rocking motion of the train soothed down the edges of Dana's nerves. Natalie, sitting next to the window, pointed out sights along the way and changed topics of conversation frequently, randomly, excitedly. This was a special day for her and a significant, transitional year as she looked forward to starting high school in the fall. Dana stayed away from any mention of yesterday's news conference and the criminal indictment. She'd answered all of Natalie's and Travis's questions last night, when she got home from work. Natalie's curiosity had been satisfied and her focus easily shifted to the pleasant events planned for Saturday: hanging out with Aunt Cheryl and a sleepover at Samantha's.

Dana tried not to brood over Travis. The chatter with Natalie on the train helped this, but not entirely.

Evan was with their son today. The boy would be all right.

Strep throat was bad enough, but even worse was the prospect of canceling Travis's plans with Ginger. Dana and Evan simply couldn't allow it, but as sick as he was, Travis just wouldn't give up. He'd lined up his arguments and delivered them in earnest last night, the forcefulness of his elocution diminished by the searing pain in his throat and high fever. By Saturday night he wouldn't be contagious, he said, and anyway, he'd be super careful not to touch Ginger or to have her touch anything that he touched. Couldn't they see that he didn't want to put her at risk? And it wasn't right to make her do the job of dispatcher alone. She needed backup, someone to answer the phone in case she couldn't, someone to help her find the addresses and guide the drivers, someone to keep her alert until late at night.

Judging by Travis's appearance, Ginger would be the one keeping *him* alert.

Evan told him, "We'll see," while Dana bit her tongue. It wasn't fair to the boy to hold out hope. She'd said this to Evan before leaving the house this morning.

Thank God for grandmothers. Dana hadn't been the least bit upset that Brenda and Travis conspired to withhold the news of his illness. They'd done it out of consideration for her. Was this a sign of skewed priorities? They'd thought of her work first, before themselves. The children were Dana's top priority, but maybe she wasn't communicating this. Maybe they saw her as not caring enough, just because she'd released herself from the guilt she used to feel about not being a stay-at-home mom.

Travis and Natalie were no longer the toddlers that Evan and Dana used to outsmart, talking in code over their heads. They were wonderfully wise, intelligent children who held strong beliefs of their own and couldn't be cheated out of the truth. She included them in many conversations about her work but withheld any information that was confidential or too disturbing. Wasn't this for the best? What were they missing by being spared the gruesome details of Rigger's wife's brains spattered on the wall, or that photo of Naomi's blue face frozen under ice?

Travis was the more difficult child to read. She couldn't tell what he'd thought about the indictment. There'd been no sign of satisfaction in his face, even though, from the start, he'd expressed an opinion that Taylor and Chloe should be charged with a crime for what they'd done.

Maybe it was the sound of it: "criminally negligent homicide." Homicide. Despite the name, it was the lowest level felony on the books. The grand jury had considered and rejected the more serious crime, reckless manslaughter. The big difference was in the state of mind. To prove recklessness, Taylor and Chloe had to be aware of, and consciously disregard, a substantial risk that their behavior would lead to Naomi's suicide. *I'm going to keep saying and doing these things, even though she's going to kill herself because of it…* A person who consciously acted this way was, well, nearly a murderer, close to a monster. Instead, the grand jury charged them with criminal negligence—a failure to perceive that their behavior was leading to that result. They were grossly unaware, self-absorbed teens. Very bad, but a more palatable theory.

One set of facts. Two possible mental states.

Dana didn't think that Taylor and Chloe had been unaware of the risk, given the evidence that they knew of Naomi's recent suicide attempt. *How* they knew all those details was still a mystery. But if the grand jury, like Dana, thought that they were aware of the risk, then the jury's vote had to be a compromise. *War and Peace.* Dana guessed that the fight in the grand jury room was really about the element of causation. Did the taunting and humiliation actually *cause* the suicide? The defendants didn't touch Naomi, didn't put pills in her mouth or hand her a loaded gun or physically push her off the bridge.

Still, maybe it was right for the jury to send a message about state of mind. Isn't this what the case was really about? A judgment of the degree of evilness in the minds of those seventeen-year-old girls. No one really knows what goes on inside another person's mind, what Taylor and Chloe were thinking and feeling when they inflicted that emotional pain. The grand jury had no more to go on than the circumstances known to the defendants at the time they bullied their classmate, judged against society's moral compass.

Dana knew that Cheryl would be curious about the case, so she'd called her this morning before getting on the train, to give her an update and to ask that the subject not be broached during their afternoon of fun with Natalie. Dana also let her sister know that she would be keeping a surreptitious eye on her cell phone, looking for a text message. The wheels of the criminal justice system never stopped spinning. Although it was Saturday, an arraignment on the indictment was scheduled for one o'clock. Taylor and Chloe would be brought into court after spending the night in jail. ADA Linda Marquette was handling the hearing and promised to text Dana the results of their pleas and bail applications. Linda didn't need any special instructions from the district attorney to know that she was not to make any statements to the press. No comment. Whatever was said in court would have to satisfy the newsmongers.

Dana's jaw tensed under the stress of a grave misgiving. Relax. Lunch and shopping. Why had she made these plans with Cheryl yesterday, at the precise moment she'd found out that the grand jury came in with an indictment? She was avoiding a personal appearance in court with Linda today. Deliberately, it would seem, but there'd been no real thought put into her choice, which she'd relegated to that ever-present subliminal conflict: the battle of priorities. And who was more important, Natalie or two teenage girls she'd never met? Two high school seniors who'd spent the night in jail because Dana had authorized a grand jury investigation.

First stop on the afternoon agenda was a favorite midtown restaurant within walking distance of Grand Central. It was a quarter to twelve. Dana was famished but also unsure if she could keep anything down.

The sidewalks had been thoroughly shoveled and salted, the curbs and gutters crusted with a foot of dirty ice and snow, jamming the people more tightly together on the pavement. Mother and daughter inched along in bulky boots. Natalie was the first to spy Cheryl, standing outside the restaurant. She was keeping warm in a waist-length, white, arctic fox coat, the collar pushed up to her chin. A matching fur hat was pulled down over her brow, her hair tucked underneath, probably in her signature French twist. Waist down, Cheryl wore gray leather pants and boots that afforded a cross between gripping sturdiness and impractical, sculpted fashion. Cheryl never fully sacrificed style to the weather. The hat obscured her features enough to make her identity doubtful, should any of her fans spot her on the street. She'd become better known of late, as her Broadway career took a back seat to small roles in episodes of television series like *Damages* and *Law and Order*.

"Auntie Cheryl!" Natalie ran up and was greeted with a big hug.

"How's my darling girl!" Half buried in the white fur, Natalie's face beamed with delight.

"Hey sis!" Cheryl turned to Dana, and they pressed cold cheeks.

Dana shivered. "Let's get inside."

"We're good," Cheryl said. "I made a reservation."

The hostess was a very young woman who showed not an inkling of recognition when Cheryl claimed her reservation by simply giving her first name.

They settled into a booth, Natalie next to Cheryl, Dana across from them. When they'd ordered their lunches, Natalie said, "I saw you on TV last week! Mommy almost didn't let me watch it."

"Oh, really?" Cheryl looked at Dana with mock indignation. The hat was off, the French bun slightly mussed, the mouth big and gorgeous, no lipstick. At forty-one, Cheryl was at the height of her beauty, something she didn't need to work at. "You think that's because I was playing a lawyer?"

"What was her name again?"

"Kelly Durant. For the defense."

"It was because the show was on a school night," Dana explained. To counter Cheryl's fake indignation, she rolled her eyes, with a little smile on her lips. "Natalie had homework to do."

"It had *nothing* to do with you being a lawyer, or acting like one, or what I mean is, *you're* the best actress, and *Mommy* is the best lawyer!"

"And I let her watch it anyway."

"You're *also* the best Mommy," Natalie added.

"I gave in. I wanted to watch it too," Dana confessed. "You were great!"

"I also get to watch Mommy on TV sometimes."

Cheryl caught Dana's eye and quickly changed the subject.

"So, what do you say to this?" The question was left hanging as the waiter delivered their food: a hamburger with fries for Natalie, a chef's salad for Cheryl, and a Caesar salad for Dana. She was glad that Natalie had expressed no anxiety today about calorie counting. Such a happy face. A healthy teen with a thin layer of baby fat, just like her daddy when he was a teen (and well into his young adulthood). Nothing to worry about. Dana looked down and squinted at the creamy dressing smothering her salad. Her stomach gave a little lurch.

Natalie asked, "What do we say to *what*?" and picked up her hamburger.

"There's a novel about a female prosecutor that's been optioned for a TV series, and I was approached by an executive producer about it. To play the lead character."

"Really?" Natalie took a big bite.

"That's exciting," Dana said.

"It's a lot of talk right now. Nothing for sure."

"Is it because…?" Natalie put a hand to her mouth to keep the food from spilling out. She chewed and swallowed. "I bet it's because you're sisters."

"That's part of it!" Cheryl laughed. "They're even considering giving you a call, Dana, to ask for your consulting services!"

"Well, that's very flattering, but I can't do something like that. I hope you land the part, Cheryl, but I can't get involved…" The conversation morphed into fantasies of stardom, Cheryl playing the life of district attorney Dana, money rolling in, the Hargrove sisters living the life of the rich and famous, Natalie getting a pony and a sports car when she turned sixteen.

Time ticked on, conversation flowed, and the world was nearly forgotten.

The sisters were drinking coffee and Natalie was finishing her Coke when Dana felt a buzz in the outer pocket of her purse, which was pressed up against her hip on the bench. She tilted her head down and pulled the phone out just far enough to see Linda's text. "NGx2. RORx2. Conditions." The defendants had pleaded not guilty—completely expected. And they were released on their own recognizance, with conditions. Not unexpected. Any violation of a condition would send them back to jail.

"Excuse me." Dana nodded toward the back. "Ladies' room." Natalie and Cheryl barely acknowledged her. They were lost in a debate over which shop to visit first.

Dana actually did use the ladies' room before calling Linda. She paused to look in the mirror and saw the sleepless night in her eyes. Outside the restroom, she found a corner in the dark, narrow hallway, people walking back and forth.

"I'm amazed I can hear you in here," Dana said, plugging her free ear with a finger. "Give me the details."

"It went pretty much the way we thought it would," Linda said. "Their attorneys gave a strong pitch for community ties and the weakness of the evidence. Very vocal about that! Judge Paterno bought it all and found that they weren't a flight risk. He isn't fond of our case and was showing some fatherly sympathy for the defendants. The conditions are pretty lame."

"And they are…?"

"The main one is no contact between the defendants."

"We've made that difficult for them by seizing their phones and laptops."

"And they're not allowed to purchase new phones and laptops or use any electronic device except as necessary to do schoolwork. They're required to continue attending school, but no social or sports events. School and home. That's it."

"No Valentine's Day dance for them."

"What a pity." Linda's voice dripped with sarcasm. "But Taylor's dress is ruined anyway, after a night on a lumpy cot in the lockup."

"Anything on the news yet?"

Linda listed the TV channels that were already airing special reports. "But I wouldn't worry about looking at any of this, Dana. Without any cameras in the courtroom, it's just the reporters putting their own spin on what happened, in their overly-dramatic voices."

"I can imagine. Thanks, Linda. Text me again if anything urgent develops."

"Will do."

All afternoon, Evan held fast to his resolution not to give in. Travis did not look good. Not at all. But he was still fighting to change his father's mind. There was some inkling of hope. Evan had the reputation in the family as the lighter touch, the go-to parent for permission on any controversial request. He adored his kids and felt their disappointments acutely, viscerally, so he gave them a lot of leeway, but today, it just wasn't possible. His son was very sick and needed rest.

Evan sat on the edge of the bed and looked at Travis, waiting for a reading on the digital thermometer in his mouth. "You don't look good, kiddo." The thermometer beeped, and he removed it.

"I'm fine, Dad. Really. I still think she can come over."

"You have a fever. One hundred point five."

"That's almost normal." His voice cracked and he winced and turned away, trying to hide the pain.

"Sorry. No can do. I'll call Ginger's mom and break the news."

"But the phone! She needs it and we have it. How can she do the job…?"

Evan understood the problem only too well because he'd put in just as much work as any SADD member when it came to the Call Central mobile phone. The brand-new Samsung Gravity, aqua blue with slide-out QUERTY keyboard, was lying on

Travis's bedside table. Yes, it had been acquired with SADD's funds, but Evan had been the one to purchase it at the phone store, register the number in his name, and program the phone in the manner directed by Travis.

"I'll take it over to Ginger's house after I drop Natalie at the Bohrs'."

Travis scrunched his brow and blinked, nothing to say. Evan's offer was a complete solution to the problem, depriving him of any further argument. Ginger would get the phone. Ginger would do the dispatch job alone.

By seven thirty, Travis was napping again and Evan was ready for driving duty, Samsung Gravity snug inside the breast pocket of his flannel shirt. He sat on the living room couch, arm around Dana's shoulder, waiting for Natalie, who was taking her time getting ready.

"I'll bet she's trying on her new clothes," Dana said.

"What did you get for her?"

"Jeans and a sweater."

"How exciting," he deadpanned. "That's it?"

"And some unmentionables."

"Oh." The mysteries of women.

"Don't say 'oh' like that."

"Why can't I say 'oh' like that?" He wedged a thumb under the scooped neck of Dana's sweater and plucked at her bra strap. She slapped his hand. With his other hand, he returned the blow with a bouncing bop of his fist on top of her head.

"Ow!"

"Okay. I give up," he said.

Still no Natalie. He kissed Dana on the cheek and whispered lasciviously in her ear: "Did you ask your sister about Sandy Bohr?"

"Yup. Cheryl knows all about her, but they never met. Sandra Steele used to be a high kicker. She was in *A Chorus Line* for many years."

"Here comes our high kicker now."

"*What* are you talking about, Daddy?"

Natalie stood at the threshold to the living room. Her hair was in a French braid (a fresh one Dana had woven this evening), and her new clothes were a good fit and modest. The jeans were tight, as was the fashion, but her hips were covered by the bottom part of the sweater, soft and fluffy, in blues and greens. She carried a small overnight bag. Here was his daughter, her own person.

"Ready, squirt? Did you drink some coffee? We wouldn't want you to fall asleep at your all-nighter."

"Sleepover, Daddy! Let's go."

Evan stood, turned, leaned over Dana, and brought his face close to hers. "See *you* later," he said, so that only she could hear.

At the Bohrs', Evan pulled into the grand, semicircular driveway, drove past the fork that led to the three-car, attached garage in back, and stopped in front of the house. A wide walkway ascended gradually to the front door, three shallow steps with a long stretch of pavement stone between each. At the top, Doric columns supported a roof over the porch landing and framed the double doors of beveled glass, frostily hinting at inanimate shapes within. The enormous house blazed with light from every window, yet it had the lifeless feel of a cold icebox. Enough electricity to serve a small village.

Evan had one foot out of the car when Natalie said, "That's okay, Daddy. You don't have to come in."

He turned and looked at her. "Just to say 'hi'…?"

Her eyes opened wide. Pleading. How embarrassing for a thirteen-year-old to be escorted to the front door by her dad, on a mission to hand her off to the next responsible adult!

"Okay, honey. I'll say 'hi' another time. Have a good time."

"Thank you, Daddy! I love you!" She kissed him on the cheek and jumped out of the car, but he didn't drive off just yet. He waited for her to run up the steps, ring the doorbell, and get an answer. Samantha opened one side of the double door. A blaze of white light shot out into the night from behind her. The girls hopped up and down with delight and made excited squeals that carried faintly out to Evan in the car. Natalie did not look back, had already forgotten him. The house swallowed her up, the door closed her in.

Evan set out on the second leg of his trip to Ginger's house. He would have to backtrack, passing his own house. The Bohrs lived on the outskirts of the school district in the wealthiest sector of town, Ginger lived closer to the high school, and the Goodhues were more or less in between. Not very convenient, but he didn't mind being on driving duty for his kids, even if it started snowing. Again. The weather channel set the odds at fifty percent. What a winter.

He hummed along to popular tunes on the Hudson Valley radio station.

He thought of Travis, Natalie, and Dana, in turn.

He smiled.

He thought of work, the summary judgment motion that was due. His smile faded, but not completely. The papers were almost ready. He planned to go into the office for half a day on Monday, even though it was a national holiday, and put the finishing touches on his submission, to have it ready for filing on Tuesday morning. Because of the holiday, traffic would be light, and the office would be quiet.

Evan had never been to the Krumins-Kavanagh house. In a way, it felt strange to be visiting the home of one of his adversaries, but this errand wasn't about Vesma or the case they had in common. It was about their kids. What an odd set of circumstances, the ways in which they'd crossed paths over the years, Dana and Vesma, Evan and Vesma, now Travis and Ginger. A small world.

As he turned onto their street, he glanced at his navigation device on the dashboard and slowed to a crawl. The red dot was taking him right about…here. He stopped, considered, and turned into the short driveway on the left side of the house, coming up to the closed garage door. A single-car detached garage. In stark contrast to the Bohrs' estate, this modest cottage made a gloomy impression of a different sort: dark except for a bright bulb over the front door and a single faint light from somewhere within the house.

Evan walked to the front door and rang the bell. He heard running footsteps and the door flew open. Ginger hadn't bothered to turn on another light. In the open doorway, she was a diminutive, solitary figure against the dim interior, and the bright bulb over the door drained all the color from her face, making it ghostly pale.

"Hi, Mr. Goodhue!" The sparkle in her voice was heartening, even if it seemed a matter of habit and a feature of her youth, not enough to disprove the possibility of darker feelings under the surface.

"Hello, Ginger. Travis is so disappointed he couldn't help you tonight."

"Yeah, well…!" She gave a little laugh.

"Here's the phone." He took it out of his pocket and handed it to her.

"Thanks for bringing it."

He was reluctant to leave, yet didn't know what else to say. Maybe it wasn't his place to inquire, but, "Is your mom home?"

Ginger turned her head over her shoulder to look back into the house, as if she could be mistaken and might find her mother inside. "Oh, she went out. She'll be back!"

"Okay, good."

She shifted from one foot to the other and looked away. "Do you think, I mean, only if it doesn't hurt his throat, could you ask, or maybe you could tell Travis to call me tonight and I'll give him a report. If he wants."

"Sure. I'll tell him."

"My cell phone is broken, but he can call my home phone. That way, the ride phone won't be busy."

"Makes good sense. Does he have the number?"

She nodded and laughed again.

"Well, good luck with Call Central. I hope it goes well."

"Me too. Thanks!" Ginger gave him a smile and a fluttery wave of her hand before shutting the door.

Natalie sat cross-legged on the floor in Samantha's bedroom, sorting and organizing piles of CDs. Half the discs were loose on the floor, and some of the plastic cases held the wrong CD. "You have so many!"

"Which one do you want to play?"

Natalie flipped the one in her hand over and read the contents. "I *love* this song, 'Pocketful of Sunshine'!" She opened the case. "Good! It's inside!" She handed it to Sammy.

"Okay, but I have that one on my iPod." Sammy grabbed a tiny plastic rectangle from her bedside table, plugged it into a stereo component, scrolled through, and found the song.

"Wow!" Natalie laughed with delight. She couldn't believe how clear and full it sounded, like Natasha Bedingfield was right there in the room with them.

So far it had been a perfect night. The minute Natalie stepped into the house, Sammy whisked her through the kitchen to the stairwell that led to a huge "game room" in the basement, where they played pool and darts and watched TV. At about ten they got hungry and nibbled on some peanuts at the bar, while they made faces at themselves in the mirror above the bottles of gin, vodka, bourbon, and scotch. The peanuts weren't enough to satisfy them, and the refrigerator under the bar held only soda and bottles of beer, so they went upstairs to the kitchen. In her stocking feet, Natalie slid on the floor of black and white squares, like a checkerboard. All the fixtures were polished stainless steel, and the room just gleamed. There were two ovens and a gigantic, two-door refrigerator, bright white inside, stuffed with food. Natalie remembered the big hamburger and French fries she'd eaten for lunch, but that seemed so long ago, and she hadn't eaten much for dinner. A big bowl of ice cream wouldn't be too much. Rocky road. Sammy loaded up her own bowl with cold pasta and piled chocolate chip cookies on another plate to take with them. They went upstairs to Sammy's bedroom, where they ate and giggled.

Samantha turned the volume up loud and started to dance and sing. Natalie danced along but couldn't enjoy it. Abruptly, she came to a halt. Sammy didn't seem to notice, until Natalie went over to the player and turned the volume down.

"Hey!"

"It's so loud, aren't your parents going to get mad?"

"Not a chance! They aren't even here."

"They're not?" Somehow, that possibility hadn't crossed Natalie's mind. It was a big house, and the parents had to be there somewhere, in a bedroom or a den or something. So she'd thought. "Where are they?"

"They went to the city, to some big reunion with Mom's Broadway friends. You remember. I told you my mom used to be a Broadway star, just like your aunt!"

"Oh, cool! I had lunch with Aunt Cheryl today."

"No kidding! Hey, we have to ask if they know each other!" Sammy turned up the music, and they started to dance again.

Natalie soon ran out of steam, feeling the weight of this

exciting day dragging her down. She went over to one of the twin beds, laid on her back, and put her hands behind her head. "You have the *best* room. I love this comforter. It's so soft. And I can't believe you have *two* beds."

"It's because I'm always having sleepovers. My mom says she's sorry I don't have a sister."

Natalie thought about this but didn't say anything. She had no idea whether a sister would be better than Travis. She'd never thought about it.

The music came to an end. In the sudden silence, Samantha plopped down on the other bed, looking exactly like Natalie, with her hands behind her head.

They both gazed upward. The ceiling was densely covered with plastic stars and crescent moons.

"That light is so bright," Natalie said.

Samantha shot up and turned off the overhead light, instantly transforming the ceiling into a black sky aglow with shining stars and crescents.

"That's awesome!"

"Glow in the dark." Samantha got back on her bed and put her hands behind her head again. "We should tell ghost stories. You go first."

"No, you."

They laid still for several seconds, thinking. The room was very dark except for the glow of the ceiling decorations and the two large rectangles on the wall that faced the front of the house. It took a moment for Natalie to figure out why the closed curtains were illuminated from behind. The house was very far from the road, surrounded by acres of lawn, garden, and the woods beyond. Finally, she realized that it was the house itself, a burning star, casting light from every window except Sammy's. In the stillness, she felt the depth of the quiet, so different from her own house, like they were alone and isolated, floating in a monstrous, shining starship.

Was that…? A flash of light on the curtains.

"I know one," Sammy said, all of a sudden. "Once there was a crotchety old man who lived in a cave—"

"What's that?" Natalie sat up. She was startled by an unexpected rush of voices downstairs, as if the front door had burst open with new arrivals. "Your mom and dad are home?" But it sounded like three or four people, talking so loudly that their voices carried up the stairs to Sammy's room.

Samantha got up and opened her bedroom door, making the voices more distinct.

"Emjay! Watcha got to eat!"

"I'm starving! Where's the kitchen?"

Footsteps.

"Hey, don't touch that!"

"Chill, man."

A screech. "Stop it!" A girl's voice. The clack of heels. Laughter.

Samantha closed the door and turned to Natalie. "Just Emjay and a bunch of his friends. The dance must be over. Want to go down and see what they're doing?"

Natalie got off the bed and walked toward the door. She was now wide awake, curious, and…scared? She didn't really want to go hang out with a bunch of high school seniors. She stopped short. "I don't know. Why? I don't think they want to see us."

"They don't have to see us. Let's go spy on them!" Sammy opened the door again. The kids were far off now, in the kitchen. The doorbell rang. Running footsteps, more voices, laughing and shouting. Samantha went to her bedroom window, pulled back an edge of the curtain, and looked down on the front entrance. Natalie peaked over her shoulder. Two cars were parked in the semicircular driveway, and another was pulling in now.

Sammy turned to Natalie and laughed, but it was hard to tell in the gray light whether her face was full of delight or fear. She grabbed Natalie's hand and said, "It's a party!" She shrieked and bounced and tossed her hair from side to side, across her face.

Natalie shrieked and bounced too, just to make it fun, adding their voices to those of the teenagers streaming into the house, filling it with life. Why, then, did she feel so alone? There was a "snap," a breaking of the tether, as their celestial starship, bursting with light and energy and sound, was sent adrift into a vast, black nothingness.

13 »   *DEEP ZERO*

TRAVIS HAD BEEN dozing when his father tiptoed into the bedroom at about nine o'clock, carrying a fresh glass of water. He placed it on the bedside table under the small pool of light from the reading lamp and sat down on the edge of the bed.

"Ginger was grateful that I brought her the SADD phone. You know, I never liked that acronym. Maybe you can think of something that goes with HAPPY! What do you say?"

"Yeah," Travis croaked. "We'll do some brainstorming, but it kinda goes with MADD." Mothers Against Drunk Drivers. Students Against Destructive Decisions. Heroes (or Hell-raisers?) Against Poor Priorities Yada yada.

"That's true. Anyway, she said that, if you feel up to it, it's okay to call her tonight. Is your cell phone charged?"

"Yup."

"Make sure you use her house number so she can keep the Call Central line open."

"Okay, Dad. Thanks." Parents sometimes liked to give little reminders of the obvious, but Dad always did this in such a nice way that Travis usually didn't mind.

A warm, open hand covered half his head, gave it a little shake, and lifted off as Dad got up from the bed, leaving his protective aura behind. There was less of a tiptoe on the way out. The door opened, letting in the faint sound of the television in the living room, and then the door was closed, separating Travis from the rest of the house.

Dad's approval made it much easier for Travis to do what he'd been planning to do all along, on the sly or not. At the very least, he had to call Ginger, to lend what little support he could. This night had turned out to be so rotten.

He sat up, feeling slightly dizzy, and reached for his mobile phone on the bedside table. Slowly and carefully, he scrolled through his contacts, and after taking a deep breath, he touched the entry for Ginger's home number.

"Hi!" she said sweetly when she answered. "Thanks for calling!" A small laugh.

"Yeah, sure." His voice cracked, even though he'd cleared it before calling. He laid his head back on the pillows to bring the room into stillness.

"Sounds like your throat is really bad."

"I'm okay. It hurts a little." With his right hand, he pressed the phone to his ear, not wanting to miss a word. "Any calls yet?" It was only nine fifteen. Of course not.

"Not yet. Do you think Dylan and Myra gave the first announcement?"

"Yeah, by now, sure they did. I guess no one's going to call for a ride 'til the end of the dance anyway."

"Mm-hmm. By then, everyone will have the Call Central number in their contacts."

"Right."

"I'm a little worried though…"

"About what?" Travis closed his eyes and tried to imagine Ginger's face with a worried look. Sometimes he would catch her in that look before it snapped quickly into a sunny cheerfulness that always warmed him to the point of bursting. Ginger's facial expressions, more than anyone else's, had a way of getting inside him, making him feel exactly what she was feeling. At least he believed in this connection. He wondered if she believed in it as well.

"Maybe no one will call and it'll be a huge waste. They'll just ignore us. I don't know why, but I think about it sometimes."

"We don't really know what will happen. It's the first night. But I'm sure you'll get some calls."

"Maybe less than we think. Some of my friends were complaining that their parents aren't letting them go to the dance because it's going to snow."

"Why is everyone always so scared of a little snow?"

"I don't know. It's crazy."

"And half the time it doesn't even snow when the weather channel predicts it."

"There's just some chance of it tonight. That's what I heard. My mom told me when she was leaving the house. She went out on a date." Another little laugh. "With a man she works with."

Travis didn't know what to say to that. There was a three-second pause, lasting a second too long. How could he say what he really wanted to say? "It would've been better if we could do this together."

"Word."

Another pause.

"No biggie," she said. "I'll be okay doing this alone tonight."

The TV was set to the all-news station when Evan walked into the living room. "All right, my love. No way am I going to watch a news program on Valentine's Day. I might get distracted if there's a sound bite from that sexy district attorney, What's-Her-Name."

"Don't make me jealous."

Evan plopped down on the couch next to his wife. "What can I say? Intelligent, beautiful women turn me on."

"Then I'd better turn the news off. I was just waiting for you, darling." She pressed a button on the clicker, making the screen go black. "I've got a DVD in the player."

"That sounds better. What do you have in store for our twentieth Valentine's Day together?"

"Aren't *you* the sentimental one, counting the years? Has it really been twenty?" Dana looked up at the ceiling and pretended to count, a little smile gracing her lips.

He sighed dramatically and said, "Counting the minutes, actually…"

"Very funny."

"…ever since we met on April 26, 1988, at eight thirty in the morning…"

"Didn't Reichert start that meeting at seven thirty or eight? He was such a go-getter."

"It was eight thirty on the dot, the beginning of that inexorable timeline, leading to the night when I got down on one knee and proposed marriage to you, Valentine's Day 1989." He put his right arm around her shoulder and kissed her on the neck.

"And now look at us. An old married couple on the couch."

"I like it on the couch." He twisted and reached across, as if to grab her thigh, when she shoved the TV clicker into his hand instead.

"Here. It's all cued up."

"Gee, thanks."

"I even got the tissue box out." She nodded toward the coffee table.

"So, there's hope yet?"

"I'm talking about the movie. *An Affair to Remember.*"

"Okay, be like that." He removed his arm from around her shoulder and pressed the "play" button.

"You're forgetting, darling."

"What?"

"That *you're* the sentimental one."

The music started to play, and Evan leaned forward, elbows on knees, in rapt attention. "I did forget something."

"What?"

"I *love* this movie."

Dana scooted closer to her husband, making thigh-to-thigh contact. "No need to be a *complete* stranger now."

The truth was, doing this project alone really sucked. The planning, the meetings, the excitement of bouncing ideas off the other kids—*that* was all the fun stuff. It wasn't as though she'd never sat alone in her bedroom in the middle of an empty house. There'd been plenty of times this year. Sean away at college. Mom at work or out. But tonight was different because she was waiting for a specific thing to happen, a thing that she had to be prepared for. It didn't really prevent her from doing anything else, but actually, it did. If she read a book or did homework or watched TV or played a computer game, she would still be waiting for this one thing to happen, and there was no way to forget it.

Travis's call had helped. But it lasted only ten minutes, and a long night lay ahead. After hanging up, she thought of calling him back, but she stopped herself. He was seriously sick and needed to rest. She couldn't be calling him just because she was lonely.

Mom had been gone an hour. "How do I look?" she'd asked, all dressed up and made up. Ginger couldn't explain the urge, but she rushed up and gave her mother a huge hug, holding on for dear life. When Mom pulled back, she had a look of pleasant surprise on her face.

Squeezed into a tight dress, sexy legs in high heels, Mom opened the door for Hernando. He came in briefly and said "hello." Ginger knew him from her visits to Mom's office. He was a nice man, and she had nothing against him, but the two of them looked so obviously like they were on a *date*, groomed and perfumed. They looked fantastic together, a strange thing to think about her mother and a colleague. When they stepped out the door, Ginger came out on the front landing and turned to the right, watching them on the short walk along the front of the house to the driveway, where Hernando had parked his car. Ginger was glad she'd done a good job shoveling the snow and spreading salt, even though Mom wouldn't like the salt on her shoes. Hernando was lightly touching the small of her back as they walked, and he opened the car door for her before circling around front and getting into the driver's seat.

Now, lying on her bed, Ginger picked up the Gravity, a quiet piece of cold, aqua blue plastic. Maybe, if she put on some music, she would stop hearing "I Drove All Night" in her head.

There were limited ways to play music in her house. She desperately wanted an iPod, but Mom said they couldn't afford one. "Maybe for your birthday." Sure. Along with a car from Daddy, right? For now, she was stuck with an antiquated Walkman. She inserted her favorite CD and started to put on the headphones but stopped. With music pumping into her ears, she wouldn't hear the phone. She pulled out the CD, grabbed the Samsung Gravity, and went into the living room. It was best to stay next to the computer anyway, so she could access Google Maps.

She inserted the CD into the computer and clicked "play," sending a tinny sound into the air. Justin Timberlake's "My Girl" just wasn't any good on these cheap speakers. She hit "stop" and stared at the screen. In the lower right corner, the digital clock showed 9:37 PM. There was also a notification on the e-mail icon: a new message from Daddy. Her finger hovered for a few seconds, then moved away.

She walked over to the front window. The curtains were closed, and she pulled the cord to open them. A few cars were parked along the street, but no one drove past. Porch lights illuminated a few of the front doors in the neighborhood, including her own. A smooth sheet of old snow covered the tiny patch of front yard, glimmering white and crusty.

Recently, Travis had been coming to her table in the cafeteria for lunch almost every day. Last week, after eating, they went outside with a few other kids for the remainder of the lunch period. It started to snow big fluffy flakes. A sharp ray of sunshine pierced a hole in the clouds as they turned their faces up to the sky, catching the flakes on their tongues.

Another day at lunch, she was sitting next to Travis and didn't know she had a chocolate milk mustache. He turned away from her, took a big gulp of his milk, and turned back with a huge white mustache on his upper lip! She cracked up, and they laughed forever.

Too bad she couldn't call him right now. Nothing was going to happen until the dance was over.

She stood at the window, peering out, listening. Now what?

She had a thought. Going back to her bedroom, she got down on the floor and reached far under her bed for the box that held her stash of candles and long wooden matches. Against the rules. A couple of years back, a teenage girl in their neighborhood had left a lighted candle near a curtain and set her house on fire. But Ginger loved candles and couldn't bear to throw them away. She hoarded them, the half-burned votives her mother used at Christmas, fancy scented ones she'd received for various birthdays, and a few she'd purchased with her babysitting money. There were times they provided a needed therapy. The sweet scents and mesmerizing flames had the power to overcome a phantom odor that persisted with a strength greater than memory, a heartbreaking, saturating presence.

Ginger set a couple dozen candles throughout the living room, on the coffee table and end tables, careful to place them on dishes or in holders. Soon, the air was filled with the sulfur of kitchen matches and a concoction of perfumes. She flipped off the overhead light and enjoyed the flames, flickering, dancing, reflecting off the windowpane.

The new look to the room triggered a familiar, urgent desire. The mood was now perfect for writing poetry. She grabbed a pad of paper and pen from the computer desk. Sitting on the floor with her back against the couch, she wrote:

Pink and white, a day for lovers,

Snow through light, we meet each other,

hearts,

and dreams,

not what they seem,

Flakes on lashes, milk mustaches,

lists,

and phones,

a girl alone…

The phone rang. It was a regular ring from the landline. Could Mom be calling? She jumped up to answer it.

"Hello?"

"Hi, um, Ginger?"

"Travis! How are you?"

"Maybe a little better. Any calls yet?"

"Nope."

"I didn't think I would be interrupting anything…"

"Nothing at all."

"What are you doing while you're waiting?"

No way would she confess to writing a poem…about him. "Not much. I listened to some music, and then I lit some candles. It makes the place feel nicer. Do you like candles?"

"Yeah, sure."

It didn't sound particularly like he did. But she didn't mind. "You sound kind of sleepy."

He denied any sleepiness, and they talked until it was clear that the effort was hurting his throat.

After they ended the call, the little clock on the computer said 10:18 PM.

Nothing happened until eleven eleven. She knew the exact time because she'd been checking the clock on the computer screen every minute since ten fifty-four.

The call came in with a blast of sound. *"I drove all…"* She jumped and answered before the first phrase was sung. "Call Central!" she announced.

"Hey! So, this is the ride phone?" The boy snickered, and there were other voices in the background.

"Yes, it is. Do you need a ride? Where are you? At the dance?" Ginger's heart was beating fast.

"Yeah, we need a ride." He snickered again. If Ginger were to guess, she'd say he was high or tipsy. "My fucking car's in the shop."

"How many of you need a ride?"

"Three. Shoulda been four. Maybe I'll just ask your fearless leader for a ride. He's standing right over there! *Yo, Dylan, my man!"*

"It's better for me to get the ride for you. I'm the dispatcher. I'll see who can come get you. Just give me your name and where you're going."

It was Julian Yarnell, Taylor Sloane's boyfriend! Yesterday, an hour after Taylor's arrest, he'd been in an accident, on the way to the police station. Never made it there. Everyone knew about it by now. After her release from custody Taylor was grounded, not allowed to go anywhere or to see any friends, so everyone thought that Julian would stay home too. Guess not.

He spoke to someone in the background. "What's Emjay's

address?" Then his voice came back stronger over the phone. "We're going to 6 Foxglove Way."

Ginger was jotting it down as she spoke. "Okay, I'll call you right back. I've got your number in my phone. Just wait on the curb in front of the gym, and your ride will come."

"Ah-ight, Lady Dispatch!" The line went dead.

If Travis had been with her, he'd have already been on the landline to Dylan, the first name on the driver "list." After all their hard work, only two drivers were available tonight: Chrissy and Dylan. Myra couldn't get permission to use her family car. Already the process was slowed down with Ginger working alone, and now she felt kind of silly about it after Julian yelled out to Dylan. But before she could call him, the phone sounded again. *"I drove all night…"*

"Call Central!" She felt the panic rise in her chest. Should she try to call Dylan on the landline while talking to the second caller? She couldn't do two things at once! It was best to take down the information quickly.

"I need to get a ride." The caller was a girl, an unfamiliar voice.

"Are you at the dance? How many people? Where do you want to go?"

The girl said there were four of them, and they were going to 6 Foxglove Way.

Okay, that was easy enough. Two rides, a total of seven people, all going to the same place. But they wouldn't all fit in Dylan's car, and he was strict about the rules, including seat belts for every passenger. Ginger gave the girl the same instructions she'd given Julian and ended the call. Too late, she realized she hadn't gotten the girl's name, but what did it matter? She had to hurry! The girl and her friends would be waiting at the curb too.

Ginger called Dylan and gave him the details. "Do you see Julian nearby?"

"I saw him a minute ago. There's a lot of people still hanging around."

"I told all of them to wait on the curb by the gym door."

"I'll find them, and I'll get Chrissy. She's here too."

"Awesome! Do you need directions?"

"No, I'm okay. I know that house. Thanks, Veep!"

Ginger ended the call feeling proud of herself. She'd arranged two rides through Call Central without a hitch! Because of her, kids would be kept safe, riding with Dylan Radner or Chrissy Farrington, the safest drivers around!

She had the urge to call Travis, to share in her glory, but then she remembered how sleepy he'd been and how scratchy his throat was. She picked up her poem instead and sat down on the couch, trying to write a new ending. She recited the poem out loud, adding various words and phrases, but nothing seemed right. Maybe she'd just keep the ending the way it was, "a girl alone…"

Twenty minutes later Dylan called in, and then Chrissy. They were now available to take other rides, but she had no new jobs to report. Ginger placed the Gravity back on the coffee table and laid down on the couch, gazing at a cluster of flickering flames, waiting.

The song was playing again and wouldn't stop. The red button didn't work. She pressed it, the music got louder. The phone turned electric blue, sizzled and sparked and hopped along the table.

Dazed, Ginger sat up and looked around the room. Some of the candles had gone out, others were puddling on their little dishes and the phone was merely ordinary looking, next to a candle. "I Drove All Night" played at earsplitting volume.

She answered too late and had to redial. "This is Call Central.

Did you just call?" A boy said that he and his two friends were at 6 Foxglove Way and needed rides home. She took the information, called Dylan, and arranged the pickup. He'd be there in five minutes. Only then did she look at the clock. Twelve thirty-three.

The time surprised her. She never fell asleep this early, and even more surprising, people were already asking for rides home from the party, little more than an hour after it started. She felt ashamed for missing the call, for falling down on the job. Dylan wouldn't be coming to get the phone from her for another couple of hours.

Five minutes later another call came in. A girl named Becky needed a ride home from the Bohrs' house. Ginger couldn't be sure, but thought it was the Becky in her class, a junior, someone she knew by sight only. She took the information and called Chrissy.

"Sorry, Gingie. I just can't go out again. My parents won't let me."

"Why not? You're supposed to drive until two at least."

"It's starting to snow. My mom is freaking out about it. She didn't want me to go out in the first place. Just wait until Dylan comes back. He'll do it."

"Okay. I guess that's all we can do."

But it wasn't okay. Dylan would be tied up for a while. He had to drop three people at three different houses. And she couldn't call him. That was his rule—no distractions on the road. She had to wait until he notified her that the job was over.

Ginger called Becky, explained the situation, and said she'd have to wait until Dylan called in to say he was free.

"You don't understand!" the girl cried. There was music in the background. "I came here with my boyfriend and he's trying to leave."

"Then go with him."

"I can't! He's trying to make me get in his car, but he's wasted! I can't tell him anything; he won't listen. Why do you think I'm calling you?" Becky sounded desperate, and maybe not so together herself, her voice a little slurred. "I ran into a closet to call you."

"Can you call your parents?"

"Are you kidding? They'd kill me. I'm not supposed to be with this guy."

"Don't they want you to get home safe?"

"You don't know my father." She made a strange sound, like a choking sob. "You have to get me a ride. I don't have anyone else to call."

"Okay. Just hang on for a minute and I'll call you back."

Ginger pressed the red button and tried to think. The silence was absolute and black, adding to her uneasiness. Becky really did sound like she was in trouble. Maybe, by some miracle, Dylan would call and save the day.

She watched the digital clock change from 12:40 to 12:41 to 12:42. An eternity. No one to help. She got up and paced the room, thinking of Becky's "wasted" boyfriend. The relaxing mood created by the candles had vanished along with their sweet perfume, replaced by the familiar, phantom odor, as if Daddy was right there, breathing in her face. The sick feeling swelled in her gut, the old fears and habits, the wariness and resentment and anxious anticipation. Why did people have to do the things they did, blinding themselves to the hurt they inflicted on others? And they never seemed to wake up, if at all, until the damage was complete and too late to repair. *I'm sorry, Gingie, so sorry!*

Her chest felt tight with panic, suffocating. No one to turn to—except herself. She'd conditioned herself out of helplessness years ago. Something could always be done. She opened Google Maps, where the single destination of the night was still on the screen, 6 Foxglove Way. Time to destination: twelve minutes.

She called back. With a click, the line was opened. Becky said, "Wait a minute!" to someone in the background. There was laughter and music, even louder this time. Was Becky laughing along? "Hello," she drawled.

"This is Ginger from Call Central."

"Oh, Ginger!" She laughed, but then her voice changed, low and raspy, lips against the phone. "I need to get out of here! Did you get me a ride?" Becky was desperate and scared again, erasing any doubt about what Ginger needed to do.

"Yes, I did. Just be in front of the house. In twelve minutes. Can you do that?"

"Shhure!"

Natalie whispered into the receiver. "Did I wake you up? I'm sorry, Daddy!"

"Natalie! What is it? What's all that noise?"

"I didn't think you could hear it in here. I told Sammy I had to go to the bathroom so I could try to call you." She really *was* in a bathroom, so it wasn't a complete lie. After leaving Sammy's room, she'd passed the closest bathroom and entered the parents' bedroom, where she grabbed the cordless receiver off a phone next to the enormous bed and brought it into the master bathroom. She sat on the closed toilet seat and stared at an enormous tub with water jets all over it. "Can you come get me? Maybe you can just say you forgot something important I have to do tomorrow, so I have to sleep at home and get up early."

"*What's* going on over there? That racket has to be keeping Samantha's parents up!"

"They aren't here, Daddy. And it's really okay, except that..."

"*It's okay?*"

"I mean it *would* be okay if there wasn't a party with all of

Emjay's friends—"

"You've got to be—"

"—and some of them are drinking. Sammy and I snuck downstairs and saw four of them in the bar."

"They have a bar there? Listen, Natalie. Go back to Samantha's room! I'll be over as fast as I can get there."

"Okay, Daddy. I'm really sorry…!"

"Don't be sorry. I'm glad you called."

An unknowable time later, Ginger was pulling into Foxglove Way, passing the cars that lined the entire cul-de-sac. She'd made it in Mom's Volvo, heart beating up in her throat, learner's permit in a jacket pocket, the Gravity in the little cubby between the driver's and passenger's seats. The phone hadn't made a sound, or was she too nervous to hear it? So many things were not quite right on the way over. It wasn't exactly snow but a mixture, some flakes and some ice pellets sounding like needles hitting the glass. The wipers were caked with ice that scraped against the windshield. She couldn't remember how the defroster worked. The window was fogged up from her breath, and she kept wiping it with her jacket sleeve to make a clear spot. Her head was filled with noise: Becky's voice, Mom's voice, her own voice reciting poetry, and a sudden thought—had she blown out the candles? Worst of all, there was something wrong with the Volvo. A horrible bumping vibration shook the car whenever she applied the brakes.

Every time that happened, she reassured herself with a memory of Travis's matter-of-fact voice: *Why is everyone always so scared of a little snow?*

At the Bohrs' house, cars were parked along the entire edge of the long, semicircular driveway, with a few gaps where some had already pulled out. The driveway was wide enough to pass the parked cars, and she pulled up in the middle, in front of the main entrance. She was blocking the driveway, and anyone coming up behind her would not be able to get out. But this wouldn't take long. Becky would be waiting for her.

The sight of all these cars gave rise to new doubts about her mission. There had to be someone here who could take Becky home, a sober driver. But maybe it was as hopeless as Becky made it out to be. Ginger didn't know what was going on inside. Becky did.

Ginger got out of the car in a hurry. Despite the thick treads on her boots, she slipped on the front walkway and almost fell. She slowed her pace and planted her feet more carefully. Becky was not waiting outside, as promised.

The front door was unlocked. Ginger entered a huge foyer, not bothering to take off her puffy winter jacket or the wool hat covering her head and ears. She looked right and left, doors on both sides. Two younger girls in jerseys and sweatpants were walking up the stairs, and a couple of teens wearing jackets were on their way to the front door.

She turned into the living room. The place was jammed, pulsating with music, everyone wearing their best styles from the dance, everyone looking…normal? Happy? There was animated talk, laughter, bags of potato chips, cookies, and soda cans strewn around, no obvious signs of alcohol or drugs. Ginger's shining coat of armor started to lose its luster. She recognized Emjay, the varsity quarterback, circulating through the crowd, stopping briefly at each cluster of kids. It looked like he was pausing just long enough to deliver a specific message.

Where was Becky?

Cutting a maze through the room, Ginger saw her in a corner, sitting on the floor with another girl. Half-lidded and flushed, Becky was propped up by the wall, her feet bare, legs splayed. The girls were talking with their heads drooped toward each other like wilted sunflowers. Becky's head bobbed up and turned. "Ginger!" With difficulty, she pushed herself up from the floor and wobbled to a standing position. Her friend did the same.

"You ready to go?"

Becky leaned forward and sprayed the word "Yes!" into her face. Alcohol on her breath.

"Where's your boyfriend?"

"My boyfriend?" Becky scrunched her brow in confusion.

"The boy who was trying to force you into his car." Ginger was beginning to feel like a fool.

Becky laughed and started to sway, planting a hand on Ginger's shoulder to steady herself. "Oh, don't worry about him! I left him downstairs with Julian and their friends."

It took another few minutes for the drunk girls to find their purses and shoes (*how are they not going to slip in those?*), while Ginger burned with shame that flared into anger — at herself more than the girls. On their zigzag to the front door, they passed Emjay, who was trying to enlist the help of a burly teammate, an offensive tackle. "Downstairs. Come on, man. Now."

Dana offered to go, but Evan wouldn't hear of it. He got dressed in a hurry.

"We could go together," Dana said, getting out of bed. "I'm so livid I could scream! That woman—"

"It's a quarter to one. Stay here with Travis."

"He's okay. He's past the worst of it."

"But there's no sense in you coming along. It's bad enough that one of us has to go out in the middle of the night. Go back to sleep." He did *not* add what was really on his mind, and what had undoubtedly crossed Dana's mind as well.

"I won't be able to sleep. Why didn't she tell me they were going to be out? Wouldn't you mention that to a mother who's sending her daughter for a sleepover?"

"I don't know, Dana. The girls are thirteen. Old enough to babysit younger kids." He wasn't convinced by this weak argument in Sandy Bohr's favor. Differences in parenting could still surprise him after more than sixteen years as a father. Here was yet another instance when the behavior of a parent awakened him with a slap in the face.

"But you would mention it, wouldn't you?" Dana was kicking herself, he could see. Killing herself about making assumptions she shouldn't have made.

"I'll get our little girl out of there, and that'll be the end of it." He couldn't say, and didn't believe, that the rest of it wasn't their concern.

"Call me when you get there and give me the details."

"You can depend on it, my love." He kissed her forehead and was out the door.

What a wretched night. At least he had the good luck of taking a route that was recently sanded and salted most of the way, but Hudson Bluffs Drive was still slick. He slowed to a crawl when approaching the switchback, a blind curve with arrows and flashing yellow lights. After successfully navigating it, he increased his speed to twenty miles an hour and soon reached Foxglove Way. With a slight fishtail, he made the turn onto the cul-de-sac.

It was alarming to see the change, the number of cars parked in the street and along the length of the semicircular driveway. Midway in, an old model Volvo blocked his path. But it looked as though the car was about to get out of his way. Two girls in dresses and high heels were getting into the passenger side of the car, and the driver was walking around front. In a minute, he could pull into their spot, run inside, and whisk Natalie away—except that, he suspected, it wouldn't be so quick and easy.

The owner of the Volvo opened the driver's door. She was

bundled in a puffy jacket, winter hat, and jeans, not wearing party attire like the others. Something about her was familiar, but in the next moment, her car was pulling away, and he double-parked in front of the house.

Evan stepped out and scanned the façade. The main entrance still blazed brightly, but the rest of the house was no longer radiating an icy whiteness, many of the lights turned down or off. Mood lighting for the party? But there was a lot of bright noise behind those walls, voices and music. A perfect hangout, he thought. A three-acre estate, no neighbors to bother. His eyes moved to an upstairs window where the curtain was pulled back and two girls were looking out—Natalie and Samantha? At just that moment, a group of boys burst out the front door, yelling and cursing.

Natalie was glad she'd called Daddy, but when she got back to Samantha's room, she felt the weight of her lie. She tried to act like everything was normal and crossed her fingers that Daddy would say it was completely his own idea to come get her.

Mostly, she regretted waiting so long. She'd been hoping that things would settle down, but more kids kept coming in.

Sammy was lying on her bed. "Did you find it?" she asked.

"Yeah." Natalie laid down on the guest bed, and they tried to go back to telling ghost stories, but it was impossible. They jumped up and opened the door a sliver, listening. "Emjay sure has a lot of friends," Natalie said.

"He's really popular but, I don't know, he never invited *this* many people over before."

They looked at each other and made little nervous screeches.

"You want to go downstairs again?" Sammy asked.

"Not really. But maybe we should go check on them, especially those people in the game room."

"Yeah. They really shouldn't be drinking my parents' vodka and stuff. Let's go see if they're still there."

They crept downstairs, but before they could weave through the throngs to get to the door to the basement, they ran into Emjay. "I think you've got to tell these people to go home," Sammy said.

"What do you think I've been doing?" He looked exasperated. "I didn't invite all of them over! Somebody put the word out. I got a few of them to leave already."

Natalie stood awkwardly by and watched. She did *not* want to be here.

"Did you get those people in the bar to leave?" Sammy asked.

"Not yet. I tried. I'm going down there again. I'll get Brent to help me." He disappeared into the sea.

"Come on," Sammy said. "There's nothing we can do." Natalie followed her out of the living room into the foyer. As they turned to walk up the stairs, a girl wearing a hat and parka and boots walked in the front door. Tiny ice crystals on her clothing caught the light as she swiveled right and left before disappearing into the living room. Something about the look on her face and the urgency in her movement made Natalie more nervous than ever.

Back in Samantha's room, only a few minutes passed before Natalie became anxious about her father. Shouldn't he be here by now? She had no sense of time, no way of knowing how long it had been since she called home. "You think any of the kids are starting to leave?" she mused out loud on her way to the window. She pulled back the curtain, just to check. Was he coming? She pretended to be watching for signs that the party was breaking up. "Wow! Come here, Sammy! Remember that girl who came in the house when we were coming upstairs?"

"No. Who?" Samantha ran to the window and stood beside Natalie. On the front walkway, the girl in the hat and parka was helping two very tipsy girls in high heels. They inched along, shuffling like geishas, then stopped dead with a little slip, one of them clutching the parka girl, sending a shriek into the air, up to the second floor.

"That's crazy! They can't even walk." The girl in the hat led them to a little strip of dirt on the edge of the walkway, and they made it to the parked car.

It was then that Natalie spied what looked like her mother's SUV pulling into the driveway. She was confused. She thought that Daddy was coming. The girls drove away, the Ford Escape pulled into their spot, and the driver got out and glanced up. Of course. He'd taken Mommy's car because it was better in bad weather. Masking her glee, trying to sound disappointed, Natalie said, "Wait! That looks like my daddy!"

Evan had just stepped from the car and was standing inside the open driver's side door when three boys emerged on the front landing. He heard a lot of the "F" word, but the rest was a jumble. The largest boy, who must have weighed more than two hundred pounds, was holding the smallest boy by his left arm. Another solidly-muscled boy was close behind them, pushing the captive in the back with angry jabs. All three were yelling and cursing, the captive yelling the loudest, struggling violently, resisting what appeared to be his ejectment from the house.

Behind them, several teens came out to watch, filling the front entrance, music blasting from the open door. A boy pushed through the crowd at the door and staggered unsteadily onto the front landing, yelling something about "Julian." Get him? Get off him? He was waving a brown object in the air. It caught the light …a bottle?

Evan hesitated, debating what to do. The ruckus dominated the entire front entrance. The faces of the four boys were contorted with rage.

The three boys moved across the landing through the Doric columns, down the first shallow step, crossing the walk to the second step, struggling all the way. The captive screamed that this was "all about Taylor" as he was pushed down the second step. In a sudden move, he threw off the hand of the big guy, slipped and righted himself, and turned around to face the boy in back, rocking unsteadily, drunkenly. The big guy grabbed the drunk boy again, this time gripping his right upper arm like it belonged to a rag doll. The captor twitched the fingers of his other hand, talking fast to his friend. Behind them, the fourth boy smashed the bottle against one of the Doric columns and advanced down the first step.

Evan had to do something to stop this! "Hey! Hey there!" he called out, his voice lost under the swell of half a dozen others. He stepped around the open car door but moved too quickly and slipped on ice, sending him down to his knees. He grabbed the hood of the car to pull himself up. A girl at the front door shrieked. Standing again, Evan saw only one boy. Where were the other three?

Everyone froze. Even the music seemed to stop.

Moving cautiously to keep from falling, Evan wedged between the parked cars. The drunk captive was closest to the driveway, down on the pavement, face up, motionless. Near the standing boy, the big boy was on the ground, holding down the fourth boy, whose face was covered with blood. The remnants of the broken bottle were on the ground next to them.

It didn't take long for the still frame to move again. In an instant, the party was over, and no one wanted to stick around to clean up. Kids started streaming out the front door.

Evan took charge, yelling directions. "Get some towels, something!" he yelled at the last boy standing. "Everyone else! Get back in the house!" He knelt next to the unconscious boy and saw blood oozing from the back of his head into a small puddle.

He pulled off his jacket and laid it on the boy's chest, took his cell phone out of his shirt pocket, and called 911. As Evan made the call, he glanced up at the house. Natalie was at the upstairs window gazing down, her eyes wide, her hands fisted and pressed over her mouth.

14 » DREAM

DESSERT AND COFFEE were long finished, the bill paid, but Vesma and Hernando lingered over their empty cups. Conversation and laughter had been plentiful, and now the moment of truth was near.

"That was delicious," she said, the last thing either of them said for a full minute. Their eyes met and held. *Do we dare to think: What next?*

The restaurant was nearly empty. They rose and floated toward the coat check. Nando, pure gentleman, held her coat open for her. They said thank you and good night to the owner, a man in the habit of standing at the portal like a priest saying farewell to his congregation. They'd partaken of his food and wine, had shared company and united with something greater than themselves.

Outside, Vesma felt an icy needle on her cheek. The sleet was just starting. Nando held her left elbow with his left hand, and with his right arm around her waist, guided her along the path to his Audi in the parking lot. They'd each had two glasses of wine and a cognac. She was aware of the effects and equally aware of her faith in his steadiness. He was sure and solid, not merely an illusion of strength like Ty had been, and this night was nothing like the early years, her nights of drinking and risk-taking with Ty. No altered state can lead her wrong with this man, Hernando

Ramirez.

At the car door, keeping his right arm around her, Nando presses the clicker in his left coat pocket, bends forward, and opens the door. He palms the upper edge of the door to press it open, and they rearrange themselves inside the opening without losing contact. The silly maneuvering makes Vesma giddy with delight. They manage to stay upright, both of his hands now circling her waist. They stand under a harsh, fluorescent light, their breath exhaled in white puffs. He presses his full lips to her cheek, lifts away, and finds her mouth. The kiss is barely begun when he pulls back again.

He is forty-three and she is forty-nine and this moment is enough for them for now. They know what it means.

They don't say a thing as he gets behind the wheel and turns the key. They sit for a long time warming the car, defrosting, melting. She hunches down into the seat, stunned, enfolded, still feeling his kiss. They glance at each other with little smiles on their faces. Finally, he reverses the car out of the spot, drives through the lot, and stops at the threshold to the street. Right or left? It's then that he breaks the silence and asks the question, very sweetly, very quietly, without assuming what her answer will be.

She says "yes."

Vaguely aware of the route he takes, she has never been to his home and has never questioned him about it in any detail. The roadways are quiet with few cars, the lights, red, green, and yellow, haloing in the droplets on the windshield. He drives slowly, their hearts gliding, their bodies enclosed in a vessel skating on ice. She trusts him completely.

When they walk into the living room of his small apartment, he turns on a single standing lamp with an orange shade, enough light to avoid tripping, to forestall inhibition. She sets her purse on the coffee table. He helps her remove the coat and drapes it on the back of a low couch. He takes off his jacket. She wanders around a bit while he goes toward the sound system. The place is tidy, distinctive, filled with South American artifacts, little statues, wall hangings, pottery, a guitar, a bookcase full of titles in Spanish. He puts on some music, Andean pan flutes, and walks over to the bookcase, where she's pretending to read and understand the spines.

"That's nice music," she says, sideways to him. "You're trying to impress me?"

"I think it's relaxing."

"So, you're trying to relax me?"

He comes up close and she turns to him. With two fingers, he draws a line from the center point of her hairline, down and across her forehead to her temple, gently pushing the hair behind her ear. In her high heels, she's nearly his height, eye-to-eye as he touches her. "I'm not trying to do anything," he says. "Everything is your call."

She shivers. Her shoes pinch her toes and she shakes them off, shrinking three inches, now looking up into his eyes, dark and liquid. Her arms find his shoulders and she pulls him in. This time the kiss is long and deep.

They're intertwined, still upright, wanting more but uncertain of the next step. On a coffee table behind her rests a purse which holds a wallet with cards that identify her, a small makeup bag, and a cell phone set on vibrate. A corner of her brain remembers who she is, the larger part has forgotten.

They pull apart, his forehead tipping forward to touch hers. His eyes question and hers answer. He puts an arm around her shoulder, and she allows him to lead her gently out of the living room. She feels the bare wood under her stocking feet in the dim hallway. At the end is a door, half open. They enter a dark room.

He unzips her dress in the back and she steps out of it, wearing her prettiest, laciest underthings because, maybe, she was hoping for this to happen. He comes around in front, admiring her, but she's suddenly shy, even as she stands in gray shadow, barely a glimpse of light cast long from the cracked door. She doesn't know how to do this, it's been so long. She starts to unbutton his shirt but can't get the top button out.

"I'm nervous."

"I am too."

He takes over and continues his own unbuttoning, pulls off his shirt and unbuckles his belt while she sits on the bed and takes off her pantyhose.

Perhaps modesty is a consideration for them both. He stops undressing before he arrives at complete nakedness and sits down on the bed next to her, thigh to thigh. He twists toward her, puts his hands gently on her shoulders and pushes her head back into the pillows, stands and lifts her legs up onto the bed. He climbs over her and lies on his side, pressed up close, and kisses her with his mouth relaxed but not open. She can feel the power of his heart, pulsing strong and steady on her breast.

She lifts a hand to his shoulder and he jumps. Ice cold! They laugh.

"Let's get under the covers," he says.

Inside the cave they warm up quickly, and soon, they've shimmied out of their remaining clothing. She has no second thoughts, welcoming his advances and creating her own, expanding into his moments of retreat and submission. Why has she resisted this for so long? Together they are pure, holy, organic, her body impressed to his, convex to concave, hollow to swell.

Becky sat in the front seat, her friend Amanda in back. They filled the car with their sloppy energy and the odor of alcohol, exhaled and weeping from their pores. All the windows fogged up. Ginger cleared a circle on the windshield with her forearm.

Becky was rummaging through her purse, the contents rattling, carelessly spilling things on the floor. "Where's my phone? You have to go back!"

Ginger kept her focus glued to the road. She'd gotten only as far as the mouth of the cul-de-sac, trying not to panic when the brakes went all bumpy as she came to a stop. She waited at the intersection with the blinker on, mustering the nerve to turn onto Hudson Bluffs Drive. "We can't—"

"That's okay! I found it!"

"Don't call that fucking dickhead!" Amanda yelled from the back seat.

"He's not a fucking dickhead! You don't know him like I do."

They'd been arguing about Becky's boyfriend, nicknamed Speed. From what Ginger could gather, he was a senior, a friend of Julian's, and the two of them, along with a few others, had been rowdy to the point of destruction down in the game room.

Ginger didn't participate in any of the conversation. She had to concentrate. The noise her passengers were making helped to control the panic rising in her chest. Two of the people in this car hadn't a care in the world about the drive home. *Why is everyone always so scared of a little snow?* But they were drunk, and this wasn't snow. It was ice. Now that it was too late, Ginger understood the difference.

I'm a good driver, and I'll get us all home, and Dylan will come for the phone. The Gravity! Dylan might have been trying to call her. Other people might have called for rides. She hadn't checked for messages and wasn't about to do it now. She had to concentrate.

She'd been sitting at the intersection long enough with the blinker on.

"Let's go!" Amanda said, slapping the top of Ginger's seat with an open palm.

"Hey!" Becky popped up from her slump, turned to Ginger, and asked, in a thick slurry of words, "How do you even have a driver's license?"

Ginger didn't answer. She'd already started her left turn onto Hudson Bluffs. The rear of the car swiveled and straightened out.

"Oh wow! Way to go, 'Call Central'!" Amanda mocked. Hoots and laughs. They really didn't care if she had a driver's license. Rules meant nothing to these girls, except as a target of ridicule.

Becky slumped down into her seat again. "This shit is kicking my *ass*."

Twenty-five miles an hour wasn't too fast, Ginger thought. She usually went thirty-five on this road.

"I *told* you that was no good. I told you."

A car was approaching in the opposite direction. The headlights blinded her.

"Speedy—what a man!"

"You don' even…"

The car passed, and Ginger exhaled.

"…know 'bout his name…"

"Speedo!"

"He wuz so fas'…the half mile…"

Coming up to the big curve.

"Track team in *middle* school. For*ever* ago! I've got a new name for him. How about Tranq—?"

And then it happens.

In the standing-still moment of Ginger's loss of control, the shock of mistake buries her excuses. Divinely, from above, she observes the scene unfolding in a slow-motion series of frozen frames: the flashing yellow lights and black arrows, the loss of traction, hands on the wheel to the left, the tail swinging out to the right in wild, ecstatic release, an arcing spasm of abandon, a scrape along the guardrail, blips of milliseconds to the other side of blindness. Screams in the night. The Volvo and its occupants are taken to final impact. All goes dark.

* * *

Pulsing, rhythmic, yellow. Ginger is not unconscious, not dead, not able to escape the consequences. Her eyes pop open almost immediately, and now there's entirely too much light. A street-lamp overhead, and behind them, the guardrail with its flashing yellow lights.

Trying to make that curve, wheels turned to the left, the Volvo had whipped out and skated on ice, skidding along the length of the guardrail, finally slipping off the end and smacking into a broad, wise sycamore. Ginger, seatbelt in place, was snapped to a halt upright, her heart beating against the strap. At once, silence replaced all sound, the bump-bumping of the anti-lock brakes, the screams and the thuds, one, two, that followed.

After a stony moment, Ginger's brain settled and became aware that two bodies were out of place. Becky was tilted to the right, her head at the intersection of the windshield and the door-jamb. Amanda was half on top of her, thrown over the back of the seat. Amanda groaned and pushed back, landing with a plop on the back seat again.

The right side of the windshield had a spiderweb crack illuminated with every blink of the flashing yellows behind them. Becky's eyes were closed.

With sudden regret, Ginger wondered why she hadn't asked them to put on their seat belts. Why hadn't she demanded it?

She did a quick unbuckling of her own, set the hazard lights, and jumped out the door. The passenger side was pushed against some bushes, too hard to get into, so she opened the back door on the driver's side. Amanda sat dazedly, with no obvious signs of injury. The sickening smell and her grogginess were familiar signs that Ginger understood—Amanda's body had reacted like a rubber band, not feeling a thing. Thrown over the seat, using Becky as a safety net. It was Becky they had to worry about. Her eyes were closed and she wasn't moving.

"Becky!" Ginger reached over the seat and touched her shoulder. Should she shake her? She controlled the impulse, remembering that it might worsen her injuries. "Are you okay? I'm calling 911."

Becky's eyes opened, and she sat up, hand to forehead, recoiling at the blood she found there.

"It's okay, you're going to be okay. I'm calling now." Ginger twisted between the bucket seats in front and fumbled with the lid on the cubby. Inside, the Gravity was aglow with missed messages. She grabbed it, pushed her way out of the car, and punched in "9-1-1" with a shaking hand. An accident, an ambulance, Ginger Kavanagh, Hudson Bluffs Drive, curve with the flashing lights. She managed to keep her voice steady. With that much accomplished, there was hope for the next call she had to make, the possibility that she could speak to her mother in that same steady tone. She pressed the digits and the phone rang once, twice, a third time. *No answer, no answer, oh thank you, no answer, I cannot talk to her because what would I say?* It went to voicemail, but she ended the call without leaving a message and leaned inside the car again. Amanda was starting to curse. "Becky, are you all right? I just called 911." The girl spoke, "yes," an okay, and Ginger pulled out again, thinking hard. A single face, a single voice came to mind. *Gingie, please call me. You can call anytime.*

Why did she know this? He would come immediately, and he would know what to do.

She pressed in the number she knew by heart, and he picked up on the first ring. When she heard his "hello," she knew she'd made the right choice. He'd never, ever sounded so good, a strong voice more reassuring than the sound of the approaching siren.

When she finished talking to Daddy, a police officer came up and shined a flashlight in her face. "You okay?"

"My father is coming," was the first thing out of her mouth.

* * *

A blissful afterglow, a fall into sleep. The vibration isn't felt, like a tree that falls in a forest on the other side of the world.

Tynan wasn't sleeping. He didn't sleep much anymore, ever since he'd stopped drinking, and it was a problem, but one that he refused to solve with pills. AA had straightened him out on that.

He hadn't heard her voice for nearly two years, and it took him a while to know who was calling. A developing adolescent voice will become lower and change slightly in character. Urgency, fear and shame will shape those changes into something entirely different. Still, he could hear the little girl inside the new sound, and her first word touched his heart like the first time she'd ever said it. "Daddy."

Much later he would understand that, in a strange way, he had been her first and only choice. Sean might have been the one, but he was too far away, in California. She'd called Vesma first, but only as a matter of reflex, not choice. When there was no answer, Gingie hung up without leaving a message, taking advantage of her mother's unavailability, a convenient postponement of her dreaded confession. The other possibilities, Andris and Stephanie, simply couldn't be called because the humiliation was too great; turning to them at a time like this would forever tarnish their status as the fun aunt and uncle. Grandpa, of course, didn't even make the list. He didn't have a car. Besides that, the phone call might have killed him.

What it all came down to was this. In Ginger's life, he was the only person who had experienced the kind of thing she was going through right now, a humiliating hurdle to be knocked down and stumbled over. He'd made so many mortal mistakes, falls from grace, hideously embarrassing, even criminal acts, and he'd emerged from the pile of them ready to finish the race, last in line but still running. A wonderful example. Hah! But she was a smart girl and must have sensed the utility in this.

The thought stopped him, bringing on a mild rebuke. He'd weaned himself from cynicism, or so he believed.

He found a better answer. She had called him out of faith in the purity of his love and with an awareness of his transformation, his readiness to parent again. Gifts and cards and e-mails meant nothing to her now. After today, even if she wanted it from him, a car on her seventeenth birthday was clearly not in her future. Five seconds on an icy road had sealed it. She wanted a father instead.

The envelope of darkness, the rise and fall of his chest and his moist breath in her hair, had lulled Vesma into a deep relaxation. A rainbow of designs played beneath her eyelids, obscuring the memory of this feeling from a time so long ago that it wasn't a memory at all but something completely new. Time did not exist for seconds or hours before she reacted to a sound and opened her eyes. There was no way to know. Had it been a voice in her head, a vibration, a dream halfway between sleep and waking?

"What is it, *mi amor*?"

He had called her "*mi amor*." There was nothing else.

Out there, in the few rooms she'd briefly explored, were the usual sounds that a house made, slightly different than those in her own home. An electrical humming of some kind, and the refrigerator turning on in the kitchen. From a distant, unknown place came a siren. People ill, hurt, in trouble.

"Nothing. Nothing at all," she said, and closed her eyes again.

In a spontaneous rush, Ginger fell into her father's arms, the top of her head coming up shoulder level, her nose pushed into a clean evergreen smell, her cheek against the thick, padded fabric of his winter coat. She pulled away again to look, to make sure it was him. This was Daddy, but it wasn't Daddy at the same time. Under the blue-gray streetlight he was steely and solid, older, weathered, square and shaven, his face intermittently splashed with red from the pulsing lights atop two patrol cars. A uniformed officer hovered nearby and watched them, holding the learner's permit and the insurance card and registration Ginger had found in the glove compartment. His partner, a female officer, was setting flares on the street. Two male officers from the other patrol car, flashlights in hand, were inspecting the Volvo. The radios on their hips emitted scratchy noise and voices. A lot was happening tonight.

"Are you sure you're all right? Did you bump anything?" Her father's chilly bare hand, smelling of soap, cradled her cheek, moved to her forehead. He gave off none of the odors she remembered and could now put a name to—the cigarettes, the sweat, the scotch. "You look intact."

"I'm okay, Daddy. I'm okay but…Becky." She nodded at the ambulance. The emergency workers had already examined all three girls. They agreed with Ginger's self-evaluation that she was "fine," her seatbelt had prevented any impact. Becky and Amanda were inside the ambulance, soon to be taken to the hospital.

"Did you call your mother?"

"She didn't answer."

"We're going to be taking her in," interrupted one of the officers who'd been inspecting the car.

"Taking her in? For what?"

"Just for a statement. Get her out of the cold—"

"Jim!" barked his partner, standing by the open door of the car. He motioned, and Jim walked over.

"You sure you're okay?" Daddy asked her again.

"Yes, I'm sure, just..."

"I'll come with you..."

"...just, oh, Daddy...!"

"...to the police station."

"...I'm so, so *stupid!*" She flew into his arms again, ripping the mantle off the levelheaded calm she'd maintained until now.

Hanging from his neck, she sobbed, wrenching his heart from his chest and sending it soaring. His girl. This was his girl! "No, you're not, you're not stupid at all. You were trying to help." He repeated the words, stroking the hair that fell below her hat.

The huddled officers finished conferring and walked toward them. Sensing something was up, Ty looked over his daughter's head into their solemn faces. The man he thought of as Officer Jim came uncomfortably close and placed his hand on Ginger's right forearm, pulling it firmly, but not roughly, from Ty's neck. "I'm sorry, Miss," he said, clamping the wrist in cold metal.

"What's going on here?"

"I'm sorry, Miss," he repeated, ignoring Ty, "but you're under arrest."

"That's outrageous! She's sixteen!"

The second officer, with his chin thrust out somewhere between the father's five-nine and the girl's five-five, was given to a bit of swagger. "Recognize this?" He dangled something in Ginger's face, a pint bottle containing an inch of clear liquid. "And these?" In his other hand, he rattled a few pills in a plastic prescription container.

What a snotty know-it-all, thought Ty, this nameless Officer Bottle! At once, four voices converged, growing louder, refusing to yield or communicate.

"What are you implying?"

"That's not mine..."

"What are the charges?"

"Driving while intoxicated—"

"She's not drunk—"

"These were on the floor in the front."

"—unlawful possession of a controlled substance—"

"…those are Becky's."

"—hasn't had a drink in her life!"

"—unlicensed driving, open container of alcohol in the car."

"We hear that all the time—"

"Let me see that! It's the other kid's!"

"—all the time. Everyone says, 'It's not mine.'"

"You have the right to remain silent…"

"I was t-taking them home, they were d-drunk…"

"Don't say anything, Gingie, I'll talk to them."

"…anything you say can be used against you in a court of law…"

"This is insane! Let her go! She's a child!"

Ty was up in Officer Bottle's face. The other two officers came behind him on opposite sides, and each clamped an arm. Memories slammed him hard in a place he didn't want to go and wasn't about to go again. Not like this, not in front of his baby. He would do this right.

They all shut up for seconds, four officers, a father, a daughter, hearts beating to the strobe of red light and the scratchy noise of the officers' radios. A stifled sob. Officer Jim, possibly hiding a flicker of self-doubt, held fast to Ginger's forearm, her wrists now cuffed behind her back. Officer Bottle had pulled back ramrod straight and just as cocky, even as he lowered his hands with the evidence they held. The other officers, a faceless man and woman, didn't loosen their grip on Ty.

He took a deep breath and found a rational tone. "As her father, I'm requesting and giving you permission to order a blood test."

"We have to take her to the station for the breathalyzer. She already blew into the handheld before you got here, but…"

"Nothing, right?"

"I'm not sure it's calibrated. It's not reliable. There's a better one at the station."

"Okay, but there has to be a blood test. Full toxicology. For all three of the kids."

Ginger's frightened eyes were bouncing back and forth between them.

"We can't do blood at the station…"

Ty shot a look at the ambulance. The emergency technician was closing the back door.

"Take her to the hospital. A doctor should examine her anyway—they could have missed something."

Officer Jim seemed to consider this before casting a meaningful look at Officer Bottle. *He knows I'm right.* A man of reason. Ty calmed down enough to look at Officer Jim's nameplate, illuminated by the overhead streetlamp. "J. Mitchell," was printed there.

"Hold on a minute," Mitchell said. He motioned to the female officer holding Ty. She walked around to take hold of Ginger while he and Officer Bottle went over to the ambulance and spoke with the attendant. There were hand gestures and nodding heads and glances at the waiting group, and then the attendant climbed in behind the wheel. While they were over there, Ty looked at the nameplate of the woman holding Ginger. "M. Rincón."

Mitchell walked up to Ty as the ambulance pulled away. "Okay," he said. "I told them we'll be getting a court order for blood on the passengers. This EMT unit has to get to the hospital and be available for other calls. We're stretched thin tonight. Another EMT unit is on Foxglove," he looked directly at Ginger, "the house you just left. We have to get over there too."

In a meek voice, Ginger said, "Did something…?"

"Never mind about that! You're going in the other car," he

nodded at Officer Rincón, "to the hospital for bloodwork. I don't need a court order for you. Since you were driving, your consent is implied by law, even if your father hadn't asked for you. After that, you'll be going to the station."

"I'm coming too," said Ty, keeping his eyes locked on Ginger's, as the uniformed woman started to lead her away. Rincón's partner let go of Ty, who started to follow them.

"On your own, sir," said Officer Rincón.

"Of course."

"Take your own vehicle."

"Sure thing. Gingie, don't worry," Ty called out after her. "I'm with you every step of the way!"

Another hazy dream, a melting, drifting, dropping, a free fall — and this time she came fully awake, eyes wide open in a new place, his bedroom with his sheets and his smell and his everyday private life surrounding her. Comfortable. She resisted a belief in her own life apart from this moment, with a creeping awareness of the need to return, now, if there was any hope of preserving what they had started together.

"Nando?"

"Hmm. *Sí, mi amor.*"

"I hate to do this to you, but I have a daughter waiting for me at home."

Not at all pleasant—pulling away, getting dressed in the dark, walking out to the cold car. All the magic of the evening had worn off, replaced with gritty sleep under her eyelids, a cottony mouth, and the chafing discomfort of evening clothes, her tight dress, pantyhose and high heels now far from sexy. She had declined his offer to borrow an oversized set of sweats to ride home in. How would that look to Gingie? But then, even in her dress, even having dragged a comb through her hair in a strange, over-bright bathroom, she didn't look like a woman merely returning home from a dinner date. It was after one in the morning, but Ginger would still be up, on Call Central duty. Vesma would have to face her. She should have called home the minute she stepped foot in Hernando's apartment, to say she'd be late.

Vesma smiled to herself in the dark car, no regrets. Everything with Ginger would fall into place. She was going to love Nando.

Her right hand rested on the soft leather of her evening bag, its contents known by touch, the small bulges and hard things inside, the outline of her lipstick, her compact, her cell phone. A short vibration erupted and stopped, signaling a new voicemail or an unopened text. She fumbled with the clasp, opened the bag, and removed the phone. There was a new voicemail from a number she didn't recognize. She listened, but the caller hadn't left a message. A guilty thought: Had her daughter called from the SADD phone, an unknown number? Ginger's own cell phone was broken.

"Something?" he asked.

But now it was too late, he was pulling into the driveway. Soon enough, she would know if Ginger had called.

"No, nothing. Don't," she said, placing her hand gently on his, preventing his move to the key in the ignition. Keys! She remembered now that she'd left her own keyring in its usual spot on the hall table and would have to ring the doorbell. Even more reason he should stay in the car.

"Let me see you to the door."

"Thank you, but no need, really. Please, stay warm."

Their eyes caught and held, tacit understanding the reward of their new intimacy. "Okay. You gonna make it in those shoes?" He glanced down.

"I'm an expert." They both smiled, and she leaned in for a

kiss. "Thank you, Nando."

She stepped out of the car and onto the icy walkway, grabbing the first post in the mesh fence that kept the deer out of the shrubs at the front of the house. She took two slippery steps, grabbed the next post and made it fine, hoping not to appear too pathetically crippled in her high heels as Nando politely waited and watched in the parked car. At the front door, finger poised over the doorbell, she tried the latch and the door opened. Of course. Ginger had failed to lock it again after Vesma left the house. They lived in a safe neighborhood, and they'd left the door open plenty of times, but still, it should be locked this late at night.

She turned to wave, and he lifted his hand in response. The Audi reversed slowly out of the driveway, and Hernando drove off.

Vesma cleared her throat, ready to say "hello" as naturally as possible. Maybe she'd work in a little reminder about locking the door. "Gingie!"

At the hospital, sitting in the waiting area, Ty palmed his mobile phone, gazing down at it, hesitating. There was no way around it. He'd have to call Vesma. But he had to think how to phrase it first.

He was aware of the small hope in his heart that this episode with Ginger would require a meeting with Vesma. He hadn't seen her in almost two years, the last time she'd dropped the kids off for a visit, and he wondered how he would look to her. Much better, he hoped, but there was nothing for comparison because back then he'd been blind to his appearance. Now, he could only imagine how repellent it might have been.

He had no doubt that she would look amazing, like always. He was afraid of that.

* * *

She heeled off her shoes in the foyer and called out again. "Gingie, I'm home!"

No response. The girl had fallen asleep or was under the headphones. Vesma laid her purse on top of a pile of mail on the hall table, not noticing anything amiss. In stocking feet, she padded into the kitchen, exhausted but happy, a tenacious little smile gracing her lips. Even the air smelled fragrant! Her own house was sweetly perfumed with love.

No Ginger. Not in the kitchen, not in the living room. Two little flames flickered in the dark. Vesma's smile started to fade. She turned on the overhead light to inspect more closely. Candles dotted the room, most of them gone out, except for two. *That* was the smell, the perfume in the air. A lavender scented candle. No damage, but wait…wax had dripped from a candle holder onto the coffee table. "Ginger! Come in here!" Anger jumped up but receded instantly. It was entirely too quiet. Something was wrong here.

She walked past the hall bathroom, the door open, the light out, and into Ginger's room, dark. Her fingers felt for the light switch. An empty bed, rumpled sheets. Such a small room. A few steps to the dresser, patting the surface, then the desk, reeling, catching herself on the edge, dropping her head to stop the veil of darkness, standing upright again. Her daughter had to be here somewhere. Her clothes, her photographs, her books, her posters, Ginger.

In a trance, arms and hands preceding, the mother went on a search. A door was pushed open, a light switched on with a disembodied hand, the tester, the sacrifice, head and body following it into the newly illuminated space. The hall bathroom, Sean's room, Sean's closet, Vesma's bedroom, bathroom, and closet. An anguished animal sound escaped her lips, a choking clamor to break free from this trap, this little house, these clothes, this skin, too tight.

Standing at the end of the hall, her vision tunneled toward the front of the house, the little table in the foyer. There, her sins and failings awaited her, hidden inside that vibrating messenger. She rushed to the table and opened her purse, where the glowing object suddenly jumped with life.

"Tynan!" What on earth… "Is Ginger with you?"

"I'm at Hudson Valley Hospital. There's been an accident." He interrupted her before she could protest. "She's okay! They've just finished taking a look at her."

"Thank God. Can you stay with her 'til I get there? I'll be right…"

"Hold on…"

"…there as soon as I…"

"…wait a second…"

"…find my keys." She'd already jammed her feet back into the high heels and was shuffling old mail around on the little table, looking underneath, patting on top.

"Vesma, hang up now and call a taxi."

"A taxi?"

"And you're not coming to the hospital. Meet us at the county police station."

15 »   MASSACRE

IT WAS TAKING much too long for Evan to call, making her mind jump to the worst possible scenario. She paced the living room, cell phone in hand. She couldn't wait any longer and called him.

"Dana, I can't talk. Hang tight. Don't worry. I'll call back as soon as I can." Was that a siren in the background? The line went dead.

Don't worry, he says.

Travis walked into the living room. "Where's Dad?"

"Did we wake you up?"

"I was already up."

"So, you must be feeling better."

"A little…but where did Dad go?"

"He went to pick up Natalie at the Bohrs' house. She wants to come home."

"Why?"

"Well, I don't know the whole story. I think Michael and his friends might be bothering her."

"See, I told you—"

"Now, that's enough. We'll just wait until we hear what happened. You ought to go back to bed."

"I can't, I mean, something's going on. I can't reach Ginger. She's not answering the phone. Both numbers."

"Hmm…"

"I called Dylan and he can't reach her either."

"Isn't he supposed to go to her house to get the phone?"

"Yeah, at two o'clock."

"That's only half an hour from now. When he gets there, he'll find out what's going on and let you know."

"I guess."

"I wouldn't worry about it. Maybe the electricity and cell service aren't working at her house."

"Maybe. Okay."

"Good night."

"Night."

He shuffled back to his room. He *did* look better, at least from the standpoint of his physical symptoms. His eyes were clearer, his skin color closer to normal, his voice less scratchy. His improvement should have lifted his mood, but he looked more down than ever. Travis was feeling responsible for Ginger. A good thing, sweet maybe, but too heavy and serious, too critical of himself for letting her down.

And was there a suggestion of something else in his eyes? Her son was falling in love. Sixteen might be the age for crushes and infatuations, but Travis was more mature than half the adults Dana knew.

The ice storm intensified. Dana could hear it on the windows. Another interminable time later, Evan called.

"I've been so worried."

"Sorry to keep you waiting, Dana. When you called, I was just finished with the ABCs, airway, breathing, circulation—"

"My God, who's hurt?"

"A boy was knocked down and fell on the front walk, hit his head. He was unconscious. I tried to keep him warm until the ambulance came. Another boy was slashed with a broken bottle—"

"*What?*"

"—and someone brought towels to try to stop the bleeding. I was also yelling at the partygoers, trying to keep them from hightailing it out of here. Most of them ignored me. I think I managed to hold the main people involved and the witnesses. There's about, oh, eight or ten here, but the police are starting to outnumber them!"

"What happened to the injured boys?"

"As soon as the EMTs took charge I had to go move the car. I was blocking the driveway, and they wouldn't have been able to get out. It took a while because I had to park on the street and walk back slowly. It's icy. When I got back, the two boys weren't on the front steps anymore. I'm not sure…maybe they both squeezed into the ambulance, one of those big paramedic vans. It's leaving for the hospital now."

"Where's Natalie?"

"Right here. We're waiting to give our statements to the police."

A sick feeling rose from her abdomen to her chest. "Oh, I can't stand this!"

"You'd be proud of me, Dana. Just like the old days, I did my best to preserve the crime scene—"

Evan and Natalie mixed up in a crime scene! "So, it's an assault? How many involved?"

"Two boys and the two injured ones. I only saw part of it. And then there's the whole issue about the alcohol. Sandy and Michael Sr. are going to have trouble talking their way out of this one…"

Dana felt an urgent call to action. "I'm coming right over. I should supervise the investigation."

"I'd advise against it. Strongly."

She calmed her racing thoughts and considered his words, his sudden change in tone. Her lighthearted, loving husband, a man of wisdom and experience, was giving her an order. He followed it up with a reminder. "You're the district attorney, not the assistant assigned to the case."

He was right, of course. She was an elected official and should delegate the investigation to her top people. She would call Indigo now, and maybe Linda too. As the DA, she shouldn't get directly involved, not just yet, not like this, especially since…

"Natalie is a witness. And I'm a witness to part of it too."

Indigo surveyed the scene at the Bohrs' estate after weaving through a mass of vehicles, both police and civilian. She tiptoed around the blood and broken glass on the front walk. Before going inside, she spoke with Lieutenant Ormand, who said he was coordinating the investigation. He gave her a sketchy report of what they'd learned from witnesses, including Evan and Natalie. She entered the house and went through the palatial foyer into the living room, where she found Dana's family on the couch, huddled together, Evan's arm around his daughter's shoulder.

"Hello, sugar. You look all tuckered out."

"I'm okay," Natalie said.

"I like the hair!" Indigo touched the top of her head, the symmetrical pattern made by the French braid. "Who gave you that 'do?"

"Mommy."

"My goodness! Your mama's a woman of many talents."

"We're thinking of opening a salon," Evan said dryly.

"I see. Keeping your options open…," Indigo looked right and left, checking for eavesdroppers, "…after all of *this*?" She laughed heartily.

Evan smiled and said, "Never a dull moment is there, Investigator Raines?"

"Well, it's time to dull it down. Take your baby home and get some sleep. Don't worry, Dad, we'll be in touch." Indigo and Evan exchanged a knowing look. This was only the beginning.

"So, we're officially excused? We're not suspects?" Evan squeezed Natalie's shoulder and shook her gently, trying to get a smile out of her.

"Free to go. The county police have your statements, and they don't need anything else from you. Linda and I have the rest of this covered. She'll be here soon."

"Linda Marquette? I thought she was head of the Bias Crimes Unit."

"That's right. Maybe this one doesn't fall into that category, but she's assigned to the Steuben case, and the boss wants her on both of 'em. Linda gets the honor of being our new expert on teenagers."

Natalie looked up sheepishly. "We're not all that bad." She was on the verge of tears, her lower lip quivering.

Indigo regarded the girl with a look of motherly compassion. "You speak the truth, sugar. Teens are my favorite people, and you're the sweetest and best of the bunch."

Emjay massaged his sore knuckles. He was in hot water up to his eyeballs. Half the senior class at his house! People he'd never invite in a million years, Julian Yarnell and his crowd. Speed. A ridiculous name! Yarnell's best buddy. Everyone knew what Speed was into. *I'll crucify whoever put the word out!*

Julian wasn't waking up, and Speed was gushing blood, from where, exactly, Emjay couldn't see. He'd gotten towels from the house but didn't get involved in the first aid efforts. Julian and Speed deserved what they got, ten times worse. Crashing the party, totally wasted. It really, really pissed him off. He didn't care about them and had only one concern. *My life is over.*

Emjay's head filled with a gallery of football stars, arrested, convicted, NFL careers ruined. There'd be no football scholarship for him now, no college stardom, his path to the NFL blocked even before it started. There had to be a way out of this. *What did that man see?* Out of nowhere, a middle-aged bald guy appeared. Had to be somebody's father, come to pick up his kid. *I'll crucify whoever called their dad!*

They needed a story. In the confusion, before the ambulance came, Emjay tried to talk to Brent, tried even to catch his eye, but it wasn't happening. Brent was helping Speed with the towels, soaking up the blood. Emjay's best friend was two hundred fifteen pounds of rock-hard muscle, an all-around solid guy. He was the player who always cleared a path for Emjay, the star quarterback, making him look good, giving him the space to show off his dexterity and speed. And tonight, Brent had gotten Emjay's back again. Brent wouldn't let him down. He couldn't! They were in this together.

The paramedics took Julian and Speed away, and the rest of it was a blur. Cop cars pulled in, one after another. Officers separated Emjay and Brent, taking them inside for interrogation. One pair walked Emjay through the living room into the kitchen, and another pair took Brent into the den. People were being questioned in the living room: the kids who'd hung around, the bald guy, and Sammy's friend. When Emjay saw this, it became clear. That little middle schooler was the one who'd called her father to come get her.

The officers asked Emjay a lot of questions. He felt trapped, his back up against the kitchen counter. The nametag of the one questioning him was in his face. "T. Davidson."

"How old are you, Michael?"

"Eighteen."

"When was your birthday?"

"February third."

"Are you celebrating your birthday today?"

"Not really."

"Where are your parents?"

"In the city at a party, kind of a reunion."

"Did they allow you to throw a party?"

"They always let me have friends over. It's not a problem."

"Can we ask your mom and dad about that?"

"Yeah, go ahead. But I didn't invite a lot of these people. They just came over on their own. I can't help that!"

Davidson asked for his parents' cell phone numbers, and the other officer walked off to call them. Emjay's only thought, his only consolation, was that his parents were spending the night at a hotel in the city and wouldn't be back until tomorrow night, when all of this would be cleared up and the house would be clean.

"Have you been drinking?"

"No." Hours ago, but that couldn't count. He'd taken a couple of big swigs of Jim Beam from someone's flask at the dance. Gave him a good buzz. Coach would kill him…

"You consent to a breathalyzer?"

"Sh-shure."

Emjay didn't see it coming. Out of nowhere, a handheld breathalyzer was in his face, Davidson telling him what to do. He read the results and said, "You're not being straight with us, Michael."

"I'm not drunk!"

"I didn't ask if you were drunk."

"That thing can't be accurate…what does it say?" He'd been schooled in blood alcohol content and knew the meaning of BAC levels.

"Point oh six."

"That's not drunk."

"That's proof you've been drinking. Are you denying that?"

"Yes, if you're talking about drinking any of my parents' stuff."

"I'm talking about drinking, period. You say your parents have alcohol here?"

"Sure, like every house does."

"Can we take a look around?"

"If you don't mess anything up."

"We'll be respectful." Davidson looked around the kitchen as if there wasn't too much to be respectful about. His eyes stopped on each little thing that was out of place. Nothing but a bunch of chip and cookie and cracker bags, cheese wrappers, and soda cans. "Why don't you show me where your parents keep the alcohol, Michael?"

Before he could answer, the other officer, who'd been off in a corner, came back and said, "They're on their way."

Emjay's heart jumped to his throat.

"How long 'til they get here?" asked Davidson.

"It'll be a while. They don't want to drive on these roads, so they're leaving their car in the city and taking the train. They just have time to catch the last one out of Grand Central at two. It arrives at about three, and they'll have to get a taxi from the station."

"Or maybe we could offer them a lift from the station?" There was a little smile on Davidson's lips that Emjay didn't like.

"We could arrange it."

Davidson turned to him again. "Okay, Michael, why don't you give me a tour of the liquor supplies. Then we'll have to have a chat about what happened out on the front steps."

Chaos, confusion. This was more than a messy house after a big party. It was a crime scene that had to be handled with care. Assault, underage drinking, and drug use. So much had gone down before Indigo arrived that she couldn't be sure where the investigation stood, whether the officers had followed the best practices, whether any of the evidence was compromised, improperly obtained, or inadmissible in a court of law.

Unbeknownst to Indigo, Emjay was down in the game room with the officers when she was in the living room talking to Evan and Natalie. After the Goodhues left, Indigo headed for the foyer and was about to go upstairs when Linda came in the front door.

"Did you know that some teenagers who'd been at this party were in a car accident?" Linda asked.

"No one mentioned it to me."

"Lieutenant Ormand said there's an officer here who was at the accident scene. Officer James Mitchell. Ormand also said that Mr. and Mrs. Bohr are on a train from the city and will get here at about three fifteen."

"Things are going to get very interesting when mommy and daddy get home," Indigo said. "I'm on my way upstairs to see the bedroom where Natalie was looking out the window."

"All right," Linda said. "I'll talk to Officer Mitchell and any other witnesses I can find down here."

At the top of the stairs, the door to the first bedroom was open, and Samantha was sitting on one of the twin beds. Indigo wasn't sure if a police officer had questioned her—no one had mentioned it. *She's probably fuming about the treachery of her best friend Natalie Goodhue.* Poor Natalie. She'd been caught in a dilemma, forced to make a choice between loyalty to her friend and loyalty to her conscience when the party started to spin out of control.

"Hello! I'm Investigator Raines. May I come in and look out your window?"

"Sure, why not?"

"A lot's going on here tonight, isn't there?"

"I wish everyone would leave. This is my house too."

"It sure is, honey. Don't worry. Things will start to settle down. Your parents are on their way home." Indigo went to the window and looked down at the front steps and walkway. It was a straight shot, crystal clear with the outside lights turned on. Natalie would have seen the action from a top-of-the-head perspective. Indigo turned to Samantha. "Is this where you were standing when those kids were fighting out front?"

"I wasn't standing anywhere." As if to emphasize this, Samantha remained glued to the bed, her hands gripping the covers. She refused to look at the investigator and kept her eyes on her lap.

Samantha was lying, but Indigo wasn't going to give her the third degree. It was expected that Samantha would want to protect her family. If need be, Indigo could work on her later. As it stood, they already had two objective witnesses: Evan and Natalie. *My God, the DA's husband and daughter!* Without a doubt, Indigo would have to pull the truth out of Samantha sooner or later.

In her usual disarming manner, Indigo continued to chatter, but her indirect methods were resisted. She remarked that the party must have been "hopping" with a lot of high school kids. Samantha protested, "Emjay didn't even invite these people!" When Indigo said that some of the partygoers looked drunk, Samantha answered sullenly, "I didn't see anyone drinking."

After a few minutes of this, Indigo said, "Nice to meet you!" and left the room. She went downstairs, intending to look for Michael Jr. As yet, she hadn't seen him.

In the kitchen, she ran into Linda again. "Officer Mitchell filled me in on the accident," Linda said. "The car lost control on a curve and hit a tree. Two passengers were taken to the hospital. They arrested the driver, Ginger Kavanagh, and charged her with possession of a controlled substance, driving under the influence and without a license. She only had a learner's permit. She says she was working on a ride center at the high school."

"Yeah, Dana mentioned that ride center." And the girl's

name sounded familiar. Had Dana mentioned that too?

"Must've been quite a party," Linda said. "A couple of the teens here are reeking." She scrunched her nose for emphasis. "And they discovered a girl passed out in the powder room. She's been taken to the hospital."

"According to Samantha Bohr, it was a perfectly well-behaved little group. I'll have to work on getting the truth from her later." Just then, two officers emerged from the stairwell with Emjay. "Well, don't you know," Indigo said. "That must be the young man of the house. I see the resemblance to his sister."

Linda introduced herself and Investigator Raines to the officers.

"Sergeant Tyrone Davidson," said the lead man, "and this is Officer Bellacosa." Davidson broke away to talk with them.

"What's going on downstairs, Sergeant?" Linda asked.

"There's a family room with a pool table, a full wet bar, all kinds of alcohol. A number of empty liquor and beer bottles. As soon as FIU is finished on the front steps they're going downstairs to collect evidence." The Forensic Investigations Unit.

"Did you get a search warrant?" Linda asked. Maybe only Indigo could hear the irony in Linda's voice.

"The boy, Michael, gave us consent to search."

"Has he been drinking?"

"He denied it at first. I gave him a breathalyzer. He blew point oh six."

"What did he say before he consented to the search?"

"After the breathalyzer, I told him he wasn't being straight with us about not drinking, and he said something like, 'Oh, I thought you were asking about my parents' liquor. I haven't been drinking any of that.' So, we asked him to show us where his folks kept it. He said okay."

"There could be a problem if the parents say their children aren't allowed to go into the bar. The son's consent would be no good. Any evidence would be inadmissible."

The sergeant looked a bit ruffled. "Go downstairs and see for yourself. The bar is in the game room. It's wide open for anyone in the family to walk through there."

"Okay. Good point."

Indigo wondered if Linda was convinced. She was also concerned about Davidson's questioning of Emjay. "Did you talk to him about the kids who were sent to the hospital?" Indigo asked.

"Yes, we just did. He and his friend Brent were trying to get one of them to leave because he was drunk and stoned. The kid's name is Julian Yarnell. He was all bent out of shape about his girlfriend Taylor. She's one of the girls who was arrested yesterday. Anyway, Emjay says he and Brent had to drag Julian outside, and he just slipped on the ice. Then the other kid—his name is Keith Westerman—was about to slash Emjay with a broken bottle and Brent stopped him. Grabbed his arm, bent it back, and he got cut."

"What did Brent say?"

"About the same thing. We're charging them both with assault, second degree." A serious felony. "For both victims. We're also charging Michael with endangering the welfare and unlawful dealing with a child, for serving alcohol to minors." Misdemeanors.

"Did they waive their rights?"

"Nope. Didn't read the rights. They weren't in custody. I didn't get the okay from the lieutenant to arrest them until a minute ago." Davidson patted the radio on his belt.

"What do you think of their story?"

"It's a coverup, like all the kids we talked to. Everyone has their lips buttoned, you know, 'we didn't see anything,' even if they were standing at the front door when it happened. We could tell that Michael had it in for these two. He and Brent ended up without a scratch, but Julian was rolled out of here unconscious and Keith had uncontrolled bleeding from the face and neck."

"We're going to need something better than a theoretical coverup to convict them of assault two," Linda said. Indigo wondered if this was a test, or if Linda hadn't been fully briefed…

"Oh, we have something better. Two very reliable witnesses." Davidson's look said *Evan and Natalie Goodhue.*

The two women turned to each other. "You or me?" Linda asked.

"I'll call her," Indigo said, pulling out her cell phone. "Sergeant, just hold on a moment while I talk to the district attorney."

Dana was finishing the call with Indigo when she heard the garage door open. Evan and Natalie were home.

A full report had been made, and Dana had given instructions. "Back-to-school day is gonna be fun," Indigo said. "Stone Ridge has taken quite a hit."

Dana mentally did a head count. Taylor Sloane, Chloe Dyckman, Michael Bohr Jr., Brent Tremont…and Ginger! "Five teens arrested for serious felonies in two days."

"It's our own St. Valentine's Day Massacre!" Indigo laughed.

"I used to think I hired you for your sense of humor."

"Sorry, boss."

"Gotta go. Evan and Natalie are home."

Husband and daughter dragged themselves into the living room. Natalie walked right up to her mother and put her arms around her waist, head on her shoulder.

Dana stroked the top of her head. "One good thing. The braid still looks nice."

"You're not mad at me?"

"Not at all. The opposite. You did the absolute right thing."

"At least it's over." Dana looked at Evan over the top of Natalie's head. She didn't have the heart to contradict her right now. "But Sammy is *never* going to talk to me again."

"Oh, I bet she will. It may take a while, but she'll understand." Well, maybe not. Dana wondered how close Samantha was to her brother. "Go on to bed now. You need some sleep."

Natalie didn't wait for any further coaxing. It was after three in the morning. As soon as she left the room, Evan grabbed Dana's hand and pulled her to the couch. They plopped down together, thigh to thigh. There were things to discuss.

"Was that Indigo?" he asked.

"Yup."

"What's going on over there?"

"The boys came up with stories about the first boy accidentally slipping and falling, and self-defense against the boy with the bottle. I could have put the kibosh on the arrests until further investigation."

"You could have."

"Yup. I could have."

"But you didn't."

"Seems Natalie is the only solid witness. How would that look when it got out? The DA declines to arrest the alleged assailants because the only witness is her daughter."

"You've got me too. I'm a witness."

"But you didn't see the whole thing."

"Missed the moment of truth. I was slipping on ice myself."

"An accident."

"In my case."

"The suspects said that the injury to the first boy was an accident. What if Natalie's wrong?"

Evan thought for a moment. "She's the most integrous thirteen-year-old I've ever known."

"'Integrous' isn't a word."

"In Natalie's case it is. She saw what she saw, and she'll explain it when she's asked. You did the right thing tonight. Both of my ladies did the right thing."

"As did my man."

"The whole lot of us."

"And we'll let the grand jury decide."

"That's what they do."

"The grand jury—the DA's cop out."

"It's never a cop out to put a case before the grand jury. Never. That's New York procedural law."

Dana considered this. He was right, even if it didn't completely allay her anxiety. Nothing in this situation should be taken personally. "I made some decisions about the parents too."

"Uh-oh."

"I told the lieutenant to charge them with endangering and unlawful dealing. It's unfair to charge Emjay and not the parents. They're responsible."

"Knowledge, my love. You need evidence of mental state."

"Emjay says his parents let him invite friends over. They split for the weekend when there's a big dance at the high school and leave tons of booze in the game room, right where the kids are likely to play pool and darts. An attractive lure, entirely foreseeable."

"Excuse me while I get that half bottle of wine in the fridge and empty it down the drain." A grin tugged at the corners of his mouth. She couldn't help smiling. "*And*," he continued, "don't forget that other piece of evidence. Sandy Bohr's convenient omission when she called you. The accused misrepresented the circumstances to the DA."

"I should have asked. My fault. Anyway, I cut the parents somewhat of a break. The lieutenant was ready to arrest and book them. I told him to give them appearance tickets instead. They need to stay home with Samantha tonight."

"So glad to hear it."

They lapsed into silence. Dana's nerves electrified the air. She glanced here and there around the living room, dimly lit by the single table lamp she'd turned on. The room seemed entirely too organized and ordinary for the circumstances.

"There's one other thing. A very big thing." She turned to Evan and looked directly into his eyes. "Ginger." No visible reaction. He didn't know. She explained.

"Oh Lord." Evan turned his head up to the ceiling. "The part about controlled substances and intoxicated driving must be a mistake."

"I'm thinking the same thing. I told Indigo to go check it out."

Evan shook his head. "First Natalie, now Travis."

They sat in the semidarkness, not moving.

Only a few hours remained until morning.

Two children were in their rooms down the hallway, fast asleep. Two children who were loved more than anything in the world. Sweet dreams. They would need them, for tomorrow would bring…

"This is a nightmare," Dana said. She tipped her head to the side and rested it on her husband's shoulder.

16 » *FALLOUT*

TYNAN LOOKED UP at the door a second before it opened, his senses in perfect sync with the inevitable. In that moment, he panicked that his looks hadn't improved as much as he'd hoped because, goddamn, just as predicted, Vesma looked incredible when she walked through that door. She was no beauty, but her tough attractiveness had always been a turn on. Her hair was kind of wild, her coat unbuttoned on a glimpse of midnight blue material clinging to her body, her step a little wobbly in high heels, her face tired but relaxed, almost flushed, with a look he knew very well. Even though the stress of their situation tightened her features, he saw the clues of what she'd been up to when their little girl had been trying to call her from the accident scene.

He resisted thinking about it, even as he was drawn, at the same time, to images of her with another man. This was the woman he had won and lost, and it was as if she'd left him all over again. But something amazing had happened tonight to make up for it. Ginger had called him! Because of that, all the pain and bitterness between him and Vesma could be borne. He'd been resurrected by the child they'd made together.

Vesma sat down on the hard, plastic chair next to his, and Ty brought her up to the moment. "We sat here for half an hour twiddling our thumbs while those guys were having coffee and donuts I guess, and now she's in the back somewhere, being fingerprinted and processed."

"This can't be happening. Our baby arrested." Ty perked up at her use of the word "our." Even so, Vesma could have been reading a grocery list. She was a cool cookie, her eyes dry.

She turned to him with a direct gaze, and he was able to see more. The quiet panic, her guilt over abandoning Ginger for… He knew what for. Their eyes held in a mutual acknowledgment of the years gone by. Their past was now a distant mountain behind them, their future a vast plain of cracked and crumbling earth stretching out before them.

"Give me the details of the accident. Everything you know."

"As best I can," he said. And he related everything that Ginger had told him and everything he'd seen on that treacherous curve in the road.

"If I'd been home, none of this—"

"If. There's always if. She's big enough to know better. I wouldn't blame yourself."

Her eyebrows lifted at this, and he wondered if she doubted his right to give such advice, even if it was only a well-meaning attempt to comfort her. Or maybe she was thinking he had just uttered further proof of his inadequacy as a parent, an unwarranted trust in Ginger's maturity.

Ty hadn't quite figured out what might be in her look when it changed again, and she moved on to the next practical consideration. "The other two kids. Are they okay?"

"No one at the hospital would tell me anything."

"I suppose I should be more worried about them—and mad as hell about the car."

"But you're not."

"No, not yet. Not with all of *this* going on." Her eyes roamed the environs, landing here and there on a uniform, the desk sergeant behind safety glass, the air peppered with short blasts from a radio dispatcher. "Of all the kids in the world, they arrest

Gingie. This never would have happened even a few months ago. It's all Dana Hargrove's campaign to crack down on teenage drinking." As if to prove her theory, two more officers walked in, each one holding the elbow of a handcuffed teenage boy. "Look at that. Rounding 'em up."

"We can't really blame the DA for a program like that, can we?"

Again, she gave him a look that suggested her surprise at hearing such an opinion, coming from his mouth. In the next breath, she expressed some of her old skepticism: "You didn't fly off the handle, did you?"

"Me?" His smile was big enough to contain all the crazy pain and joy of this night. "Veshetska!" His eyes were moist. He couldn't hide it. She accepted his old nickname for her and regarded him in a way that said she understood how much this night meant to him and how hard he'd tried to do everything correctly.

If she suspected the angry edges, he couldn't blame her. He didn't regret his momentary rage when the officers rough-handed Ginger and made those ridiculous accusations. Now, as he stumbled through foggy memories of confrontations with armed men in uniforms, he wondered if he had a past with any of those four cops. He doubted it. They all looked so young. And he'd gotten them to listen when he demanded the blood tests—a major accomplishment.

But he doubted his ability to get anything else out of them on his own, no matter how much showmanship he might be able to muster. Vesma would do the rest. She was the real savior like she always had been, putting on her façade of authority with a rational, calm exterior under fire, the level head and articulate tongue, a woman who wore a steel breast plate against emotion, riding through it.

She had always made it to the other side, seemingly unscathed, while the demons were eating her alive inside. He knew her well. Still did.

"Damn!" she said, letting one of her shoes drop. She crossed her leg and massaged the foot. "I should have changed."

Another little reminder of the emotion under the surface. Too rattled to think about changing her clothes. He looked down at the curve of her instep and smiled. He didn't mind seeing her in those shoes. Didn't mind at all.

The rational half of Vesma's brain fully understood the reason behind the cardinal rule against self-representation: A lawyer who represents herself has a fool for a lawyer. The same holds true if the client is a close family member. Emotion and personal involvement interfere with reason and judgment. This case also presented a twist of professional ethics. As the owner of the automobile, she was a potential witness, not to mention a potential defendant in a civil lawsuit. If she'd been thinking clearly, she would have called an attorney for her daughter. Immediately.

But the circumstances worked against reason. Still dreamy from her Cinderella evening, Vesma came home to the shock of a lifetime, made worse by the surreal backdrop of a suburban police station in the dark, early morning. Sitting with her ex-husband so soon after intimacy with a new love, she was forced into an unwanted closeness as they agonized over the predicament of their tender, vulnerable teenage daughter. The arresting officer, Maria Rincón, allowed Vesma only a brief visit with Ginger, whose tear-filled kitten eyes evoked the most primal defensive impulse. The thought of Ginger spending a night in jail was intolerable, especially because (dare she think it) everything had been her own fault. She was stabbed with shame, remembering that moment, right before leaving the house, when Gingie rushed up for a hug and clung to her as if the world depended on it.

Vesma had cut that wonderful moment short with an urgent need to get away, to be with Hernando…

Rudely thrust onto this bizarre outer planet, Vesma did what came instinctively. Much later she would understand the biggest reason for her forgetfulness about cardinal rules. She couldn't call another lawyer until she came to terms with her own shame and humiliation. At the police station, these insecurities conveniently yielded to a more aggressive instinct to attack and fight.

If she'd rolled over and done nothing, her daughter would have been locked in a cell overnight until a bail hearing could be held at the local criminal court. From the moment Ty related the facts, Vesma's plan was to engineer Ginger's immediate release on a desk appearance ticket, setting a future court date. Luckily, "Officer Bottle" (true name Robert Whitehead) wasn't the "arresting officer" assigned to the case. Vesma needed only to convince Officer Rincón that Whitehead's zeal was unwarranted. They'd now seen Ginger under artificial lights for two hours and had a negative blood alcohol result from the supposedly more accurate breathalyzer in the station. Still, the intoxication charge could go forward, pending the results of Ginger's blood test for drugs, and the possession charge could stick, based on the pills found in the car. The last name on the prescription bottle was unknown, and the source of the pills had to be investigated. Vesma was convinced that, when all the facts were in, the only remaining charge would be unlicensed driving.

A fleeting thought: was she duping herself? Maybe this was an opportunity for tough love, a taste of hard reality. Punishment. Was the working mother out of touch with her daughter's world? The thought quickly vanished. Vesma had implicit faith in her daughter's character. That faith was enough, an instinctive knowledge of her right to act on it.

Vesma told Officers Rincón and Whitehead of her experience in the criminal justice system and pummeled them with logic and reason. The other girls were obviously intoxicated, not Ginger. Erratic behavior? She was very upset, that's all. Her story made sense. It was Becky's pint bottle and pill container that spilled out of her purse onto the floor of the passenger side of the car. Ginger was a member of SADD, a proven crusader against this kind of behavior. There would be witnesses to her character.

The officers stepped away from Vesma and conferred behind the desk. Body language: Whitehead was obstinate, Rincón was tenacious. The arresting officer broke away and walked over to Vesma and Ty.

"Okay" she said, pulling a ticket pad from her back pocket. "Let's get you out of here."

After that, Ty had a few more moments to relish. They walked out of the police station together like a family, daughter between them, father's arm around her shoulder, mother holding the girl's hand. Sixteen years ago, against the recommendation of the pediatrician, they kept her in the bed between them after Vesma nursed her in the middle of the night. A nightlight remained aglow near the baseboard next to the bed. In that orange-tinged obscurity, Ty would wake up, feel the warm bundle next to him, and remember where he was, who he was. A new father. He would stroke the soft hair and dewy forehead, inch down to push his nose into her cheek, feeling the tiny stream of moist air from her nostrils. He was sober and alive.

Vesma and Ginger were dependent on him again. They had no car. He was the man of the family. Approaching the parking lot, he barely noticed the activity around him, civilian and police vehicles, people getting in and out of their cars. A lot seemed to be happening tonight, but the only people who mattered to him were right here, by his side.

He drove his '95 Skylark slowly, carefully. The ice storm had stopped, and the roads were better, salted and sanded.

They were quiet, except Ginger in the back seat, who occasionally let out a sob with an apology, using her childhood names for them. "I'm sorry, Mommy. I'm sorry, Daddy."

"It's been a long night," said Vesma. "We'll talk in the morning."

"I'm sorry. Thank you for getting me out."

"You're welcome. We'll talk later."

That was also Vesma. When it wasn't business, when it was life or love, she could sit on it and let it brew and bubble. She would live through the bad times until she couldn't bear it anymore, and then you were thrown out on your butt—and rightfully so, but it was a shock because she'd been so good at holding everything in.

He wiped the thought from his mind. For now, for twenty minutes, they were a family, all very tired, driving home in the wee hours when they should be asleep. There was sadness and remorse in the air, but the silence was not awkward or stressed. There was familiarity and comfort in their mutual company, a vision of how things could have been.

When he stopped in the driveway, the dream ended and a new one began.

Vesma opened the door, enough to make the dome light come on, and she turned to him, looking directly into his eyes. The dimness washed the years from her face and she was twenty-six again, the first day they met. When she spoke, he knew the illusion was faulty, that they would never erase the years, but the good was there, along with the bad. They would accept the lessons and move forward. "Thank you, Ty." Warm and genuine. She placed a hand on his shoulder, and when she lifted it, they had crossed a barrier.

"My pleasure." Their eyes remained locked a moment longer before Vesma moved for the door and Ty came to his senses.

"Gingie." He swiveled around in his seat, suddenly fearful that all the gains of this night would be lost.

His daughter leaned forward over the seatback and threw her arms around his neck. "Thank you so, so much, Daddy." She rasped intensely into the collar of his jacket.

"Gingie, if you want...," he said as she slid along the seat toward the door, "call me tomorrow, or anytime you feel like it."

She looked back one last time and said, "Okay, Daddy. I will."

And he believed she would.

Vesma didn't think that Ty or Ginger had seen him getting out of his car in the parking lot of the police station. Didn't see Vesma make eye contact with him and the exchange of silent questions. If they'd noticed, they would have said something. They both knew Hernando.

On the ride home, her mind was again preoccupied with images of him, when she should have been thinking only of Ginger. She'd already thought of him once during the hours at the police station, when she was considering who she should hire. Only two names came to mind, the best criminal defense lawyers she knew, Hernando Ramirez and Wendel Bridges. Maybe a third, Frederick Carlyle, but he was a big gun and currently on trial in the Perry Rigger murder case. She fantasized for all of one minute about her daughter standing at the defense table in court next to her new lover and instantly rejected the idea of hiring him. Bridges would be the one to call, but she'd have to wait until later in the day. Four thirty on a Sunday morning was an ungodly hour, and there was no immediate rush. Ginger did not have to appear in court until Thursday.

So, there was nothing to stop her from calling Nando at the first opportunity, was there? As soon as Ginger went off to sleep,

Vesma grabbed her cell phone, closed herself in her room, kicked off the shoes (finally!), and fell onto her bed. Would his business at the station be finished? Probably not. She could guess why he was there. Every defense attorney got calls in the middle of the night from potential clients who'd been arrested, and she was curious about his new case. She relaxed back into the pillows and made the call.

"Hello, Vesma," he said in a professional tone. She was no longer *mi amor*. Any lingering afterglow of their evening together had vanished. "I'm still at the police station. I'll call you the minute I get home."

Nothing to do but wait. After ending the call, she became aware of her physical discomfort, her jazzed sleeplessness. Except for the short "nap" at Hernando's apartment, she'd been awake almost twenty-four hours, was still running on adrenaline, and was still wearing this goddamn tight dress. She went to the closet and undressed slowly, changing into loose-fitting pajamas.

Between the two of them, her business at the police station was the more mysterious. Hernando might be wondering why Vesma was in a cozy threesome with her ex-husband and daughter so soon after their lovemaking. Or, maybe he'd jumped to his own conclusions.

When the phone rang, she was lying on the bed, wide-eyed, her heart thumping with thoughts of all the many things she had to do to help Ginger. To help herself.

"Were you asleep?" His tone had softened.

"Wide awake. Will we ever get any sleep? It was lovely seeing you again so soon!" She laughed, but the attempt at lightheartedness fell flat.

"Did your husband say anything to you?"

"Ex."

"Ex-husband."

"No. I don't think he saw you."

"Tell me what's going on." There was genuine concern in his voice.

She stumbled on a few words, aware, suddenly, that she feared his reaction. She erased that thought. This was a man who daily represented people accused of crime and never mistook the accusation for the person he was representing. She launched into the story, trying to control the unexpected tremor that took hold of her voice.

"Thank God Ginger is all right."

"Yes, thank God."

"And you can be proud of how you handled it."

She considered his words, finding no truth in them. "How can I be proud of any of this?"

"You convinced the officer to release her. That was no small task."

"Maybe. But I'm thinking of the bigger picture, how we even got to this point—"

"You're thinking that you should have been home last night. Is that it?"

She responded with a deep intake and noisy release of breath, nothing more. He didn't need to answer his own question. Merely posing it was an admission of involvement, the undefined extent of his responsibility. She wondered if he resented being drawn into this, no matter how unintentionally.

But his next question conveyed the opposite sentiment. "How can I help you with this?"

"Nando, I'm sorry, but—"

"May I give you my opinion? You shouldn't represent her. You're too close to it."

"I know. I'm not planning to. At first, I was thinking of asking you..."

"To represent Ginger?" He paused long enough to make her wonder if she'd insulted him. Was this whole mess just too much to ask of anyone so soon after beginning a new relationship? He was wondering how he could have made such a mistake, getting involved with an older woman who had a past and carried around extra baggage, a troubled teen.

But his silence meant something else. He was weighing the risks. "I can't possibly represent her. I'm also too close to this. There could be questions."

Of course. She saw it now. If she was sued, there'd be questions about her responsibility for Ginger's actions. *Where were you when the child took the car without permission?* Even Nando was a potential witness.

"You're right," she said. "I'm going to call Wendel Bridges."

"He's a good choice. I don't want to give Ginger any legal advice, and I don't want her to think of me only as a lawyer. I want our relationship to be something else."

His declaration went so far beyond what she could have imagined that, this time, her intake of breath was a gasp of love.

"I want to get to know her," he added, "and I want her to like me."

"Oh, she will! How could she not? When this is all over we'll arrange something, we'll have dinner together, or—"

"I want to know her because she's a part of you."

With that, the pooled tears streamed down her cheeks. "What…what can I say, Hernando?" She wasn't any good at this. She hadn't let her guard down in such a long time.

There was another brief silence, one he was obliged to break. "We need to talk about another thing…"

"The reason you were at the police station? I'm sorry. I've been talking only about myself."

"It's okay. Now that you've told me about Ginger, I have to rethink this. I wanted to refer a case to you. A couple of clients came my way from that party on Foxglove where Ginger picked up her passengers. The homeowners and their son have been charged. I was going to keep the son and give you the parents, or vice versa. It would be a conflict to represent all of them."

"No need for three lawyers?"

"I don't think so. The parents are a united front. They can have a single lawyer."

"Well, it's nice of you to think of me, but…"

"I know. You're out of the criminal defense business, even though you just accepted that criminal appeal."

"That's different."

"Oh yeah, I forgot, that's completely different," he teased.

"So, you don't believe me." She smiled. The easy way he had about him was beginning to cheer her up. "Not much different, I admit. I just need the money."

"That's why I thought of you for this new case. These people have mega bucks."

"Who referred you? Or maybe you know them?"

He hesitated, clueing her in that he had his own secret. "The father, Michael Bohr Sr., is a plastic surgeon. My ex-girlfriend—"

"Good. Now we can talk about *your* ex—"

"Dr. Bohr was her surgeon a couple of years ago. I spoke with him in the recovery room about her post-operative care. Somehow, we ended up talking about our respective careers. He remembered me from that."

"Elective surgery? How nice of you to help your girlfriend."

"There's nothing to read into this, *mi amor*. My ex was a woman of low self-esteem who failed to see how fantastic she looked just the way she was—"

"Sorry, I wasn't implying…" She apologized even as she wondered about the "fantastic" looking ex. "Anyway, how did everything turn out?"

"Doctor Bohr did a professional job, thank you, but my ex is a woman I no longer care to think about. To get to the point, the doctor called me at about three thirty and asked me to meet him at the police station. His son, Michael Jr., was arrested and being processed. The parents were given appearance tickets for this coming Thursday."

The same date as Ginger's court appearance. "Thursday's going to be a busy day. What are the charges?"

"Michael Jr.—they call him Emjay—was involved in a fight. He's charged with assault two, along with another boy, Brent Tremont. This is interesting. The alleged victim is the boyfriend of one of those girls arrested for cyberbullying the other day. Did you hear about that case?"

"I did indeed."

"The other misdemeanor charges have to do with alcohol. Kids at the party got into the liquor supplies, and all three of the Bohrs are being held responsible."

Dana Hargrove on the warpath. Why did this bother her? She should let it go. Her past with Dana was the past, and Ty, of all people, agreed with the DA's zero tolerance policy. Vesma's main concern should be to protect Ginger and herself. "Let's say, for argument's sake, I was in the business of criminal defense..."

"Okay."

"I shouldn't represent any of them anyway. Potential conflicts. Ginger was at their house and saw what was going on. She could be a witness against any of them."

"So, I guess that seals it. I can't give you the case, big bucks or not. I know what I'll do. I'll keep the parents and recommend Thalia Derrick for Emjay's case. You know her?"

"Yes."

"This case is right up her alley. She'll pick it up and meet the kid in court. I'm too tired to do an arraignment and bail app today."

"I know what you mean!" She smiled again and felt that he was smiling too. Some of the magic they'd shared in the night came rushing back.

They chatted a while longer and said "good night" before changing it to "good morning." It was nearly six o'clock, but still dark.

Vesma slept for a couple of hours and then got busy making calls while Ginger was still sleeping. A red light on the house phone indicated new voicemails, but she ignored it, for now. First, she needed to call Bridges. She gave him the facts, and they agreed to meet in his office on Tuesday. Next, she arranged to have the Volvo towed to a body shop. Then, she called the hospital. She was concerned about Becky and Amanda and wasn't going to avoid them out of fear of a lawsuit. If anything, a show of concern might help. But the hospital stonewalled her, claiming that the patients couldn't be identified with the information Vesma gave them. Ginger hadn't been able to give her the girls' last names. Maybe one of them would be identified by her incoming call to the Call Central phone.

Ginger had left the aqua blue Gravity on the hall table. In another small victory from last night, Vesma had convinced the police to return it. They were going to keep it for evidence, even though they found no incoming or outgoing calls for twenty minutes before Ginger called 911. The accident couldn't be blamed on cell phone distraction.

That small rectangle of plastic looked strangely cheerful, new and shiny. Unlit. Officer Rincón had turned it off after checking the call log, and no one had thought to turn it on again. Vesma pressed the power button and the phone jumped to life. Multiple alerts. Calls from Dylan Radner and Travis Goodhue at various times during the night, up until about three. She should wake Ginger up and tell her to call these boys now.

But the doorbell rang. "Hi. I'm Dylan Radner," said the young man at the door.

"Come in, please." He stepped into the small foyer and she closed the door. "Ginger is sleeping. I'm so sorry she didn't call you, but it's been quite a night."

"Yeah, everyone was worried. I kept trying to call. I was going to tell her I'd pick up the phone today because the roads were getting too bad, but I couldn't get in touch."

"She was in an accident."

"I know. Travis found out from his mom, and he called me just a little while ago."

Yet another reminder of Dana. For all Vesma knew, the DA might have authorized Ginger's arrest. "Dylan, would you let me hold onto this phone a bit longer? I was going to look through the call log to see if there's any information that could help us."

"Sure, no problem. Call Central is on hold, at least for today."

"I'll bring it back to you. Actually, I can't. I don't have a car."

"That's not a problem. I'll pick it up when you're ready. My number is in the contacts."

"Thank you."

She opened the door for him, and he was about to step out when he turned and looked at her. Dylan had a dark intensity about him that perfectly illustrated his commitment to the cause. "We were kind of surprised by what Ginger did," he said.

"Weren't we all."

"But SADD is going to support her. One hundred percent."

Vesma thanked him, and he turned to go. Just then, the house phone started ringing. In the living room, she picked up the receiver and looked at the display. Boy Number Two was calling. Travis Goodhue.

Mom was letting her sleep late, not knowing that she'd slept for only a few hours and was pretending the rest of the time. She laid in bed immobile, making no sound, becoming even quieter than silent, trying not to breathe when she heard Dylan in the front hallway. Then she heard the house phone ringing, but Mom didn't answer it.

She should have called Dylan and Travis last night, but she was overwhelmed by humiliation. The terror of the accident and the arrest made her forget about the Gravity until Officer Rincón questioned her about it. When the officer turned the phone off and gave it back to her, she didn't turn it back on again. She didn't want to see what she knew would be there.

She'd screwed up so badly. What could she possibly say to them?

After Mom said goodbye to Dylan, she waited another long while. Why hadn't Mom come to knock on her door? Maybe she was hiding too. Maybe she thought she had things to explain.

Ginger couldn't stay in her room forever. She went to the kitchen. Mom was sitting at the table with a cup of coffee. She glanced up but didn't really let her eyes stay for long. The coffee cup was more interesting. "Sit down, Ginger. Did you get some sleep?"

"Yeah. Some." She took a seat on the other side of the table.

"Do you want something to eat?"

Ginger shook her head.

Mom didn't press food on her but started to talk about the lawyer she'd hired and what might happen in court on Thursday. Legal things that kind of floated into Ginger's ears and fell into a crack in her mind. Mom didn't once ask why Ginger had taken the car, why she'd thought any such thing was remotely rational, and Ginger didn't ask Mom what she'd been doing last night that made her unavailable for an emergency call from her daughter. They were even, kind of, in a way, but not completely. Mom was still ahead. She asked her to do some unpleasant things, like find out Amanda's and Becky's last names and home phone numbers. She was thinking of calling the girls or their parents to see how they were and to apologize, but first she was going to ask the new lawyer what he thought.

"Before you do that, you owe Dylan and Travis return calls. They already know what happened last night. Travis's mom told them."

"Okay, I'll do that." Ginger took the cordless receiver of the home phone into her bedroom. No way did she want to touch the Gravity. Travis would be first. Somehow, he was easier. Dylan almost felt like a parent at this moment, the person she had to answer to.

She sat on the floor propped against her bed, phone in hand. How different everything was from last night, daydreaming in the mellow glow of flickering candlelight, feeling ticklish butterflies as she wrote poetry about Travis. She was safe and sheltered then, with good things to look forward to, when she still had the chance to be smart enough to avoid the biggest mistake of her life.

She started to cry, big choking sobs, and cried uncontrollably for a good ten minutes. Then she blew her nose and got up the nerve to call.

Travis said he was feeling better, and he'd been dying to talk to her. "I called you like about a hundred times," he admitted.

She told Travis the reasons she took Mom's car. He was as angry as he could get for a person who never got angry, his voice like an impossible scream because he had maybe never screamed in his life, and his throat was still sore. It came out more like a crippled yelp. "Why didn't you call me first?"

It seemed, especially now, that he always did everything correctly and always behaved perfectly in every situation, and never, ever could anything that he did be described as "wrong." She couldn't stand his disappointment in her. He was right and she was wrong, but he was also sad and frustrated by regret, not critical of her. If anyone could forgive her, it might be Travis.

The tears started to spill again as she tried to explain the rest of it. The words twisted her tongue into a big, choking blob, and when her mouth unscrambled, and the story tumbled out, it was a mixed-up mess of fact and admission.

When she had finished, he said, "I still can't believe they arrested you. Were you scared?"

"It was so, so scary."

He became quiet. If he had been with her at that moment, she believed he might have put his arms around her. She could bury her head in his chest, and they could be quiet together, breathing the pain in and out, no need to talk anymore. But over the phone, the silence had no face or heartbeat.

She waited, looking down at the floor with an elbow on her knee and the fist pushed into her forehead. He was not the kind of person to talk about problems as a way of figuring them out. He was the kind of person to think about them first.

Finally, he said he wanted to see her, but he couldn't today. His parents wanted him to have complete rest so he could return to school on Tuesday, after the three-day weekend. "I wish I could be with you," he said, making her chest rise and fall in one slow heavenly release. There was nothing secret held back in his voice, nothing underneath the words.

When they hung up, she was feeling a little bit reassured. But right then, she couldn't face going through another conversation like this, couldn't face calling Dylan just yet or finding numbers for Amanda and Becky. She called her daddy instead, because he was the one person she didn't need to explain anything to.

17 »   *STRATEGY*

PRESIDENTS' DAY, AND the lawyers were hard at work. Vesma was in her office trying to concentrate, despite her curiosity about what was going on in Hernando's office. Dr. and Mrs. Bohr had come calling. Emjay had stayed home, licking his wounds after being bailed out on Sunday. Emjay's friend, Brent, had also made bail.

Vesma avoided bumping into the Bohrs in the hallway of their suite of offices. She was dying to be included, but it wasn't proper. Later, over lunch with Nando, they'd talk about the case, and then she'd leave work early, to spend time with Ginger. The girl was at home, working on a term paper. Vesma hoped. It was heartbreaking, seeing Ginger so despondent, but it wouldn't help matters to hover. The prescription: a full morning apart, followed by an afternoon of quality mother-daughter time, no judgment on either side. Where were you? Why did you do that? They wouldn't ask these questions. They were past the why of it and were solidly in the present, cleaning up the aftermath.

Ginger wouldn't be tempted by any moving wheels—the Volvo was still in the shop! A bad joke. Vesma had taken public transportation to work. She was reminded that Andris called last week and mentioned that Ginger had taken the bus to Pa's house. A surprise, but Vesma hadn't let on to Ginger that she knew. It was a secret of some sort and...what? An expression of loneliness?

A silent rebuke? She made a vow to follow her daughter's example and spend some time with Pa. The past was the past. Maybe, if things went well with Nando, Pa would like him better than Tynan. Twenty years ago, Pa's refusal to acknowledge Ty's good qualities, at a time when alcoholism hadn't yet obliterated them, turned out to be prescient, but for the wrong reason. She couldn't fault her father for trying to warn her.

The one bit of good news this morning was that Becky and Amanda were fine. Vesma had called their parents and extended her apologies—not a guarantee against a lawsuit, but she was keeping her fingers crossed. The hospital had kept Amanda only a few hours. Becky had stayed more than a day, not for the minor bump on her head. Ginger hadn't been driving very fast. Becky had to detox from drunkenness and a double hit of Percocet. The name on the prescription bottle was still under investigation.

Vesma had planned to spend the full morning on Yusuf Nashid's case, but she pushed it aside in favor of work on her new case, the criminal appeal. Every defense tactic for Nashid seemed hopeless, every argument contrived and silly. Judge Tenzler had already lambasted her, and even Hernando thought the case was a loser, suggesting that her main concern should be to collect her legal fees. Cut and run. Still, she had a duty to make the best possible argument for her client, so he could keep at least part of the settlement money from the medical malpractice case.

One of her strategies now seemed completely hopeless. She'd planned to argue that Yusuf was just as much a "victim" as the plaintiff because he'd sustained injuries in defending himself against his brother's use of a knife. Vesma looked back and understood that the defense had been her idea, and she'd done everything but put the words into Yusuf's mouth. If they pursued this strategy, they'd have to file a motion in criminal court to vacate his guilty plea on the ground of newly discovered evidence—the pocketknife. She'd already drafted the papers but hadn't filed them because she had serious doubts. The motion shouldn't be filed unless Yusuf fully understood the consequences and still agreed to the tactic.

Vesma called Green Haven to leave a message for her client. When he called back, he asked, "Did something happen on my case?"

"We go to court on Thursday. I'm preparing the papers. Do you remember we talked about the motion to set aside your guilty plea?"

"Yes, as a way to keep the money, if we can."

"That's part of it."

"What's the other part?"

"If you succeed in vacating your guilty plea, we'll have to go back to court on the criminal case. I just want to make that clear."

"Why will we do that? The case is over. I have seven years left to serve."

"If the guilty plea goes away, you're no longer convicted of manslaughter and the case starts all over again, on the murder charge. You testified at your deposition that you were not guilty of murder because your brother came at you with a knife."

"I said not guilty of murder because I pled guilty to manslaughter, isn't that so?"

"Correct."

"I was given sixteen years instead of twenty-five or more. I will not go back to criminal court on this."

"If you truly acted in self-defense, you should think about this carefully."

"'Self-defense' was your word, Ms. Krumins, the minute I said that my brother carried a pocketknife. I was justified because he dishonored my family. He had a knife, but mine was bigger, and I killed him. Sixteen years for his life. A justified killing. I should not be punished at all, but the legal system doesn't see it that way. I will not go back and have this changed to twenty-five years or more in prison."

The man was playing with words more deftly than any attorney could. Under the law, "justification" and "self-defense" were two ways of describing the same defense. Did he understand this? It didn't matter to Vesma. She was more than willing to give up the fight when he made this final, emphatic point: "You are *not* to make any motion to upset my guilty plea."

One thing Hernando had always wondered: how such a large man could perform delicate, intricate surgery with those stevedore hands. Dr. Bohr was at least six-two and powerfully built from weightlifting at the gym. He remained cool and controlled next to his blistering wife, former Broadway star Sandra Steele. Sandy was petite, almost a foot shorter than her husband, with freshly dyed, champagne-blonde hair.

"Let's get down to business," Hernando said. "I want to give you an idea of what you're up against with these criminal charges, so we can plot the defense strategy."

"Criminal defense!" Sandy exclaimed. "I love this. We're criminals, Michael."

The doctor did not seem to be enjoying his wife's company today. "Who did you think they were, those men in uniforms with guns? Jehovah's Witnesses?" Cool sarcasm.

Hernando, with his usual finesse, quickly smoothed things over. "It was the DA who decided this was criminal. She might set the policy, but we'll give her a run for her money." He always stopped short of promising absolute success to his clients. Anything was possible in criminal court.

Hernando's charm and good looks must have impressed Sandy, who arched her back and leveled her gaze. "District Attorney Dana!" she said, affecting a bit of the coquette. "God knows I didn't vote for her!"

The husband kept quiet and fumed. Perhaps he'd voted for Dana Hargrove. Perhaps he'd liked her campaign promise to combat crimes related to alcohol and substance abuse. He crossed his arms on his chest and shook his head with his eyes closed, shutting out his wife or the DA or the world or his son or himself. One of the above was to blame.

Sitting this close to the Bohrs, across the desk from them, Hernando could detect the strain and years in their faces. Sandy was a woman in her early fifties, doing her best to look thirty-five, but the red in her tired eyes and the venom in her voice weren't helping. Dr. Bohr's face was pitted with acne scars, a rugged look, an incongruous rejection of plastic surgery for himself. Their investments in gym workouts and alien tanned skin in the dead of winter took them only so far. There were deep crow's feet cut into the corners of Sandy's eyes, a receding "W" hairline marking the top of the doctor's head, and purple shadows underneath both sets of eyes from their recent sleepless nights. And something else. They exuded a faint odor from their well-scrubbed skin, a familiar scent that Hernando often detected in the presence of his clients—the eau de cologne of fear.

"Actually, Sandy," said Hernando, "you hit on a possible defense tactic. We could argue that this is *not* a criminal matter. It's a political stunt. Is she going to arrest every parent of a teenager who has alcohol in the house? Or did she pick you as the scapegoats?"

"I can imagine how stressful her job must be," Sandy said in a phony voice. "I'll bet Mizz DA has a bottle or two in her own house!"

"Exactly. If you want, we can make this into a media case. We have a choice: either lay low and 'no comment' everything or send the story out the way you want it. Stir up some public support and apply pressure on the DA. Of course, if we go this route, I wouldn't want you to talk to the press. Anything you say can be twisted and used against you in court. I would do all the talking, but I can spin it so that your rights aren't compromised."

They considered this for a moment before simultaneously blurting: "I say, go for it!" and "Not on your life!"

Dr. Bohr was the naysayer. Hernando's proposal seemed to turn a key in him. He opened his eyes wide and boomed, "I'm *not* authorizing *any* statements to the press!" His dormant power had surfaced.

Nando flat-palmed it, pushing at the air between them and shaking his head. "Not a problem at all."

"Reporters twist things worse than any DA could. And they'll have plenty of fuel with these assault charges against Emjay."

"Those are valid concerns."

"I thought a little public pressure might help," Sandy whimpered in a more conciliatory tone. "This is such a mess. It was supposed to be a perfect night, a perfect weekend! I didn't even care that Sammy invited the DA's very own daughter to our house. What harm could there be in a sleepover, I thought? I talked to that woman and told her it was *fine*. What a mistake! Little did I know—"

"Did you tell 'that woman' we'd be out?" the doctor asked. "You didn't mention anything to *me* about the sleepover. I can't imagine the Westchester County DA would want to send her daughter overnight to a house with only a couple of teens and no adults. She's in the public eye."

"Well, she never asked me."

"You should have told her."

"Do you know how strange it is to talk to a public official about a sleepover? I didn't feel like saying much of anything."

Dr. Bohr shook his head. "We never should have gone to that reunion. Emjay was at the dance, and we knew he was going to hang out with his friends afterward, and you allowed Sammy to have a friend over… We were ignoring the kids."

"No, Michael. They aren't kids, they're practically adults. The only thing I did wrong was not telling that Hargrove woman 'no.' We couldn't possibly miss the reunion. *Everyone* was there, the entire original cast. Can you imagine?" She gave Hernando a direct look. "It's been three decades since *A Chorus Line* opened! It was my big break into the business. I hadn't seen some of those people in years! We couldn't miss it, we just couldn't."

"*You* couldn't," her husband said.

"Don't you dare! Don't pretend it was all me! I saw you having the time of your life, singing 'Dance: Ten; Looks: Three'! Bellowing 'tits and ass' right along with everyone else!"

Nando leaned forward and coughed into his hand to cover a smile.

"Well, look where it got us." Dr. Bohr turned to Hernando. "Don't say a word to the press. It'll blow over. People have short memories. It will be forgotten! Especially when we're exonerated. You have to get us out of this, Hernando. I can't have any kind of conviction on my record, even a misdemeanor. It will hurt my practice and my standing with the AMA."

Hernando sensed the need to exert a calming influence, a return to rationality with a bit of legalese, something devoid of emotion. "As I see it, the DA has two problems with this case. First, we have a good argument to suppress the physical evidence. If you didn't allow Emjay to drink the liquor in your house, then he wasn't authorized to consent to a search of the area where you stored it. Second, the biggest challenge for the DA is proving *mens rea*. The circumstantial evidence has to show that you knowingly endangered the kids. *Knowingly*. They can't prove this mindset if you told the children to stay away from the liquor in the house, or alcohol in general. Anything you said to the kids along those lines would be admissible as *res gestae*. Is there any evidence like that we can use?" He didn't know how to give them a bigger hint.

Sandy looked indignant. "Well, *of course* we told Emjay and Sammy they could never touch the liquor, didn't we, Michael?"

"We sure did." He looked less than positive.

"We wouldn't be in this predicament if it wasn't for that Yarnell kid and his friend, those, those...," Sandy struggled to find the right word.

"Punks," suggested the doctor.

"Thank you, dear." She smiled at her husband and patted his arm, almost grateful that he'd put her in her place a moment ago. "Those punks showed up at our house very uninvited! They don't even run with Emjay's crowd! Crashed the party, stinking drunk, and God knows what else in their systems! Julian was in a rage about the arrest of his no-good girlfriend, the cyberbully! Those punks were the ones who started it, you can be sure of it."

Yes, well, now those punks were in the hospital, thought Hernando. Julian in a coma. Keith recovering from near life-threatening wounds. Things didn't look good for Emjay, based on the statement of an unnamed witness in the police report. Everyone knew the witness was the DA's daughter, Natalie Goodhue. On top of this, there were a few things Sandy wasn't mentioning about her own legal troubles, like the drunk girl passed out in the powder room and the empty liquor bottles strewn around the game room.

"Emjay's attorney will get the toxicology results on Yarnell and Westerman," Hernando said. "Their blood is going to show extreme intoxication, and that should help your son's case." But not the parents' case, he was thinking, unless those boys were drunk *before* they got to the Bohrs' house. That part of it depended on witness testimony.

"Emjay was just defending himself. There's no question about that." Sandy pitched forward in her chair. "When the DA's husband came, Emjay stood his ground and didn't run. Why would he stick around if he had something to hide?"

Maybe because he lived there? Hernando thought. To the mother, this was proof of her son's innocence, while the father just shook his head and retreated into his shell, seething and dazed. Emjay's prospects for a Division I college, a sports scholarship, and NFL recruiters, had all gone down the drain in one crazed, unreal night.

"That's for Thalia Derrick to sort out," said Hernando. "She's the best attorney around for this kind of case. Your son is in good hands."

"Poor baby! He was scared out of his wits being arrested like that! This is so wrong."

"A justification defense is top of the list for him. Assailed by drunken party crashers. But you're not charged with assault, so let's concentrate on *you* for now." He grabbed his Penal Law and flipped to a page he'd bookmarked. "Here's the first charge. Endangering the welfare of a child under the age of seventeen. You commit this crime if you knowingly 'direct or authorize' a child to engage in an activity involving 'a substantial risk of danger to life or health.'"

"Guilty as charged! I admit, we allowed Emjay to play football." Sandy winked. "How many times did I tell him to go out for drama instead?"

"Very funny," Dr. Bohr said under his breath.

"As I said, your mental state will be hard to prove." Hernando flipped to another page. "You're also charged with unlawful dealing with a child. There's a complete defense to this if you successfully complete a program in alcohol awareness training. Are you willing to do that?"

"With my professional credentials?" The doctor looked incredulous. "I need alcohol awareness training?"

"It *is* a complete defense."

"I suppose we'd consider it, but why do we need it if we didn't commit the offense?"

"The DA has a slim chance; it's a tough hurdle. The offense is committed only if you 'give or sell or cause to be given or sold' alcohol to a minor."

"Like I opened the bottles and passed them around. Here you go! Have another!" Sandy shook her head.

"Right. We'll argue that you didn't 'cause' liquor to be served just because it was in the house. I don't know of any other case in New York that's been prosecuted on a theory like this."

"So, we're a test case, is that it?" the doctor asked. "Does the physical evidence help them? When do we see the list of the items the police took?"

"Usually we serve a written demand, but the assistant DA on this case, Linda Marquette, is sending the list today. You can thank DA Hargrove for this policy. She believes in open book discovery to the extent of the law. She's not into obstructing the defense from investigating or preparing for trial."

"I suppose they took some empty bottles. Is that the crux of their case?"

"A big part of it," Hernando said. And lack of parental supervision, he could have added, but the thought was already on everyone's mind. The doctor himself had admitted that they knew of Emjay's plans to "hang out" with friends after the dance.

"Those bottles could have been empty before the kids even got there," Sandy said. "Blaming *us*, when they have *no* idea what went on in the house!" Her anger was back in full bloom. She looked at Hernando. "You have kids, don't you?"

"I haven't been so blessed."

She shot out of her chair, stepped away and whirled around, clutching her elbows across her abdomen. "Do you have *any* idea what we went through? Getting a call from the police at two in the morning? 'We're taking your son in!' My heart's *banging* in my breast!" She arched her back and pounded with a fist to illustrate. "Minutes to decide if we risk our necks driving home in an ice storm or dash for the last train. The dream weekend is *ruined*. Sunday brunch is *canceled*. I'm pleading with the police to leave my son *alone* until we get home. They couldn't care less about Samantha. Can you imagine what *she* went through? Cops all over the house, arresting her brother, searching, rifling through our underwear drawers for all I know. Can it possibly get *any* worse?"

She was staring at Hernando, challenging him, but he didn't have to answer her "question." She didn't skip a beat.

"You bet it can! At the train station a pair of cops push us into a squad car. When we get home, there's blood and glass on the front steps, stale alcohol smell and vomit from party crashers in the house. Emjay's handcuffed like a thug, and Sammy's crying her eyes out! I'm thinking it can't get any worse, and then a cop pulls out a fat ticket book. 'We're charging you with hosting an underage drinking party! You're just lucky the DA told us not to arrest you!' *Lucky*, he says!"

With a huge, sucking breath, the tirade ended in a torrential flood of theatrical tears.

"Thanks for coming in on your day off," Dana said.

"What else are we good for?" Indigo intoned. "I live for this place."

"Ditto," Linda added.

"I'd be here anyway, working on Rigger," Ted remarked.

"Proving once again that I hire only the best." High caliber workaholics, all of them. "I need your input on the quote-unquote St. Valentine's Day Nightmare. The events of the weekend have thrown us into crisis mode."

They sat around Dana's corner table, picture windows framing them on either side. Oddly, for the first time in a week, the sky was a cloudless, brilliant blue. In the east, a small white ball, the size and sheen of a hard candy, peeked between two buildings. A thaw was predicted. Inside the district attorney's office, it was more like an inferno. Just six weeks into her new administration, Dana was feeling the fire. The press was in scandal heaven. So many arrests with interesting angles to choose from. And the commentators knew how to hit a nerve.

"You might remember the op-ed piece in the County News last week about the Steuben case. The editor implied that I wouldn't arrest the cyberbullies because I didn't want to tarnish the reputation of the school district. I called the editor and demanded that she never, ever print the names of my children again."

"So far, she's complied…in a way," Ted ventured.

"Skating the line," Dana said. "No names but plenty of references to the 'DA's husband' and 'daughter.' Even the 'DA's son' was mentioned as a participant in Call Central. The press had plenty of sources for this information."

"I have proof it wasn't me," Indigo said with a wink. "No one's calling it the St. Valentine's Day Massacre."

Dana smiled and said, "You can use that one in your memoirs." No way was she accusing her trusted, inner circle of talking to the press. She'd called them here for another reason. "So," she said. "You tell me. Am I too close to this? Should a special prosecutor be appointed for any of these cases? We've got seven defendants to think about. Taylor Sloane, Chloe Dyckman, Michael Bohr Jr., Brent Tremont, Michael Bohr Sr., Sandy Bohr, and Ginger Kavanagh. Did I forget anyone?" She rolled her eyes.

"Sloane and Dyckman are off the list," Linda said. "You have no conflict of interest. Your family has nothing to do with that case."

Ted and Indigo agreed. Linda took the opportunity to give an update. The DA's tech wizard, Bytes, would soon have a full report on the content of Taylor's and Chloe's cell phones. AT&T was still stonewalling Linda on her subpoena, but it no longer mattered. Bytes had found dozens of text messages stored on the defendants' phones.

"Okay, let me know as soon as you have his report. Another thing, about this afternoon…" Dana and Linda exchanged a meaningful look.

"I'm less visible, Dana. I should go."

"I disagree. Stay here and work on the case. I'm not hiding from this. I'll attend the funeral. The media is already going to be there, and if anything, my presence might distract them from the family. The Steubens should be given room to grieve."

There was a moment of silence before she went on. "Okay, let's start with Ginger Kavanagh. I've assigned that case to ADA Charlie Walsh in the Local Criminal Courts Bureau. The charges are unlicensed driving, intoxicated driving, open container of alcohol in the car, and criminal possession of a controlled substance." Dana reviewed the evidence and her son's involvement, including his phone calls to Ginger that night, both before and after the accident. No one at the table could think of any conflict of interest that Dana might have. "Travis isn't a witness to any material facts," Linda said.

"But he *does* have a huge crush on Ginger," Dana said, "as long as I'm being meticulously honest."

"Well, that's a different story." A tiny smile twisted Ted's lips.

"Poor baby," Indigo moaned.

"I can see the headline now," Linda said. "DA's son goes steady with jailbird."

Indigo clenched a fist at Linda. "Run to the tabloids with this and you'll regret it."

Everyone laughed. Dana added, "Seriously, if he knew I told you about that…"

"No worries, little mama." Indigo reached over and patted her forearm.

"What's the status on the pills, Indigo?"

"Becky says she got the pills from her boyfriend 'Speed,' true name Keith Westerman. He was the kid who got slashed with his own broken bottle in the fight on the front steps. He's still in the hospital with deep cuts down the side of his face and neck, just missed the jugular, lost tons of blood, shards of glass embedded in the wounds." Indigo and the rest of the team shuddered. "As soon as he's fit, we're going to question him. He had a bottle of pills on him too, and we think he's a grunt in a prescription pill ring that's working the high school. Narcotics has tips from a few doctors about stolen prescription pads, and one of the doctors was on these pill bottles."

"Let's hope this pans out," Dana said. Wouldn't that be a fortunate outcome for the St. Valentine's Day Nightmare? Busting a drug ring. "On to the next cases. All four of the defendants are Linda's."

"Thanks so much," Linda said dryly.

"Dr. and Mrs. Bohr are charged with misdemeanors and will be appearing in the town justice court on Thursday. Their son Emjay and his friend Brent were arrested for felony assault—we'll need a grand jury indictment to proceed." Dana summarized the evidence against those four defendants, including Evan's and Natalie's potential testimony. "My biggest regret, I admit, is that I allowed Natalie to have a sleepover with her friend Samantha."

"Did you know the parents were going to be away?" Ted asked.

"I was led to believe they'd be at home when I talked to Mrs. Bohr on Friday, but she didn't actually say it. I realize now that I just assumed it."

"The media could sting you on that if they wanted to," Ted noted, "especially since we're faulting the Bohrs for not being at home."

"Well, if they do, I won't be able to respond. There's no way

I can comment in public about a phone conversation I had with a defendant, which reminds me, this is another connection I have to this case."

"Your phone call with Sandy Bohr isn't relevant," Linda said. "If the defendants try to attack your character as part of their defense, no judge will allow a stunt like that."

"Gee, thanks," Dana said.

"I agree, but I have other concerns about the case against the parents," Ted added. "We've never prosecuted a case like this, only cases where the defendants are at home, actively hosting the underage drinking party."

"I'm aware it's a first. But the community wants this problem addressed. Some parents make drugs and alcohol readily available, then turn a blind eye."

"I agree with you there, but we're limited by the Penal Law. The evidence of mental state and causation is weak."

"Take the strongest possible view of it, Ted. These parents knew their son would have friends over after a huge event at the high school. They kept a well-stocked wet bar in the game room — an attractive lure for teenagers hyped up after a dance. Then they left town for the weekend, without a second thought. Emjay himself blew point oh six on the breathalyzer. It shows impaired judgment and tolerance of other kids drinking."

"Okay," Ted conceded. "Maybe it's enough, especially the case against Emjay. He was there, allowing this to happen. It's closer for the parents."

"Linda and I discussed some options. We can offer a plea to a lower-level misdemeanor on both charges."

"Also," Linda said, "they have a potential defense on the unlawful dealing charge. If they go for that, we have no problem with it, right Dana?"

"Right."

"They can take alcohol awareness training and the charges

are dropped. Even if the case gets dismissed, it serves as a wake-up call to the community."

"Of course," Dana posited with grim sarcasm, "I could just dismiss the case now and duck any questions about my conflicts of interest."

"Or make that inquiry worse," Ted answered with a wan smile. "They could say the DA dismissed it because she didn't want her child involved."

"So, I'm damned if I do, damned if I don't—is that what you're saying? Time for a special prosecutor?"

"Not necessarily," Ted said.

"I need your honest view on that. Natalie is a witness against all of the Bohrs..."

"Except Samantha," Indigo said.

"Yes, that's a different story. According to Natalie, that's a friendship ruined forever."

"Natalie's only doing what Samantha could be made to do. She's a witness to everything. I just can't get her to talk," Indigo said.

"We could compel Samantha with process, but that isn't going to work. The assault case has to go into the grand jury with the witnesses we have. The boys were seriously injured. Julian's still in a coma. His mother called me this morning and demanded that I throw the book at Emjay and Brent. She insinuated that I might be inclined to go light on them to protect Evan and Natalie."

"That would never be part of the equation."

"I appreciate that thought, Linda, but we have to look at this from the public's point of view."

"The only possible reason for going easy on Emjay and Brent is the one I doubt Mrs. Yarnell mentioned when she called you. Her son's blood alcohol level was through the roof. The defendants are claiming justification. They're both going to testify in the grand jury."

"We have evidence to refute self-defense; you've seen Natalie's statement. Plus, the severity of the injuries to Julian and Keith indicate unnecessary force."

"I won't be able to get around putting Natalie in the grand jury," Linda said. "We might not need Evan, at least not until trial. He didn't see the whole thing. But Natalie is the star witness."

"A star. Maybe that will make her feel better!" *Oh, Natalie.*

Ted jumped in and got directly to the point. "To answer your question about conflicts, Dana, I don't think it's a breach of ethics for you to handle these cases. It would be different if you were a witness but…a family member?"

"I shouldn't be on a case if my personal interests could adversely affect my professional judgment. That's the general rule in the code of ethics."

"If you're talking about your interest in protecting your family, a special prosecutor wouldn't make any difference."

"How so?"

"If you were inclined to keep your family out of this, you could still do it behind the scenes."

"Influence them to recant?"

"Or something similar. Make them useless to any special prosecutor."

Ted's opinion did not come as a surprise. Dana had been reassuring herself with exactly these arguments. But it was helpful to hear this viewpoint expressed independently, by a colleague as exacting and ethical as her first deputy.

"I agree with Ted," Linda said. "Better to jump into this without delay. Get all the facts before the grand jury."

"Yes, but clothed in secrecy." Everyone understood Dana's implication. The grand jury was closed to the public.

"Well, suppose someone has a bug up their ass about it," Indigo said. "They can ask the court to review the record or open it to public view. But that ain't gonna happen…"

"Why not?"

"Because this isn't a white cop shooting an unarmed black man. For example. This is a bunch of drunk teens from suburbia in a fight."

Trust Indigo to put things in proper perspective.

"And even if someone convinced the court to disclose the transcript," Linda said, "which is pretty hard to do, I'll make sure there's nothing in there to raise an eyebrow."

"Okay," Dana said. "I'm inclined to agree with all of you." She paused a moment longer. Had she forgotten anything? Policy, competing interests, ethics, public opinion—the path to justice snaked through a vast, amorphous minefield. Always, the ticking clock urged her on. Decisions couldn't be postponed. Cautious steps had to be taken immediately to avoid a worse outcome: festering injustice wreaked by indecision. "I'm going forward with these cases. Linda, let me know whatever you need for the grand jury. I think we should shoot for Wednesday."

Linda's eyes sparkled with confidence in her marching orders. "Will do."

"That'll be it," Dana said, "except for you, Ted. Stay behind just a minute to let me know about Rigger."

Linda and Indigo left the room, and Dana sat across from her first deputy. He looked drawn and pale, proof that he'd been burning the midnight oil, feeling the weight of his high-profile murder case. Maybe the public attention on the St. Valentine's Day Nightmare had lessened the pressure on him. Not by much.

"How's Rigger going?" She knew better than to comment on Ted's physical appearance. Tomorrow, in court, he would rise to the task at hand.

"The defense case should finish up tomorrow. Rigger's shrink will be testifying about his so-called narcissistic, paranoid personality disorder. Closing statements and instructions to the jury on Wednesday. We've already spoken with Judge Sinclair about Rigger's defense, and she's buying Carlyle's arguments on extreme emotional disturbance."

Dana was well aware that Rigger's attorney, Frederick Carlyle, was a forceful advocate. "Is he still arguing that the defendant had a reasonable excuse for losing it with a baseball bat?"

"Yup."

"Just because his wife wasn't backing down from inviting the in-laws to dinner?"

"You got it."

"That's ridiculous. How could any jury find that reasonable?"

"That's what we're arguing about. The statutory definition of 'reasonable.'"

"What's Carlyle say?"

"That Rigger's excuse should be judged entirely subjectively, from his viewpoint, in his situation as he perceived it. The judge agrees with Carlyle that the excuse is 'reasonable' if it makes sense for a person with Rigger's emotional and psychological makeup, with all the stresses in his life, financial and otherwise."

"That's crazy right there. The word 'reasonable' in the law has always been used to mean the average reasonable person."

"That's what I've been trying to get through to the judge. The appellate courts apply a combined subjective-objective standard. Judge Sinclair's definition blows any objectivity out of the statute."

"So, any defendant who comes up with a unique excuse for flying off the handle can get his murder downgraded to a manslaughter? The statute can't possibly mean that."

"I'm doing some more research today, gathering case law to show the judge tomorrow."

"Good luck, Ted. You're on the right track."

* * *

Just as predicted, Belknap, Rose, & Goodhue, P.C., was eerily quiet, the hallways dim. Evan didn't think anyone else had come in, but he couldn't be sure. He'd been holed up in his office, finishing his papers for the summary judgment motion in *Hafeez versus Nashid*.

So far, it had been easy enough to lay out the facts and the law. The Son of Sam statute clearly favored Evan's client. Last week, Judge Tenzler had shot down Vesma's defenses—not in the nicest way, but the fact remained that her arguments were meritless, a grasping at straws. Her client had a right to some money for medical expenses, and Vesma had a claim to her legal fees. It was time to make a decision. Should he put every argument in his papers, even the weak argument to block her legal fees? It was a gray area. It poked at his conscience. There were three possibilities: fight Vesma's claim, stay silent, or concede the point to her. Given Judge Tenzler's demonstrated prejudices, Evan feared that she would lose out entirely unless he actively took her side.

Evan turned away from his computer and gazed out the window into spotless azure. His mind went to Saturday night, so much colder than today, when he dropped off Natalie, then delivered the phone to Ginger. The first house: a stately, radiantly white mansion at the end of a private cul-de-sac, acres of buffer, lawn and trees. The second house: on the grid, middle of a narrow, darker street lined with modest bungalows, square patches of lawn under the snow. A lonely porchlight. A girl of sixteen, alone, self-reliant, sweet as anything, responsible, courteous, smart, a life ahead of her. Light auburn hair, the color of her name, sunny smile, white skin, ghostly pale under the harsh, single bulb. Single mother, financially strained. Father, an alcoholic. Everyone knew it. Had known it for years.

Travis's friend. A girl he admired, and maybe more.

Evan turned back to his computer and started typing up a proposed settlement agreement. He would send it to Vesma along with the motion for summary judgment. A choice. Would she be distracted by Ginger's case and drop her resistance? Evan wasn't trying to take advantage. He had a fair proposal that conformed to the law, with a few concessions on his part, taking the gray areas into account. He'd call Malikah today to get her authorization. All around, the settlement would save everyone a lot of time and expense.

The desk phone rang, prying him loose from his internal strategy session. "Dana."

"You have a minute?"

"For you."

"I've just had a meeting with my brain trust, but I never got the chance to ask you what I asked them."

"Am I part of the trust?"

"You're the main brain. But I want you to dig deeper for this one. I want you to bypass your brain and give me your instinctual, gut reaction."

"So, I'm the main gut too?"

"Here's the question. Gut reaction please. Should I recuse myself in the Foxglove party cases and ask for a special prosecutor?"

Evan said nothing, pretending to be thinking about it when he'd already mentally analyzed the question in detail, twenty-four hours ago.

"You know what I mean," Dana said. "Gut reaction, but from an outsider's point of view. Pretend we're talking about someone you don't know, the district attorney of Des Moines, Iowa, or somewhere. This fictional DA is faced with the same circumstances I'm in. Her husband and child are witnesses against the defendants. Should a special prosecutor be appointed?"

"My gut says 'no.' The professional judgment of the DA of

Des Moines isn't impaired, and she'll prove it by conducting business as usual." And she'll try to assuage her daughter's angst. He didn't need to remind Dana of that part.

"My brain trust agrees with you."

"Glad to know I'm just as brainy. And just as gutsy."

"There's no comparison, darling. But, I suppose…"

"You have something else you want to tell me. I know that tone of voice."

"I *do* have a confession. I thought it wise not to rely *entirely* on the advice of people who work for me and my husband."

"Thanks for the compliment."

"You know what I mean."

"I do."

"I called Patrick and asked his opinion." Patrick McBride had been Dana's mentor in her years at the Manhattan DA's office, first as her bureau chief, then as the elected DA.

"No kidding. How *is* Patrick?"

"Retirement is treating him well, if you could call it retirement, being a member of every criminal justice advisory board in the state."

"I can tell that Patrick gave you the okay to go ahead on these cases."

"How can you tell?"

"If he'd said 'no-go,' my opinion would be worth diddly-squat and you wouldn't be praising my brain."

"I don't think so. I needed your independent judgment."

"Well, you got it. Now that you have the approval of the brain trust, the main brain, and the supreme brain—I almost said the supreme being—I think you can go forward without further doubts."

"I can, and I should, but…"

"Another but."

"There's something else that's still bothering me. Ted

mentioned it too. He said it a little nicer than this, but—am I no better than those people? Leaving the teens unsupervised? I allowed our child to sleep there without making sure that an adult would be at home."

"How about Emjay? He's eighteen."

"Be serious."

"Okay. Seriously, you're asking me about something that didn't happen. You did *not* allow her to go over there without any parent in the house. You thought the parents would be there."

"I *thought*. How sloppy was that?"

Dana had made one concession: She allowed Indigo to drive her to the services at the First Presbyterian Church. They were a few minutes late, and the parking lot was full. After circling it, Indigo dropped Dana at the side walkway and pulled out of the lot to find a parking spot on the street. This way, Dana avoided the reporters. She counted three news vans at the curb, the reporters waiting to pounce when the services were over. At least they'd been respectful enough to wait outside—or perhaps the church had warned them that entry onto the property would be considered a trespass.

The church was packed, the service had just begun. Dana paused in the back until she spotted a seat on the left end of the last pew. She slipped in. A few pairs of eyes went her way and showed signs of recognition. She was not a churchgoer at this or any church, and she refused to pretend any religious adherence for the sake of appearances or politics, yet she found meaning in the ritual and valued the comfort it provided. As the pastor spoke, handkerchiefs and tissues came out. Bowed heads, shuddering shoulders, teary eyes, soft exclamations. The death of such a young person was especially wrenching.

A few minutes later, Indigo entered the church and squeezed

in next to her. Circumspectly, Dana scanned the people in attendance, most of them visible only from the back or side. The Steuben family was in the front row, Bernard and Dierdre. A girl of about twenty next to the mother had to be the sister, Olivia. Next to the father were three gray-haired grandparents. Naomi was a few feet in front of them, inside a closed coffin draped with an enormous flower arrangement. Dana couldn't help it. An image came to mind, a blue-white, bloated face under ice.

A chilly draft cut through the high-vaulted chamber. Dana shivered. Her eyes wandered. She saw a few people vaguely familiar to her, parents from the school district. By contrast, most of these people would know who she was from television or newspapers.

Indigo softly elbowed Dana's upper arm and nodded toward the right side of the church, halfway in. How had she missed them? Chloe Dyckman sat between a man and a woman, undoubtedly her parents. Calculated appearances, pure and simple, everyone playacting. Did the Dyckmans think this would help Chloe's case? Had they given no thought to the Steubens' feelings?

The pastor read the poem "Gone from My Sight" by Henry Van Dyke and a verse from the Bible. A hymn was sung, a eulogy delivered by a cousin. Of course, the parents and sister were too distraught to speak. At the close of the services, Dana stood and hesitated, debating whether to go forward. A long line of people waited to give their respects to the family. The Dyckmans were not in that line. They made their way for the door, glancing at Dana on the way out. Mr. Dyckman's expression, more of a glare, seemed to say, "How dare you?" Perhaps they hoped that the five o'clock news would feature a video clip of them exiting the church.

"I'm going up to pay my respects," Dana told Indigo.

"Okay, I'll wait back here."

As Dana started for the front, the pastor spotted her and whispered something to Mr. Steuben, who nodded his head. The pastor approached her in the aisle. "Ms. Hargrove. The family knows how busy you must be and would like very much if you could come forward right away."

"I appreciate that, thank you." Cutting the line was not her style. She was a servant of the people, district attorney of a suburban county, not president of the United States. In some ways, being a public figure was anathema to her, but today, she graciously accepted the pastor's invitation. She *was* a busy person, no doubt about it.

The pastor escorted Dana to the front pew. She offered her condolences, in turn, to the grandparents, Mr. and Mrs. Steuben, and finally Olivia. "I'm so very sorry for the loss of your sister," Dana said, shaking Olivia's hand.

Olivia surprised Dana by placing a hand on her shoulder and leaning toward her. "I need to talk to you," she rasped into Dana's ear. "It's very important!"

"Please call or come to my office just as soon as you can. Do you have my number?"

"Yes! I'll call you."

Dana walked away, puzzled by the encounter. What did Olivia want to tell her?

Indigo met her in the aisle, and they stepped out of the church together. "Want me to get the car and meet you in the lot? We can try to duck these goons."

"No. Let's walk down to the street. I don't mind giving a statement."

Indigo flashed a dubious look and said, "You're the boss. I'll beat 'em up if they get too ornery." They walked down the path together, a united front.

The first reporter to rush Dana blurted, "District Attorney Hargrove! People want to know how it's possible to commit murder by Facebook post!"

"It's my job to present the evidence to a grand jury, the voice of the community. They returned an indictment. The charge isn't murder. It's criminally negligent homicide, a lower-level felony. The indictment is a formal accusation only. We trust the court system to render a just result in this case."

The moment she stopped talking, five reporters jostled and elbowed each other, flinging questions at once. Dana tried to speak over them: "I have no further statements about the case. The Steuben family is mourning the loss of their daughter. Please be respectful and allow them to grieve in peace."

Dana started walking right into the fray. There was no other way around. "Stand back!" Indigo shouted, holding out a hand.

As they pushed through, reporters blasted her with questions about this case and the others, the St. Valentine's Day Nightmare. "How can you charge Dr. Bohr when your own daughter was there?" In the ruckus, the nastiest jab was hurled behind her back. "Madam District Attorney! What do you say to people who call you 'Hypocrite Hargrove'?"

Oh, my Lord. For the first time in her life, Dana had the urge to pray.

18 » WITNESSES

OLIVIA SEEMED RELUCTANT to talk on the phone, so they arranged to meet in Dana's office on Tuesday morning, the day after the funeral. Dana would have liked to invite Linda to join them, but Olivia asked for a private meeting with the district attorney. It seemed a delicate matter, and Dana didn't want to do anything to intimidate the girl.

"My parents are so upset that…" Olivia broke down and seemed surprised by it, more distraught than she realized.

"Take your time," Dana said, handing her a tissue. "Sometimes the emotion catches up with us unexpectedly."

The young woman worked at composing herself. Under the red nose and eyes, her face was pleasantly sturdy and plain, framed with dull-brown hair falling to mid-back. In snug jeans and a black turtleneck, she looked healthy and strong, with no extra weight. She blew her nose and said, "We're all upset, so I'm staying around a few more days before going back to school. Everybody's wondering what we could have done to prevent this."

"It must be so hard for you and your family."

"It is. The last time I saw my sister was at Christmas and I practically ignored her. I did love her so much. I really *did*."

"I can tell that you loved her, so I'm sure that she knew it."

"I don't know. I hope so. She was very quiet and kind to

people, never said a bad word. And she was really smart. A genius in math."

"I've heard about that."

"So, all of that makes it hard for me to be here. It doesn't seem fair to my sister. For me to talk to you, I mean."

"Why is that?"

"Because I'm going to say something to help one of the girls who killed her. I mean, one of the girls you *arrested* for killing her. I know they didn't actually kill her, but they were so cruel."

"Which girl?"

"Taylor. I feel sorry for her. I was thinking of finding out who her lawyer was and talking to that lawyer, but then I thought about who has the real power over this case. Sorry, but that's what everybody says. That you're the one who decides to charge someone with a crime."

Olivia's perception wasn't entirely accurate, but close enough. "I do make those decisions," Dana said, "but they won't stand up if a jury or a judge doesn't agree. I think your instincts are correct. It's important to come to me with any evidence you have, especially if it favors one of the defendants. I have a legal obligation to consider that evidence and disclose it to the defense."

"Okay, then I feel better about telling you. What I want to say is…all of this is Chloe's fault."

How did that make any sense? The evidence pointed to Taylor, the one who wrote the vilest messages to Naomi, while Chloe merely went along for the ride. So it seemed. In the next instant, Dana understood. Everything snapped into place, if Olivia was alluding to… "What makes you say that?"

"I know her. I'm not very proud of this, but I dated her older brother Tim for about a month when we were seniors. Good thing I figured him out before it was too late…" She shuddered in disgust. "That family! They're all gorgeous, that's why people are attracted to them. That's why I was attracted to Tim, you know, but he would take *anything* he wanted from you. Make you feel like he was God's gift. He'd say things like, 'I don't normally date girls like you,' and I felt so lucky."

"What did he mean by that?"

"You know." She looked at Dana like it was obvious. When Dana said nothing, she explained. "He could have gone out with really beautiful girls, not someone so average."

What a total… Dana mentally completed the sentence with several descriptive nouns for Tim. She wondered if Olivia understood his game. "Why do you think he wanted you to feel grateful?"

"Grateful. That's a good word. That was part of it. Mostly he would charm you to death and act like he was entitled to anything he wanted. If you didn't give it up, there was this whole guilt trip, comparing you to all the pretty, popular girls he'd been with. 'So-and-so does this and that,' you know. After a few weeks, he started getting real pushy with me, but I'm stronger than that. I ended it and got away. Other girls weren't so smart."

This made sense too. Last week, when the Sloanes voiced their dislike of the Dyckmans, Dana ordered Tim's criminal sheet and found that he'd been arrested for sexual assault in the late spring of his senior year. The complainant had been a junior at the high school, and the case ended in a negotiated disposition, a misdemeanor. The ADA on the case said she salvaged as much of the case as she could with a plea bargain when the victim developed serious cold feet and refused to testify.

"So, Tim isn't a very nice guy, but how does that reflect on Chloe?"

"They're—how do you say that? Like from the same cookie cutter. I spent some time at their house and saw enough of her there and at school to figure out a few things. Chloe and Tim both have this way about them, this personality that's just…*wrong*."

"What do you mean by 'wrong'?"

"Okay. Here's an example. I'm at their house, and she's there with Taylor. She says, 'That's Naomi's sister!' Both girls have these big sparkly smiles like they're my best friends. Right there, that's so ballsy. You know they're two years younger than me, right?"

Dana nodded.

"They're both beauty queens, you know, but Taylor's kind of dumb, a follower. She listens to Chloe like she's a goddess, believing everything she says." Olivia paused and rolled her eyes.

"Did something else happen?" Dana asked.

"Sorry." Olivia shook her head. "This is about the sweater. I tell Chloe she's wearing a beautiful sweater. It's expensive, you could tell. She says, 'I think it would look better on you' and takes it off right there. She's wearing a tight T-shirt underneath, showing herself off. She tells me to try it on, so I have to take off my own sweater. Tim's in another room, so that's no problem, but still, she's looking me up and down. When I put it on, she says, 'It's so perfect on you, Olivia!' I try to give it back, but she won't take it. Says it's mine, she's giving it to me. So, I wear it to school the next day. She's standing in the hall with Taylor and some other girls. Their little entourage. I say 'hello' and 'thank you for the sweater,' and she says, really loud, 'I was *wondering* where that sweater went! You must have taken it when you left my house yesterday!'"

"Why do you think she did that?"

"I don't really know why she does most of the things she does. This is just one example. I saw her do stuff like this all the time. She gets people to do things, then twists it around to make you think she didn't get you to do it. The truth is never the truth, and she smiles the whole time, like you're an idiot. She's right, you're wrong. She's a manipulative liar, and I can't even figure out why. This sweater thing…why would she want to lie about that? She doesn't seem to understand that she's lying. I think it makes her feel superior. Kind of a control thing. I was older than her, I was dating her brother, and she made me feel like a fool. She did this a couple of times with me. Even then she might have started getting ideas about what to do to Naomi…" Tears started to roll down her face.

Dana patted Olivia's arm and gave her some time while her own thoughts were set in a whirl. Was the seed planted two years ago?

"Last fall," Olivia continued, "Naomi told me that some girls were being mean to her. She didn't give the names, but I just *knew*. Right around then Naomi took those pills and practically died… Did you know about that?"

"Yes."

"Well, I had to tell Chloe to back off! I called her. I had to! I told her what Naomi had done and how sensitive she was. It didn't do any good, did it? I made it worse—" She broke down again.

The missing link. Naomi's own sister gave Chloe the details about the suicide attempt. Dana hoped she would use the right words to dispel Olivia's sense of guilt. "You did everything you could to protect your sister. No one is responsible for what Chloe and Taylor did except Chloe and Taylor."

When Olivia calmed down again, she described other instances of controlling behavior, times when Chloe picked on Taylor, telling her what to do or directing her to fix something in her appearance that didn't need fixing.

"I don't know if I can explain it any better."

"I'm getting the picture," said Dana.

Olivia looked off into the distance, searching for something. She turned to Dana and said, "I just thought of the right word. Taylor was a puppet, just like a puppet in Chloe's hands."

At the end of their conversation, Dana thanked her for

coming in and tried to impress upon her the value of her contribution.

"I just want everyone to be treated fairly. Naomi most of all, but also Taylor. It would make things worse if someone got an unfair punishment. I don't think Naomi would like that."

"I wouldn't like that either," Dana said. "Justice is always our goal."

When Olivia left, Dana picked up the phone and called Linda to fill her in.

"We're on the same wavelength, Dana," Linda said. "I've just been going through the transcript of their text messages that Bytes prepared. Chloe is directing Taylor every step of the way, putting the words right into her mouth. She's a control freak."

"The text messages might be enough to show the dynamic between the defendants, but it would be better to get these girls analyzed by a psychiatrist. If we go to trial, the evidence is relevant to their mental state, and if we negotiate, it's relevant to disposition."

"But we have no authority to order the exams," said Linda. "There's no indication they're unfit to stand trial, and they haven't said they're going to present their own expert."

Dana thought a moment. "There should be another way. First off, we're going to disclose this evidence immediately. We're obligated to hand over exculpatory evidence, anything that can help the defense. The relationship between the defendants might indicate that Taylor is merely Chloe's instrument. There's also some possibility that Chloe is incapable of forming the mental state. We don't know until we have the psychological workups. Give the attorneys the transcript of their text messages and the gist of Olivia's statement without revealing her identity. I'm betting that Taylor's attorney is going to order a psych eval, hoping it will convince us to go easy on her."

"But Chloe's attorney might not want a psych eval on her

client—she seems to be the more culpable one."

"My guess is she'll want to order one just to test the waters. They won't be obligated to use it, but if it benefits Chloe, they'll bring it up when we discuss disposition."

"And if they keep quiet about it, we can read something into it. We'll know that Chloe's shrink confirmed what we're thinking…"

"That Chloe is a sociopath."

Natalie sat all alone at the front of the room, twenty-three strangers staring at her. She couldn't believe that Mommy used to do this all the time, what Linda was doing, standing in the back of the room, asking her questions.

For three days now, everyone had been super nice, trying to make her feel good about doing her "civic duty." Mommy, Daddy, and Travis. Of course, Samantha hadn't been super nice. She wasn't speaking to her. Tuesday, the first day back at school, Sammy had looked the other way when she saw Natalie coming down the hall. The absolute worst was English class, where they sat next to each other in assigned seats. Natalie's head hurt from the effort of keeping her eyes straight ahead, on the teacher. There would be many more days like that one ahead. But today, Wednesday, she was excused from school so she could testify in the grand jury, a room full of strangers, most of them with gray hair.

Linda Marquette could be counted as one of the gray-haired ones, but she was, most of all, one of the people who'd been super nice. She'd come over to the house last night to talk about the grand jury, explaining exactly what would happen. There were no surprises, really, except the way Natalie felt when she first walked into the room. Getting "prepared" for twenty-three people staring at you is a lot different from actually being stared at.

No French braid today. Natalie thought she might never wear her hair like that again. She wore it down in a half-ponytail and fought against her habit of fishing for a strand to twist around her index finger. She began to relax—a little—after Linda got through all the "warm-up" kinds of questions. Her name, her age, how she knew Samantha, why she was at Samantha's house Saturday night, who dropped her off, what they did when she got there, and what the game room and bar looked like, including the lined-up bottles of alcohol and the beer in the fridge.

"Did you see Samantha's mom or dad in the house?"

"No. At first I thought they were there and I just didn't see them. It's a really big house. Later, Sammy told me they weren't home."

"Did you see anyone else at the house?"

"Yes."

"When?"

"It was kind of late. We were in Sammy's room and started hearing people coming in the front door. We peeked down the stairs and saw her brother Emjay and some of his friends."

"Why do you say they were his friends, Natalie?"

"Well..." She thought about that. Hadn't Sammy told her? She also remembered how her mother and Linda said it was important to give straight observations, not "opinions" or "conclusions." "I think Sammy told me, but also, they looked like Emjay's age. I knew there was a dance at the high school, and they were wearing clothes you would wear to a dance." She felt very proud of this answer. One of the jurors was looking at her with a sparkle in her eye, kind of like a grandmother. Wouldn't that be funny if Grandma Brenda was here? Natalie thought to ask her later whether she'd ever been on a grand jury.

"Can you estimate how many people came to the house?"

"I didn't really count them. We walked through a couple of times. Kids just covered the whole place. The living room, the kitchen, and downstairs in the game room."

"What did you see in the game room?"

"There were a bunch of high school students down there and empty beer bottles and alcohol bottles all over. I remember two of the kids really well because they looked so drunk. Two boys. They were sitting at the bar, and they each had a different bottle of alcohol. I mean, those big bottles."

Linda turned to the stenographer. "Let the record reflect that the witness is holding her hands with a space of about one foot between them. Go on, Natalie."

"The two boys were drinking from those bottles, and they were also very loud. I was kind of scared."

Linda showed Natalie photographs of Julian Yarnell and Keith Westerman to establish the identity of the two boys.

"What did you do then?"

"Me and Sammy went back to her room. I told her I was going to the bathroom, but I snuck into her parents' room to look for a phone. I called my dad. He said he'd come pick me up."

"Why didn't you ask Samantha for a phone?"

Oh, this was awful! Natalie felt like a liar all over again. Why hadn't she told Samantha she wanted to call home? "I felt embarrassed, I guess. I was supposed to stay the whole night, but I really wanted to go home. It was noisy, and I didn't like the way some of those kids were acting."

"What happened while you waited for your dad to come?"

"We heard even louder noises, a lot of shouting, and we looked out Sammy's window. You can see the front of the house from there."

"Tell us what the lighting was like, outside and inside."

"The lights were off in Sammy's room." Should she mention the fluorescent stars and crescents on the ceiling? It probably didn't matter. "And the outside lights were on, so you could see the part in front of the house, you know, after the little roof that covers the porch and those column thingies. There's a long path or pavement, kind of, with a few little stairs in it going to the driveway."

"What happened then?"

Natalie's heart started to pound harder in her chest. This was the difficult part because—didn't Julian and Keith really deserve it? Emjay and his friend were trying to get them to leave. Wasn't that the right thing to do? But did they have to do it *that* way?

"Sammy's brother Emjay and a friend of his—a really big boy—were dragging and pushing Julian out of the house. He was one of the ones who was drinking in the game room. He looked really drunk and was yelling a lot of stuff I couldn't hear."

Linda showed Natalie a photograph to establish that the "big boy" was Brent Tremont. "What did the three boys do next?"

"Brent was holding Julian's left arm, and Emjay was pushing and jabbing Julian in the back. They pushed him down the front stairs. Then Julian threw his arm up like this and broke away from Brent."

"Let the record reflect that the witness has thrown her arm up in the air as if to push someone away. Go on, Natalie."

"Julian looked like he was going to leave, but then he turned around and walked back. It wasn't exactly like walking…"

"What did it look like to you, the way he was moving?"

"He took a step toward Emjay, but he looked unsteady and loose. He was drunk and wobbly. Kind of falling forward almost, but he didn't fall. He just stood there and swayed a little and kept yelling at Emjay, waving his arms around, but he didn't try to hit anyone. And then…" She closed her eyes briefly, seeing it again. "…Brent grabbed Julian's arm and squeezed it so hard he couldn't get away. It was Julian's right arm this time because he was facing Emjay. Brent is so big and strong he only needed one hand to hold Julian. With his other hand, Brent was going like this to Emjay, like 'come on, come on!'"

"The witness is holding her hand out in front and waving it toward herself repeatedly in a scooping motion. Please tell the jury what happened next."

"So, Brent was waving like that, and Julian was just tipping side to side and couldn't break loose. Emjay had his face like two inches away from Julian's face, yelling at him, then Emjay stopped yelling and stepped back. He kind of froze for a second, like he was thinking about something."

"Could Emjay have safely walked away from Julian if he wanted to?"

"Yes."

"Did he walk away?"

"No! He looked like he was thinking for just a second, and at the same time he did like this once..."

"The witness punched the palm of her left hand with her right fist. Did I describe that correctly, Natalie?"

"Yes. And then Keith came up behind Emjay. He was yelling and waving something in the air behind Emjay's back."

"Did you see the object that Keith was waving?"

"At first, I couldn't really tell. It just looked like a brown thing. But he waved it in the light and I saw these sharp edges. It was a broken bottle."

"What happened next?"

"Everything just happened at once! Emjay punched Julian in the face with his fist. He punched him really hard! It was so fast. Brent let go and Julian flew backward and fell and hit his head. The back of his head kind of bounced on the pavement. Keith was right behind Emjay and he rushed at him like he was attacking Emjay with the bottle, but then Brent grabbed Keith and stopped him. He..." Her lip quivered, and tears were forming in her eyes.

"It's okay, Natalie. Take your time."

She sniffed, wiped a tear away, and said, "Brent was way bigger than Keith too! He twisted his arm back and pushed his hand with the bottle into his face and they fell on the ground. I couldn't see Keith anymore because Brent was on top of him. When he moved a little to the side, I could see Keith better. Blood was gushing out of his face!"

"What happened next?"

"My father came and tried to help Julian, but he just laid there and didn't get up. He never woke up!"

Ted was having his own problems in court Wednesday morning while the Bohr case was in the grand jury. Lecia buzzed Dana and said he was on the line.

"We've just had the charge conference," Ted reported, exasperation in his voice. "Judge Sinclair rejected my requested instruction to the jury. I objected and asked for a five-minute recess. I'm in the hallway just outside the courtroom now. There's another possibility I want to run by you."

"Seems like our hands are tied. You did your best to convince her."

"I gave her at least ten case cites from the Court of Appeals, but she's still going to give the jury incorrect law on extreme emotional disturbance. I want to move for a mistrial."

Oh no. Perry Rigger must be rubbing off on Ted. His new idea bordered on delusional. "She will deny the motion."

"When she does, I'll demand a continuance to file an emergency article 78."

"A special proceeding against the judge? On what ground?"

"On the ground that she's acting outside of the law."

Dana shook her head and rolled her eyes. She knew how frustrating it was to work with a judge who wouldn't back down from an unsupportable position, but they couldn't respond with insane, no-win tactics. "The Appellate Division will not buy that argument. We can't file a special proceeding every time we disagree with a judge's instructions. The criminal justice system would come to a complete halt."

"But it's so hideously wrong! Her instruction almost rubber-stamps his defense. If the jury comes in with manslaughter instead of murder, we can't appeal or retry the case. Our hands are tied!"

She'd never heard Ted so worked up. "I wish there was another way to go with this. I just don't see it."

Silence. Then a sigh. "Okay. It was a long shot, I know."

"It isn't over until it's over, Ted. There's still a chance, and I know you'll give a great closing argument. You always do."

In Natalie's room that night, Dana sat on the bed with her daughter, arm tight around her shoulder. The girl sobbed, shuddered, and agonized.

Natalie's pain was Dana's pain, a mother's pain. Natalie's youth and innocence sparked memories of Dana's early days as a rookie prosecutor, when she was naïve, emotionally charged and overloaded. Back then, and even today, she kept a steady stream of rational arguments in her head, an internal mantra of ineffectual self-assurance. Deep in the muck of her criminal caseload, she was pulled apart by conflicting agendas in her quest for justice, that elusive goal. Rarely were the paths to right and wrong clearly marked. The pureness of her compassion for people—the victims, the witnesses, the defendants—was often diluted by her personal investments in reputation, appearance, and righteousness.

Today, they'd done the closest thing to right. She just wanted Natalie to believe it, to feel it.

After Natalie testified this morning, Evan drove her home while Dana stayed at the office, awaiting word of the outcome while keeping busy, trying to shut out the humiliation of having seen and heard five news sources repeating the phrase "Hypocrite

Hargrove." Meanwhile, Linda was presenting the rest of the prosecution case, witnesses that saw teenagers drinking the Bohrs' alcohol, evidence of Julian's and Keith's blood alcohol levels, and medical evidence of their injuries. After that, the two accused boys testified, in turn.

Close to five o'clock, Linda came to Dana's office to deliver the news. Dana had duped herself into believing that this grand jury vote would mean no more and no less to her than any other vote. She was absolutely sure of this, even though Natalie had been on her mind all day. But in the moment before Linda spoke, Dana felt a panicky breathlessness, her heart pounding hard and fast.

"Natalie did very well," Linda said. "Articulate and believable. As we predicted, the defendants came in and said it was self-defense. A lot of what they said conflicted with the medical evidence, and to me, it sounded like they'd gotten together to nail down their story. They even used some of the same words. They testified that Julian threatened them and lunged at Emjay. Brent grabbed his arm to try to stop him, Emjay pushed Julian with a flat palm, and he slipped on the ice. Then Brent defended Emjay against Keith's attack with the bottle."

Two versions of the same event, two witnesses against one. A star quarterback and an offensive tackle against a middle schooler. Believe Natalie, and the boys committed intentional assault against the two victims. Believe the boys, and they were justified. But Linda and Dana knew that three witnesses to the same event should produce three versions. Each individual perceives an incident through the lens of a unique perspective, emotional makeup, and experience. Unbiased witnesses, that is. Here, the boys had a motive to distort the truth. If the grand jury overlooked that motive, and if they thought that the supremely unlikeable "victims" had put Emjay and Brent in a difficult situation, the scales could have tipped in the defendants' favor.

This way of looking at the case fell outside the boundaries of the law, but juries weren't immune to the power of emotion.

"Did the jury have any questions?" Dana asked, delaying the ultimate question. She was steeling herself for the result, still unsure of it. Her radar seemed to be broken. She couldn't read Linda's face.

"They wanted to hear the justification instruction again, and they had some questions about how to apply the law to Brent's assault on Keith. That was the closer case. Keith escalated the fight with deadly physical force—the broken bottle. Also, Keith's attack came a split second after Emjay had already clocked Julian, so it wasn't justified as a defense of his friend. Brent had a good case for defending Emjay against Keith's attack, but Brent is much bigger and stronger than Keith and he overreacted. He could have twisted that bottle away instead of aiming it for Keith's face and neck."

"Melees like this are always hard to sort out. How long was the jury deliberating?"

"It wasn't quite *War and Peace*, but they worked on it a good long time. Almost two hours."

"And…?"

Finally, Linda's unreadable face was subtly transformed by inner satisfaction. "Emjay and Brent were indicted for assault in the second degree for the assault on Julian. But the grand jury dismissed the charge against Brent for assaulting Keith."

Dana exhaled, hopefully not too audibly. "And the alcohol misdemeanors…?"

"The jury dismissed the endangering charges against Emjay but came in with two counts of unlawful dealing with a minor. Although there was testimony of widespread drinking, the jury charged only the counts based on Julian and Keith. So, clearly, Natalie's observations of them in the game room tipped the proof over the top."

The vote was fair, and Dana counted the outcome as a success. Of course, an indictment did not guarantee an end to Natalie's involvement. If the cases against Brent and the Bohrs went to trial, Natalie would be called to testify, and worse, she'd be subjected to cross-examination. *If* there was a trial.

For now, Dana assumed that Natalie would be pleased to know the vote. But when she got home, the girl was moping in her bedroom, visibly distraught. The news only upset her more.

In between big heaving sobs, Natalie agonized, "There's going to be a trial now, isn't there? I'm going to have to testify again!"

Dana sat down on the bed and put her arm around her shoulder. "We don't know that yet. A lot of criminal cases get resolved without a trial." What an unsatisfying answer! Dana wished she could remove the anxiety of all the unknowns that would hang over them in the months to come, until the case was finally over.

"Oh, they're going to have a trial! I know it! They don't think they're guilty! I'm going to send them to jail, and I don't even know if that's right!"

"Well, the parents definitely aren't going to jail, Natalie. And the boys—we don't know what the sentence will be. It's possible they won't get any jail time." Again, a lot of unknowns. "What do you mean when you say you don't know if it's right to send them to jail?"

"They were kicking drunk people out of their house. Shouldn't they be allowed to do that?"

"Sure, but that isn't the only thing that happened, is it?"

"Yeah, I know. They also practically killed them. But what about Julian and Keith being so awful to begin with? All four of them were terrible." She shook her head. "It's confusing—I don't know what's right!"

Welcome to the world of criminal justice, Dana thought.

Never any easy answers. "These are really good questions you're asking. If there's a trial, the jury will have to sort all of this out."

"And the trial jury might also decide that Emjay and Brent aren't guilty, right? Especially if…"

"Especially if what?"

"If they don't like the victims. Maybe that's not very nice to say… They're both still in the hospital."

"The jury isn't supposed to base the verdict on whether the victims are 'bad' or 'good.' No one deserves to be assaulted. But we also give juries the leeway to show mercy to the defendants. Sometimes, the jury is influenced by extra facts that the law doesn't strictly allow them to consider. We can't always help that."

"Extra facts." Natalie concentrated on that one for a moment. She'd been thinking so hard that her tears were nearly dry. She sniffed, rubbed an eye with the back of her hand, and said, "I know the extra facts in this case—Julian and Keith are a couple of real stinkers!"

Dana's heart swelled, filling her to bursting. She pulled Natalie into her arms and rocked her gently on the bed. They stayed that way for a long time, Dana humming softly into her daughter's honey-colored hair.

Yesterday and today had been so hard. Mom told her to jump back into things, to face people now and get the tough part over with. Ginger considered playing hooky, but she'd never done that before. She sucked it up and made it through all her classes, taking a couple of breaks in the restroom, locking herself in a toilet stall to cry.

Everyone in SADD was being nice about it, Travis especially. But Ginger avoided most of them as best she could. If she happened to look anyone in the eye, all she saw there was disappointment.

This morning, Mom mentioned that maybe they should go visit Grandpa soon. Strange, but everything was different now. There'd been so many times when she'd said, "No, we're busy," when Ginger had suggested a visit.

"Did you tell him?" she asked. "About me?"

Of course not. Mom hardly ever talked to Grandpa. She turned away and shook her head. "No. I don't think he has to know, do you?" Testing. *She knows about my trips to his house.* And if she did, was that so bad? It wouldn't stop Ginger from visiting.

After school, she couldn't face her friends or the empty house, so she took the bus to Grandpa's. Tomorrow was her court date. Maybe she would tell him about it, maybe she wouldn't.

But the minute they were sitting at the kitchen table with their cookies and milk, everything came out. At the end of her story she said, "I know I let everyone down."

Hunched over the tabletop, he shook his head and clapped a knotty hand to his forehead. "Ginger, my child." Maybe he thought she was her mother. He palmed back along the spotted scalp, through the scatter of white hairs, and looked up. "When I was a boy, the age to drive was fourteen."

"But people still had to follow the rules, didn't they?"

"You were helping the girls. That was your purpose, wasn't it? You're a good person who made a mistake, that's all."

"But it was the stupidest mistake ever made by anyone. I could have helped them another way. I don't know why I did it. When you were thirteen you didn't take your mother's car, did you?"

"We had no car."

"You walked everywhere?"

"Not everywhere. We were on the farm with wagons and horses and tractors. And to Rīga we took the train and used the streetcar when we were there. The big city."

"Hadn't they invented cars yet?"

He chuckled. *"Mans Dievs!* Yes, there were many cars! But we could not afford to buy one."

"Okay. Now I'll be just like you. No license, no car."

"Not such a big problem. Who needs a car? You took the bus, didn't you?" He smiled, and the pink spots came into his cheeks and his eyes widened, scrunching his forehead up into a mass of wrinkles.

"Right, who needs it?" She laughed.

"Who—needs—it!" His palm came down hard on the table with each word, rattling the tin of cookies. He pushed it closer to her, inviting. "Here, have another one. You are a good girl." She took a brown rectangle with slivers of almonds on top. The buttery crunch of it, the explosion of flavor, the gooey gobs that stuck in her molars—all of it was so wonderful that she felt like laughing and hugging the world with her grandpa in it!

She chewed, swallowed, took another, and tears rushed into her eyes. "But Grandpa! I did such a stupid thing! How can you possibly love me anymore?" She'd forgotten that she'd never heard him say he loved her.

"Stupid things are not the person." He reached across the table, put his cool, bony hand on hers and shook it, the pink spots rising even brighter in his cheeks. *"Es tevi mīlu. Es tevi ļoti mīlu."*

Grandpa didn't translate, but she felt sure he must have been saying that he loved her. Either that, or she was a good girl. But he was wrong on that one. Sorry, Grandpa, good girls don't get arrested.

19 »   *RESOLUTION*

"Busy day today," Evan said. It was a quarter to seven, and all four members of the Goodhue family were around the breakfast table. Everyone was feeling the need for mutual support at the start of their day.

"You look better this morning," Dana said to Natalie, putting a hand on her shoulder. "Are you up for facing a new day?"

"Sure, I guess so." She was still a bit down in the mouth. "I've already had practice ignoring Sammy at school."

"You're a regular expert by now," Evan said around a mouthful of toast.

"Maybe things between you and Samantha will get better when the cases are finally resolved," Dana suggested. "I'll let you know later what happens in court today on the alcohol charges against the parents."

"But not the assault case…"

"No. I'm afraid that one will take a while."

"About court today, Mom, I wanted to ask you…" Travis sounded tentative and kept his eyes fixed on his cereal bowl. "If I go to Ginger's court case, you won't mind, will you?"

"No but, well, yes. It's at two o'clock. You should be in class."

"I'll go only if they get it postponed until after school, at three thirty. Everyone in SADD wants to go, to support her."

"You know something about Ginger's case that *I* don't

know?" That would be an interesting turn of events. She'd have to chew out ADA Walsh for not keeping her informed.

"Yesterday we asked the principal, Mr. Beggs, if he would excuse us at one thirty. We could walk to the courthouse and be there by two. He said 'no.' Then we started thinking it would be good if the case was heard at three thirty instead of two. Alicia said she'd work on it."

"Alicia? How can she…? Oh, I see." A little negotiating, behind the scenes. Questionable? "If the case is postponed until after school, then, yes, I give you permission to go."

Evan pushed away from the table and stood. "Do *I* have permission to go, Mommy?"

"Yes, you have permission to go to court too, if you're talking about the Son of Sam case."

"Yup. But before I visit my favorite judge, I have a few things to do at the office. Enjoy the rest of your breakfast, everyone. I'll try not to be jealous." His look at Dana said, *You okay with this?*

"Go on," she said.

"You have at least five cases today, and I have only one and you're telling *me* to go ahead. How does your mother do it, kids?" He walked around the table, kissing them each in turn on the top of the head.

"You exaggerate, darling. Only two cases are in court today, and they get handled by my very able assistants." Evan might have been thinking of three others. The assault case against Emjay and Brent was on the long course for trial. The Sloane and Dyckman case was put on hold after Linda disclosed the new evidence and both attorneys requested psychiatric evaluations for their clients. The fifth case was still in the investigation stage…

Dana and the kids finished eating their toast and cereal in silence. Evan was always the life of the party, and when he was gone, they felt it. Reluctantly, they got up from the table. No one moved away immediately. They stood for a moment, looking at one another, shell-shocked. The day would be a very difficult one for all of them.

Dana, the magnet, held her arms out to her children, and they rushed in. She pulled Natalie close with her right arm and Travis with her left, squeezing them tight. "I love you guys so much!"

This time, the Honorable Friedrich Tenzler did not insist on a private meeting with the attorneys in his chambers. The judge took the bench, and the clerk called the case of *Hafeez versus Nashid*, a stenographer taking down every word.

Vesma had too much on her mind to haggle over Evan's proposed deal or to obsess over Judge Tenzler's behavior. She wanted to get this over with, to be with Ginger.

This morning she'd gotten her client's okay and called Evan to seal the deal. Out in the corridor, before setting foot in Tenzler's courtroom, they signed all the papers. Still, the settlement needed court approval or it wouldn't fly. She wondered if the judge, who'd been so clearly biased in Evan's favor, would rubber-stamp their deal without a hitch. The terms were not as entirely one-sided in the plaintiff's favor as the judge might have liked, but nearly so. Two hundred thousand for Vesma's legal fees in the med mal case, one hundred thousand for Yusuf's future medical expenses, and the balance, eight hundred thousand, to the plaintiff, Malikah Hafeez.

Vesma had come to terms with the fact that the case was a dog, with only a few gray areas to play with. Evan, always the gentleman, was being particularly gentlemanly in conceding these points to her. His about-face was sudden, but she wasn't going to look a gift horse in the mouth. If the case had been assigned to a decent, fair-minded judge, Vesma would have likely won these points anyway, in time, after more expense and litigation.

Today, in open court on the record, Judge Tenzler would do well to treat her with at least a modicum of respect, unlike the last time, when she considered filing a complaint against him. He opened on an appropriate note, using a tone that was, if not innocuous, merely whiny.

"Good morning, Ms. Krumins, Mr. Goodhue."

They stood and returned the greeting.

"Today was the deadline for submission of your summary judgment motions. Instead, I'm told that all motions have been withdrawn. Care to explain?"

"Yes, Your Honor," Evan said. "We've agreed to withdraw our motions because we've reached a monetary settlement. With the court's approval of our agreement, we stipulate to the dismissal of this case. We believe the terms are compliant with the law." He gave a fully signed copy of their agreement to the clerk, who handed it up.

The judge started to read it. Facing the bench, Vesma heard activity behind her, the polite click of business oxfords and women's heels as people quietly entered the courtroom. The judge said nothing for a full minute, interrupting his reading with intermittent glances at Evan, Vesma, and the audience. Unusually quiet for a man who loved to talk the ears off everyone within range. Holding the document in both hands, he rustled the papers and grew agitated, working against an internal struggle. Vesma felt something coming. She suspected it wouldn't be good.

An explosion. With an audible groan, Judge Tenzler slapped the agreement down hard and fumbled around the desktop for a pen. "All wrapped up neatly!" He scribbled his signature on the last page. "You've done your homework, counselors. You've researched the law. This is exactly what a jury would have come up with. So ordered!" He thrust the papers to the side, and the clerk, always one step ahead of the judge, was already there. "George will give you conformed copies. Case closed. Now, get out of here!"

Well, surprises never ceased. Was it something Judge Tenzler ate for breakfast? Evan and Vesma thanked the court and walked to the clerk's desk. With a glance into the audience, Vesma saw a bevy of corporate attorneys with shiny briefcases in their laps, waiting their turn. Apparently, a case far more interesting than *Hafeez versus Nashid* was about to be heard in Judge Tenzler's courtroom.

The judge twitched his fingers. "Come forward," he said with a smile on his lips, and multiple suits marched up the center aisle to the counsel tables.

Two media cases were scheduled for hearings in the courtroom of Town Justice Leroy Jones today. Morning session, *People versus Bohr, et al.* Afternoon session, *People versus Kavanagh.*

Jones, a part-time town justice, wasn't used to quite this much hubbub in his court, which handled local misdemeanors and traffic offenses. He heard cases on Thursdays, with occasional special sessions, and was engaged in his own law practice the rest of the week, specializing in criminal defense. Judge Jones was a stickler for proper criminal procedure and a staunch enforcer of the constitutional rights of the defendants who appeared before him. He was also the father of Alicia Jones, treasurer of the SADD chapter at Stone Ridge High School.

It was a small courtroom, packed to the gills. At the counsel tables, Linda sat by her lonesome on the left, and Hernando Ramirez sat with his two clients on the right.

"All rise!" intoned the court officer. Judge Jones entered and assumed the bench. With an audible rustle of scraping chairs, rustling papers, and random coughs, the spectators, attorneys, and defendants were seated again. The judge surveyed the room with a gleam in his warm, brown eyes. "Are we all here, or can we squeeze another busload in?" Everyone laughed. "This is a first." He turned to the sketch artists at the side of the room. "We put you over there because this is my best side." Laughs again. "Good morning counselors and defendants. Please enter your appearances."

The attorneys stood. "Assistant District Attorney Linda Marquette for the People, Your Honor."

"Hernando Ramirez for the defendants Michael Bohr Sr. and Sandra Bohr."

"All right. I understand there's a related case that was moved out to superior court because of a felony indictment, is that correct Ms. Marquette?"

"Correct. Michael Bohr Jr. and codefendant Brent Tremont were indicted for assault in the second degree. That indictment also charges Michael Bohr Jr. with two counts of the class A misdemeanor of unlawfully dealing with a child based on the same events as the charges in this case against his parents, Michael Bohr Sr. and Sandra Bohr."

"All right. This court has no jurisdiction over the misdemeanors against the younger Mr. Bohr since they're joined in a felony indictment." The judge turned to the defense table and said, "Defendants, please rise and stand next to your attorney." They did as instructed. The Bohrs were a fine-looking couple, all spruced up for court. The doctor was in a well-tailored suit, a hint of embarrassment under the professional mien. Sandy looked more like herself today, expertly made up to enhance the fading beauty. Emjay sat in the first row of the audience, alert, wide eyed, and square shouldered, in sport jacket and slacks.

The judge addressed them. "You've been charged with two counts of unlawful dealing with a child in the first degree. This offense is committed when you give or cause to be given an alcoholic beverage to someone under the age of twenty-one. How do you plead? Let's start with you, Mrs. Bohr."

She glanced briefly at Hernando, who nodded his go-ahead. The defendants had discussed their strategies with counsel and were prepared for their day in court. "Not guilty, Your Honor."

"And you, sir?"

"Not guilty," said Dr. Bohr.

"Are we putting this down for trial, or have you folks been working out a disposition?" The judge scanned the attorneys' faces.

Hernando spoke first. "Your Honor, Dr. and Mrs. Bohr are not interested in pleading to a lower-level offense, even if the prosecutor were to make that offer. It's our position that, number one, they did not 'cause' alcohol to be given to minors within the meaning of the law. Number two, the police conducted an illegal search. Their son's so-called consent was invalid because my clients didn't allow him to use the area that was searched. We request an adjournment for defense motions."

The judge turned to Linda. "What do you say, Ms. Marquette?"

"There was absolutely nothing wrong with the search, Your Honor, and if we go to trial, the evidence will show that these defendants violated the statute. But we have no objection to an adjournment for motions. The People will need two weeks to file opposition."

"All right, adjournment for defense motions granted. But let me suggest that you make use of this time for an additional purpose, counselors." The judge turned to look directly at Hernando. "These defendants have no prior convictions for this offense. I would hope you've studied the law on this…"

"You're reading my mind, Your Honor!" Hernando flashed his charismatic smile. "That's the second reason we're asking for an adjournment. The Penal Law provides an affirmative defense for alleged first-time offenders who complete a program in alcohol awareness training. Although my clients maintain their innocence of these charges, they've signed up for a program in a show of good faith." Hernando pulled two pieces of paper out of his briefcase and handed them to the court officer to give to the judge and the ADA.

Judge Jones looked at the offering. "This is an acceptable program. Ms. Marquette?"

"It's fine with the People," Linda said. She'd been wondering whether the Bohrs would go this route since it could signal their implicit acknowledgment of guilt. Why do the program if you didn't do the crime? Obviously, the Bohrs just wanted this case to go away. If they passed "alcohol school," the charges would be dismissed. A clean slate.

"All right. We'll adjourn to March 19 for program results. Meanwhile, I say this to the defendants: Take this training seriously. The instructor will know if you're merely biding your time. People were injured on your property. This case shows how a little inattentiveness to underage drinking can open the door to serious harm..."

As the judge spoke, Dr. Bohr leaned down to his wife and whispered animatedly into her ear. Sandra Bohr nodded subtly, keeping her eyes on the judge, not wanting him to think she was being disrespectful. She didn't need her husband's reminder. She was mindful of the mission she'd set out to accomplish today, the performance she'd perfected in front of a full-length mirror at home. It would smooth over the rough spots with Michael, and as for Emjay...he was foremost on her mind. Behind her, in the first row of the audience, Emjay was calm and collected, doing a fine acting job of his own. But she felt the rest of it, the nervous tension, anger, and frustration jazzing the air with electric current. A young man's future stood in limbo because of a mere scuffle, a show of self-defense, and a few knocked heads of punks who deserved far worse than they got! Every plan out the window because of *that* woman, the person who held all the power over her son!

The gavel was about to come down when Sandra Bohr blurted, "Please!"

A stunned hush came over the room.

"Is there something you wish to say?" asked the judge, glancing at Hernando for a sign of approval or disapproval.

"Yes please, if I may. It's about what you said just now, about inattentiveness."

Hernando didn't stop her. He knew what this was about and showed no concern that her remarks might damage their case.

"Go right ahead," said Judge Jones.

Sandy Bohr stood as tall as her short stature allowed in heels. She pulled back her shoulders and projected her voice from her diaphragm. "I'd like to say," she looked at her husband, "we'd *both* like to say that there's something inaccurate in the news reports." Her voice acquired volume and depth as she reignited her theatrical training. "It really doesn't seem fair to that little girl the way some people are speaking about her mother. I'm referring to the daughter of the district attorney."

In the background, the scratching sound intensified. Colored pencils frantically scribbled Sandy's likeness onto artists' pads.

"Last Friday, the day before Valentine's Day, I spoke to Dana Hargrove on the phone. She asked if my husband and I were okay with our daughter inviting her daughter for a sleepover. It was clear that she thought my husband and I would be home Saturday night. I didn't tell her we would be out. I *should* have told her."

Scritch, scratch. Everyone waited, all eyes on the former Sandra Steele of Broadway.

"What I'm trying to say is, the newspapers should be more careful before they print such complete bunk! The DA is no 'hypocrite'!" Sandy smiled prettily, flashing plenty of lip gloss, as a murmur of loud whispers rose in the audience.

* * *

Dana had asked Lecia to keep tabs on the local news stations to let her know of any breaking stories. Reporters often jumped on the wire before the ADA in the courtroom could call Dana with an update.

A bit after eleven, Lecia skipped into her office. "You're gonna love this, Dana. No longer hated, double H deflated!" Lecia hit the power button of the flat-screen TV panel on the wall.

"And you look elated! Did you ever consider a career in rap?" Dana slipped her slim five-foot-eight length out from behind the desk and went over to Lecia, who was fiddling with the TV clicker.

"Here we go," Lecia said when the local cable station was on the screen. "They'll loop it again in a few seconds." They waited through a commercial about a dumpster service for construction debris, and then a reporter came on, standing in front of the court building, microphone in hand.

"Chapter one of the St. Valentine's Day Nightmare was heard in court today, the case known as 'The Family Affair.' Dr. and Mrs. Bohr, the homeowners who allegedly hosted that wild party on Foxglove Way last weekend, pled not guilty to serving alcohol to teens. They want all the charges dropped by next month if they go to school for alcohol awareness training! Town Justice Leroy Jones strongly encouraged this outcome, and the prosecutor seemed to have no problem with it.

"But the real surprise came when Sandra Bohr stridently accused the newspapers of printing, and I quote, 'complete bunk,' by calling the district attorney 'Hypocrite Hargrove.' As you know, the Bohrs are accused of leaving town the night the teens went wild at their house, even though the DA allowed her own daughter to spend the night there. What we didn't know, and what Mrs. Bohr revealed today, was a phone call between the two women last Friday. Mrs. Bohr says she led the DA to believe that she and her husband would be home. 'It's all my fault,' she says. 'I didn't tell her we'd be out'!"

The camera went to an artist's sketch of Sandra Bohr standing next to Hernando Ramirez, as Judge Jones looked down from the bench.

"Doesn't she look good today?" Dana said.

"Especially since we like what came out of her mouth!"

"That takes a load off. Thank you, Lecia."

Minutes after Lecia stepped out of the office, Linda called and related all the details. Shortly after that, ADA Walsh phoned. Charlie Walsh was a bright kid, one of her younger assistants in local criminal court who hadn't yet graduated to felonies.

"The Kavanagh case has been changed from two to three thirty," he said.

"Are you aware of the reason?" Dana asked.

"No. Judge Jones's law clerk just called and told me. No explanation. Is there something behind it?"

"It was rescheduled to make this an after-school fieldtrip for half of Stone Ridge High School. Students Against Destructive Decisions will be there in full force, including my son. The judge's daughter is a member of SADD."

"So, the daughter… Do we think she engineered this? Is it a problem?"

Dana wasn't going to get excited about potential conflicts in a misdemeanor unlicensed driving case. The judge's daughter was a friend of the defendant. The judge's daughter asked her dad to change the time of the proceeding. Did this make Judge Jones biased in favor of the defendant? It went both ways. Alicia also strongly believed in following the traffic rules. That much Dana knew from Travis. "It's not a problem. We aren't going to open this can of worms."

"All right. It should be an interesting afternoon. Will you be coming?"

"Possibly. I'll let you know."

An elected district attorney rarely attended proceedings in a town justice court, and Dana had thought that her presence at the emotionally-charged St. Valentine's Day Nightmare cases could generate unwanted speculation and rumor. But things had changed for Ginger's case. It looked like SADD would be in the spotlight, and Dana's reputation had miraculously improved, thanks to Sandra Steele!

A few minutes later, she received a call from the child who never, ever bothered his mother at work, even for a raging strep infection. Travis was between classes at school, and he wanted to know if she'd heard that the time was changed. Was she still okay with him going to court? Dana assured him of her approval. She couldn't suppress a big smile and was glad her son couldn't see it. His overabundance of caution about this afternoon was another sign of his emotional attachment to Ginger.

At one fifteen, Lecia buzzed. "Ted's on the line, and I was just about to come in to turn on the news again."

"Rigger. Thanks, Lecia. I'm going to get the news from Ted before I watch any anchorman's spin on it." She switched to the call. "Hello, Ted. That didn't take long."

"Yesterday afternoon and this morning. They were out maybe five hours altogether."

"I guess their stomachs are growling for lunch. Are you calling with good news or bad?" Dana could already tell from Ted's tone that the news was not good. Although a heinous crime like this *could* result in a quick verdict of guilty on the top count, the opposite was the norm. Finding a fellow human being guilty of the ultimate crime is a difficult job, usually requiring long deliberations.

"Not good. Man one. They went for his EED defense. I told you, Dana. The judge basically rubber-stamped his excuse. The jury was allowed to find it 'reasonable' under the circumstances.

They bought it."

Silence.

"I feel like I let everyone down," Ted added.

A rare show of self-criticism from her first deputy. "You did an outstanding job, Ted. This is a difficult area of the law, and the judge saw it differently."

"I suppose."

"We'll push for the max at sentencing. The range for manslaughter in the first degree is five to twenty-five years. Even Judge Sinclair wouldn't give this guy less than the max."

"I don't know, Dana. I don't know."

Ginger had never been so nervous in her life. Travis told her that everyone would be there to support her. She couldn't tell them to stay away, so she'd prepared herself as best she could: *I will not break down. I will be strong.* A hundred times in her head. There were things she wanted to say.

The anticipation was exciting and terrifying. Like never before, the intensity of the world was concentrated in every face and smell and color and sound and texture, a confusion of everything unbearably wonderful and cataclysmic. She imagined how it might be, speaking to every important person in her life at once as the feelings coursed underneath, real and raw and sucked in under her breath, clenched tight in her chest until they broke through. Likely would. She'd never been any good at controlling her emotions.

She'd gotten over some of her shame by admitting the part that was her fault. The other part of it was so unfair. How could anyone think that the pills and the alcohol were hers?

Her attorney Mr. Bridges was a nice man, grandfatherly, and very smart. The other day at his office he told her that she didn't have a legal defense to unlicensed driving and suggested that the judge might be more lenient if she believed she was acting under an emergency. Did she want to testify that way? "No," she said. "There really wasn't any emergency. I was wrong. I'm going to plead guilty to that, because I'm guilty." He thought that was a fine expression of responsibility, and so did her mother. "I'm not guilty of anything else," she hastened to add.

Ginger entered the courtroom with her mother on one side, Mr. Bridges on the other. A sea of familiar faces stared back. Devraj, Alicia, Sarah, Cameron, Larissa, and Dawn. Dylan, Myra, and Chrissy. Travis. So many more, all the SADD members who'd ever shown up to a meeting. Up ahead, in the front row on the right side, were Uncle Andris and Aunt Stephanie. She didn't see Grandpa. Good. It would be too much for him.

Dylan stepped into the aisle and came right up to them. He offered his hand to Mr. Bridges and said, "I'm Dylan Radner, president of the SADD chapter at Stone Ridge." They shook hands. "If it's okay," Dylan said, "I'd like to tell the judge a few things about Ginger. She's completely against alcohol and drugs. It's impossible for that stuff in the car to be hers."

"Thank you, son. I'm sure Ginger appreciates the gesture." He glanced at her with a smile. "But we're not having a trial today, so I doubt the judge would allow your statement or testimony. I'll let you know."

Ginger met Dylan's eyes. Had she ruined everything for Call Central? This was her biggest regret. People on both sides of the issue had been talking to Mr. Beggs about it. If she thought it would help, she'd go right into the principal's office and try to convince him that the group shouldn't suffer on account of her own stupid mistake. She hadn't found the nerve to approach him, and that's why so much depended on the impression she would make in court today.

When they reached the front row, Ginger noticed Travis's mom sitting on the left side of the aisle. Ginger's mom also noticed her, and the two women stared at each other longer than seemed polite. Mom had such a funny look on her face. Was she angry at the district attorney? There was also a little smile on her lips and a shine in her eyes. It was the kind of look that old friends gave each other when they were thinking of more than just what was going on at that moment.

Mom gave Ginger's shoulder an affectionate squeeze and went to sit next to Uncle Andris and Aunt Steph, who gave her encouraging smiles. Ginger returned their smiles as best she could, even as a wave of sadness washed over her. The person she really wanted to see was missing. Would he be coming?

At the front of the room, a very young man stood at the table on the left. He didn't look much older than Dylan. Ginger and her lawyer stood at the table on the right, and then a court officer told everyone to rise. Judge Jones came into the courtroom.

This was so strange! She'd seen Alicia's dad before, acting like a normal dad at his house. No way had Ginger ever imagined him in a black robe, looking down at her in judgment. He was a very cool dad, and she really liked him, so in a way, it made her more comfortable. The judge greeted everyone, made a few jokes, and asked for "appearances."

"Assistant District Attorney Charles Walsh for the People."

"Wendel Bridges for the defendant, Ginger Kavanagh."

The judge announced the charges against her. Four of them! Driving while intoxicated, criminal possession of a controlled substance, possession of an open container of alcohol while driving, and unlicensed driving. "Now, Ms. Kavanagh, I'm going to go through these charges one at a time and ask for your plea, guilty or not guilty. If you have any questions about the charge before you enter your plea to it, let me know."

The assistant district attorney said, "Your Honor…," like he was about to make a little speech, but Ginger cut him off! "I understand all the charges, Judge Jones. My attorney explained everything, and I know exactly how I want to plead!" She glanced at Mr. Bridges, who gave her a look of approval. Was that rude of her to interrupt ADA Walsh? She didn't care. She had to do this! "I plead guilty to unlicensed driving and *not* guilty to the other three charges! I'm absolutely not guilty of those!"

"Have you discussed this with your attorney?"

"Yes, I have, and I need to say some things. May I talk?" That sounded so stupid! *May I talk?* Already her voice was shaking. Could she do this?

"Yes, you may."

But then, she couldn't. The silence of a hundred people pressed into her from all sides, squeezing her into a little block of ice.

"Go ahead, Ms. Kavanagh."

"I, I'm…" she stammered, and remembered to take a deep breath. "I'm the vice president of Students Against Destructive Decisions at our high school. We fight drug and alcohol abuse. The stuff they found in my car, that bottle and those pills, were not mine. I don't use drugs or alcohol, and I try to be an example for other kids." Her lips quivered around that word. Some example!

She took a moment, another deep breath. She had so much more to say! "But I *am* guilty of driving without a license. I want to apologize to everyone. I made a big mistake, and I'll never make it again. I was trying to help the girls I picked up from the party, and I'm glad they're all right now. I apologize to them and to all the members of SADD. None of them would ever make the mistake I made, and I think they should be allowed to continue with Call Central. It's a good program." With tears in her eyes, she turned to her friends in the audience. "I'm sorry I let you down." Her voice was shaking badly now. She turned back to the judge. "Most of all, I want to apologize to my mother for using her car without her permission." She turned around again and found her mother's face. "I'm sorry, Mom." Any last bit of control Ginger possessed was completely lost now. She collapsed into shuddering sobs, and Mr. Bridges patted her shoulder in a kind of helpless-father way.

After the days of distress and preparation, she'd broken down in public after all. But maybe it wasn't so bad to face these people all at once and to show them exactly how she felt.

While she tried to bring her sobbing under control, the best thing of all happened.

"Your Honor," said ADA Walsh. "If I may."

"Yes, please."

"At this time, the People have an application. We move to dismiss the charges of intoxicated driving, criminal possession of a controlled substance, and unlawful possession of an open container. After further investigation, the People are unable to prove those three charges."

Well, the whoops and cries were so loud that Judge Jones had to bang the gavel over and over again! The hammering was forceful, but the judge really didn't look mad. A big smile was on his face. And Ginger didn't mind that, maybe, ADA Walsh had wanted to say this at the start, when she rudely interrupted him. She still would have said what she wanted to say.

When everyone settled down, the judge said, "That leaves a single charge against the defendant, unlicensed driving." He looked directly at Ginger. "The court accepts your plea of guilty to that charge."

Mr. Bridges said, "Your Honor, the defendant stands ready for sentence now." Ginger had told her attorney she wanted this over *today*. She understood the possible outcomes and didn't want him to ask for leniency.

"People? Any recommendations?"

"We defer to the court's discretion on sentencing, Your Honor," ADA Walsh said.

"All right," Judge Jones said. "This is the sentence of the court. You are to pay a fine of three hundred dollars, your learner's permit is revoked, and you may not apply for a learner's permit again until your seventeenth birthday. That concludes these proceedings." The gavel came down.

In the clamor that erupted, Ginger was aware of a few things. The judge left the room by a side door. Mr. Bridges leaned down to her and said, "Well done." District Attorney Hargrove walked up to the prosecutor's table and spoke to ADA Walsh. Mom came up to their table and gave her a big hug. Ginger looked out over Mom's shoulder into the audience. In the blur of faces, only one came into sharp focus. Travis was standing tall and still among the moving bodies. His eyes sought hers, and she stared at him for a long time over Mom's shoulder. His expression changed slowly from seriously thoughtful, to more relaxed, to very happy, full of wonder, smiling broadly. He looked awesome.

Mom let go of Ginger, and her eyes stopped here and there on one smiling face after another. God, she loved these guys! As people moved out of their seats and into the aisle, a lone figure came into view. There, at the back of the room, Ginger's father stood up from his seat in the last row, a spot she hadn't seen when she first walked in. From the look on his face, she knew that he'd been there all along. She also knew that, from now until forever, he'd always have her back. Everything was up to her.

TWOSOMES

Friday, March 27, 2009

IN KEEPING WITH a Goodhue tradition, Friday night was pizza night at the family dinner table.

"Still picking the mushrooms off?" Evan eyed Natalie's fingertips.

"What am I supposed to do? It's part of the tradition, especially since Tug ate the last pepperoni slice."

"Nats!" Travis Ulrich Goodhue was not fond of his babyhood nickname.

"You can give them here," Evan said, lifting his paper plate. Natalie reached over and tipped her plate to let them slide onto his slice.

Dana soaked up the happy energy and love at this table, pushing the big news of the day out of her mind. Ted had felt somewhat vindicated when Judge Sinclair sentenced Perry Rigger to the maximum term the law allowed for manslaughter in the first degree. A tragic case, imperfect justice, but could anything ever be made right when a life was taken in such a brutal way?

"Mom," Travis said. "Did you know about the announcement at school today?"

"About what?"

"The Naomi Steuben scholarship fund. Mr. Beggs made an

announcement on the P.A. system in the middle of class. He said that any senior can apply."

"What's that all about?" Natalie asked.

"Naomi's parents started a college scholarship fund in their daughter's memory. By the way, the Dyckmans and the Sloanes each made big contributions to it."

"Was that part of the court deal?" Travis asked.

"No, it wasn't. The fund is set up for anyone to contribute. The Dyckmans and Sloanes gave on their own, and I'm glad they did. Taylor and Chloe have other conditions they have to meet before their records are cleared."

"That's what I don't get," Travis said. "Everyone knows they pled guilty, so how can their criminal records ever be cleared?"

Earlier that week, Chloe and Taylor pled guilty to criminally negligent homicide, but only after the judge promised them "youthful offender" status and a sentence of probation. Their psychiatric evaluations had convinced the court that treatment would afford a better outcome than prison. Their crime had been the product of a pathological, symbiotic relationship. Taylor, with her need for approval, was Chloe's instrument, and Chloe, with her need to dominate, had little control over her sociopathic tendencies. Under the youthful offender law, their criminal records would eventually be sealed, as if they'd never been convicted, but only if they met a long list of conditions, including many hours of community service and psychiatric treatment. Of course, all social media was off limits for the girls.

"I know what you mean," Dana said. "In a way, it seems fictional that their records will be cleared, but it makes a big difference for their future. Any opportunities for employment and other privileges won't be hurt by a criminal record. It's a clean slate for them, and they have every chance to make the best of it."

"But what's it like having them at school?" Natalie asked her brother. "Isn't it kind of creepy?"

"They don't have too many friends," Travis said. "They don't act like they own the place anymore. Their whole clique disappeared. Julian's friend Keith hasn't even been back to school."

"That's 'cause he practically died," Natalie said.

"Oh, he's fully recovered from his injuries," Dana said. "He lost a lot of blood at the time, and he has lasting scars, but that's not the reason he isn't in school. He dropped out after he got arrested for peddling illegal narcotics. He's facing some serious criminal charges." Dana's office had closed in on the prescription drug ring at the high school, and it turned out that Westerman was one of the key players.

"What about Julian?" Natalie asked. "Is he getting any better?" She scrunched her brow in consternation. It had been only ten days since he'd emerged from his coma.

"He hasn't come back to school," Travis said. "Not as far as I can tell."

"It's a slow go from what I understand," Dana said. "Brain injuries take a lot of time. I believe the doctors are hopeful. Most of his speech is back, but he has some partial paralysis on one side of his body."

Dana was afraid that Natalie would ask—again—about the status of the criminal case against Emjay and Brent, but Travis spoke up first. "Hey, Dad, I just thought of something. Did anyone ask you to be the lawyer on their case? Either side?"

"You mean the Yarnells against the Bohrs?" Evan and Dana exchanged looks. The Yarnells were suing the Bohrs to get money damages for Julian's injuries, and the Bohrs were countersuing the Yarnells for Julian's trespass on their property. If the criminal case against Emjay ended in an assault conviction, the Yarnells would easily prevail in their civil lawsuit—but both cases were still ongoing. "No one asked me to represent them, but if they did, I wouldn't touch that one with a ten-foot pole."

"Why not?"

"Conflicts galore," Evan said. "You going to finish that, Natalie?" He reached across the table and grabbed her half-eaten slice, hoping to divert attention away from *Yarnell versus Bohr*. It was bad enough having to worry about Natalie being called to testify in the criminal case against Emjay and Brent without also having to worry about her being summoned into court for their civil lawsuit! The cases had put a rift in the community, and Natalie's avoidance of Samantha at school was still a sore spot. As for the wild night on Foxglove, only one case against the Bohrs was resolved. The parents had passed alcohol awareness training with flying colors, and the charges against them were dropped.

"I propose a toast." Evan raised his soda can high. "Here's to Mommy for the good fight against drugs, alcohol, and cyberbullying at Stone Ridge!" Dana dipped her head in modest acceptance of the tribute as her husband and children clinked soda cans. Among the successes she counted in this mess were the arrests in the prescription pill ring, the heightened awareness in the community about parental responsibility, and this: "Did you know, kids, that your mom is going up to Albany next week to talk to the governor and top legislators? She's spearheading the movement for more effective laws against cyberbullying."

"Awesome, Mommy!"

"Really cool!"

But Dana's moment of glory was soon over.

"May I be excused? I have to get ready," Natalie said.

"Me too," said Travis, already pushing away from the table.

"Go on you two," Evan said. "We leave in fifteen minutes."

Travis was already on his way out of the dining room. Natalie rushed over to her father, threw her arms around his neck, and kissed his bald head. "Thank you *so* much, Daddy!" She ran off to her room.

"Well, I guess it's Friday night," Dana said.

"For some of us."

She got up and started to clear the table, but Evan stopped her and took her hand. "Leave that. We have fifteen minutes to plan *our* Friday night." He led her into the living room, and they sat down on the couch. "As I recall, our Valentine's Day was rudely interrupted this year."

"What is there to plan? It seems to me that we're locked into the 'kids first' stage of life."

It was true. Evan was on driving duty tonight. Although Travis had passed his driving test, the restrictions on his junior license did them no good for tonight's plans. Travis and Natalie were both going to the multiplex to see different movies. Travis would be meeting Ginger there, and Natalie would be meeting her new best friend, Maggie. After the show, the kids planned to have ice cream in the Sweets Shoppe across from the theater. Travis had gotten Natalie to promise that she and Maggie would *not* sit *anywhere near* her brother and his "date" while they ate their ice cream.

"Not just 'kids first.' It's 'old married folks last'—for tonight anyway." Evan was referring to the driving arrangements. Vesma had said she would be "unavailable" and asked Evan to drive Ginger home. No doubt this meant that she was going on a date with Hernando. Maggie's mother had offered to drive Natalie home, but Evan told her he didn't mind taking Maggie home instead. He would be out in the car anyway, taking Ginger home.

"But all isn't lost," Evan added.

"How's that?"

"By my calculations, we have a good three hours together here, all alone…"

"I'll pick out a movie…"

"…on the couch." He put an arm around her shoulder and nuzzled the nape of her neck.

"I know how much you like it on the couch, darling."

OPUS NINE BOOKS

All works published by Opus Nine Books are dedicated to the nine members of the family headed by John and Kate Swackhamer at 3 South Trail, Orinda, California — a large world under one small roof.

DEAR READER,

As I write the afterword for this updated edition, the sixth (and last) Dana Hargrove novel is on the horizon, to be published in January 2022. For more than a decade, Dana, her family, friends, and colleagues have been a big part of my life. I hope you'll get to know them well!

Each novel is a standalone, finding Dana at a different stage of her personal life and career. Here they are, with the years in which each story takes place:

Thursday's List (1988)

Homicide Chart (1994)

Forsaken Oath (2001)

Deep Zero (2009)

Seven Shadows (2015)

Power Blind (2022)

Let me know what you think! Now's the time to return to your online bookseller and post a reader review of any length on the webpage for *Deep Zero*. Or, send me a message through the contact page on my website, vskemanis.com. While you're there, subscribe to my blog and take advantage of the free e-book offer for one of my story collections.

To keep up with the latest news about my books and life, look for V.S. Kemanis on Goodreads, BookBub, Facebook, Twitter, Instagram, and YouTube.

Thanks for reading!

V.S.K